Opus Pistorum

Other Books by Henry Miller
Published by Grove Press

Tropic of Cancer

Black Spring

Tropic of Capricorn

Quiet Days in Clichy & *The World of Sex*

Sexus

Plexus

Nexus

Opus Pistorum

BY

HENRY MILLER

GROVE PRESS, INC./New York

First Hardcover Edition published in 1983

Library of Congress Cataloging in Publication Data
Miller, Henry, 1891-1980
    Opus pistorum.
    I. Title.
PS3525.I5454064   1983   813'.52   83-80498
ISBN 0-394-53374-7

Manufactured in the United States of America

GROVE PRESS, INC., 196 West Houston Street, New York, N.Y. 10014

10 9 8 7 6 5 4 3 2 1

CONTENTS

VOLUME I

"Drop your cocks and grab your socks."
—Canterbury.

BOOK 1

Sous les Toits
de Paris

God knows I've lived in Paris for long enough now that I shouldn't be amazed at anything. You don't have to go deliberately looking for adventures here, the way you do back in New York . . . all that's necessary is to have a little patience and wait, life will seek you out in the most unbelievably obscure places, things happen to you here. But the situation in which I now find myself . . . this pretty thirteen-year-old naked on my lap, her father busy taking down his pants behind a screen in the corner, the buxom young whore sitting on the couch . . . it's as though life were viewed through a distorting glass, recognizable images are seen but discredited.

I've never seen myself as a cradle snatcher . . . those men you watch being hustled away in the public parks, always a bit shabby, a little shaky on their pins, explaining that the child had dust on her dress and they were brushing it off . . . But now I must admit that Marcelle with her hairless little body is exciting me. It's not because she's a child, it's because she's a child with no innocence . . . look into her eyes and you see the monster of knowledge, the shadow of wisdom . . . she lies across my legs and squeezes her naked figlet against my fingers . . . and her eyes mock my hesitance.

I pinch her lengthening legs, cover one entire cheek of her restless ass with a palm . . . the roundness and shapelessness of childhood have scarcely left her body. She is a woman in miniature, a copy as yet incomplete. Her cuntlet is damp . . . She likes it when I tickle it with my fingertips . . . she's feeling the front of my pants for my dick . . . her fingers frighten me when they sneak into the front of my fly. I hold her arm . . . but she's found my bush. She clutches my coat and pulls herself so close to me that I can't keep her away from my dick, she begins to play with John Thursday . . . well, she'll find him hard . . .

The whore sits shaking her head . . . Such a child . . .

such a child, she says . . . these things should be forbidden by law. But she watches every move eagerly. In her trade one can't afford to feel excitement, whores live only when they've learned to sell their cunts and not their passions . . . but I can see emotion coming into her body, her voice is already thick with it . . .

She calls Marcelle to her. The child doesn't want to leave me but I set her off my lap . . . I'm almost grateful to be rid of her. Why does she want to be a—well, a bad girl, she's asked. She doesn't answer, she stands between the girl's knees and the whore touches her bare body. Does she do these things every night with papa? Yes, every night when they're in bed . . . she is defiant, triumphant . . . And when papa's working, when he's away in the daytime? The little boys try to make her do things sometimes . . . she never does it with them, nor with the men who want to take her for a walk.

Her father steps irritably from behind the screen. The young lady will be good enough not to question the child . . . he produces a bottle and the three of us have a drink of stinging brandy. There is a thimbleful of white wine for the daughter.

I sit with the whore on the couch. She's as grateful for my presence as I am for hers, she has forgotten her trade or she'd take her clothes off when I reach for her leg . . . instead, she lies back and lets me feel up her dress . . . her legs are big and solid.

Marcelle is on her father's lap in the chair. She plays with his dong and he diddles her between the legs . . . she raises her little belly and he kisses it, her spread legs show his finger sliding up in her tiny hole. Her mousetrap stretches when she puts one of her fingers in with his, and she laughs . . .

The whore's body is hot, and when she spreads her legs I find that she's wet between them. She has a bush as big as my hand and as soft as feathers. She lifts her dress in the front, takes my dong out and rubs John Thursday's nose against her whiskers . . . will I pinch her breasts, she moans, and would I be offended if she asked me to kiss them, perhaps to bite? She's catting for a fuck, that she's been paid to come here has nothing to do with it now . . . she'd probably give the money back and something extra besides just to get a cock into that itch under her tail now . . .

Marcelle wants us to look at her. She's bending over her father with his prick in one hand, gesticulating with the other, and calling loudly for an audience. She's going to suck him off, she tells us, don't we want to watch her put it into her mouth? Her old man beams like a hashish addict, everything's rosy now. He's halfway out of his chair, waiting for the little bitch to take it.

I wonder if her pleasure is half as much as it seems to be . . . she's been taught, that's seen at once, it hasn't all come out of her imagination. She rubs her nipples with the end of her father's dick, puts it where it would be between her bubs if she had any, and cuddles it . . . then she presses her head against his belly, kisses him there, kisses his thighs, kisses his bush . . . her tongue looks like a red worm hiding in his black hair.

The whore grabs my hand and holds it between her legs. She's so hot that she almost screams when the filthy little cunt suddenly pops her father's cock between her lips and begins to suck it. Such things cannot be, she exclaims, and Marcelle goggles over and smacks her lips a bit to prove that they can . . .

Marcelle wants me to fuck her. She leaps onto the couch and pushes her way between the girl and me . . . there's something so fascinatingly horrible about her that I can't move. She slides into my arms, pushes my cock with her naked belly, opens her legs and places my dong between them . . . I turn onto my back to get away from her when I feel her bald cuntlet touching the end of my dick, but she's straddling me at once.

"Fuck the dirty little cat!" The whore leans over me with

narrow, excited eyes . . . she pulls the bosom of her dress and pulls it half off her shoulders . . . her teats press my shoulder. I hear Marcelle's father too—"Fuck her! I must see my little darling be fucked!"

Marcelle stretches her tiny split fig, holds it open and pushes it down against my dong . . . the little monster gets it in somehow . . . I watch my dong stretch her to twice her size. I don't know how she manages to take so much . . . but her bald cuntlet seems to gobble me up, it takes my cock in and in . . . for a moment I have an urge to throw her beneath me, spread her child's legs and fuck that splitting little trap until it bursts, open her and open her with my dong, fuck her baby womb and fill it with jism again and again . . . She's fucking me now, has her sweet ass against my bush, the bareness of her cunt hidden by my hair . . . she's laughing, the puppy, she loves that cock in her . . .

I throw her from me, push her off the couch, but she doesn't understand that I don't want her, or if she knows she doesn't care . . . She clings to my knees and licks my balls, kisses my dong with her red lips—suddenly I see that they're painted—and takes it in her mouth before I can stop her. She sucks me, and I'm almost coming . . . she gurgles and pants over my cock . . .

"You loony bastard!" I yell at her father. "I don't want to fuck your damned kid! Fuck her yourself if you have to have her laid!" I shove my dong into my pants and Marcelle runs to her father. "I must be as nuts as you are to have come here in the first place . . . I'm certainly not drunk . . . Now get to Jesus out of my way!"

"Papa!" Marcelle cries. I think she's frightened by my violence, but she's not . . . not that little monster. She shines her amber eyes at me. "Get it now, Papa! Get the little switch so she can beat me while he fucks me! Oh, Papa, please!"

I absolutely run out of the house. I'd kill somebody if I didn't get out, and I tremble so badly when I'm on the street that I have to stop and rest against a fence. I feel as though I had just escaped from something dark and bloody, something out of a nightmare . . .

"Monsieur! Monsieur!" It's the whore following me. She clutches my hand desperately. "I threw his money in his face, the dirty old pig." She sees me reaching in my pocket. "No, I don't want any money . . ."

I pull her behind a fence into what must be a lumberyard. She stands solidly against me, holds her dress around her ass and lets me fondle her bush. She's so hot that her cunt has wetted her legs farther down than I'm interested in feeling . . . her cunt opens against my fingers and she takes John Thursday out.

There's a pile of boards to lie on. They're rough and damp, and she'll probably spend the rest of the night picking splinters out of her ass, but none of that matters . . . she wants to be fucked, and she'd lie on a bed of nails if she had to. With her legs spread she hooks her high heels into a crack and raises herself while she tucks her dress around her middle.

"Monsieur . . . Monsieur," she sighs. You'll never know, you wonderful bitch, how grateful I am for this night . . .

I dig John Thursday into her whiskers. He hadn't a brain in his bald head, but left alone he can fend for himself. He can manage somehow. He slips through her bush and butts her rectum.

She has a flood coming down from her tail, this whore. There's no stopping it . . . you could stuff towels, blankets, mattresses between her legs, and it would still pour down to engulf you. I feel like the little boy who had to stop the break in the dike and had nothing but his finger. But I'll plug it, I'll fill it with my dong. . . .

What was it like? That's what she wants to know, that's what she keeps asking me. She can't forget that hairless cuntless cuntlet even when my cock is nudging into the very gates. The way it stretched and closed over my prick stays in her mind, she says. That little bare body slipping against me . . . ah, if I could have seen how it looked to someone else! But what was it like?

And when the dirty little puppy held my dong in her mouth, that painted baby mouth, and sucked it, what did I feel then? Oh, such a wicked, wicked little girl she is, that one, to even know such things exist! And so on. But won't I just lift a bit, at her hips, to make it easier for Jean Jeudi to slip into his stable. . . . Monsieur!

An army has marched through her legs . . . an army uncounted and nameless and half forgotten. But she'll remember this night. It's an event in her life when she gives it away for nothing, that won't be forgotten so easily. I push my cock into her ripe fig and she pulls at my coat to keep me down and close to her. She's not a whore now . . . she's only a cunt with an ache that must be rubbed away . . .

The ache won't remain long. I'll fuck it out, fuck out the memories too of those others who had you. Who were you with tonight? Who screwed you? Does it matter and can you remember even now? In a day or a week they will have marched on to join those others who have come before. But I will remain, you won't pass this one by so easily . . . my cock is in you, and there it will stay, even after I am gone. I will leave something that you will never forget, I will give you a little parcel of joy, fill your womb with a heat that will not cool . . . You lay beneath me with your thighs strained apart to receive it, and your whore's mouth whispers words you have said a thousand times before to a thousand men. But that doesn't matter. Before me there were no men, and after me there will be none. It is not your fault if you have no unused phrase for what you feel . . . it is enough that you feel . . .

I club her thighs with my dong, taking it out of her and pushing it into the soft wound again and again, taking her anew time after time. They have left her ravaged and open, easy to take and easy to fuck, all those others. But I fill her, she knows she's being fucked this time. She pulls her dress away from her shoulders again and offers me her teats. I rub my face against them, sucking and biting.

I grab her ass in both hands and crush the meat while I slip my cock toward her womb. If it hurts her, neither of us know or think about it. My balls lay in a hot pocket, a hairy nest under her tail. The boards rattle under us like the jangling bones of a skeleton.

Jism gushes out of my dong as freely as water out of a hose. The whore suddenly puts her legs around me and holds me tightly . . . she's afraid that I'll stop and she hasn't come yet. But I fuck her for a full minute longer, coming into her womb even after the fire in her has been quenched and her legs fall to my sides again . . .

The whore lies sprawling on the pile of lumber after it's over. She doesn't try to cover herself . . . she acts as though she had forgotten where she was, and she seems to be completely fucked out and contented. But I'm afraid that she'll remember and try to wheedle her few francs out of me, want me to buy her a drink, pay for a taxi, tell me of her ailing mother . . . I take the first bill I find in my pockets, wipe my cock on it, and lay it crumpled on her bare belly weighted with a coin.

The streets receive me, as bleak and foreign as before . . . .

Tania's letters will find me, no matter where I go. Two arrive, one in the morning and the other by late post. She is lonely! . . . .

. . . . . think I will go crazy if I have to go another night without a fucking by you. I keep thinking about that big prick and all the wonderful things it does, and I would give anything I own if I could just feel it again, and take it in my hand. I even dream about it! It isn't enough to have Peter fuck me. Sometimes it is hard to keep from coming to see you, even when I know you would probably be angry with me and not treat me nice.

Don't you ever think about me and the good times we had together? I hope that you do and that sometimes you wish I were there in bed with you, sucking you off, playing with your cock, and fucking, Mother wishes you were here to fuck her too, I can tell because she talks about you so much. She is always asking what we did, just what happened on the times when you fucked me and even what we said! I don't think she is letting anybody but Peter fuck her now. She has Peter and me go to bed with her every night and she makes me suck her off a lot. I don't care, I like to do it, but I wish that you were here so that I would be fucked more often. . . . .

And so on. "Love from Tania," closes this letter. The second one is longer. Tania has discovered a new thrill and, as she writes, I have to tell you about it right away. Isn't that strange? It's because I would like to have you do it to me. Everything that anybody does to me would be better if you were the one who did it to me. I guess that's because you have such a big cock. When I think of how big your cock is I feel goosepimples come up all over me. And I was even thinking of you part of the time when he was doing it to me!

I was so glad to have a man fuck me again (Mother watches me like a hawk) that I could hardly wait to take the time to undress when we went to his room. He wanted to lie on the bed so we could play with each other, but I kept getting so hot that I couldn't stand it, and he had to fuck me. I was acting so crazy that he was afraid I might jump out of the window or something. Oh it was wonderful to feel a man fucking me again. Peter is kept so busy fucking Mother that he isn't so much good any more, and this was the first time that I have had a good one since you went away. He dragged me all over the room! He had already fucked me twice when he told me that he was going to show me a new trick, but he didn't have any trouble getting his prick hard. I just let him put it in my mouth and sucked it a tiny bit, and in a minute it was just as good as ever! Then he laid me on the floor on some soft pillows and had me lie on my stomach while he started to fuck me up my ass.

It was wonderful, of course, although it wasn't as wonderful as when you ram that big cock of yours into me that way, but then I was just a little disappointed because it wasn't really new after all. Then I suddenly felt something new and strange. At first it felt as though he had come and the jism was going into me, but then it began to squirt hard and I knew that he was making pip in me! Oh what a queer and wonderful feeling that was! His big cock was stuffed into me and nothing could get out, it all went up inside. It was so hot that I felt as though I was burning all through me, and I could feel it squeezing into every bit of my insides.

It seemed as though he would never stop, and it crept up and up in me, making me feel all swelled up like a pregnant woman. When he was all finished he took his prick out very slowly and said that if I held it in, it would all stay in me. You can't imagine how I felt after he had taken his cock out, lying there with a man's piss inside me and feeling it all through my stomach every minute.

Then he took me into the bathroom and I let it come out again, litres and litres of his pipi pouring out of my ass while he stood in front of me and made me suck his Jean. . . .

I'll confess . . . . it gives me a hard on to read Tania's letter. I know the little bitch so well . . . so fucking well, I might say . . . that I can imagine the entire performance as well as though I were there. I can close my eyes and see every gesture, every move she would make. I go marching back and forth across the room with a dong that would do credit to a stud horse. I don't know why the thought of pissing up that smooth round ass should evoke such results, but I can't get rid of the damned thing.

I go for a walk, feeling that one leg drags slightly. I'm bait for every whore on the streets, and they all make a pass at me . . . they're experts at judging a man's condition. But it isn't a whore I want. I want another Tania, but one with whom it will not be necessary to become so deeply involved.

I do not find her on the streets.

Ernest has a wonderful view from his window. An art class, the real thing, where the students take turns in posing for each other because they're so poor that they can't afford a professional model. When I'm up in his place we sit and watch them for a while. I like the spirit the people in that place show. They goose the model as they go past, give her bubs a pinch, tickle her in the crotch . . . she's a nice tight young blonde with wide hips and she doesn't mind a bit. Ernest tells me that there was a young fellow posing the other day and the girls bothered him so much that if their sketches were honest they must all have shown him with a hard on.

It's a fine thing to see art come to life. Back in New York they used to have phoney sketching classes where the bozos who mooched around the burlesque houses used to go. Fifty cents paid at the door and they gave you a half hour of looking at a naked cunt. All done, of course, with the strict understanding that you weren't really looking at a cunt at all . . . you were looking at something called Art. But these youngsters—they're all kids, even the instructor—know what it is they're after, the girl on the soap box is a naked girl with a bush around her cunt and juice between her legs! She's something alive, to get your hands on and your prick into, and if the boys stop to give her a feel, if they pinch her ass and do their work with their cocks up . . . their work and the world will be the better for it.

Ernest tells me that he's always had good windows . . . all but one time. The one he didn't like was one which gave him a view into the apartment of a couple of fairies . . . the real things, the kind that even your grandmother would recognize on the streets. It wasn't so bad just having to see them sucking each other off or sucking off their boy friends, Ernest says, but they were continually bringing home sailors and being beaten up the next morning. The mornings were awful, he tells me, and besides there was always their wash with the silk pants hanging out the window every morning.

The most convenient was at a place where he lived with a whore named Lucienne. The house she worked in was next door and Ernest could look over and see the bed where she took her clients. It was very comforting, Ernest declares, to be able to look over and see his Lucienne at work and know that the rent was being provided for.

This leads into a discussion of the women with whom Ernest has lived at one time or another. The list he makes astonishes me until I discover that he is cheating. Any woman with whom he has spent more than ten minutes he counts as having lived with.

"Shit," he says, speaking of one when I challenge her position on his list. "I took her to dinner, didn't I? And didn't she sleep in my bed that night? Bed and board, if you give them that they are living with you."

Ernest is astonished to learn that I've never laid a Chinese. I'm astonished myself. With all the chop suey joints back in New York you'd think I'd at least have gotten next to one of the waitresses. The subject of races comes up, and Ernest is prepared to give me advice on all of them. Don't try the Japs or the Chinks in the whorehouses, he warns me. They're all shaved and bathed and perfumed but they carry a skull and crossbones between their legs. They take on any man who comes along and wow! SYPHILIS! The galloping kind that carries you off in six months, nothing that you can pass off as a bad cold. The far Eastern brand of the syph, Ernest insists, has a special deadliness for the Occidental race. It all sounds like shit to me, but Ernest is positive enough to scare me away from the Orientals forever.

Then, when he has the piss scared out of me, Ernest tells me that he knows of a nice little cunt who's quite safe. She's not a whore, just a nice Chink girl who he knows, and there's not a chance of catching anything. Her father has an art shop, one of those joints filled with salvaged junk that was probably thrown out of the palaces with the garbage a few hundred years ago, Buddhas and screens and ratty chests, and so on, and the girl helps with the place and waits on the young blades who come in looking for a jade necklace.

Ernest writes the address on an envelope and gives it to me. I may have to buy something just to keep up appearances, he says, but it's a certain fuck if I work it right. He isn't going with me . . . he has a date with some cunt who paints and he's going to try to fuck her into doing a portrait of him for nothing, but he assures me that it will be all right.

"Find out if they sell cocaine, will you Alf?" he asks. "I promised to get this cunt of mine a little . . . she's never tried it. I'm afraid to go back to my old neighborhood for it. I owe them a little bill yet and they're sore because I moved away . . ."

Armed with this address I take a stroll down to this shop after I've done my two hours in the office. On the way I change my mind half a dozen times, and I almost go off with a black wench who gives me the signal from a park bench. There was a time in New York when I spent almost every night in Harlem. I was nuts about a black cunt for a few weeks and wouldn't touch anything else. I got over that, but I still like it, and this girl is so husky and black . . . shit, she looks healthy enough to withstand a barrage of germs. Ernest really has frightened me with all his talk about catching something. But I pass her up and go on.

I never know how these things are done. When I'm stinking drunk I can talk to any cunt on the street, make the most insulting propositions without batting an eye, but to go into this joint cold sober and make my little speech . . . it's too much for me. Especially when I find that the girl is one of those cool, poised bitches who speaks perfect French. I expected to have trouble understanding her accent, and instead she makes me feel that I speak French like an American tourist.

I don't know what the fuck to say. I haven't even the slightest idea of what I want to buy, if anything. She's a pretty cunt, I'll say that, and she's as patient as she is good looking. She shows me everything in the damned shop . . .

I like her looks, especially the odd way in which her nose is flattened against her face and pulls her upper lip up. Nice ass and bubs, too . . . something there I hadn't expected. I've noticed that most of the Chinese women I've seen appear to have no teats, but this cunt has a beautiful set. Still, they're not quite the thing to begin a conversation around.

Using Ernest's name doesn't help matters a bit. I was sent here by a friend, I explain, and I mention Ernest, but she doesn't know him! So many people are in the shop every day, she suggests politely . . . I find that I have bought a hanging, a gorgeous thing with dragons to hang on my wall. The cunt smiles and wants to give me a cup of tea . . . her old man rattles out of the back of the shop and whisks the hanging from under our noses . . . he's going to wrap it.

I don't care for tea, I tell her. I was thinking of going around the corner for a pernod, and I would be charmed if she would accompany me. She accepts! I can't say a word . . . I stand gaping like a fish and she trots back through the shop.

She comes back wearing a trick hat that makes her look more Parisienne than the Parisiennes and she carries the package under her arm. I still haven't invented anything clever to say and our departure out of the shop is made even less graceful by a little bastard of a street urchin who tosses horse turds at us from the gutter. But the cunt has wonderful poise . . . we march down the street with a grand air and I'm soon at ease . . .

Questions! She wants to know who I am, what I am, my entire history. Also the matter of my income comes up. I don't understand what she's leading up to, but she begins to talk about jade. There is a little trinket, she tells me intimately, which has just been smuggled in, a true gem of the emperors which must be sold for a mere fraction of its worth . . . and she mentions my month's salary almost to the sou.

I'm curious. There's obviously something fishy, and I get the impression that she wants me to understand that she's shitting me. Where can this stone be seen, I ask. Ah, everything comes to light, then! It's not safe to have it about the shop, she tells me . . . so she wears it on a silken cord tied around her waist, where its cool caress on her skin speaks of its safety. The purchase would have to be made in some secluded spot far from the shop . . .

It's a wonderful game once I understand how it's played. This cunt really has imagination about selling her body. But her asking price! I begin to haggle with her and over the third pernod we agree that a week's salary will be the price of this piece of jade. I'll have to live on credits until the ghost walks again . . . I've never paid so much for a tail, but this cunt makes it seem to be worth it.

I don't doubt that she has a French name like Marie or Jeanne, but in the taxi going to my place she coos something that sounds like the piping of a flute . . . Bud of Lotus, she translates it, so I call her Lotus. It's all such a marvelous fraud . . .

I add my part to the show. As soon as I have her tucked away in my rooms, I run down to buy some wine from the concierge and serve it in the small green glasses that Alexandra bought for me. Then, when Lotus is to show me the stone, I spread the lovely old hanging on the floor for her to stand on.

The bitch must have played a year in burlesque to learn a strip routine like the one she showed me. Artfully, she leaves her stockings and shoes on after everything else has been tossed off. And there's a red silk cord around her belly with the piece of jade hanging in her bush. It looks very neat, that little piece of green stone, snuggling into that bit of black. She leaves her clothes heaped on the dragon spread and offers it for inspection . . .

The stone is the cheapest sort of junk, of course, but it's what's under it that I'm interested in. Lotus doesn't mind when I pay no attention to the thing . . . she smiles quickly when I pinch her thighs and run my finger between her legs. There is an odor about her that reminds me of the tiny scented cigarettes that Tania used to smoke . . . she smiles down at me while I sit on the edge of the chair and run my finger into her tail. She says something in Chinese and it sounds fascinatingly filthy.

I've forgotten all of Ernest's dire warnings by now. With the dong I've got I'd probably fuck her even if she did have a dose, and trust to a quick cure . . . but it's so fresh smelling and pink that I'm positive everything's all right . . . she lets me pull her fig open and sniff at it . . . then she moves away from me again. She breaks the cord at her waist and drops the stone into my palm.

I fuck her on the floor, right there on my new hanging with a pillow tucked under her head. I won't let her take off her stockings, not even her shoes. To the devil with the embroidered dragon . . . if she gouges his black eyes with her heels, if we leave a stain that won't come off, so much the better for it. I go after her fiercely . . . a French whore would object to such violence, the biting, the pinches, but Lotus smiles and submits.

Do I enjoy to squeeze her teats roughly? Very well, she presses them into my hands. And if I bruise them with my mouth . . . she gives me her nipples to bite. I put her hand on my dong and watch her long almond-colored fingers squeeze around it. She murmurs continually . . . in Chinese. Ah, she knows her business well. Her customers pay well for that spicy breath of the Orient and she knows what it is they buy.

Her legs and belly are quite hairless . . . it's only at one spot that the well-kept goatee covers her. Even her ass, the damp skin around her soft cul, is bare. She spreads her legs when I touch her rectum. Her thighs are beginning to feel hot and slippery close to her fig. Her abricot-fendu is almost as small as Tania's, but it has a more mature feel about it . . . it seems softer and more open . . .

John Thursday interests her. She pinches his neck and pulls his whiskers. I stop feeling her up and she sits cross-legged between my knees to play with him. Her con splits open like some ripe and rich fruit, and her stockinged thighs press against my knees. The stockings and shoes provide an anomalous touch that I like.

I couldn't tell by looking at her whether she was excited or not. But that damp patch around her silky muff gives her away. It spreads and shines between her thighs, and the smell of cunt slowly cuts through the odor of the scent she uses. She pats John Thursday's head and tickles my balls. Soon she's stretched out full length between my legs with her nose pushing along my dick and into my bush . . . her hair is blue-black, straight and shiny . . .

I don't know what they teach their women in the Orient . . . perhaps cocksucking is neglected there, but Lotus has had native French teaching. Her tongue curls into my hair and smooths against my balls. She licks my dong, kisses my belly with her flat lips . . . her slanting eyebrows arch together when she opens her mouth and bends to let John Thursday poke his head in . . . her eyes are wild slits. Her arms slip around me and her teats are warm against my balls as she sucks me off.

I scramble over her . . . she sits up with my dong still in her mouth, still sucking it, but I push her flat and crawl down to her open crotch. I rub her bush with my cheek and my chin, tickle her bonne-bouche with my tongue. I lick her thighs and even the flat crease between them . . . I want only to feel her thighs close and draw me in, pull my mouth to that deep-split fig. I throw both arms around her waist and pinch her ass while I lick the cunt juice from her skin and from the spread mouth that offers itself. Quickly she throws herself upon me. Her conillon presses my lips and her legs are weak and open. Her juice drips into my mouth while I suck the hairy tail.

She seems to tremble when she feels my tongue in her cunt. She can't think of enough things to do to my dong in return . . . she bites it, licks my balls, does everything but swallow the whole works. She even pulls her fig further apart with her fingers, until I have my tongue so far in that it must be tickling her womb. Suddenly there's a flood. She's come, and she almost bites my prick in two. I let her fuck my mouth with her juicy thing . . .

I want to see what she looks like, what she'll do when John Thursday blows up in her teeth . . . I lie on my back again and watch her work over him. Her head rises and falls slowly. The look of surprise . . . She's found something warm coming into her mouth. Then her slant eyes close. She swallows and sucks, swallows and sucks . . .

The Chinese, I've been told, or I've read someplace, measure a fuck by days rather than hours. When I ask Lotus about it she laughs . . . She'll stay all night if I want her. And could she please take her stockings off now?

I'm hungry and I suggest going out for something to eat, but Lotus puts me right. When a man buys a Chinese woman, she says, he's bought a woman, not something to fuck like a goat. She brings all her talents to him . . . and Lotus can cook. I like the idea, so we dress and go out to buy some food.

As soon as we're in the place again we take off our clothes and Lotus makes a meal with a towel pinned at her waist, covering her front but leaving her ass bare. I lie on the couch and she pauses to kiss my cock each time she passes me . . . she's an agreeable cunt and she doesn't mind if a pot burns while I'm feeling her up . . .

After we've eaten we try the bed. Lotus thinks it would be nice if we did the tete-beche again, but I want to fuck her . . . I jump onto the bed after her and immediately ram my dong up her tail. She stops talking about the so wonderful tete-beche when she feels what John Thursday is like under her ass.

It doesn't make any difference to Johnny what color she is. She's warm and wet and hairy around the edges, and that's all he requires. He really spreads himself. He fills all the cracks and crevices, and when he's in I tuck his whiskers around to cover the corners. A few swabs with him and the girl begins to glow . . . she wiggles her round, yellow ass and begs me to take the itch out of it . . . it doesn't matter that she jabbers most of the time in Chinese, we understand each other perfectly. Her small feet cross between my knees in back . . . her soft, naked thighs are stronger than I thought . . .

She's a positive relief! I think of Tania, remember that bookkeeper with his half grown daughter, and laugh. The white world is upside down . . . a man has to find a Chink for so simple a thing as a quiet, normal fuck. Lotus laughs with me, without knowing why we're laughing . . . perhaps if she knew she'd be laughing at me. She's a good cunt. I start to fuck the hell out of her. It's a great thing to have a bitch who can laugh while you fuck her.

And she's no whore! A concubine, rather. Lotus brings her passion as well as her talent for cooking . . . it's accidental that money's involved. The money simply buys a jade trinket . . . If she pants in your ear, it's real, if she moans softly you may be sure it's because she *feels*. She has life in her body, juice to oil the works, and she gives them ungrudgingly . . .

I play with her bubs and she wants me to suck them

again. The nipples, I discover, have a lemon ring about them like a Chinese moon . . . Ah, Lotus, you'll soon find that you have a Chinese firecracker in your cunt . . . I'll singe your ovaries with Roman candles and sky rockets will flash through your womb . . . The spark is catching . . .

Lotus may fuck in Chinese, but she comes in Parisian French.

Later in the night we become very gay over our wine and Lotus teaches me a few filthy Chinese phrases, each of which I forget in turn as I learn a new one. I fuck her again and again and in the morning I find she's gone, leaving a cheap jade trinket tied with a silk cord to my tired prick.

Visitors! Two of them. Sid, whom I have not seen since the night when we gave Marion such a hell of a going over at his place, and a cunt. Or a female. They perch politely on the edges of their chairs and we talk delicately of the weather or literature or something equally safe. She's a Miss Cavendish. A Miss Cavendish, with no first name. You need only hear her hoity-toity "How do you do?" to know that she is something that will be forever England.

Miss Cavendish, Sid explains, is a friend of his sister who lives in London. The explanation seems purely conversational and it seems that the visit has no purpose save a politely social one. But Sid goes on to say that Miss Cavendish is going to teach in Lyons and, since the job does not begin for almost two months, she plans to spend some time in getting acquainted with Paris.

One has to be civil, even with a female who wears tweeds and cotton stockings. I ask cheerful questions, just as I will cheerfully forget all about her tomorrow. And where is she staying?

Her glasses gleam as she turns toward me. "That's one of my problems," she says. "Sid has suggested that I might be able to get an apartment here." She takes a look at the place as though she were just seeing it. "It appears very nice . . . and inexpensive?"

"Oh sure," Sid assures her. "Alf, you'll fix things, do all the arranging, won't you?"

I'll arrange to wring his fucking neck! But there's nothing to do . . . she's moving in somewhere in the house. Anyway, she has nice legs, and there's an outside chance that she may be good for a fuck. But what a fine fucking friend Sid is! I wish that I could see her without her glasses . . .

When she is settled, says Miss Cavendish, we must not forget her, for Paris can be very lonely for a single girl alone . . .

Evening visitors . . . Anna, back from the grave, and ten minutes later Alexandra. Anna is sheepish about our little party of a few evenings ago. She laughs about it, with embarrassment spilling over the edges of her laughter. About what happened to her after she ran out of here without her clothes she is very vague. I don't press the subject. As soon as Alexandra arrives Anna remembers that she has another appointment. This time I remember to get her address.

Alexandra pours her troubles over my head like a libation. She is certain now that she is going for a trip to get away from Tania and Peter. Readjustment, she calls it. She sits on the couch and shows me her thighs while she calls the roll of the great sinners of history who have ended in the arms of Jesus. Perhaps . . . who knows? . . . she may even turn to the church herself, she confides.

"But would it be necessary to confess the details?" she wants to know. "Would the church have to know everything?"

I really don't know, but it's simple enough to see what she wants to be told. I give it as my opinion that Jesus would probably like to know the whole works. Alexandra shudders deliciously. If she could only escape the children, she says, everything would adjust itself. But they seem to have an evil grip on her. And Tania . . . she's far worse than Peter now that she's been to bed with her mother. She comes parading her naked little body into the room and there's no escaping her . . .

"I don't know what the end of it is to be," she says. She pauses, glances at me and quickly looks away. "Something really too depraved to mention occurred last night . . . I tell you only because I know that you understand. She tormented Peter into . . . into making his water right in my face while she had her mouth against my con. . . ." She wrings her fingers in distress. "The moment was . . . but you understand. In passion the mind is clouded . . . I believe I may have said something . . . perhaps I said that . . . I liked it. She called me a filthy name . . . and bit my thigh. The mark still remains."

Never a word, of course, of the times when she's pissed in Tania's face. That little depravity is passed over and forgotten. She lifts her skirt along the thigh to show me the place where Tania bit her. The white flesh bulges over her garters. And the mark, as she said, remains . . . a round, perfect imprint of Tania's teeth high up and on the inside, a few inches from her cunt. She raises her knee and parts her legs while I examine it. I squeeze her leg and begin to feel her up.

She didn't mean that this should happen! Not much! She's made herself and me hot with her little slide-lecture . . . she knows what she's after, this bitch. But if it's a sample of John Thursday she's after . . . his head is already up. I lay her skirt up to her belly and slip her pants down.

What an ass she has! She could harbor a nest of white mice in the bush between the cheeks and never know that they were there; they could live cosily with never a care in the world. I tickle the hair and she begins to warm up. Her fingers go into my fly and John Thursday leaps out.

While we lie there playing with each other she reveals

more of her adventures with those fuck-nutty kids of hers. She talks more freely as she becomes excited. Peter, it seems, now believes that sucking off a man makes him more potent. . . . it threatens to become a habit. I'm glad that I'm out of that asylum, but it's nice to hear what goes on there . . .

Do I guess, she asks me, why Tania has such a grip on her? It's because she likes so much to have her cunt licked . . . and Tania does it so shockingly. Nothing stops her. If it weren't for that perhaps she could break away. And while she tells me this she rubs her bush into my hand. It's an invitation, she's waiting for me to bend down and give her fig the same treatment that she describes, but she's disappointed.

I squeeze my dong between her thighs and rub her abricot-fendu with the end. She throws one leg over me and the split spreads. Alexandra reaches under her ass and sets my cock into the place where she needs it and manages to get a little of it in. She's so hot that she doesn't want to take the time to undress. I tell her that I won't fuck her with her clothes on. . . .

We compromise. Tania has told her so many things . . . yes, she even knows that her precious Peter sucked me off that day before I left . . . and will I fuck her the way Tania says I've done it? She wants me to do everything . . . . everything that I've ever done to her daughter.

She sits up to take her clothes off, and as soon as we're both naked I yank her off to the couch and put her to her knees in front of me. I wipe my cock in her hair and give it to her to kiss. Ah, I pull her face into my bush and let her lick it. A moment later I have it in her mouth, swabbing her throat. A few choice names go well too. She gobbles deliriously when I call her the bitch she is, in embroidered synonyms. . . . .

She slobbers over the end like a kid with a juicy lollipop. John Thursday is a mess but at least he's having his beard shampooed . . . She tries to lick my bush while she's got him in her mouth and almost succeeds in smothering herself. Then, when she's really working over my dong, when I've got her loving it so much that it hurts, I take it away from her.

Alexandra's too large to be tossed around like Tania, but I push her onto the couch and flop her legs up in the air. The whole underside of her, everything that's between her legs, sticks up. She raises the very devil when I suddenly push a finger up her ass and tell her to be quiet or I'll put my whole fist up there. With three fingers stuck into her rectum she's positively dizzy, but this is what she asked for, and I'm determined that she's going to get the whole thing.

She doesn't object when I turn my ass in her face and make her kiss it. She even licks the cheeks without too much fuss. But when I tell her to spread the cheeks and run her tongue over my rectum . . . ah, that is really too much! She can't do that, not even if her daughter did, she begins to tell me, but I put it against her mouth and make her kiss it anyway.

Shit, there isn't anything they won't do if you give it to them in the right way. In about three seconds I feel Alexandra's hot tongue slip into the bush under my ass and then she begins to lick it. I have to teach her the little game Tania invented, and soon she's running her tongue up my rectum and letting me shit it out again. And it makes her hotter, too . . . . she holds my dong in a death grip . . . if anyone tried to take it away from her she'd probably begin to tear the joint apart, pull down the walls with her finger-nails.

She must know what's coming next, but she pretends not to, so I make her name all the possibilities. Finally she hits upon it, speaking hesitatingly and as though hoping that she guessed wrong. It won't be, she suggests, that I intend to put my prick into her rectum. For a favor and a prize for guessing correctly I let her have another taste of John Thursday.

Oh, but not that, she pleads. She had forgotten, when

she suggested this, that I had done that to her daughter . . . but now she remembers . . . how the little thing was stretched and stretched and almost split . . . OH, ho! She doesn't know how it's accomplished, my prick is much too big.

She's faking, the cunt. And I finally win an admission. Well—doubtfully—perhaps she did consider it now and again . . . . it would be hard not to think about it after having watched me do it to her daughter. Yes, she might even have desired it to be done. I pinch her ass. What about it now, I want to know? Doesn't she want me to do it? Well. . . . DOES SHE? Yes, she thinks that perhaps she does want to do that.

I'm after her at once. I pull her around and set John Thursday knocking at her back door. She kneels with her legs far apart and hangs her head while I work him in. She doesn't object as she did when I first put my finger into her rectum . . . in that she is very much like her daughter. She simply waits for it to be accomplished.

Her rectum isn't as tight as I expected it to be. Either she's shoved candles up it or she's played this game before, I decide. My dong doesn't actually fall in, but there's none of the trouble I had with Tania, and quite soon I have it up there.

"You've done this before," I tell her. She is shocked. How can I possibly think such a thing? It's abnormal, to do such a thing as this! That's what the bitch tells me . . . it's abnormal!

Let it be abnormal, then. I fuck her this way because I like it, and she likes it too. Just to make certain, I pull my dong out. She looks around and reaches for it immediately.

"Please!" That's all she says, and it's enough to tell me what I want to know. But I tease her with it, start again to put my cock in and snatch it away. I like to hear her ask for it. I make her call herself a sucker of pigs, a five-sous licker of ass-holes, a whore who fucks dogs in the gutter. "Please put it back! I was lying . . . I like to have it done to me. . . .

Peter does it to me . . . Tania's seen him do it . . . Peter does it to me, yes, my own son pedicates me! Put it in and fuck . . . . Your cock is so much bigger than my son's. . . . My cocksucker son . . . ah, it's so wonderful to feel your prick there! Your wonderful prick that we've all sucked . . . my son and my daughter and I . . .

Tania's letter comes to my mind . . . now she wishes that I would come to see her and try the new tricks which she has learned. Well, if the girl isn't here, there's nothing to keep me from trying it with her mother. . .

Alexandra positively screams when she feels the scalding piss let into her ass. I don't know what she thinks, but it's a marvelous feeling for me. I keep my dong all the way into her and piss a stream. She begs me to stop, but I couldn't if I wanted to. I go on filling her with it until I feel her belly swelling in my hands. She moans that she's coming . . .

I pull her from the couch and she writhes before me on her knees. Its hot inside her, she whimpers, it's making her come in a way she never felt before. . . .

"Lift your face. . . ."

She clutches my knees and turns her chin up. "I know what you're going to do . . . Quick, now, ... while I'm coming. . . . please do it. . ."

She kisses my cock and presses it to her lips while I piss, lets some of the piss fall into her open mouth . . . Then, when it's finished, she stays on her knees and sucks my prick until another taste wipes out the old. . . . . .

Miss Cavendish is a fucking nuisance. Or, to speak more correctly, a non-fucking nuisance. In plain language she's a cock teaser, all promises and no follow-through. In three days of living here she's invented three hundred excuses for three hundred visits . . . or so it seems. If it isn't the faucet that drips it's her clock that won't tick. Instead of running down to the concierge she comes tapping at my door. The faucet needs nothing more than to be turned completely off and all that's wrong with her clock is that it hasn't been wound, but no matter . . . she has her excuse to come in and tease around a while.

The glasses have disappeared, and she's really quite good-looking. The tweeds and cotton stockings seem to have been packed away too . . . she blossoms out in organdy and silk. And she has thighs. . . .

The thighs I discovered the first time she came in to see me. It's easy to do, I suppose, to show just so much and no more, to drive a man nuts by letting him almost—but not quite—see that extra four inches. The hard part is to keep him from knowing that you're quite aware of what you're showing, and at that Miss Cavendish is not so good as she might be.

I thought at first that she was catting for a lay. But a few feelers put out in that direction put me off that trolley! She hasn't the slightest intention of letting her pants down for a man . . . at any rate, not for me. . . . but she teases and teases until I'd like to toss her out on her ass.

It isn't just with me that she plays her little game . . . Sid was certain that he was going to lay her, told me all about it, and even offered generously to put in a good word for me. Now he comes around with the news that she must use the douche bag that hangs in her bathroom to clean her ears with. He can't get anywhere.

Women like that can make a nervous wreck of you if you take them seriously. Two hours of carrying a dong in your pants and you're ready to go back to masturbation. And you can't help but take Miss Cavendish seriously. She's under foot too much of the time to be ignored. I have my nails bitten to the quick. . . .

Christ, you can't even cop a feel from her. She talks nothing but fuck. It's fuck-fuck-fuck every minute that she's around . . . but nothing direct, of course. Grandma might have called her a flirt or a coquette. She knows naughty stories about little boys and little girls . . . but try to touch that ass! She'll bring in a new pair of pants that she's just bought and ask you to admire them . . . . even lift her skirt and give you a comparative squint at the ones she has on . . . . but don't try to get too close to the pair she's wearing!

Then, when you're ready to give up in disgust, she becomes somebody else. The rules are changed, and she comes and sits on your lap. Then it's permitted to give her a little squeeze on the behind or play with her garters, but before you get anything more than a terrific hard-on she's gone again and you get a who-the-hell-do-you-think-I-am look the next time you try to touch her.

Last night Sid and I tried getting her drunk, but that didn't work worth a shit. Oh she got a little edge on, she laughed easily, and she even let us have a few peeps at her cunt . . . by way of those wonderful accidents she contrives to have happen. But that was all. When she had teased up to the point where the tension was becoming unbearable, she went home.

I'd let it go and forget her, but the bitch simply won't let me. This morning she came into my room with nothing but a bath towel wrapped around herself . . . a big bath towel, but only a towel nevertheless, to ask how the lock on the bathroom door works . . . .

Ernest is in bed when I call. He's been waiting to hear from me, he says, and he's glad to hear that Anna has turned up whole in mind and body. But he's more interested in my story about the little Chink he sent me to. I don't tell him that she cost me a week's pay. . . . .

It doesn't matter that I forgot to find out about the cocaine. He's off that cunt already, he says. She didn't want him after all. What she was after was a young Spanish cunt that she'd seen him with a few times, and Ernest is disgusted. The Lesbians are taking over the world under our very noses, he insists, under our very noses. A moment later he's made an epigram . . . it's cunt that they're taking from under our noses . . . from under our very noses.

Ernest acts uneasy, and I think that he may be expecting some cunt along. He lies with his knees drawn up and the covers bulked around them and apparently intends to stay in bed all day. I ask if he's feeling well. Oh yes, he's fine, just a bit tired . . . and he fakes a yawn. Well, I tell him, I guess I'll mooch along . . . and just then something moves under the bedcovers, at Ernest's knees.

I've seldom seen a man look so sheepish as Ernest . . . . When I see what he's been hiding I have to laugh.

"Which sex is it?" I ask him. Ernest pushes back the covers and a girl of ten or eleven climbs out from beneath his knees.

"Another two minutes and you'd never have guessed it," he says. "But now look, Alf, Jesus Christ, keep quiet about this, will you? You know how it is."

The girl pushes back her straight black hair and wipes her forehead, on the sheet. She complains that it was too hot under there . . . she was ready to die. She sits on the edge of the bed and stares at me.

"How the hell long have you been keeping this around?" I ask him. "What do you do? Give her peppermints to get her up here?"

She's the daughter of the people who keep the bar next door, Ernest tells me. And, he says defensively, she doesn't visit him only . . . . . everyone in the neighborhood knows about her.

"It isn't as though I just picked her up somewhere," he says. "Shit, there isn't a fucking thing I can teach her . . . she knows everything now. Just ask her a few questions, you'll see that I'm not shitting you. It's only that she's learned to fuck a little earlier than most girls do."

The girl spreads her legs and shows me her bare figlet. She even pulls it open to be certain that I get a good peep.

"You can fuck me if you want to," she pipes up. "Only I've got to let Mr. Ernest fuck me first."

Does Mr. Ernest fuck her very often, I ask her? No, this

is only the third or fourth time she's been here. He was just ready to fuck her when I came in. . . .

"Go right on," I tell Ernest. "I don't want to spoil anything." The girl has begun to play with herself with one hand and she's using the other to shake Ernest's cock up.

Ernest thinks that I don't understand. He's not doing anything that anyone else might do, etc. etc. On the other hand, I do understand, I assure him. I came close to doing the same thing myself. . . . in fact, strictly speaking, it might be said . . . . So Ernest feels better.

"By God, Alf," he says, "you ought to try her once. I never thought I'd see the day when I'd admit it, but it really does give you a kick." He pushes the bedcovers back with his feet and sits up. He gives the girl a pinch on her ass and sets her shoulders straight. "Look at her. Isn't she a little beauty? She'll be a fine cunt when she grows up. And she's filthy as hell . . . you ought to hear the line of gab she can toss out at you when she gets sore. And Christ, the stories she tells me! I don't believe half of them, but the half I do believe is bad enough. Did you know that they have a smell even when they're as young as this one? It's just sort of a suggestion, but it's there all right, all you have to do is get your nose close enough."

The girl stops playing with herself and grabs his dong with both of her hands. She knows enough about pricks to understand what makes them big. . . . she bends over and lets her hair tickle it while she slides her fingers up and down.

"It's not like this was all I liked to fuck," Ernest goes on. "Shit no! I'm only trying this as a change. And she's big enough. . . . it doesn't hurt her or anything. Jesus Christ, Alf, she's getting laid anyway. . . . I might as well try it and find out what it's like."

He'd be singing the national anthem in a minute, but the girl has him so excited that he's begun to stutter. She brings her mouth very close to his cock time after time and then draws away just as her lips are about to touch it.

"She wants to charge extra for sucking you off," he explains, "but she always forgets about it and does it anyway."

"Charge extra!" I shout. "Do you mean that they know enough to sell it at her age? By God when I was a kid. . . ."

" Sure she sells it. But that doesn't make it any less of a good fuck. . . . ."

The girl stops playing with his dick and starts to diddle herself again.

"You see that?" Ernest says. "She's nuts about that cunt and the feeling she gets out of it. The money part doesn't have anything to do with it, some dope probably gave her a few sous once and she found that she could get money too. But Jesus, Alf, when you get your prick into that little thing, when she starts to wiggle under you and rubs that little belly against yours . . . . I'm telling you, it's like nothing you ever tried before."

"I don't want to talk," the girl complains suddenly. "I want to be fucked."

"That's the way it is, Alf . . . . just like that, just like she said. Now watch her when she feels it between her legs. Shit, you'll think she's going to kill herself getting onto it. But she's plenty big enough inside. It's just the way it looks . . . . she doesn't take it in her cunt, she wraps herself around it. . . . . ."

She doesn't touch Ernest's cock when he gets himself arranged over her . . . she grabs his bush, a handful in each fist, and holds onto that. She lifts her ass a good six inches from the bed and seems to throw herself downward. It's amazing, but she has half of his dick into herself with just that one movement.

"The first time she did that I thought she was a goner," Ernest declares, "but that's how she seems to like it . . . can you see it? Christ, I used to hold a mirror behind her ass just to watch it. You can see the whole machinery with this little cunt, not a hair to hide the facts of life. And you ought to see. . . ."

Whatever it is that I ought to see, Ernest forgets it. The girl has begun to wiggle, and each time she gives her ass a

40 ·

shake it squeezes his dick in a little further. Ernest wasn't cheated when they were handing out pricks, either, and it really does begin to look as though the girl might do something to herself that can't be repaired without some fancy hem-stitching.

Her cuntlet stretches and stretches, until it's more than twice the size that it ought to be able to reach. But never a squeak out of the little mouse . . . she shakes her tail and tightens her legs around Ernest like a veteran. When it stops going into her it's because there isn't any more . . . all that she's left outside of herself . . . except Ernest . . . is a mop of hair and a pair of balls.

"Just take a good look at it now, will you, Alf," Ernest begs me. "Just as a personal favor to me. I want you to take a look at it and then tell me it's possible. Christ, I have had bad dreams about it at night, but I can't leave her alone. Ah, you little bitch, that's it. Wiggle some more! Jesus, I never had anything that was more like fucking a snake. . . ."

"What to Jesus are you going to do when you knock her up?" I ask him.

"What was that? What did you say? Knock her up?" Ernest becomes very excited. "Stop shitting me, she's too young to get knocked up . . . isn't she? Hey, what about that, Alf? How young can you knock them up? They have to have hair, don't they?"

"Like hell they have to have hair. All they have to do is have a hole to put it in, and you can get them in a fine family way. You mean to say you don't use anything with her?"

"Don't shit me any more, Alf. Anyway, I'm not the only one that fucks her. They couldn't prove anything on me. . . . could they? Hell, I'd drag the whole neighborhood into court, everybody around here lays her. Look, Alf, you wouldn't believe it if I pointed out some of the guys she tells me she's been fucked by. Even some of the women, honest to Christ! Not whores, either. Just people around here."

He lies there with his cock shoved into the girl's tail and

argues with me about the possibility of getting her knocked up. But the girl gets tired of hearing us talk. . . . she wants to be fucked, she says, and if Ernest isn't going to fuck her the right way she won't come to see him any more. So he swabs out her figlet a few times and then lets her take a couple that should have knocked her teeth crooked.

"Get this," he says. "See her ass twitching, sort of? She swears she's coming when she does that. Do you suppose she really goes? That's all that happens. . . ." He goes to work fucking her again. "But Holy Jesus, when I come in the little bitch. . . ."

He grabs her ass and half lifts her off the bed. His dong drives in and the bed groans. . . . or perhaps it's Ernest. The girl keeps her legs far apart to help him go in as far as he likes, and I imagine that I can see her belly filling out. . . .

"God, she takes gallons," Ernest gasps. "Imperial gallons . . ."

I'm actually shaky on my pegs when it's over. I'm in worse shape than Ernest, and he doesn't look exactly like a daisy. The girl passes the whole thing off with innocent nonchalance. She wants to know if I'd like to fuck her now!

"Go ahead, Alf," Ernest advises me from the bed. "You won't find anything like it again. But you'll have to do it on the floor or someplace . . . I simply can't move an inch from the spot I'm in . . ."

I tell the girl that I don't want to fuck her just now . . . some other day, perhaps, but she comes over anyway and rubs her baby ass against my knee. If I'll feel her up a little, she tells me, I'll want to fuck her.

"They all do after they've felt me," she informs me. "Put your hand between my legs . . . . you can feel Mr. Ernest's jism coming out of me now. . . ."

But I don't, I insist, I don't want to screw her, and I don't care to feel of Mr. Ernest's jism. Then would I like to be sucked off? No! Played with, perhaps? Or if there's anything else I'd like . . . . she slips between my knees and presses her belly against my cock. . . . I have a real dong on, she can feel that, and she can't understand why I can have a hard on and not want to screw her. She suddenly asks if I'm a fairy! Or if I haven't any money, she says she'll let me do it on credit just this one time.

Just this one time! The French Caution appears early. But even the inducement of credit fails to sway me, so she finally decides that I'm really serious. Well, she says, perhaps some time again. . . . Mr. Ernest will tell me where I can find her . . . she'll expect me. . . .

Miss Cavendish! A bitch on wheels if I ever saw one. This morning I got a look at her in the altogether as they say. It's some trouble with the toilet this time . . . she can't make it shut off and it's driving her out of her mind. Just why it should choose the moment when she is dressing to drive her out of her mind I don't know . . . . these things are beyond the scope of normal intelligence. But there's a noisy toilet and of course I'm the boy who's picked to do something about it.

It takes about fifteen seconds to lift the top from the thing, loose the float and replace the cover, and in that time Miss Cavendish manages to get out of the few clothes she had on when I came in and strut calmly from her bedroom to meet me as I'm coming out of the bathroom door. Oh, she's terribly shocked and dreadfully embarrassed, of course. She simply hadn't dreamed that it was anything which could be fixed up so quickly . . . she'd expected to be quite safe, running around the house that way . . . she's carrying a small, white scarf and she drapes that eloquently in front of her.

That bitch! She stands and fumbles the scarf until she's sure that I've had a complete exposure . . . teats, belly, cunt . . . the whole layout. And it's not bad, that I have to admit. Anna, perhaps, has better bubs, but Anna's an exception, you can't class the headlights she sports with the accessories that most women carry. And I note that Miss Cavendish has one of those big, deep navels, the kind that you could keep a horsechestnut in. What I can see of her cunt isn't a hell of a lot, since she's standing, but she takes care to keep her thighs apart so that daylight comes through them . . . . her mop hangs down in a reddish tuft.

She stands on one foot and then the other, giving me the full benefit of all angles, and when I have the complete plan blueprinted she turns slowly . . . ah, you can be sure it would be slowly! . . . presents herself in profile, and gives me the full read while she ambles back to the bedroom. And there I stand with a dong on and nothing to do with it.

I'd give my back teeth to fuck that cockteaser! Not because I think that she'd be such an incomparable lay, but because she makes me so fucking mad. I'd like to get my prick into her bush just once, just for the satisfaction of hearing her say a few well chosen words of apology to John Thursday . . . just to knock her off her high horse, take some of the starch out of her sails, put a spoke in her wheel, and a half dozen other metaphorical phrases which add up to fucking the nonsense out of her.

It's Arthur who has the wonderful idea. Sid and Arthur and I are in a bar, all just a little bit tight, and Sid has told Arthur the sad story of Miss Cavendish, to which I add my little piece from time to time as the occasion seems to call for it. Arthur, of course, is certain that we haven't been very smart about the bitch. Now if he had her, things would be entirely different. In fact, since we've let him in on a good thing, he'll help to make things different for all of us. The wonderful idea is that we'll go calling on Miss Cavendish and fuck her. There isn't the slightest chance that it can't be done, Arthur says, because there are two more of us than there are of her.

"We'll go up and talk to the young lady," he explains, "and we'll try to get her to fuck us peaceably. But if she won't—zingo! We'll rape the bitch!"

Sid applauds heartily. If only he could think of things like that, he says. But his mind doesn't work that way, he never sees the simple, obvious conclusion . . . So we go calling on Miss Cavendish.

She's quite glad to have visitors, she says when she lets us in . . . although we can see that she wasn't expecting anyone. She spreads the negligee she's wearing and lets us have a peek at her legs, leads us in and immediately provides a hospitable drink. While she's out of the room Arthur whispers to us that this is going to be easy, we won't have to rape her after all . . . didn't you catch the way she eyed him when she made that crack about being properly dressed? He gets the horse laugh.

Talk begins to roll around the room . . . Matisse . . . Gertrude Stein . . . I don't have to listen to take an intelligent part any more, I simply say the names, for no one listens to anyone else anyway. I keep my attention on Miss Cavendish. She's giving Arthur the works . . . her knee becomes uncovered again and again and the negligee falls open halfway up her thigh. The poor dope goggles at her and waits for the thing to come open far enough to let him see her fig . . . but if I know her there's a pair of pants under that negligee and Miss Cavendish has every intention of keeping them there.

It takes Arthur an hour to work his way to the couch at the same time that Miss Cavendish is there. Well, he'll find out . . . She lets him pat her knee and feel her up a bit . . . he can pinch her thigh from outside the negligee, but she won't let him get his fingers under it. When she leaves the couch he follows her, mooches around the place after her like a dog following a whiff of fresh meat. Sid and I pretend to be having an argument so there won't be any interference . . . it's rather funny to see someone else getting spiked . . .

Miss Cavendish has trotted out her naughty stories . . . and a few personal reminiscences designed to let Arthur believe that she might be a tiny bit naughty herself. The next time she's out of the room he tells Sid and me that we're a pair of lunks.

"She's dying for it," he says. "What the fuck's wrong with you bozos, anyway? Why she's like ripe fruit, all ready to fall off the tree into your hands. She's doing everything but asking out loud for it."

Here Miss Cavendish's voice cuts in. There's something wrong with the light in her bedroom. Won't someone come and see . . . ? She's afraid of electricity. . . .

"There it is, Art," Sid says. "Now she's asking for it out loud. So you just run in there and see what you can do. If you need any help we'll be right in."

Arthur hasn't been in the bedroom more than a minute when there's a scream and the cunt comes dashing out with Arthur close behind her. The negligee's half off, and as I expected, she's wearing a pair of pants under it. She runs into Sid's arms and snuggles her bare belly against him. Arthur, she gasps, attempted something unmentionable back there in the darkness.

Sid turns sternly to Arthur. "Why you nasty man, you," he says.

Arthur's tongue is hanging out and he doesn't see anything funny.

"Just give me the damned bitch," he says, "I'll give her something unmentionable to mention! Look at my fly! Who the hell do you think opened it? She did. The bitch, she had me in there with my cock out and everything and then she wouldn't give it to me. Hand her over, I'll fuck her."

"That wasn't the agreement," Sid argues. "We were all supposed to screw her, not just you. Where'll we do it, here or in the bedroom?"

The difficult Miss Cavendish can't believe what she hears. She leans back in Sid's arms to see if he's kidding, and finds that he's holding her tightly with no idea of letting her go. She demands to be released. Sid gives her bubs a squeeze and tells her to be a nice baby.

Then, when she decides that we're serious about it, she begins by demanding that we leave at once and ends by pleading that she didn't mean to do any harm . . . she was just joking, innocently.

"Then how about a fuck," I ask her, "a nice, innocent fuck, as a sort of joke?"

We can't talk to her that way! She'll scream if we don't release her at once or sooner! She'll have the police in to investigate if we make a false move. Ah, she'll see to it that news of the outrage reaches the proper authority!

"Look, Sid," Arthur says, "I can't stand this kind of talk . . . it makes me sick at my stomach. Anyway, she might scream at that, and it hurts my ears to hear a woman yell, so let's fix her up so she can't make those noises."

Sid gives her one more chance to come across peaceably. She won't, she screams. What kind of a girl do we think she is, that we expect her to let three men misuse her? Arthur stuffs a handkerchief into her mouth and ties it behind her head.

"Say something," he tells her, and Miss Cavendish says "goo" in I think a British accent. "That's fine," he admires. "Now, you cockteaser, you're going to find out what fucking is like. You're going to be raped on your own god damned bed, since you won't let anyone in it any other way."

She kicks and scratches, but the three of us are simply too many for her. We carry her into the bedroom and toss her into the bed. Sid and Arthur hold her while I strip her.

I've never raped anybody in my life before this. It always seemed pretty silly to me, but that was before I ran into this teaser. Now I'm for rape one hundred percent, and I've seldom enjoyed taking off a woman's clothes as much as I enjoy stripping this cunt. I feel her up, give her a squeeze here and a pinch there, and the more she squirms and blubbers into the gag, the harder my dong gets.

Since it takes two of us to hold her down it is decided

that the fairest arrangement all around is for us to fuck her in the order that we know her, one at a time. That makes Sid first, and he's in fine shape for it, too. Miss Cavendish takes one look at him with his pants off and squeezes her eyes shut. I can feel her trembling under me. I might feel sorry for her if I wasn't so fucking sore about the way she's acted. . . .

Sid takes his time about everything he does, even rape, it seems. He tickles her crotch and feels her up, beginning down at her feet and taking a long time to work back up to her bush again. He runs his hands over her belly, plays with her bubs . . . then he spreads her legs and takes a peek into her fig. She's no virgin, he announces. . . . .

Miss Cavendish is scared shitless. Possibly she thinks that we've already made plans to get rid of the body when we're through with her. But she still fights like a cat whenever she can catch enough breath . . . Sid has anything but an easy time making her hold still long enough to get his dong under her ass.

Arthur and I both lean over to watch his cock go into her . . . Sid opens the bonne-bouche and rubs his dick against the struggling, straining thighs. Miss Cavendish stares mutely from one to the other of us. Somehow she manages to slip the gag partly away, but fright seems to have taken her voice . . . she doesn't scream . . . she begs us, in a terrified whisper to let her go.

"Please don't do this to me! I won't ever tease anyone again, not so long as I live . . . I swear it! Oh, please . . . please! I'm sorry that I was such a beast . . . it won't happen again! Don't shame me any more . . "

But she's far too late with her good resolutions. Sometime later we may talk reasonably with her, but as Arthur tells her, she has a lesson to learn first. Sid slips his dong into her mop . . . her thighs strain away. Arthur and I stop playing with her bubs and give Sid a clear road. Her belly quivers and quakes and I notice that her nipples are erect . . . they stand up, large and dark in the center of the dark eyes of her teats. . . .

"NO . . no . . no . . no. .no . . . ."

Sid has squeezed the end of his prick into her tail. He forces it in . . . his balls brush against her smooth legs. He keeps her thighs spread and slowly gives it to the bitch. Her belly recoils from his as he leans against her and begins to fuck her. She moans. She doesn't want to look or have anyone see her face . . . Sid holds her head and makes her open her eyes.

"Now, you bitch, how do you like it? This is what you've been teasing us for ever since I've known you . . . why don't you smile? Aren't you happy, you lousy cunt? Feel that prick in your cunt, God damn it! I want you to feel it! Here, maybe this will help you know what you've got in there!" He fucks her so hard that it's impossible to tell whether it's her struggling or the fucking that tosses her about the bed. "You won't be so tight when I've screwed you . . . it won't be so easy for you to keep your legs crossed when you have some poor bastard sweating to lay you . . ."

For the first few minutes the cunt fights him. But nothing will let that dong out of her tail now, not before Sid's finished. She finds that it's no use . . . she can't push him off . . . her struggles become weaker . . . she's defeated. There's nothing for her to do but let it be done. She becomes still.

"Ah, now she's becoming reasonable," Sid declares. "Maybe she's learning again that it's nice to be fucked . . . she must have liked it once . . . somebody's screwed her before this. We should have done this last week . . . I think she enjoys being raped! You fucking teaser, you won't do your act so easily tomorrow! Listen, stingy pants, there are three of us. Get that . . . three of us. Three cocks just like the one you're being fucked by right now, and we've been kidded by you for a long time . . . don't think that one fuck each is all you're going to get . . . we're going to fuck you once and twice and three times . . . God knows how often, until we've fucked ourselves out on you. We'll give you a night like nobody but a whore ought to know . . . shit, maybe we'll go out and get some of the boys and sell fucks off you, maybe you'd like to be a whore . . . But you won't be so spry when this is over, you won't be ready to hop through the daisies. . . ."

He's really fucking the piss out of her by this time. He's got the juice coming out of her by spoonfuls and he must have her womb opened up too. When he's ready to come I expect the bed to come down under us . . .

"Here's a little something to warm your cunt," Sid yells at her. "Maybe there won't be enough to fill you right up to the edges, but don't worry . . . you have plenty more coming . . . Hold her, you guys . . . She'll jump a mile when she feels it. . . ."

"Don't do that!" She begins to beg again . . . having Sid's jism dropped into her trap seems worse to her than just having him fuck her. "You can't do it to me!"

But Sid goes on and shows her that he very well can. He pulls his dick out and as a parting insult shakes the jism off the end onto her belly. Miss Cavendish hides her head under the kicked up covers and moans.

Sid has accomplished at least one thing . . . he's opened her up so far that it isn't the slightest bit tight when I climb on her. And she doesn't fight me so hard, either. Oh, she doesn't exactly throw her legs around my neck and shout a welcome . . . she raises a minor bit of hell. Not another one, she pleads . . . we won't make her go through that torture again will we? Haven't we had our revenge?

It's really nice to hear her beg after the way I've been treated in the past few days, and I tease her a while before I fuck her up, just to hear it. I've been going nuts thinking about putting my tail up her legs and now that the time has come when I can do it I get everything out of it that I can . . . I tickle her bush with my cock, feel that fucked-open split that she's been such a bitch about . . .

"Hey Sid," I yell, "she's got something coming out of her cunt! I think it's jism . . . it's all over her legs. What'll I do about it?"

Sid takes a look at her and declares that it's at least half cunt juice.

50 ·

"Shove your cock in her and push it back in," he advises me. "We don't want her to lose any of it . . . we have to keep her nice and juicy for the next round . . . and if we decide to raffle off fucks on her or something, we want her to be nice for the boys . . ."

"Jesus Christ, will you stop talking and give her a fuck, Al?" Arthur protests hoarsely. "I can't just feel her teats any longer . . . I'll come right in her face. Honest to Jesus, if you don't give me a shot at her I'll have to shove my cock down her throat, and we don't want to have to fuck a corpse . . . . so soon."

The girl is wrapped up in the covers by now, but I untangle her before I put my prick up her fig. I want to see all of her, I want to be able to feel everything and see just who and what I'm screwing. I let John Thursday sniff in her hair. . . . .

There's a tide sloshing around inside her . . . Sid must have tossed her one hell of a juicy cud . . . either that or she's a damned wet fuck. My dong is positively submerged. John Thursday has to swim for his life in there. But it doesn't interfere with his pleasure.

"Come knocking at my door again sometime, will you?" I beg the girl. "Just come around tomorrow and rap three times. I'll be there, Johnny-on-the-spot." I slip my prick deeper and feel her become limp under me. "What do you have . . . a clock that needs winding? A cunt that needs fucking? Just call on me, rap three times and I'll fix you up. . . . ."

I smack her bare ass. . . . God, it's a treat to be able to do that! . . . I grab her bubs and lick them. Even if she has to be held while I do it, I CAN DO ANY FUCKING THING I WANT! I stretch her conillon, let my prick head into her womb. . . . .

The room becomes sea-sick. Her cunt smells like the sea, and the world rocks like a boat. I lose sight of things . . . I scatter jism like spray. . . . .

Arthur can't wait to have his turn. He pushes me off and gets between the girl's thighs. She's too weak to do a thing to stop him now. Her legs open weakly and she does not even attempt to keep them together against him.

One shot and he's in. He wiggles his cock under her ass and tries to climb in after it. She doesn't try to hide her face any longer . . . she simply lies there and lets him fuck her . . . it's no effort to hold her.

Sid puts his prick into her hand and tells her to play with it. She closes her fingers. I put my dick in her other hand . . . it's still wet. . . .

"Don't fuck me any more . . . please don't fuck me any more . . ." She seems too weak to talk above a whisper.

Arthur stops fucking her. "Maybe we are fucking her too much," he says. "I don't want to hurt her even if she is a cockteaser."

Sid climbs down and looks into her fig. There's nothing wrong with her, he says. It can't be hurting her . . . it's as fresh looking as when we started, just a little more open.

"Go to it," he says. "If there was anything wrong she'd let you know about it. Listen you cunt . . . yes, YOU! I want you to tell the truth. . . . . . are we hurting you, or aren't we?"

He looks so damn fierce that the cunt's afraid to lie. No, she says, whispering, it doesn't hurt her a bit. But she can't stand any more . . . . . she'll never tease us or anybody else again. . . .

Which is all that Arthur wanted to know, of course. He pops his cock into her abricot-fendu and does his bit to widen the chamber. He groans like a tired camel and leaves her with a thick flood that soils her thighs.

"See this," he says, pointing out a patch of jism on the bed. "Tomorrow when that itch comes again you can sniff these spots and play with yourself . . . or you can chew on the sheets if you like to eat it."

Sid reaches between her legs, smears his fingers with jism, and rubs them against her lips. "Lick them off, damn you," he says. "Maybe we'll let you suck us off if you like it . . . maybe you'll suck us off anyway . . ."

"I wouldn't trust that cunt to take my cock in her mouth," Arthur says. "I'd probably wind up with only half a cock and one ball. For Christ's sake, Sid, don't be nuts, don't give her a chance to set her teeth in you. I've been bitten by bitches, I'm telling you, I know what it's like. . . ."

Sid bends over Miss Cavendish and whispers in her ear. "How about it, you cunt?" he asks. "I'll bet that you've tasted cock before now, haven't you? Oh, don't be so fucking coy about it, you're among friends . . . . . your nearest friends. Did you ever have a prick in your mouth?"

BOOK 11

The French
Way

Miss Cavendish doesn't want to play our game any longer. I can see her viewpoint . . . Sid's fucked her, I've fucked her, Arthur's fucked her, and she's had enough. As a final spit in her face Sid is prying into her private life . . . and Miss Cavendish is very British. Sid wants to know if she has ever sucked a cock, but he won't find out, certainly not the way he's going about it.

Of course she's deserving everything that's happening to her tonight . . . every time the hollow voice of conscience gives a burp I remember the teasing this bitch gave me; it helps a great deal to keep me from feeling sorry for her. The really remarkable thing, when you turn the case of Miss Cavendish over in your mind, is that she hasn't been raped before this. A cunt who acts the way she does might as well wear a tag: "Forceful Persuasion Solicited." After a few experiences with Miss Cavendish you begin to feel violent. That she's managed to escape for so long is simply another indication of the general helplessness of the male sex.

Take Sid, for example . . . he's been hanging around for a long time and as many things have happened to him as happen to most people, but if the three of us hadn't happened to get together tonight he would probably never have done anything about this bitch the way she was treating him. For that matter, I let her have pretty much her own way with me until tonight. Well, I don't suppose that there will be much tapping on my door from now on . . . I suspect that her solitary household here will run more smoothly, with fewer calls for assistance. . . .

Arthur is almost in tears because he believes that Sid is going to have his dick bitten off before his very eyes. It's an actual phobia with him . . . a couple of experiences of his own have given him a bad case of the shits on the subject. He pleads with Sid to leave well enough alone. Throw her another screw, he says, and to Jesus with being sucked off . . . . at least for tonight. Some other time, next time we lay Miss Cavendish, when she's not so overwrought and liable to excesses in one direction or another, it would be a fine thing, he suggests.

"How about that?" Sid says to Miss Cavendish. "Do you think you'd feel more like sucking us off some other night? Say . . . night after next?"

Asking Miss Cavendish how she's going to feel two nights from now is like asking a drowning man if he's considered where he'll spend his next summer vacation . . . she hasn't the time to think about it, but she hopes that there will be another night to put an end to this one. It occurs to me that the reason she hangs onto Sid's and my cocks may be because as long as she has them in her hands we can't fuck her. She stares at the ceiling, looking very long and very naked stretched across the bed, and Sid plays with her cunt. When he pinches it, jism bubbles out.

Arthur thinks we ought to screw her again and at once. "Full measure," he says. He gives a little lecture on the subject of our obligation both to those who came before us and those who are to come after. The first lay, he declares, was for pleasure only . . . the second is a responsibility we have taken onto our shoulders. The second round, it seems, is the one that really counts, the one that takes the nonsense out of her.

"Shit, don't you see how it is?" he says, sounding the slightest bit drunk. "Now we've got her so she won't tease us again. . . . but that isn't enough. We have to fix her so she won't tease anybody, and that means we have to give her another . . . shit, anybody can see that."

Just how this conclusion is arrived at is not as clear as it might be, but no one disputes Arthur's logic. Sid tells him to go on and fuck her.

"I'd do it myself," Sid says, "but I can't bear to take my dong away from her. Doesn't she hold it nice? Just like it was a flower or something." He chucks Miss Cavendish under the chin.

Arthur swats his dong a couple of times. It's limp as a rag, and it's apparently going to stay that way.

"It isn't that I don't feel like screwing her," he explains. "But Jesus, I just climbed off her. You can't expect it to bounce right up again. How about you, Alf?"

When Arthur says that, I can feel the cunt's fingers twitch and tighten on my prick. She's still scared, and it seems that she's finding out if I am in condition to take her over. John Thursday's in fine shape. . . .

"Don't do it anymore . . ." Miss Cavendish without her glasses is remarkably good-looking, and she almost succeeds in making me feel that we're playing her a dirty trick. "I won't inform on you, I promise, if you don't do anymore to me. . . . . . ."

She won't inform on us! Female logic is enough to make a man slit his throat. She's been criminally . . . actually criminally teasing Sid and me for days . . . before that . . . God knows how many men or how many years. She's thrown that cunt in our faces and then snatched it away at the last minute often enough to make gibbering idiots of us, and chronic masturbators as well. But now . . . SHE's going to refrain from informing on US! I almost throw my cock up under her tail . . . if John Thursday had feet only his toes would be sticking out.

"This one's for the time you needed me to set the mousetrap," I tell her, and in goes my cock again. "And this one's for the time you wanted me to hang your pictures while you skittered around in a bathrobe that kept falling almost off. And this one's for the window that got stuck . . . the closet that wouldn't open . . . the wallpaper that came loose. . . ."

I have a list that could go on for several minutes, but I never could talk as fast as I could fuck. I hammer my dick into that bitch's fig until it's ready to split completely. But she's too unresisting now . . . I give her ass a pinch to put some salt under her tail . . .

"She's a hell of a cunt," Arthur says disgustedly. "Either she wiggles too much or you can't get a move out of her. Maybe we ought to teach her how to fuck as long as we are here. Fuck, damn it, or I'll piss in your ear . . ."

Miss Cavendish comes back to life sufficiently to inform Arthur that she isn't going to be intimidated. We may be able to rape her, but she won't be coerced . . . we can subdue her body, but not her will, etc. etc. . .

"Maybe we'll have to put the screws on, Sid," Arthur says.

"Yeah, it looks like we'll have to make things a lot clearer . . . look, bitch, did anyone ever lay a fat turd over your pretty nose and then wipe their ass on your hair? Then give you a bowl of piss to wash in? Or take pictures to peddle on the Boulevard des Capucines and maybe send to some of your friends back in England? No, I didn't think so . . ."

Miss Cavendish quiets down at once. Arthur chimes in . . . he has always wanted to make some photographs to end all photographs. He has some ideas . . . Miss Cavendish with a Roman candle firing out of her ass and a black turd held in her toes, patriotically waving the tricolor. . . Miss Cavendish standing on her head or hung by her toes in a corner while a mangy street dog . . . or perhaps a fat little boy . . . tries his aim on her . . .

"Or would you rather be a nice girl and fuck?" he asks.

It is very difficult for Miss Cavendish to make herself bump bottoms with me. But Sid and Arthur have scared the piss out of her . . . she believes us capable of doing anything. Sid calls for more enthusiasm . . .

"Allegro con moto," he shouts at her. "Jesus, what a lousy motion you've got! Hey, is that the way you think people fuck? No wonder you don't lay. . . ."

"That's strictly a play-with-yourself motion," Arthur advises Sid. "It gets to be a habit, sort of . . . but if you put your prick up their ass a few times that goes away."

"Will you shut up?" I yell at them. "She'd be all right if

you'd leave her alone . . . shit, I've paid good money for worse fucking than this . . ."

Miss Cavendish doesn't care for the compliment. She tries to look reproachful but succeeds only in looking slightly dazed. My cock slips out of her fig and she holds her ass up so I can get it back in . . .

Arthur swears that she's beginning to like it . . . Sid says that he's merely imagining things.

"She isn't supposed to like it," Sid says. "If she likes it then we aren't doing it right. How about that, Alf . . . do you think she likes it?"

I can't think about anything but my cock . . . it's lost up in her tail, and I'm coming. . . .

Sid's ready to take her next. The bitch doesn't even close her legs after I'm through with her . . . she keeps them spread and waits for Sid to climb on . . . We've stopped pretending to hold her, so I sit on a chair and watch from across the room.

Sid fucks her for a long time. When things begin to get too hot for him and he's ready to pop off he stops and rests, and Miss Cavendish doesn't know any better than to stop too. If she'd gone on fucking he'd be finished in half the time, but as soon as he stops poking his dong into her she quits too. I become tired just from watching them . . .

"You know, she's really not too bad," Sid says critically during one of the pauses. "If we come up here real often we might be able to make a real cunt out of her. Say . . . well could you spare two nights a week, Arthur?"

But the threats are having less effect on Miss Cavendish now . . . perhaps she's convinced that nothing worse can happen to her or perhaps she knows that we're shitting her. She looks at Arthur's cock . . . it's been swelling up in her hand.

"Stop shitting around and get her fucked, will you?" Arthur complains. "I got this thing up again, but it won't stay that way all night . . ."

Sid rams his dong under her ass and closes his arms around her like a crab . . . Miss Cavendish lets out one little squeak and then everything is quiet. Sid is shaky when he pulls his dick out again . . .

Arthur takes a squint into Miss Cavendish's bonne-bouche. How to Jesus, he wants to know, is anyone going to fuck a trap like that? It has to be bailed out first . . . otherwise he might just as well stick his prick into a pail of hot milk.

Sid tells him not to be such a dope . . . all that's necessary is to give it to her from in back. Just put her on her belly and it will be all right . . . everything will run forward in her then, he explains.

"Here, we'll turn her over," he says. But before he touches her, Miss Cavendish rolls over by herself.

"That's fine," Arthur says rather surprisedly. "Now just stick your ass up to where I can get this thing under it . . ."

It's really funny to see Miss Cavendish shove her behind up and then look around to see what's going on. I begin to laugh and when Sid and Arthur start too Miss Cavendish looks as uncomfortable as I've ever seen a woman look. Arthur smacks her on the ass . . . She hides her face in her arms when he screws her . . .

Sid makes a farewell speech while he is climbing into his pants. Modesty! Miss Cavendish covers herself with a sheet and keeps her eyes turned away until we're all safely in our clothes. We have found her hospitality bewitching, Sid tells her . . . perhaps we may call again tomorrow . . . say at nine? . . . and he has a friend or two who would like to know her . . .

Ernest sits rolling a cigarette, spilling most of the to-bacco down his coat front. Ernest grew up in Oklahoma and never allows you to forget it. He talks of going back there some fine day, but he never will. He can't go back because there never was such a place as the one where Ernest thinks he grew up . . .

He admires the hanging I bought from the Chinese cunt. Very nice, he says, and does everything seem to be all right with my cock? In that case, then, perhaps he may take a stroll down to her shop himself one afternoon.

And what about his little girl, the one I found him in bed with a few morning ago? Oh, that little bitch! But wouldn't he like to get his hands on her! He kicked her out one day when he had a cunt coming up to his place, and she wrecked the place next day when he was out. She pulled his books from the shelves, tore all his papers in the desk, cut his mattress with a razor, then took a shit just inside his doorway where he stepped in it when he came in.

"Kids," he says. . . . "Christ, they're horrible, especially the precocious ones. That little cunt, for instance . . . she's as vindictive as a woman and she has the awful imagination of children. Jesus, it scares me to think of kids . . . they like Red Ridinghood and the wolf in bed . . ."

Ernest wants to know if I'd like to see his Spanish cunt, the one his Lesbian painter was after. She hangs around in some spic joint where you can see a real Spanish flamenco. . . .

On the way out I stop and listen at Miss Cavendish's door. There isn't a sound in there. There hasn't been all day, and a telegram has been stuck on the knob since morning . . .

A hag, evil and old as the witch of the fairy tales, tends the cloakroom. In America, no matter how slimy the joint, they'd have something young and sexy to park your hat . . . but these people are realists . . . to them a good-looking bitch in a cloakroom is a waste of the worst sort. Anyone can hang up your coat, but a handsome cunt can be put to better use . . . Ernest whispers to me that you make appointments for the back rooms with this ancient broomstick galloper. . . .

The joint is full of Spanish sailors, pimps and whores. Those I can pick out. The others . . . God knows . . . you'd have to read their police records to learn what or who they are. Ernest finds his cunt immediately.

"Hands off," he says from the corner of his mouth as we go to her table. "And stick to the wine here . . . it's safer."

The place has a sour stink of old food and stale beer. I'm glad that we ate before we came here. . . .

Ernest needn't have warned me about his cunt . . . we don't like each other. She's pretty enough, and I suppose I could lay her without having to turn out the lights, but we simply don't attract each other. She and Ernest begin to argue about the Lesbian . . . she thinks he's being stupid about it . . . the Lesbian gave her presents, and Ernest doesn't. I begin to feel bored . . .

The little orchestra pounds away on the jerky tunes . . . One thing about those fellows, they're persistent! One at a time three women dance . . . they all have gold teeth. It's all so terrible that even a tourist would know that this is authentic . . . the real thing . . . An hour drags off like a lamb chicken . . .

Without any warning whatsoever a girl comes onto the floor. She's veiled, but you can see that she's young and a very pretty cunt. The bozos who've been making all the noise put their guitars down . . .

"Flamenca," Ernest says, "they tell me she's the youngest girl dancing it. . . . I mean really dancing it."

For all I know it may be just so much shit . . . but people who claim to know have told me it takes ten years to make a flamenca. Ten years to learn to do a dance that takes ten minutes! It's one of those things that don't interest me very much . . . it all seems like such a fucking lot of wasted effort, like learning the Bible by heart. But anyway, it's supposed to take ten years, and therefore the women who dance the flamenco are all past the age where they ought to be doing that kind of dance.

But this girl! Ernest's girl sees the way I'm watching her and tells me that the flamenca performs again, in a room upstairs, to a more restricted audience. She ripples her shawl, clicks the castenets. The dance begins, and you can see at once that this cunt knows what she's about. The idea of the flamenco seems to be that if it gives you a hard on it's well done. . . .

"What's her name?" I ask, as the cunt whirls by and gives me a look that spells bedroom. "What about this dance she does upstairs?

"You have to see Grandma out in the cloakroom about that," Ernest says. "The girl's name is Rosita. . . . but watch out! That little rose has thorns." . . . . .

She warms your blood, this cunt. She puts pepper under your tail. . . . John Thursday sniffs cunt somewhere in the air and raises his head. Ernest and his bitch are playing with each other under the table. If the dance lasted another three minutes Rosita would have everyone in the place jerking off. . . .

The girl swirls off with a twist of her ass that wraps her heavy Spanish skirt and the petticoats under it around her legs. I turn to Ernest. I have to know if this show upstairs is a fake.

"Look Alf," he says, "All I know is that she dances naked upstairs. I never saw it or anything."

"Why don't we go up and take a look at it . . . all of us?"

But ladies aren't allowed. It's for men only, and Ernest doesn't want to leave his cunt now. Well I'll go up . . . I go out to the cloakroom and haggle with Granny. . . . I simply have to see it.

Upstairs, in a room without windows and without air, there are about twenty men sitting at tables and gabbing. Not so many sailors here . . . mostly greasy men in business suits and wearing flashy diamonds as big as your balls. . . I grab the only good place left and order wine.

They don't keep you waiting long. In America, at a show like this, they'd jack the price of drinks up four times and then hold out on you until the rent for that month had been collected. But here as soon as everybody who's coming up is there, the girl comes on. . . .

Rosita appears at one side. Naked, shit. . . . she's worse than naked. . . . She wears a high comb and the mantilla is long . . . the end of it just touches her ass. Red slippers with very high heels, BLACK STOCKINGS! The stockings come high on her thighs, and to keep them up she has tied the garters very tightly . . . the skin pinches out over the edges . . . Over one arm she carries a lace shawl . . . also black. Then. a touch of the old crap, a rose in her hair.

She doesn't begin to dance until she's paraded across the floor, giving us all a chance to see just what we're getting. My cock comes up like something on strings . . . A sailor tries to grab at her ass, but she twists by him. I wouldn't have been surprised if he'd tried to bite it.

She has hair, this cunt, and you can see it through the lace shawl that she droops from her arm so that it just covers her bonne-bouche . . . Her mop looks more like the black fur of some animal than like an ordinary bush. But she carries the shawl so well that you never get a peep at her trap until she's ready to show it to you.

Whether you'd call her young or not depends on where you grew up and what your tastes are. . . . she's eighteen, and she has bubs that make you think of going on a milk diet. They're big and they wiggle, and the nipples are like red knobs . . . Her ass wobbles every time she takes a step, and around her waist there are the marks of the corset she's just taken off . . . they make you think of the whip. . . .

She's left the veil off, and while a Spaniard would probably have reservations about her looks (they look for the woman; they know their girls don't last long), she's just the kind of cunt I would go looking for if I had an itch for some Latin tail. I take a look around the room. Every eye is fixed on her like a rubber stamp. Christ, she must feel that she's being eaten every time she comes out to dance. . . .

I don't know what they pay girls to do this sort of thing. It's not like being just another whore. . . . Take a whore . . . a man comes to her with an itch in his britches and she does her best to fix it up. It's a service, really a kindness of the whore. But to go out in front of twenty men every time you perform . . . to go out and deliberately put that itch in their pants . . . that's really whoring. What it amounts to is going out there and being asked to be ravaged, teasing men up until every one of them is fucking the Jesus out of you in his imagination. Then, when you've taken it, what can there be left for you? Christ, they'll have to invent a new currency . . . . there's nothing in the Bank of France to pay for that . . .

Rosita's heels tap the floor like pebbles on a roof. She throws her head back, and her teeth gleam . . . her teats rise, and her belly is thrust forward . . . the shawl sways . . .

John Thursday sticks out like the sawed-off limb of a tree. If I wanted to I couldn't keep him down . . . not with that bitch throwing herself in front of him . . . She whirls across the room and her shawl seeps up . . . her belly is dark and hairy . . . a fingerline of hair twists up it from her bush. . . her fig is a red bulge, split moistly down the center. . . looking fecund and open.

Her heels stamp louder and her teats jump with every step she takes . . . her eyes begin to look slightly drunk.

"Dance, you cocksucker, dance!" someone shouts in Spanish. Everyone in the room laughs, and Rosita tosses a dark smile over her shoulder. Someone pinches her ass. She shrills and leaps away, changing the leap into a bold drunken step and the cry into a dancing shout . . . Her hips squirm wildly . . . . .

"Ah!" the cry comes from many throats as the dance changes. She's fucking now, fucking some image in her mind . . . Fucking all of us . . . She throws her ass forward and back. . . You can almost see the fingers running across her belly, down her arms, along the moving hips. . . . .

No one in the room moves now . . . Rosita lays her hands on her hips, turning slowly until she has faced every table, offering her cunt to every man . . . Hungry eyes bulge from inflamed faces on every side. . . she is ringed, walled in by lust . . . wherever she turns there is a pair of eyes to take her . . . She cowers into a smaller and smaller circle until she is standing in the center of the floor turning slowly on tip-toe.

Every man who watches her now . . . . they see her before them, supplicating pity . . . Rosita falls slowly to her knees . . . . her head bows as she reaches forward . . . her mouth seems to meet something with a wolfish, obscene noise . . . She is forced backward, bracing herself with arms that cannot resist the pressure that strains downward against them . . . Her knees spread as her body goes back . . . the men begin to howl. . . .

And the bitch can laugh then! She rocks with high, contemptuous laughter, letting her body fall backward, spreading her knees further, showing her cunt up . . . The room growls angrily. Rosita's laugh rises like a tide of hysteria over the muttering roar that creeps toward her. . . .

"Filthy beast!" a man spits at her as she laughs in his face. A sailor tosses his beer. I can feel my balls creeping in my pants . . . Christ, can't the bitch see what's doing? Some of these bozos are drunk enough to beat her to death . . . One big bastard knocks over his chair and sways toward her . . . he stands over her and raises his fists over his head . . . Rosita laughs and his face grows livid . . . the muscles bunch heavily in his arms . . .

Somehow the cunt is on her feet. The big guy reaches towards her like a bear . . . and she throws her open shawl in his face. As she runs to the door someone catches her mantilla . . . the comb is yanked from her head and her hair falls down over her shoulders. . . .

I know one thing . . . in three minutes there'll be twenty men at the cloakrooms arguing with Granny. Shit, maybe they line up at Rosita's door . . . I run down the stairs. . . .

"Quick! That girl who dances upstairs . . ."

The hag takes my money and counts out the change in a saucer. Number three along the back hallway . . . She's a very nice child, willing, and sure to please . . .

Rosita is sitting on a small iron bed smoking a tobacco-wrapped cigarillo. She is exactly as she was when she ran out of the room . . . her breath still comes quickly. . . .

"I thought it would be you," she says. Then she adds, "I hoped it would be you . . ."

All of her customers may get the same line . . . that doesn't matter. I look her over and grab for her fig. She laughs and throws the cigarillo away. Her belly feels hot and slightly sweaty.

Her eyes, while I'm taking off my clothes, remind me of those of the men who watched her dance. She looks at John T. as though she'd like to bite his head off . . . She's hot, there's no question about it. . . .

"Look," she says. She spreads her legs and gives me a peep at her conillon. There's a juice between her thighs; she has a small river under her ass. She lies back in my arms while I feel her up . . . suddenly her teeth prick my arm like hot needles.

I can give her what she wants . . . she grabs my balls and rubs the knobs of her bubs against my chest, then her fingers catch my dong by the throat. . . . she yanks John Thursday's beard and tickles his chin. She makes a soft, pleased sound like a cat, when she finds how hard he is. When I feel her up she begins kicking her toes into the bed . . . the covers become a mess, hard and lumpy under us . . . Rosita squeezes my thighs between her legs rubbing her bush and her cunt against me . . . she's playing with herself against my leg, and that hairy belly is tickling my hip.

I drag her from the bed and put her on her knees, exactly as she was at the climax of the dance. She looks up at me. . . .

She knows what I want . . . My dong quivers in front of her. . . . She places her hands against my knees and bends . . she takes my prick in her mouth and sucks, waiting for me to force her backward. . . .

Laugh now, you bitch! Try to laugh with that cock in

your mouth! Try to spill your laugh around the edges, into my bush, it will catch in the bristles. . . . I'll push your laughter down your throat, cram it into your belly and out your ass. . . . I'll make your laugh a slobber, and after I've come, your laughter will be choked with jism . . . when you giggle little squirts of jism will come out of your ears . . . and for hearty laughter you will have special tears of jism . . . . to drip from your nose . . . . .

Rosita's braced arms give under my pushing . . . her knees spread and she drops back until her hair sweeps the floor. I kneel, keeping my cock in her mouth, and she sucks, digging her fingers into my hips. I feel her belly rising and falling under my ass . . . I give her bubs a pinch and make her lick her slobbering off my balls . . .

She can't swallow the jism when I come! Her head is too low and she chokes when she tries to do it . . . but I hold her, I keep my dick in her mouth until things are steady again, and then I find that she's still sucking it. She hasn't stopped, not for an instant, and she has a mouthful of jism that she can't swallow.

I lift her up, put one arm around her, and get my hand in her hair. She shakes her head . . . she won't swallow it. She turns away from me and we wrestle on the rug for a few moments. Suddenly she laughs and opens her mouth to show me that it's gone.

She lies on her belly while I sit on the floor and she begins licking my dick again. Her tongue wiggles around my balls and she kisses them. Did I like her dance, she wants to know? It's like that every time she dances, she tells me . . . she shows them everything, and they end up growling. One night a Negro, a big black fellow with blue lips, slashed her with a razor . . . she shows me a fine, raised line diagonally across her belly. . . . Afterward he came in and fucked her and stayed all night. . . . the only Negro she ever allowed Grandma to send to her room.

I wonder why there hasn't been someone else along to bang at the door yet. Oh, but that isn't the way she does it.

Sometimes she takes one . . never more than three after she's danced. Now and then she lets two men in at once, but never any more. She could have them all if she wanted to, but she only did that once. Fifteen men, one right after the other just after she'd danced! And they were so rough she was afraid . . . she had to have two of them thrown out.

How long had she been dancing? She doesn't know . . . she thinks she was twelve when her father had her take off her clothes and dance naked for some men . . . he kept a bar back home in Madrid. She remembers that she was scared . . . one of the men wanted to fuck her and her father caught him playing with her on a dark porch later . . . her father knocked him down the step. . . . She lied and said that he really hadn't done anything to her . . . . she'd been kissing his prick and putting it into her mouth. . . . .

Telling me this, she kisses my dong and puts it into her mouth. I'm getting another hard on . . . she licks my legs and my belly. She likes me, she tells me . . . if I hadn't come to her room she intended to go downstairs and look for me. Would I like to arrange to stay all night? It won't cost me any more, and she'll guarantee that she can give me more erections than any other girl in the place . . .

I explain that I'm with friends, that I'll have to go down soon . . . and the cunt actually appears to be disappointed. She puts my prick in her mouth and sucks me off for another few minutes . . . then she gets up and lies on the bed with her legs spread. She strokes her bush as though she were in love with what's down there.

John Thursday appears to have forgotten that he's just had a French lesson. He's up and ready to keep an appointment with the split peach lying in halves between Rosita's thighs. When I go to her the cunt sticks her legs up into the air, waving them and her arms like crabs waving claws.

Rosita has a big cunt once it's opened and spread before you . . I wish that I had a flashlight so I could look into that dark hole. It looks like the Hole of Calcutta . . . I can almost imagine the bodies of all the men who've ever tried to fuck it lying in a pile inside. With a hole like that you ought to be able to look in a straight line to her back teeth.

But I have a dong to fill it . . . I grab Rosita's waving legs and push them up until her knees are on her teats. My end of her is all ass and cunt . . . nothing else. I slip my prick under her tail and it disappears into the center of her bush. Doesn't she wiggle them? Even before I get my cock into action she's hopping as though I'd shoveled a bucket of hot coals into her furnace door. She reaches down to her ass and yanks my balls until I'm beginning to worry about the hinges coming loose . . She's coming, she howls . . . I suck her teats . . . I've got an erupting volcano on my hands.

I haven't really begun to fuck her until that first hurdle is taken. Then I settle down on her, go to it as though I expected to spend a few years there. . In three minutes I have her gasping . . . in five she's asking for mercy.

When I come it's like lying on the bed and feeling the room flop over a couple of times. It hits me hard in the pit of my stomach. Everything's distorted, but I hear Rosita cooing . . . it's hit her too.

She's a loony bitch . . as soon as I'm off her she throws herself on her belly on the floor . . . she kisses my feet and bites my toes . . . I have to stay, she says . . . I can't go and take such a wonderful cock out of her life. She wants me to stay all night . . . all week . . . it won't cost anything. She looks at my clothes . . . she'll buy me a new suit . . . a lot of new suits. What she's saying is that she wants me to be her pimp . . . her last one she tells me, got drunk and fell out of a window a month ago . . .

Shit, I haven't time to be anybody's pimp . . . and besides I couldn't stand the Spanish temperament for more than a couple of weeks. I try to explain, but she won't listen . . . she's got a bug in her head and the more I explain the more she insists. Her voice raises and she begins to get sore. I get sore too . . . I had a swell fuck, but I didn't pay money to fight with anybody. I yell back at her. Finally I begin to dress.

I'm standing with everything on but one shoe . . . when I see the wicked little knife in her hand. I grab a brush from the bureau and peg at her. I miss, and so does she . . . the knife slithers against the wall and falls.

I go hopping out into the hall on one shoe . . . Rosita runs for the knife again. We yell at each other through the open door until I see her lift her arm again . . . then I slam the door shut. There's a sound like that of bone shattering . . . it's the thin door panel . . . the black point of the knife is pricking through. She has a strong arm, that crazy whore . . . and much too good an aim. I put on my other shoe and get the fuck out of there.

Ernest isn't downstairs. He and his cunt are off playing bumpbottom I suppose. I get my hat from the withered old bitch at the cloakroom. Did I have a good time she asks? I must come again sometime. . . . . . .

Miss Cavendish is no longer with us. The neighborhood, she told the concierge, was not quite what she wanted . . . so she packed her things and took a sneak. Sid says that he saw her on the boulevard Saint-Germain a couple of days ago. When she saw him, he said, she positively ran in the other direction, jumped in a taxi and disappeared.

In the meantime I see a Spaniard behind every street post. I'm certain that the cunt Rosita has put a couple of her boyfriends after me . . . I expect the knife in my back every time I walk down a dark street. It's gotten so that I take the corners wide and jump when a kid comes running out of a doorway. I'm hoping I can keep myself intact until Rosita finds something else to occupy her time and mind.

Jesus, these cunts! If they don't own you they want to kill you, or if they don't want to kill you they want to kill themselves. It's in France, and especially in Paris, that you become fully conscious of the awfulness of women; it's no accident that the French novel has come to be a by-word for a dither and fuss over who loved who and why not. There's something in the very air which makes you constantly aware of the tricks and intrigues of women.

Carl's Toots, for example. She's off now to catch herself a rich American. Living with Carl has become too impossible, she tells me. The truth probably is that Carl is running short of money . . . if she found that Carl had just come into a few hundred thousand I imagine she would find living with him much easier. Anyway, Toots has found her rich American and she's getting him ready for the hook. She tells me she'll probably marry him. He owns a chain of grocery stores in America and he hasn't any family or any kids. But before she can get him to marry her she has to get him to lay her . . . without looking like a bitch. He's a very moral old bastard, Toots tells me . . . he doesn't even try to feel her up . . . it has her worried.

Alexandra is having a moral convulsion. A letter from her, and she has gone back to the church . . . not the Greek Orthodox of Russia . . blazing Roman Catholicism. A priest calls on her three times a week to instruct her, and she's sent the children off to the country. Her letter is mystic . . . a mystic letter from that cunt! It's all I can do to finish it. There doesn't seem to be an answer called for . . . Alexandra has found the answer to everything. . . . . . at least for awhile . . .

Anna is feeling low. I meet her on the street—she's not going anywhere and neither am I, so we get drunk. She wants to cry at first, but a few drinks fix that. At first I think she has the rag on, but that's not what's wrong . . . . . it's just that she's a woman she says, and without talent. If a man felt the way she does he'd beat his mistress or go to a prize fight. She's restless, the days go by and she does nothing with them. If she could only paint or write books! Or even if she had a job to go to every day. But she can't paint or write and she doesn't need a job . . . she'd get tired of getting up every morning after a week . . .

I'm positive that what she needs is a good fuck. Something happens in women's heads when they're deprived for too long of that little parcel of happiness between their legs. I ask when she's been taken to bed last.

She's been taken to bed often enough, Anna says, but it hasn't been as good as it ought to be. To tell the truth she hasn't been coming . . . the man who's keeping her is too old to fuck her as often as he tries to and he makes a bother of it. . . . If he'd just try to give her a good lay once every two weeks or even once a month! But no, he has to show her what a man he is and it isn't any good.

To tell the truth, Anna finally confesses, she hasn't come since that unmentionable night at my place . . . since she got scared and ran out without her clothes. Not of course, that she believes in doing that sort of thing. But what she did that night . . . the way she acted . . . frightened her so that she resolved to be faithful to her admirer. He's the only one who's laid her since that night when she let the three of us gang up on her . . . and as she said. . . .

Anna doesn't mind giving me a feel, but she doesn't think it's nice to play with each other with so many people around. Nevertheless I slip my hand under her dress and tickle her thighs until she's squirming on the seat. It becomes more fun with each drink, and Anna eventually moves her chair around so that she can slip her fingers into my fly, too.

In the back of the taxi while we are being driven to my place, things become a great deal warmer. I pull Anna's dress up and take her pants off, and she brings Jean Jeudi out into the night air. She lets me tickle her crotch, but I mustn't try to play dirty finger with her . . . the driver would smell it. Shit, if he doesn't smell it already there's something wrong with him. I grab her and try to play with her anyway. Anna falls drunkenly off the seat and puts her head in my lap. She'll do THIS, she whispers, if I'll be quiet until we arrive. I let her do it . . . I lean back in the seat and watch Anna sucking my dong until we stop at my door.

Then upstairs, the surprise. Toots is curled in front of the doorway, stinking drunk and asleep. She doesn't wake up when I shake her . . . she moans and begins to make a racket, so Anna and I take her by the heels and drag her in. . . . Anna is laughing.

Toots lies sprawled in the center of the floor with her legs apart and her dress up to her belly. She's wearing pants but her bush sticks out around the edges between her thighs. Anna tickles her and she kicks her feet.

Anna gets a crazy idea. She wants to undress Toots and she thinks I ought to fuck her while she's asleep! My God, the purity of women! And Anna's a moral cunt, too . . . at least as moral as women ever get to be. There's something in a woman's make-up that makes them a fuck of a lot more interested in other women than you think they ought to be. Take two men and one woman, and one of the men passed out, and the chances are ninety to one that the only one who got his prick played with would be the one who was still on his feet. It's certain that if anything happened to the lush, it would be the woman's idea.

Anna unfastens Toots's dress and takes it off carefully over her head. Then she sits down with her skirt tucked up in such a way that I can see her cunt and begins to feel Toots up. It's more curiosity than anything else . . she wants to see what the cunt does when she feels somebody's hands on her . . . but it looks damned queer. She knows all the best places, too, being a woman. . . .

Toots doesn't do anything at first. She lies like a rock while Anna gives her teats a squeeze and a pinch and takes off her brassiere. Anna tickles her belly and her crotch . . . she begins to feel her thighs and rub them.

"I feel like one of those damned Lesbians," Anna says. She means it . . . she tries to laugh, but her voice sounds strange. I pour myself a drink and sit down to watch . . . on top of having Anna suck my prick in a taxi, this business gives me a bastard of a dong.

Anna doesn't touch Toots's fig. She rubs all around it, pulls Toots's pants down and almost off, reaches between her thighs to give her ass a feel. Toots half wakes and wiggles . . . she reaches for Anna's hand and holds it . . . then pushes it across her con. Anna giggles but she's blushing in a way I never saw her blush before. She plays with Toots's bonne-bouche, touching the upper part of the split but not putting her fingers into it.

"She's dreaming of you," she says.

Toots must be dreaming of something . . . she closes her legs and holds Anna's hand between them, then opens them as far as they will spread.

"So this is what it's like to be a man," says Anna. "I used to wonder . . ." She slips her finger into Toots's abricot-fendu and moves it around. "My God, it feels queer . . . I'm glad I'm not a man! All that hair tickling your finger . . ."

"Stop shitting me, Anna. Your own hair has tickled your finger plenty of times."

"That's different," she tells me. "Besides I haven't played with myself since I was a girl . . ."

Anna wants me to climb on Toots and fuck her. Fuck that, I tell her . . . if Toots ever comes back to life I might screw her, but to put meat up her legs when she's a corpse . . . it's a sheer waste of cock. When I lay a cunt I like her to feel it, to know what's going in and to yell at the right times.

Anna lays her head along Toot's thigh and pets her belly. She's never had her nose so close to a cunt, she tells me . . . it's an odd smell when you get so close.

I leave her there while I go out to take a piss . . . . I have to do something or John T. is simply going to drown in his own water. When I come back Anna sits up very quickly . . . She's wiping her mouth with the back of her hand. She's been licking Toots's fig, the bitch! I can tell it just by looking at her, and she knows it's no secret . . . she pushes off her shoes and curls her toes.

"Don't stop on my account," I tell her.

"Listen Alf," she says, speaking very quickly, "you have to believe me . . . I never did such a thing in my life! I just wondered. . . . I wanted to know what it was like. . . . I think I. . . . I must be pretty drunk . . ."

She is pretty drunk. And I believe her, of course. Shit, haven't any reason not to believe her . . . Anna's no girl lover. But she's a filthy bitch . . . I don't imagine that there's much she wouldn't try if she were hot enough and drunk enough.

"Well, what is it like?" I ask her.

She doesn't know. Really she just doesn't know, she says. She was just starting it when I came back. I tell her to go on from where she left off . . . as long as she's begun it, now's no time to leave off.

"Damn it, I think you'd like to see me do it," Anna says. "I think you'd like to watch me lick this girl's cunt in addition to everything else you know about me . . . things that nobody should know . . . that should never have happened."

"Oh stop farting around and do it! What the fucking Jesus do you think I am? Christ, if you don't I'll come over there and hold your nose in it, like a cat that's shit in the wrong place . . ."

Anna takes off Toots's shoes and stockings and pants . . . she gets down on her belly and looks into that split fig, taking a good peek. It looks like a sideways mouth she says, with a curly beard growing all around it. . . . She runs her red tongue along Toots's thigh and into her bush . . . she licks over the mop and touches Toots's cunt with the end of her tongue. It slips in . . .

So unexpectedly that even I jump, Toots wakes up. Bang . . . . . like that, with no warning. She sits up and stares down at Anna, who hasn't had time to move. One look around and then at me to get her bearings. Then she grabs Anna by the hair and yanks her head away from her fig.

"You dirty whore!" she yells. "No wonder I had such

dreams! Pervert! Look at your mouth! Oh my God, wipe off your dirty chin!"

She shoves her pants into Anna's face and mops off the juice. I begin to laugh at them . . they look so silly, those two bitches, each glaring at the other and each scared shitless of the other. I explain to Toots . . . it's all a mistake, etc., etc. and when I've told my little story she suggests we have a glass of wine and become friends again. Whatever else you might have against Toots, she's better tempered than most cunts . . .

Just the same, Toots says, Anna shouldn't have done that. Now Toots is hot, and when she's hot as she is now she can't cool off unless she's fucked and fucked and fucked and FUCKED! She and Anna fall into each other's arms, drunkenly amiable. Toots wants Anna to undress.

"I want to see if those things are real," she says pointing to Anna's bubs.

Anna's proud as a pigeon of those teats she sports . . . . the one sure way of getting her out of her clothes is to admire her front profile. She strips . . . and why she has to take off her shoes to show her teats God alone knows. But I can't complain . . . Here I am in my own place, with the rent paid, drunk, and with two swell-looking and naked cunts on my hands. Jesus, I feel like the lord of the manor. . . .

They park their asses, one on each side of me, on the couch. I put an arm around Toots and an arm around Anna and give their teats a feel. When you have a normal pair of bubs to compare them with, Anna's seem bigger than ever. She opens my fly and takes my cock out. . . . Toots wants to play with it too . . . they both begin diddling me. . . .

There's one thing very wrong with having two bitches ready to fuck at the same time. Having only one cock is bad enough in itself, but the real trouble is the one who is fucked last is liable to get angry and never get over it. The logical thing to do is to screw Anna, of course. . . . Toots is the big game hunter these days. But still, I don't exactly

relish trying Toots's good temper too far . . . one bunch of
spics dogging my footsteps all day is more than I can handle
as it is. . . .

Fortunately there is a friendly solution. Toots, it appears, really liked having Anna lick her fig . . . she
shouldn't have made such a fuss, but she was startled, etc.
And if Anna would like to do it just a bit more . . . but just a
bit . . . . and then if I would fuck her . . . oh, but just a
bit . . . . she'd like that too, and I'd still be able to fuck
Anna.

Anna is doubtful. She doesn't really do that sort of thing
she explains . . . it was just a caprice. But, well, she's so
positive that Toots won't say anything to anyone . . . and of
course I won't . . . We end up with me sitting at one end of
the couch, my feet toward the other end, and Anna lying on
her back with her head in my lap. Then Toots gets on her,
kneeling with her legs outside of mine. John Thursday is
lost somewhere in Anna's hair, and I can't see Anna's face
because it's under Toot's ass . . . but I can hear her sucking
. . . she's chewing the Jesus out of Toots's fig . . . Toots puts
her arms around me, shoves her bubs against my cheek,
and sucks my tongue. . . . . . .

Anna seems to be doing her part since she's been persuaded. Toots wiggles and puts her mouth against my ear.
Over her shoulder I can see Anna diddling herself. . . . .

"She's licking my ass," Toots whispers to me. She looks
down at Anna . . . "Please, please put your tongue in it . . .
up . . . in there . . . put it in . . . put it in . . ."

I can't see what's going on down there but Toots keeps
me informed. Anna's put her tongue in Toots's rectum, and
it's so soft and squirmy! What a pair of cunts I have here!
I grab Toots's foot and feel around her ass with my fingers. . . . .

And that bitch Toots! She throws her teats in my face,
gives them to me to suck and bite, then reaches down and
grabs a handful of Anna's hair and my dong with it . . .
Christ what a way to have your cock played with! If I don't

get fucked in a minute I'm going to come into Anna's permanent.

Toots is ready for it, too. She gets up, takes a look at Anna's face, then turns around and sticks her ass out for Anna to kiss. And Anna, the filthy cunt, kisses it! She licks the cheeks . . . licks between them . . . finally presses her mouth between them and gives Toots a kiss, a regular smacker.

I jump up and throw both cunts together on the couch. . . . I spread Toots's legs and hold Anna's head down against her bush . . . I want to see her licking Toots's fig . . . . and I do. She pushes Toots's thighs further apart and acts as though she were trying to go into it head first. . . . . .

Toots is beginning to feel crazy, too . . . . . . she wants to try tete-beche with Anna. They get together and go after each other, and Toots is just as filthy as Anna. . . . They lock together like a Chinese wood puzzle, their arms around each other's waists, their heads under each other's tails, their fat asses sticking out, each with a head beneath it. . . . Toots is on the outside, and I climb up next to her . . . I can look into Anna's mop and watch what Toots is doing to that slippery peach she's biting.

Suddenly the lights go out and we're in darkness so black that I can't see a thing. I've been pushing my cock against Toots's ass trying to get it in . . . but Anna gets it and begins sucking it . . . she slips it out of her mouth . . . . the crazy whore . . . she's licking my dong and putting it into Toots's cunt at the same time! Well, if she wants to watch the works she can . . . I start fucking Toots and Anna is licking both of us, sucking Toots's fig and even while my dick is going in and out of it!

Being drunk and in the dark it is much easier to do something than it might ordinarily be . . . Anna takes my cock again, sucks it, and puts John Thursday's nose against Toots's rectum . . . I get in it and Anna's still trying to lick it . . . .

It's too easy to forget where you are though . . . These

cunts act as though they were on a full-sized bed. I'm pushed to the edge of the couch and when I feel myself falling, I grab . . . . all of us go onto the floor . . . . I feel an ass sticking up . . . . I climb on and try to get John Thursday back in where he was . . . . Anna yells and pushes me off again . . . someone's got my cock in her mouth . . . . the other is licking my ass and climbing over me . . . . I smell cunt and then there's a bush over my face . . . I can't tell which one it is but I suck it anyway . . . My eyes are becoming accustomed to the dark. I can see the dark outline of a head moving up and down while one of those cunts sucks my prick . . . . the other one is trying to play with it and I have a finger in her rectum. . . . . .

The lights flicker on again. Toots is on her knees sucking Anna's ass . . . Anna is the one who's squatting over me with my dong in her tail.

"Turn the lights off and fuck me!"

Toots grabs me and wants to go to the couch. I throw her on it and spread her thighs. . . . But I leave the lights on. . . . I'm seeing her as it is now but in the dark I might lose her. . . .

Anna must be dazed. . . . she sits on the floor and looks at us, shaking her head as though to clear it. Toots's trap takes all my dong at once . . . she keeps asking me to turn out the lights . . . until the tickle in her tail takes her voice away . . . . . she's burning up; . . . it's like embracing a furnace. I'm fucking her like an ape but she can't get enough of it.

She goes limp in my arms. . . . she's come and passed out again. I keep screwing her until Anna grabs my knees . . . she wants it now. She pulls Toots off the couch and jumps on me, scratching and biting like a tiger. We wrestle until I get her beneath me on her belly . . . Not that way, she gasps . . . But John Thursday squeezes his head into her rectum and wiggles up until he's neck deep . . . Shit if she doesn't split now, she never will. . . . . my dong spreads her like a wedge . . . . and when I've got it in she likes it . . .

While I'm ramming my cock into Anna I can look down at Toots lying sprawled on the floor with her legs apart so that I can see her fucked-out, juicy cunt . . . . it spreads while I watch it . . . it yawns cavernously, and I get the impression of standing on the edge of a smouldering volcano, peering over to see the sulphurous pit . . . I'm falling downward into the heart of that burning maw; flaming, brilliant sparks rush by me as I drop into the heat, the mystery. . . .

My face is being slapped. I push the hands away and sit up whirling. Anna is talking to me . . . I must have gone under. My God, if you came like that the first time you'd probably shit your pants and then cut your dick off with your old man's razor. . . .

Anna says she wants another lay . . . but first there's a little matter to attend to in the bathroom . . She wobbles out of sight and I sit on the couch looking down at Toots. Jesus, if Carl could see his swell cunt now he'd chew his tongue off. . .

I find Anna asleep in the bathroom. She's sitting on the crapper, snoozing as peacefully as a baby. I'd leave her there but she'd probably fall off . . so I carry her into the bedroom and tuck her away. While I'm giving her a little feel before pulling the covers up Toots calls me from the other room. She comes into the bedroom and falls across Anna. . . . . Anna is completely gone . . . she doesn't even move when Toots wraps her legs around her neck and rubs her fig with her mouth.

Toots wants to play the head to tail game with me. Shit, Toots is one cunt I could lick all night . . . I watch her wash my whiskers, and when she has my prick in her mouth I jump into her mop . . . I lick her thighs and her belly and before I arrive at her cunt she's so hot she's trying to turn her womb inside out.

These bitches are like something you dreamed about when you were fifteen . . . they don't wait for you to get it hard and ask them to suck it . . . they take it when it's soft and maul it in their mouths until you have an erection. My prick looked like a wilted candle when Toots began to suck it . . but she straightened it out, she takes the wrinkles and creases away . . . .

The room is heavy with the stink of cunt juice. I smell of it, the bed smells of it . . . it's sneaked into every crack and corner of the place, and I wonder that the cats in the neighborhood haven't assembled to howl outside the windows.

At times like this I can't think of anything better . . . To have a fat ass in your hands, a cunt to hide your nose in, and a hot bitch trying to pull your cock off with her tongue . . . . that's all a man could ask for in this world or any other. I lick the cunt juices from Toots's thighs . . . if I push my dong any further in her mouth it will come squeezing out of her rectum, past my nose like a fat, red turd.

She's coming and I fill her mouth with jism . . . But she doesn't get all of it . . . some of it goes onto the bed. That bitch staining my sheets! I make her lick it up and then I can't think of anything better to do than wipe my cock on her hair. . . .

With both the cunts asleep on my bed there's no place for me except the couch. But I'm not so positive that I care to be about when they wake up, head to tail, and begin to contemplate their sins . . . so I take my toothbrush and go to a hotel. They're curled up like kittens when I leave them and Anna is poking her nose into Toots's bush. . . .

I don't want to die. Today I take half a dozen of my books to the binders . . . two of them are beyond repair and have to be discarded. I hadn't noticed they were dying, that the paper was becoming too brittle to hold the thread . . . but they're finished, and I bought them only last week or the week before . . . . when I was in America of course. Where else but in America could you buy a book so shoddy that it was ready for the ash heap before the man who bought it? But time is passing.

These pricks who tell you that in five or fifty years they will be ready to give up the ghost . . . how in Christ's name can a man say something like that? There's too much to see, too much to do, and as long as you're alive it should be impossible to get tired of possessing that tiny spark of consciousness . . . .

As long as you're alive! But we live in a land of ghosts. The world is half dead before it's born. People straddle their lives with one foot in the grave and the other still sticking in the womb . . . they never grow up and they're old from the first second they utter the first squawk of protest on finding they're out on their own. . . . . .

Alexandra comes to see me after an exchange of notes. She's up to her ears in Catholicism, and beyond. . . . Satanism is attracting her. She talks of magic, black and white, of the Rosicrucians, of succubi, and incubi, of the black mass . . . . Oh, she has it all pat, she knows all the words, and she acts so serious that I'm ready to believe that her mind is affected.

She has decided now that she has to learn something about a certain defrocked canon who is supposed to have gathered about him a group of devil's disciples and celebrates the black mass here in Paris. From him, she hears that women have been known to receive the faculty of incubacy! And it would be so charming to be able to go to bed, be visited by, let us say, Byron, or some man who, for reasons of prudence, etc., etc., is otherwise unattainable.

And she believes that stuff! She's been reading tons of books on the subjects, she tells me, and her confessor is quite angry with her. Do I know for instance, she inquires, that there are over twenty-seven known societies scattered about the world, the members of which have dedicated themselves to the worship of Anti-Christ? She speaks of spells and incantations, of fevers and various maladies transmitted by means of hypnosis and spirits. Hell, to hear her talk you'd think that she consorted with spooks and goblins every night. Even alchemy enters the conversation

. . . she has lists of the great fakirs of the ages linked up in her head, and I'm told that in France alone there are twenty-seven transmutists' furnaces lighted at night.

It's impossible to fuck a woman in that condition. I'd as soon lay some cunt from an asylum. To tell the truth, I'm glad to be rid of her, and when she's gone I still feel the chill she's left. It isn't the demons and larvae that bothers me.

Toots makes her contribution to my week. Toots and Peter! The rich American Toots has been trying to snag expresses a desire to meet some other, any other, Americans living in Paris . . . he is homesick and subject to that disease which makes tourists feel that a person who has been anywhere within two thousand miles of their original home is a brother to be bothered and beshitted with effusiveness and confidences. So Toots brings him around.

He's not such a pain in the ass as I expected him to be . . . that may be because both he and the cunt are feeling gay . . . . they have made a grand tour of the neighborhood bars. He isn't so old, either . . . why he hasn't laid Toots before now isn't clear . . . . . she's getting desperate . . . . She sits on his lap and wiggles her ass for him, right there in front of me, but the best he can do for her is to give her a pinch and go right on talking.

Toots appears to have made up her mind that it's tonight or never . . . . . she's been trying so long to get him that she's done almost everything but come right out and ask him to screw her. She begins to tease . . . soon she's rubbing his shoulder with her bubs, his knee with her thigh . . . Jesus, I can see all she's got, and while her 'Henry' sits there and goes on about what Paris must have looked like in the Middle Ages, I've got a dong that I could put on exhibition.

She's catting for a fuck as openly as a heifer in the spring . . . and it looks to me as though she wanted a fuck for its own sake as much as to tie this Henry to her. Oh, she's a bitch, there's no doubt about that . . . never a bit worried about what went on here the other night . . . called me up

the next day and asked how I was feeling! While Anna . . .
Anna creeps away and hides for a day or a few weeks before
she comes out to show her tail again . . . .

Then my bell rings and it's Peter. He's ridden in
from the country with a farmer and he has a letter from
Tania which she could not mail because they're watched so
closely at the place where Alexandra has tucked them away.
I can't take the letter and chase him away . . . not when he's
come all that way. He comes in . . . and don't Henry's eyes
light up when he sets eyes on that cute little prick! Shit, he
might as well have dumped Toots onto the floor on her ass
. . . he doesn't even pretend to hear what's she's saying
anymore.

Peter gets the idea right away. He sits down and becomes coy . . . all he needs is a tiny lace handkerchief to
swish. That little cocksucker! Toots's rich American is be-
witched . . . He gives him a glass of wine and he flutters
around with the first spark of life he's shown all evening.
Then he and Peter sit there and goggle at each other.

Toots sits next to me on the couch. Perhaps, she suggests
sarcastically, Henry and the boy would feel better if we left
them alone! Why don't they simply fall into each other's
arms? She is hopping mad at first and then it all begins to
amuse her. She comes right out and tells Henry what a joke
it is . . . that she's been trying to tie him up and marry him.
And here he turns out to want a pretty boy instead of her!
She must be drunker than she looks . . . certainly she's
disgusted. If I were Henry I'd take her over my knee, pull
down her pants, and slap her ass for her. But he thinks it's
funny too . . . the pair of them sit and laugh and have a glass of
wine on it, and Peter blushes and looks pretty.

"Why don't you . . . oh whatever it is that you do," Toots
asks Henry. "Take him in the bedroom . . . Alf won't mind.
But I'd like to see it, to have the satisfaction of knowing
what he's got that I haven't got."

Peter dangles his long hands over the arms of the chair.
He manages to look shocked . . . something I've never seen

Peter do before. Henry frowns . . . perhaps he thinks that Toots is being somewhat crude . . . but these bitches can be a hell of a lot cruder than that. Suddenly Toots hoists her skirts and shows us her bush. It's like having a blinding light suddenly turned on you when she aims that thing at you. She almost throws it in Henry's face.

Why, she wants to know, is there something wrong with it? Does he see worms crawling around in it, has it turned green, or does it stink? If that isn't better than a boy's asshole to put a prick into, she'll eat it . . . and if he has to have a round hole, she has a rectum herself!

She makes a mistake in flinging that bonne-bouche in Peter's face, though. He looks at it, sniffs it, and pushes one of his long fingers up it before Toots sees what's happening. Henry thinks that's funny too, but when Peter puts his arms around Toots's ass and gives her mop a kiss, he's as startled as the cunt.

Toots pushes her skirt down quickly, and demands to know what he is this pretty one . . . fish or fowl? Both, I tell her and she shakes her head. The depravity of the people I know.

Henry wants to have a good time. He's a long way from home and for once in his life he tells us, he can do exactly as he pleases. So why don't we make this a night? We're all friends here, we know what the world is like, etc., etc., he grows quite philosophical about the matter. Finally he turns to Toots. He'll make it worth her while if she's agreeable. Toots tells him to shove his money up his ass . . . but there's no reason why we shouldn't be gay.

I'm not so positive I want to take my pants down with this Henry around . . . but he acts straight enough with me. I decide that he is interested only in someone like Peter. In that way he's a lot like Ernest, except that Ernest is cunt struck, too.

He has a small confession to make, Henry has. Since he's known Toots he has often thought of what she must be like when she's being screwed . . . oh yes, he's thought about fucking her, but he simply doesn't get hot over women anymore, the way he used to! But he would like to see her being laid. It's easy enough to see that . . . every whorehouse in Paris has a peep show . . . but he's never seen a nice girl, someone he's known, do it.

Shit, I'm not putting on any entertainment for this rich bastard! But I have an erection that seems to be a permanent attachment, and if I don't fuck Toots I'll probably have to go out later and pay some whore . . . I pull her onto my lap when she passes by. She snuggles her ass against John Thursday and lifts her skirt for me to give her a feel.

Toots is as much ready to be laid as I am to give it to her . . . her thighs are burning and they have juice between them. And her mop . . . . it's the original burning bush . . . I feel like a man about to dip his finger into a pot of hot lead when I tickle her fig. She spreads her legs and that swell stink of cunt spills around the room.

Jesus, I'd fuck her on the steps of the Palais de Justice, in the center of the Place de la Concorde before a full military review! I throw her legs up in the air and pull off her shoes . . . she tumbles off my lap and lies on her back in front of me while I take off her stockings. Peter's almost shitting his pants with excitement.

Toots lies on the couch and wiggles while I'm undressing . . . she's trying to get Peter to come over and kiss her bush again . . . but before she can persuade him I'm climbing on her. I have my dong up her tail before she knows what's happening, and she begins to kick the couch so hard that I expect the springs to fly out and sail across the room.

Peter is sitting on Henry's lap . . . his fly is open and Henry is tickling his dick . . . Peter reaches into Henry's pants and begins diddling his cock . . . the place is taking on the air of a madhouse. Toots squeals like a pig under the knife.

Yes, squeal, you cunt! You have a knife in your belly, your womb is butchered, your con feels its edge . . . .

Peter undresses, and when Toots sees him standing naked, his dick hard and erect, she begs him to come over and let her feel of it. That little bastard, he wears a two-sided coat, he changes from one sex to another like a chameleon. . . . . he stands and lets her play with his cock and feel his balls and pinch his legs. Then when he thinks she's liable to be agreeable about it, he wants to put his cock in her mouth.

Toots doesn't say any of the things you might expect her to say. She looks at him with an expression that says she thinks it's a wonderful idea . . . lets him rub his balls over her mouth . . . and then she kisses them. A fine cunt like her kissing that cute bastard's balls! It's enough to make you want to strangle her, or at least beat some sense into her head. I fuck her as though I was driving a pot into her abricot-fendu but a goat could butt her between the legs and she'd enjoy it . . . . she simply grunts a bit and licks Peter's bush.

Should she do it or shouldn't she, Toots asks her Henry? Is he shocked now or should she show him something that will make him remember for the rest of his life what a marvelous cunt he could have had for a wife? A question like that is silly . . . there's only one answer, and everybody knows it . . . She puts one arm around Peter's ass and he leans over the couch. Then she puts his prick into her mouth, pulls the skin back afterwards and sucks it.

I'm more sober than anyone in the room, including Peter now that the wine has settled in his stomach, but I feel the floor rocking gently . . . Then it hits me . . . I'm coming and I feel that I must be putting my cock almost through the bitch. But she's holding back. . . . I soak her womb with jism, but she won't come. Afterward my mouth feels as though I had eaten a spoon of salt. I get up to pour some wine.

Henry is shocked now. Certainly not after I've fucked her? Why one can see . . . just look between her thighs, all that coming out of her cunt . . . . but Henry doesn't know Peter. If there's jism in a cunt that simply makes it so much the sweeter for him. . . . He bites Toots's thighs, tickles her belly with his long red tongue . . . . then kisses her trap.

Henry clucks his tongue like an old woman . . . and

Peter seems to enjoy shocking him . . . he puts his tongue into Toots's trap and brings it out dripping . . . then gobbles up the juice that's fallen into her mop. He sucks her clean, and if there is a single spermatozoon who's escaped with his life he must be hiding in a corner and hanging on with his teeth.

But when Peter's through sucking Toots's cunt, he's through, and she can't manage to keep him at it. He pulls his cock out of her mouth, rolls her over as contemptuously as though she were his sister Tania, and plays with her. And Toots enjoys every minute of it.

Oh, she must be insane, she says, to let this boy, this mere child . . . . this cocksucker, in fact, have her this way. But her insanity doesn't appear to worry her particularly. She lets him suck her teats, bite her belly . . . go over her thoroughly. And when Peter, having her on her belly, hoists her ass up and gets behind her, she's positively docile.

His hard little dick gives her a thrill, too. It may not be as satisfying as the full-sized dongs she's accustomed to, but when a woman's being fucked in the ass it doesn't take a horse to fix that itch. . . Peter takes her hands in his and puts them on her ass, and she lies on her face with the cheeks spread waiting for him.

Toots isn't a child like Tania . . . she has a full sheet aft, and Peter has something to work with. It isn't hard for him to get his cock in where he wants it, and she's heavy-assed enough to take it all before she begins to feel it. He hangs onto her bubs like a monkey and rough-rides her.

Henry watches Peter's fat little ass bouncing. . . . . I think of a tom cat watching a succulent and foolish bird. He's sitting there with a broad grin splitting his face . . . when I turn around again he's standing behind the couch feeling Peter's ass and goosing him. Peter throws him a look and waits . . . then Toots's Henry has him, his cock in his ass.

Toots looks around, sees what's happening and practically turns a handspring. She never even imagined anything like this before, she says . . . oh, what slime she's wallowed in since coming from Italy! Peter tells her to be quiet or he'll piss up her ass . . . whatever else, you have to admire his aplomb.

Jean Jeudi is looking up . . . Trust him . . . no matter what good sense may tell you, if there's a cunt in the neighborhood all for it. Toots sees him and stretches out her hands . . . . bring it to her, she begs.

There's no limit for a woman who's as crazy for cocks as Toots is . . . you could stuff her trap, rectum, mouth and ears with them, give her one in each hand and a pair to tickle with her toes . . . she'd want another between her teats or rubbing her belly. She almost tears my prick off getting it into her mouth . . . she holds my legs to keep me from taking it away from her again.

My God, what a melee! Peter squeals that he's going to come . . . Henry is fucking so doggedly that there's no question but that he's about to let his dong explode. Toots is too busy sucking me off to do anything but make those filthy, slobbering noises. Ah, Gay Paree! This must be what people mean when they talk about bohemia. . . .

I take Toots's head in my hands, lift it and stare into her eyes. Shit, she's so groggy with excitement that I don't believe she even knows who I am or where she is . . . But she knows that she's sucking a prick . . . the veins in her throat and temples are swollen and throbbing . . . I give her teats a squeeze, and under them her heart is racketting like a drum.

Ah, what fucking whores these nice girls are! She doesn't even have the decency to close her eyes when I come and she starts to swallow it! But then she's coming too . . . . and Peter . . . Christ, the whole fucking world is having an orgasm!

Tania's letters are not recommended for insomnia. Alexandra must have picked a remarkably remote place to send the children . . . if there's a cock within ten miles it can usually be depended on to find its way to that girl before long, but Tania complains that she's burning with fevers and frustration. Peter and she are watched and kept apart, and her only amusement is a puppy whom she is corrupting in anticipation of his eventual development:

> —he is such a baby that he can't fuck at all. He doesn't have any idea of what it is, and when I lie down with my legs open and put him between them he only wags his tail and turns over on his back. That's because he thinks that when he turns over on his back I'm going to suck his little hose! He likes that already, even if he doesn't know what it is. Isn't it wicked, telling you that I'm such a bad girl? Yes, your Tania sucks a funny black doggie's pip thing, a tiny weenie cock like your thumb but with a baby beard of whiskers on the end. Isn't it funny to think of a prick with whiskers on the end? . . . . .

And this too: . . . . .

> . . . sometimes when I'm playing with him and know that it's time for him to go out and dig his little hole I undress and lie down naked, holding him on my stomach until he does his pipi, sometimes on my teats and sometimes on my legs and over my little you-know-what! I found out how to make him lick me, too. I put milk on myself, between my legs and on my conillon, and oh, how long and flat and wet his red tongue is! Pretty soon I won't have to put milk between my legs, I hope . . .

There are the usual details of her daydreams, in which I appear to figure largely, and then something which surprises me:

> . . . . But it will be all Mother's fault when she comes to find me being fucked by goats and pigs! All her pretty talk when she put me

away here! And that pretty business about her church! I know very well that she's doing something queer with that man, Canon Charenton! I've heard about things of that sort before, she needn't think I'm completely ignorant. . . . .

So Tania knows about that! And even the man's name! Where she gets her information is a mystery. . . . .

Ernest has done me a great favor. Unwittingly he has perhaps saved my life. And I think very well of that life of mine. . . . . .

At ten in the evening he comes to my door . . . with a bloody sleeve. In his coat there's a huge rent, but his arm is barely scratched. Someone waiting in the hallway tried to take out his gizzard with a knife. Luckily Ernest was as drunk as usual and managed to stumble at just the right second, as the knife swooped at him.

We bathe the cut with whiskey . . . . you can't trust these spicks to use a clean blade, and they sometimes go so far as to rub garlic on the edge to help make the wound fester. Then a clean handkerchief around his arm and Ernest is as good as new. He knows that I've been followed since that night with Rosita, so he's not worried about the knife being intended for him . . . . all he has to do to keep his skin whole is to keep himself out of situations where he might be mistaken for me.

But me . . . what the Jesus am I going to do? I'll be damned if I'm going to move again. Besides, it would be the simplest thing in the world for anyone who's really watching me to find out where I've gone . . . .

To settle it Ernest and I go out and get drunk, and Ernest tells me a long and not very coherent story about an inventor he's met and who he thinks is going to let him screw his wife and maybe his daughter. All night long Ernest tries to head me toward that Spanish joint to have what he calls a show-down with that Rosita cunt. We'll take the place apart, Ernest says. Ernest is too drunk to take a newspaper apart . . . .

Alexandra is positively possessed. Or so she tells me. Her confessor is pissing his pants these days . . . . I suppose it's distressing to have a conversion backfire on you. But he can't tell her that she's imagining things, send her to a psychoanalyst, because he has to play ball with the power of darkness. That's one of the rules of mysticism . . . you have to admit the existence of the reverse side, and if Alexandra were to claim that the devil himself calls for tea every afternoon, her confessor would be obliged to swallow the whole story.

The machinery which makes the thing go is tremendously complicated. Besides, this stuff which Alexandra tells me of the Protestant religion is absolutely vapid and without imagination. She talks of miracles and visitation as though they occurred day before yesterday and if I read the papers I'd know all about them . . . . then I learn that I've been listening to an account of something that happened in the fifteenth century . . . .

What about this Canon Charenton, I ask? Is he performing miracles these days? Alexandra's astonished . . . so Tania was right about the dame . . . apparently about his reputation as well. Alexandra wants to know how I learned about him. I refer her to her demons.

"He's a remarkably gifted man," she tells me. "And through his offices things which might be called miracles have been known to occur."

"Such as the inculcation of incubacy?"

Yes, Alexandra admits, she's seen him several times and now . . . he has the faculty. She has only to think of whom she would like to be laid by, just before she goes to sleep, and soon after her eyes are closed that person appears to her. And it's not dreaming, she hastens to inform me! She's had erotic dreams all her life, and they were never like these visits she's been enjoying lately.

Well, there's no arguing with her . . . I ask her what's necessary for her to do to receive this gift. She's vague about that. Well, yes, when I ask her outright, she slept with Canon Charenton . . . that was part of it. Jokingly I ask her if she had to make a pact with the devil . . . and she takes me dead seriously! No, she didn't have to make a pact—she took part in certain ceremonies.

What about these creatures who come to call and share her bed, I ask? Are they demons and do they have any special properties? Surely Satan must reward his followers with some special fucking machinery?

"They're simply men . . like you. Yes, I've called you to my bed, dear! But oh, such wonderful . . . such really terrible fucking as they do!" She watches my face, probably to try to learn whether I'm taking in all this shit. "Of course you know nothing about it. . . ."

Actual demons, she tells me, are possibly more entertaining . . . and also more dangerous. They take the shape of men . . . beautiful men, she says . . . but they have very remarkable pricks . . Adaptable pricks, in two, and sometimes three sections. There are authentic accounts of these, of course . . . there are authentic accounts of all the wonderful things Alexandra talks about.

The general form is a prick in at least two parts, the first branch of which is long enough to reach the woman's mouth while the second is thrust into her cunt. The third branch when it is present, appears to wiggle into the female's rectum where it may, because of its property of changing size and shape, squirm like an eel through her intestines until the end of it finally emerges from the mouth to meet the first.

Once these fellows are evoked, though, according to Alexandra, they may become hard to control and possibly get out of hand altogether. There have been instances she says, where these delightful bogies have ridden women for days . . . . until incantations, prayers, or reverse magic drove them off. Decidedly they're not people to be too chummy with . . . .

"This Charenton celebrates a Black Mass, of course?" I ask.

"Yes. Oh, I suppose I may as well tell you the truth . . . .

in order to receive this faculty of incubacy I . . . was obliged to allow myself to be used as the altar."

Ah! Alexandra has mentioned the altar before. A naked woman, of course . . . sometimes on her belly, so that her buttocks are used; more often on her back . . . I'd like to see that . . .

I tell Alexandra that I want to see this performance. She's doubtful . . . it isn't put on for curiosity's sake, like a whorehouse show. Only good Catholics, or very bad Catholics, are given the opportunity to witness it. She'll speak to Canon Charenton however. The blasphemy of having an unbeliever present might appeal to him. . . .

Just before she leaves I mention that there is a small service which she might do for me . . . I tell her about Rosita and what has happened to Ernest. Now, if she would have a very small spell cast to rid me of this nuisance, I would be very much obliged.

"If you could fix it so she would jump into the Seine I'd appreciate it," I say. Alexandra smiles . . . it's possible that it might be done just that way, she tells me. . . .

She leaves without once having made a move or said a word which might hint that she was looking for a lay. Her imaginary boyfriends must be taking good care of her these days. . . .

At the office I come across a small item which almost makes me shit green. Rosita D'Oro, etc., etc., a cabaret entertainer, has committed suicide. For the past few days it had been noticed that she acted strangely, and last night, at the conclusion of a performance (undoubtedly the upstairs flamenco), she rushed to the street and disappeared. (How in Jesus name does a naked woman DISAPPEAR?) Several hours later her body was found in the Seine!

It's unnerving . . . not that I believe in the potency of Alexandra's magic, but because I called it so accurately. My God, I didn't want the girl to kill herself, but because I spoke of it and she did it I feel a responsibility in the matter.

Over a period I begin to see things in another way. She

wasn't through with me yet . . . every day that she was alive
I stood a good chance of not being alive. It's a great weight
off one's shoulders, not having to worry about a knife in the
back. . . . .

Ernest calls, carrying under his arm an object which he
assures me is a beautiful piece of twelfth-century pottery
. . . an antique which he picked up for next to nothing.
Ernest is forever picking up something priceless for next to
nothing . . . . and they are all very much like this object
which he has now. It looks like nothing else but a bidet, but
he tucks it cautiously under his feet while he tells me about
this inventor he mentioned a few nights ago . . .

"We're sitting there having dinner, Alf, and I couldn't
help it . . if you saw her you'd know what I mean. I began to
feel her up under the table, right there with her nutty husband carving the meat and everything! Shit, you know how
those things happen . . . pretty soon she had my cock out
and was jerking me off. And that's how we were when that
bastard had to drop his napkin!"

"So he caught you at it? What did he do?" I ask.

"That's just it, Alf . . . he didn't do a thing! And his wife
. . . she didn't even bother to take her hand off my dick.
She went right on pulling at my prick while he peeked at us
under the table! Then guess what he does . . . he begins to
talk about how sexual excitement interfered with digestion!
Honest to Jesus, Alf, I'm telling you straight. I couldn't just
sit and listen to him and let that cunt of a wife play with
me. . . . I made her stop. Then, when dinner was over he
asked if I was going to stay all night. I tell you, Alf, that
bastard is plain cracked."

"Well, did you stay?"

"I did like Hell. What kind of a fuck would that be?
Jesus, if you're going to lay a man's wife you don't want him
to just up and give her to you, like a cigar after dinner . . .

that way it's you who looks foolish instead of him, the way it ought to be . . . Maybe that bastard isn't as dumb a cluck as he looks. . . ."

While Ernest goes on talking the mail comes. A note from Alexandra . . . she's fixed everything with the Charenton bozo. I'm to go with her to the next Black Mass he celebrates.

Alexandra calls for me in her car. I've been expecting her. A note arriving yesterday informed me that her precious Canon Charenton was holding his Mass tonight . . . location unspecified. Since she neglected to name the time, I've been waiting since a little after eight. It's around ten-thirty when I'm finally startled out of my doze by the bell.

Alexandra is more animated than she has been the past few times that I have seen her. She asks me, when we are entering the car, if I mind if she continues to drive. She's keyed up to a high pitch, as nervous as a schoolgirl with her father's car and a hot date, and she'd merely be restless if she didn't drive. Besides, she knows where we are going, a little bit of information which she does not care to impart to me, apparently.

I don't know how Alexandra's goblins have been treating her recently, but she's quite willing to have me feel her as we drive along. She laughs when I ask her about her spooks . . . she reminds me of one of these irritating bastards of priests you sometimes meet . . . . the ones who will take off their collars and shoot craps with you. Alexandra, the attitude declares, is as willing as anyone else to enjoy a bit of amusement at the expense of her religiosity.

She's been placing herself in the persons of women she knows, she tells me, enjoying their pleasures along with them. She takes her eyes from the road to glance at me and smile. It was a very enjoyable evening at Anna's party, she says.

How in the name of Jesus she found out about that I don't know. I'm not taking in any of her crap, but not Ernest or Arthur or Sid could have told her about it. And if

Anna herself has been talking, she's even a worse bitch than I think her to be.

The street stretches out interminably, and I pass the time by lifting Alexandra's skirt over her thighs and playing with her. She doesn't mind if I tickle around her crotch . . . it doesn't interfere with her driving. She hasn't anything on under her skirt, and by the time I've worked my fingers up to her abricot-fendu I find her things already damp.

The street lamps become farther and farther apart, and the paving becomes worse as we approach the ramparts. At least the approach to the altar is successful, I'm thinking . . . . . it would be too much a disappointment if this affair was held in some busy street in the heart of the city. As we drive on and on I try to worm out of Alexandra some idea of what I may expect, but she's a clam. All she'll tell me is that I'll know everything in a few hours. . . . . .

Abruptly we swing down a side street, into a sort of alley, and out of that into a lane. The car stops under the shadow of a high wall. As we get out I see not the slightest sign of life or human habitation. Marching behind Alexandra, with my hand under her dress and on her bare ass, I am led through a heavy wooden gate in the wall. We follow a bad path to a low building of stone, and as we enter I find that we are in a dimly lighted passage or hall.

"This place," Alexandra explains to me as I follow her through a succession of ammoniac-smelling vestibules and rooms, "was once the chapel of an Ursuline Convent. Until a few years ago it had been used by a farmer as a barn. . . ."

She brushes my hand from her ass as we enter a somewhat larger, but no better lighted room in which a number of people are seated about and whispering. So far as I can make out, they comprise the usual assortment of religious fanatics, with the exception that the cunts are perhaps more juicy looking and the fairies more obvious. There are no introductions, of course . . . . Alexandra puts me on a couch and leaves me to my own devices while she goes off somewhere. I try to enter into a conversation with a somber-eyed and very pretty cunt who's sitting close to me, but she's lost in meditation and gives no sign of hearing me . . . . too bad, because she's a fine-looking bitch. When one of the male bitches comes up and wants to talk to me I give him the same treatment that the cunt gave me . . . evidently it's acceptable, for in a moment, he goes away.

Alexandra returns after several minutes. In the dim light I can't see the flush on her face but by touching her I find that her cheeks are burning. She's breathing quite heavily and her eyes are bright.

"I've been conversing with the Canon," she tells me. The cunt next to us shoots her a glance like a dagger.

There's a stink about the place that has been strangling me. The incense burners are venting clouds of smudgy smoke. I question Alexandra about it.

"Myrrh, datura, leaves of henbane and dried nightshade," she says, sniffing as though she actually enjoyed the stench.

Just then a hush comes over the room, and several kneel before their chairs. The Canon enters, preceded by two chubby choirboys, and wearing the usual sacrificial habit with certain additions and modifications. On his head he has settled a crimson bonnet with a pair of velvet-covered horns protruding at the top. He looks about, and his eyes settle on me. He nods his head and solemnly turns away. Then, with no further pause, he kneels before the altar, mounts the steps, and begins to say mass. The choirboys quietly begin to distribute censers and deep copper dishes filled with that stinking, strangling mess of burning rubbish.

The ceremony of the sacrifice goes on . . . . most of the women are crouching over the smouldering dishes, inhaling the smudge that comes up from them. . . . The Canon genuflects and drones Latin . . . one woman silently begins tearing her dress from her body . . . suddenly she rushes up the steps, tears two black candles from the holders, and throws herself across the altar, naked. Whimpering, she lies there, a candle held in each outflung hand, guttering and dripping wax over her white wrists, while Canon Charenton lays his hands on her belly and passes them over her.

One of the choirboys brings in a pitch-black rooster and hands it to the Canon along with a small knife . . . Holding the bird high above his head, the man slits its throat, holding it for a moment until the blood drips and spatters onto the woman's heaving teats, and then drops it onto her belly, where it scrambles senselessly in a smear of crimson. The blood gathers in the woman's loins, then trickles down into her bush and cunt . . . . As the decapitated cock drops to the floor, the Canon throws himself between the woman's spread knees and sucks the blood from her cunt. . . . .

A long, vile and impassioned prayer to the powers of evil is begun. And whatever you may think of its intention, or its probable chance of success, you have to admire the facility of language which the Canon displays in that prayer. I find myself inwardly applauding . . . it's as fine a prayer as I've ever heard, although I can't say that I'm entirely in sympathy with all the opinions the Canon expresses . . . . . . It ends, and the choir boys tinkle their bells . . . .

It's the signal for the place to really become a complete looney house. The faithful begin undressing themselves and each other . . . . a moaning and chattering and an ecstatic wailing commence. The Canon pulls up his robe and I see that he is naked beneath it . . . he ties it up with a cord, and the woman on the altar reaches for his prick . . . Before she can touch it, the Canon has drawn the choirboys into him, and both of the cute little pricks fall on their knees and begin playing with him and each other. They kiss his balls and let him put his cock in their mouths while the woman behind drops the candles and cries something unintelligible. Suddenly I see that one of the children is not a fairy but a young girl. . . .

Alexandra has become as crazy as the rest of the Canon's congregation. She's holding her dress up and showing her bush to me and anyone else who cares to see it, and with her free hand she's reaching inside my pants. I push her away and someone else grabs her. While he's feeling her up she takes his dong out and plays with it.

The Canon is preparing for the Communion. He pisses into a bowl of consecrated wine, then into the mouths of the altar boys, who spit into the bowl. He mutters the phrases, takes one of the wafers from the tray and wipes it on the cunt of the woman . . . . he tosses it among the howling congregation, who scramble over it . . . the fouled bowl of wine is dealt out in small silver cups. And some of the bitches actually drink that mess! Most of it, however, is flung in the direction of the altar after a preliminary ceremony of touching the cup to the lips or cunt.

Lifting the altar boys in his arms, Canon Charenton lays first one and then the other across the belly of the woman on the altar. Then, while they howl and squeal, they get his prick in the rectum. . . . Afterward the man wipes some more of the wafers over their asses and flings them out. . . .

One woman and a young girl approach the altar. After first kissing the Canon's cock they throw themselves upon the woman there and hold her head between their thighs . . . her tongue flashes out and she sucks them. . . . More follow, then some of the men . . . The Canon begins to fuck her as the women come up to her and then move on.

A large wooden image of Satan himself is trundled out on a wheeled platform. It is complete in detail, with a large, but thoughtfully, not too large, prick and a pair of enormous balls. Women cluster around it, throwing themselves before it to kiss the red cock . . . Climbing over the bodies of the others, one of the cunts clings to the image with hands and legs . . . . . she squeezes her bonne-bouche over the enormous dong and fucks it until she drops, coming . . . . Another woman puts her mouth upon it . . . two cunts are playing with a third girl and a man behind the thing. . . .

I feel something soft and hairy pressing my hand. Arms

encircle my neck, and a young girl whispers in my ears while she puts her fingers into my fly. . . . She wants me to fuck her, she says, and she rubs her naked fig against my hand again. . . . She has a very pretty little girl friend, who would like to be screwed too. Her trap is wet and her breath has the sweet stink of cunt on it. I push her on her ass, and she smiles sweetly at me . . . but she is carried off by a man who passes by with another bitch under his arm . . . she grabs his dong and fights the other woman for it. . . .

In a corner I see a girl of about sixteen being held by two older women while a small band of men take their turns at fucking her. She's screaming, and scratching but one of the women is obviously her mother . . . so it must be alright. I watch them screw until she suddenly falls limply in a heap. She's evidently fainted but the men go on screwing her . . .

Among the women I find a few who, sobbing and writhing on the floor, are left to themselves. They are going through all the postures of women being laid, and I see one come with a violence that leaves her shuddering and too weak to move for several minutes afterward. Obviously they imagine themselves to be ridden by incubi, and their pleasures are so convincing that it gives me the creeps to watch them.

Canon Charenton has finished with the woman who acted as altar. She is lifted up now and her blood-smeared belly and breasts are licked clean. Then she is carried to the image and, much like a battering ram, shoved at it, ass first. The red prick enters her cunt, then her ass. Holding her roughly half a dozen men and women fuck her on the image. . . .

Something else takes my attention. . . . One of the women has rebelled and is reviling the entire affair, shouting prayers and screaming for a thunderbolt to strike the Canon dead. She is quickly subdued, her arms are bound, and she herself is placed on the altar, where she continues to howl . . . . She howls through one fucking . . . through

two, and a third. . . . Then she weakens . . . she relents . . .
a few moments later she is on her knees, sucking the ass of a
woman who is herself licking the cunt of still another. . . . . .

My head is swimming. The din is bursting my ears, and
the murky smoke is so thick that my lungs ache with it. But
the crazy show goes on. . . . Almost at my feet, two men are
grappling with a young blonde. One of them finally succeeds in getting his dong into her rectum . . . . then the
other rams his dick into her fig! And while both of them are
fucking her that way she is chewing and sucking a large
piece of red rubber formed in the shape of a cock. . . .

On the altar, a woman of about thirty has discovered the
dead body of the chicken. Pushing the loose skin back along
the bleeding neck, she exposes the raw, bony flesh. She
clutches it as though she were holding a prick, moving the
feathered skin backward and forward . . . . . then she places
it suddenly into her mouth and sucks until her lips are
smeared with blood. . . . .

A girl who walks as though drugged falters up the altar
steps. Her dress has been removed, but she is still wearing
her underclothes, stockings and shoes. At Canon Charenton's feet she tears the brassiere from her teats, rips her
pants to shreds, then licks his thighs and places her lips on
his cock. Soon she's lying apart from the others with a
woman who is feeling her up and spreading her thighs. . . .

I have not seen Alexandra taking part in any of the ceremonies. Finally I discover her. She is standing near the wall
naked but alone. Her eyes gleam in the flickering light . .
Her expression is one of almost Satanic delight. Her teats
are swelling with each heavy breath she takes, the nipples
erected and dark.

Finding her clothes where she has dropped them, I
push through to her side. At first she fails to recognize me,
but as I shout in her ear she starts and tries to wind her
arms around my neck.

"I want to be fucked," she moans, "I want you to fuck
me . . ."

I have such a hard on that I can't walk without limping,

but I'm not going to fuck her in that place. Since she won't put her clothes on and won't even hold them when I give them to her, I put them under my arm and drag her along behind me. She doesn't want to go . . . she scratches and bites my hand, kicks and screams for help.

There's such a racket . . . such an infernal squeaking and pleading for help all about us that I don't understand how she can be heard. But suddenly Canon Charenton sees us. He rushes down the altar, tripping over his habit. Knocking people to right and left, he comes at us with fury in his eye. But his worshipers undo him . . . women cling to his knees, pull at his clothing, fling themselves headlong into his arms. We make the door, and somehow I manage to find my way back through the vestibules.

No sooner are we outside than something in Alexandra collapses. She stumbles behind me as I drag her through the garden toward the wall. Her hand is jerked from mine as she trips, and she rises to her knees on the wet grass with both arms stretched imploringly toward me. "Alf!" she cries, "Alf! I want to go home!"

BOOK III

La Rue
de Screw

Arthur's luck is simply fantastic. Especially when you see it in action . . . if the amazing things that happen to him occur before your eyes there's no discount for an active imagination, as there would be if you only heard about them. Taking a walk with Arthur is like buying a ticket to the land of the elves, and if you come across a colony of people living under toadstools it's not to be regarded as anything out of the ordinary. Still, Arthur, himself, never grows accustomed to himself . . . he's as amazed as anyone when he finds himself in these impossible situations. When he talks about them it's not with the air of a man who believes himself and his life to be intrinsically amusing— while you, you pitiful dullard, never have any adventures— but more like a stage magician who one day discovers that his illusions are performing themselves without his trickery. He's as mystified as anyone, he tries to make his adventures sound more plausible by deprecating them, but if you know Arthur you understand that what he manages to make sound like a bad lie is really the husk of something that has come to life from the works of the brothers Grimm.

There are times when Ernest doesn't do so badly, either. For a while Ernest had a genuine, one hundred percent American Indian cunt to play with. . . . She was here teaching the students at the Academy of Design to draw swastikas . . . the old primitive horse cock, and Ernest says that most of her designs come straight from the advertisements in the Metro. I forget where Ernest met her, but for a while he was playing Big Chief Standing Prick, and he swears that he got drunk one night and scalped her bush with a barber clippers. Swell cunt, he said, too, but the trouble was that he couldn't forget she was an Indian, and Ernest is from a state where the only good Indian is a dead one or one who buys a new Buick hearse every year, and he was afraid that she might go on the warpath some night and polish him off, so he finally gave her the go-bye.

But shit, everybody knows there are Indians, and if there's any place to find a real one it would be Paris. Arthur's good fairy wouldn't take up his time with anything so commonplace . . . if Arthur had an adventure with an Indian she would be certain to have two cunts or something equally esoteric.

Arthur and I are walking along the rue de l'Estrapade admiring the afternoon display of cunt and feeling the pernods we have tucked away under our belts. The sun is shining . . it's just an afternoon like any other, and there's nothing about Arthur to tell you he has a spell on him. Then there's a purse lying in the middle of the sidewalk, with people walking past it and over it and almost stepping on it, but never seeing it. Arthur picks it up and we sit down on the curb to see what's in it.

No money. The fates never tempt Arthur. He doesn't have to make a decision to be a good, honest boy and be rewarded by the good fairy. There isn't a sou in it, so the question of emptying the purse and dropping it in a trash can doesn't come up. From the first there's nothing to do but return it if it appears to be worth returning.

Handkerchiefs, hairpins, some paint to put on fingernails, a mirror, a file, some pills to keep women from feeling cramps, some other pills to be taken if they don't feel them, a photograph, a couple of letters, a packet of matches . . . it's as dull a collection of junk as I've ever seen. I'm disappointed, and so is Arthur. You'd have thought we'd at least have got a drink or two out of it.

We read the letters. They are too dull to finish. The photograph is somewhat better . . . . a smiling blonde cunt who is pretty much on the juicy side. Arthur turns the picture over and over while he looks at the address on the letters. What do I think, he wants to know . . . is this the cunt who owns the purse? Does she look like that name? Isn't she just the kind of a cunt who would be named Charlotte? She looks good for a fuck doesn't she?

The address is in the neighborhood . . . we can walk

there in a few minutes . . . and Arthur wants to take the
purse there and see if we can get a peep at the cunt. The
least she can do, he says, is give us a drink, and if she's a
whore, maybe a fuck . . . . maybe both, Arthur says, it's a
good purse.

"But suppose she's a hag," I ask him. "I don't need a
fuck so badly that I'm going to ride an old hag just to keep
you company."

She's no hag, Arthur says. Even if she isn't the girl in
the picture, no hag would know a girl who looked like that.
The cunt sticks together, Arthur says positively. But even if
she is a hag, there's always a chance of a drink, and we don't
have to fuck her.

"I don't know, Art. . . . I don't think it will work." The
sun is just warm enough to stir the alcohol in my head, and
we sit on our nice comfortable curbstone and think it over.
"Maybe if it was one of us it would . . . but I don't think
we'll both get a lay out of this. We ought to flip a coin or
something like that . . ."

Arthur won't hear of it. We found the purse together
and we'll return it together . . . . either that or he'll drop it
in the postoffice and let them return it. Besides, what if it
was snatched and dropped? He's going to need a witness or
I'm going to need a witness . . . to prove that it was somebody else who snatched it and took the money. Somehow
we get into an argument about who took the money. . . . .

In the end we both go. On our way we stop off at a bar
and have another drink. There we get into another argument, this time about what we'll do if the cunt isn't home or
if some man opens the door. It is decided at last that if she
isn't home we'll keep the purse and come back again . . . if a
man receives us we'll either paste him or hand over the
purse, depending on how tough he looks and how drunk we
are when we get there.

The concierge is stone deaf, and Ernest has to take out
one of the letters to show him who we're looking for before
he'll let us in. Then he shoos us down the hall . . . . straight

back and on the ground floor. We knock and the door opens at once. There's a piping voice almost at our feet.

Arthur looks at me in consternation and then looks down again. It's not a child and I don't suppose you could call it a woman. It's a midget.

Arthur stammers something and holds out the purse . . . . . if she can't understand what he's saying, she at least recognizes that and knows why we've come. She asks us to come in. Arthur nudges me in ahead of him. I feel that we are walking into a doll house. . . .

We're offered the drink at once . . . the woman seems to understand how badly we need one. She leaves us sitting on the couch while she goes out to get it for us.

Neither Arthur nor I can say a word. We look at each other without laughing and then look at the place she has. Some of the furniture, like the couch, is full size . . . a lot more of it has either been especially made or cut down.

The quart bottle of scotch whisky she brings back looks almost as big as she is. For the fourth or fifth time Arthur explains just how he happened to find the purse . . . it's all he can think of to say, and each time he tells the story we're thanked and made to feel progressively idiotic.

There isn't anything in the rule books about a situation like this. What in the name of Jesus can you say to a midget, anyway? Obviously they must have things to say, but a midget . . . shit, those little people live in an entirely foreign world. I wish that we hadn't come. . . .

She's pretty, too. At least, she's pretty for a midget. She doesn't look quite so babyish as most of them, either. . . . She's more like a tiny copy of an ordinary woman. She has good legs, an ass that you'd have to call cute, and her bubs. . . . I suppose you'd say they were big for her size. A look at Arthur tells me that he's taken all this in too. . . . The whisky is good and makes me feel better. I accept another.

Ten minutes later she's making goo-goo eyes at us. . . . She's asked us about ourselves, what we do, etc., and we've been told that she's resting between circus tours. All in that high thin and rather sweet voice which reminds me of some kind of a bird. I give Arthur the sign—it's no good sticking around here—and we make as hasty an exit as we can with decency. Won't we please call back again sometime, she says as we go. Her name is Charlotte. . . . Charlotte. . . .

Arthur and I march in a beeline for the nearest café. Arthur asks a hundred questions, whether of himself or me, I don't know . . . . at any rate they're not answered. Do they have hair like an ordinary woman, he wants to know, how big are their cunts, do they make any kind of a fuck? He rubs his hands together. By Jesus, if he only had the nerve to go back there and find out . . . . she was willing wasn't she, Alf? She was ready to be laid, wasn't she, Alf?

We sit for a long time at a table and let the saucers pile up. I keep trying to imagine what she would be like in bed, of those tiny fingers playing with your dick, and all the rest of it, and the title of it runs over and over my brain like a trickle of water. Afternoon with an Elf. . . .

Toots comes to see me for she is going away . . . leaving Paris and perhaps for good. With her American, of all people. She and Henry have come to some sort of an agreement. . . . I can't discover whether they are to be married or not, but it appears that they are. Being a very practical person, Henry has concluded that having Toots around is a very cheap form of insurance against any unpleasantness which might otherwise arise out of his attraction to people like Peter. He's taking her to London and from there probably to America.

Toots tells me this sitting on my bed while I finish shaving, for she has called rather early. What do I think of it, she wants to know? I try to think of what I think of it, but it's altogether too much effort.

After a pause Toots asks, too casually, for Anna's address

. . . she'd like to say good-bye. I pretend that I don't know, Anna moves about so much. That cunt! If she'd come out and say that she wanted to play head-to-tail with Anna, I might give her the address.

Toots goes out with me while I have breakfast. The service is remarkably improved this morning . . . . that's another value of a cunt as beautiful to look at as Toots. But I have no appetite. Toots is beautiful and I've laid her, and now she's going away . . . who could eat under those circumstances? It does not help to remind myself that I'm not in love with Toots, never have been and never could be . . . I ought to be in love with her, that's what counts, and I ought to feel terrible. Out of sheer sympathy for the person, I'm not, I have no appetite. It may be a long time before another cunt as lovely as Toots walks into my life . . . or out of it.

On the street we meet Carl. He looks very forlorn as he walks along with us. I'm making an appearance at the office, it's pay day. At the door I hand Toots over to him, thinking I probably will never see her again, but half an hour later, on my way downstairs, I find her waiting in the foyer. She's ditched Carl, and now she wants to go home with me.

She talks about Paris. Now that she's leaving she thinks that I ought to leave too. New York, Berlin, perhaps. One of the phenomena of this place is that it induces everyone departing from it to believe all those who remain are simply frittering away their souls and their substance. The general notion seems to be that you may be sucessful in Paris but that you have to go somewhere else to cash in on it.

Toots is still trying to persuade me to leave Paris when we get to my joint. But once we're inside with the door closed behind us and the bed waiting to receive us, her tune is forgotten. She's come up here with me to be laid, and there's no nonsense about it. I've hardly pushed the door shut when she's put herself in my arms, rubbing herself up to me and feeling for John Thursday. Right there, two steps inside the room, I begin stripping her.

She has no pants on . . . I discover that the first thing. Say what you will for hidden sweets; I like things out in the open, all of it where you can get your hands on it when you want it, with no laces and straps and ties. Feeling her up, I lift her dress up until I have her ass bare and that mighty interesting fore view showing, too. Then, even though she's just getting her fingers into my fly, I move back to get a good squint at her.

She stands transfixed, holding her dress up, showing what little girls are made of. Hairy and pink, and a sweet little stink, we used to say when I was a kid . . . Only her eyes move for a moment. She looks down at her fig and then at John T.'s stable. Finally she tucks the dress up somehow and struts across the room, parading back and forth like one of those beauty contest bitches that you never see any place outside of the newsreels. Bare ass, bare cunt, belly belly . . . What an eyeful she makes, and she knows it, too. That's one of the things that makes Toots unusual . . . . that she should know what a swell-looking cunt she is and yet not be stingy about that trap she has between her legs.

No wonder Carl was going nuts. Anyone would go nuts, having a cunt like that around and never being able to fuck it. He'll be better off to have her gone . . . not that he or anyone else would listen to such an argument. I certainly wouldn't. While I'm watching her do this strutting act of hers I suddenly realize just how awful it must be to have a dose and a beautiful mistress, both at the same time. Awful? It's horrible . . . . it freezes my spine to think of it, having her undressing and showing off that ass with the hair between the cheeks when she turned around, bending over to pick something up and letting her bubs swing out and sway a little, passing her hands across her belly, scratching herself . . . and you sitting there with your dong wrapped up in a sling . . . I resolve to be doubly careful in the future.

Toots backs away from me when I try to get close enough to give her another feel. No, she's not pulling any stunts, she's telling me. But if I get my hands on her and she gets hers on me, if I begin to squeeze her ass and play with her teats . . . why then, she'll surely commence playing with Jean Jeudi . . . . first thing we know he'll be up under her bush . . . and then where will we be? On the floor of course, and the bed is so much more practical as well as comfortable.

She falls face down on the bed and covers her face in the pillows and the crook of her arm, leaving her bare ass as a problem which it's up to me to solve. Her thighs are apart . . . shit, she's a yard wide from knee to knee . . . with the garters pinching them tightly through the silk stockings. Her hair is coming down . . . there's a small pile of pins beside the pillow. From the rear she looks as though she needed a supply of pins to use between her legs . . . the hair spreads out and over her thighs like a kind of moss, very long and very curly. Anna flashes through my mind . . . Anna with her soft, oily goatee hiding her bonne-bouche. Then I remember that Anna and Toots came to know each other very well on that wonderfully drunken night when they met here. Toots must know almost as much about Anna's soft goatee as I do . . . . and Anna knows things about Toots that I'd think twice about before learning for myself.

I have a very fine sort of memory for things of that type. I see things quite clearly and exactly as they looked, with none of the fuzzy edges that things sometimes have, as when, for instance, you dream about them. I spend a moment more in remembering it before I get onto the bed and give Toots the paddle on the ass which she's obviously expecting and over which she therefore raises a loud howl.

She raises herself on one elbow and turns to give me some kind of Hell . . . but she sees my dong—which is really a dong by this time—and reaches for it with the hand that was rubbing her ass. I let her dig into the whiskers after my cock . . . her ass is very interesting, one cheek

116 ·

pink and the other one white. The marks of my fingers begin to come out slowly, like a photographic plate being developed.

Her Henry does that, she confides while she's trying to
get Johnny's head through an opening that's too small for
him. Rather too often and too hard, she thinks. No, he
hasn't shown any interest in the thought of screwing her,
she adds quickly before I can get the question out. Not the
slightest interest. But he does give her a smack on the ass,
and when she jumps and squeals he positively roars with
laughter. Do I think that possibly he may be a sadist? Oh!
Suppose he beats her? Won't that be horrible? And she
shivers and sighs when she thinks how wonderfully horrible
it would be if he strapped her or had the vice of the brush.

Christ, the machinery of women is a completely asinine
mechanism once you get the hang of how it operates . . . I
tell Toots, since it's what she wants me to tell her, that
Henry is without a doubt a modern version of Gilles de
Rais. Ah, she likes that! Possibly, she thinks, he has friends
who are addicted to the same strange pleasures . . . possibly he has them in to enjoy foul orgies of pain and lust. . . . .
She lets her imagination carry her along . . . in a few moments she is picturing herself, a trusting young bride (if
only she could be a virgin in the bargain!) being summoned
forth to provide entertainment for her husband's guests.
Shit, if I don't stop her she'll have herself believing these
fantasies, the marriage will be off, and all my fine leave-
takings will be wasted. . . .

I pull her dress over her head but when I have it halfway off, with her arms secure and her face covered, I give it
a twist in back and imprison her. She writhes . . . delicious!
But that isn't what she is saying . . . she's demanding,
pleading to be free . . . it's that soft note in her throat that
gives her away. I feel her up, pinch her teats, test the firm-
ness of her thighs . . . at last I examine her conillon in the
most minute detail. She wriggles her toes, she kicks—but
not too vehemently—and groans from the pleasure of it.

Her armpits look particularly naked and helpless, for some obscure reason. . . .

When I allow her to be free she's offended. Now—she won't have anything to do with me. But at the same time she kicks her shoes off. I'm so very strong she sighs. Which is nothing but the sheerest nonsense. I doubt very much if I could even lift myself on a chinning bar these days . . . it's all I can do to carry a fairly well-fed female from my couch to the bedroom.

What do I intend to do, she asks as I'm squirming, trying to take my pants off without standing up. There are three things which I might do, she tells me, and then she proceeds to enumerate them for me . . . What would cunt be, what would the bitches do without the words to be whispered or shouted or sung. I could screw her . . . or make her suck my cock . . . . . or put it up her rectum, I've been notified when I'm naked at last. What am I going to do? She wants me to tell her first, wants me to give her a sort of brief outline. Ah, Toots, you're such a bitch. . . . I'd be cheating you and myself if I let you pass out of my life without doing all of those things to you at least once more! Yes, I'll screw you . . . ass, mouth and cunt . . . until you have been marked forever by the passage of my prick . . . I'll put my dong in your hair, in your ears, let you jerk me off and come with the end of my cock held tightly against your nostrils . . . I'll fill your body with fucking, and your mind with fucking and your soul with fucking . . . Your hair will be forever sparse where my cock has rubbed it thin. I'll give you a fucking too great for you to hold within yourself, a screwing too big for your life and your experience . . . it will enter you, fill you to overflowing, spill into your children, and your children's great-grandchildren . . . ten generations from today your descendants will start from their sleep with the shock of a dream which will live forever in the cells and fibers of the line that springs from your ripe loins.

I grab Toots around the middle and lay my head on her

thighs. She grabs my cock and kisses it in an ecstasy while I bite her soft flesh and rub my nose over her belly. The soft stink of her abricot-fendu is as sweet as the odor of grapes rotting in the sun. . . . Toots licks my balls and her tongue curls through my bush . . . her mouth is wet and lax. . . .

With my teeth I begin to tear the flimsy silk stockings from her thighs. I rip them to shreds, gnaw at the light garters until I've bitten them in half. Soon all that is left is a fragment, like a badly made sock, fitting one ankle.

Toots throws her thighs apart again and again. Oh she wants it, she's ready to die if I'll just pop my tongue into her slit, run it under her tail and lick her! But she can't wait for that alone . . . she takes my prick in her hands, chokes it until John T. is purple black in the face . . . then she slides one hand under my balls, holds them together in her spread fingers and arches her head downward to slide my dong into her mouth.

Hair creeps over Toots's belly like a fine veil. I follow it with my tongue up her navel to her long, ripe fig. It runs in a thin wavering line over flesh that tastes like salty milk. . . . I tease and torture her by pretending time and time again that I'm about to thrust my tongue up her tail, then licking her thighs instead. She's crazy from frustration . . . she slobbers and sputters over my cock until her head looks as though it might bob off entirely. When she's least expecting it I stuff her cunt with my mouth and begin to suck it . . . I am closed in by her thighs, and my tongue twists in and out of the slippery mass of wet hair. . . .

She's going away . . . she probably will not see me again . . . so Toots, who was first Carl's and is now truly anybody's, is as bawdy and bitchy as though she were completely and unresponsibly drunk. Later, not then, but when she's about to leave with some excuse about an appointment, it occurs to me that she is quite probably making the rounds of all her friends giving them all a taste—Hell, a full draught—of complete and filthy whorishness.

She begs me to come! In the same hopeless way that

women plead to be screwed, Toots pleads with me to let my prick explode in her mouth. She wants me to come in her mouth the first time, when I have plenty of jism . . . when it's thickest and most full of the taste of my cock.

John Thursday's as willing as I am to let her have it that way . . . His beard actually appears to be trembling . . . then Toots's thighs become tighter, and against my groin I am able to feel her throat move as she swallows the jism. . . .

She hasn't come . . . I go on sucking and licking her con, and Toots goes on sucking and pulling my cock so hard that my balls ache. If I want to keep it in one piece I'll have to take it away from her . . . and when I do she begins to spout a flow of language almost as crimson as some of Tania's better effects. She confesses most of her erotic history (why this compulsion for confession in women?), beginning with her first and ending with the latest of her failures with temptation. And I learn, to my complete astonishment, that she once allowed herself to be screwed by a Chinaman. That's her word . . . Chinaman. And since Toots has good sense for the value of words, I understand that she does not mean Chinese college student, but more likely some skinny-shanked laundryman . . . a Chinaman.

Why in the world a Chinaman I can't imagine. I've never known a woman who was laid by one, never even heard of one who expressed a desire to be laid by one. They're little, they're bandy-legged and hollow-chested. I am wholly unable to imagine any woman getting a good fucking or a good, juicy miscegenatory thrill out of such an experience.

Toots is licking my balls, running the end of her tongue behind them and down my thighs . . . She kisses both cheeks of my ass, then licks them, as though she had just gathered courage, she presses her lips kissingly on my ass hole and sucks it! That appears to give her the final thrill she's been waiting for, the bitch . . . She pushes her tongue against my rectum and as it's slipping in, she comes . . . Juice comes from her as though a hundred little valves had suddenly been released. . . .

Her interest in my ass is lessened at once. But she's been making me hot again with that, and I am beginning to sport an erection once more. I'm not ready to let her stop. I keep pushing her head back between my thighs until she begins to suck my rectum again and I make her keep at it until I have a dong that's in shape to screw again. . . .

It may be her interest in my ass that makes me take such an interest in hers. It's a fine, womanly ass, with plenty of meat and plenty of hair. And that place, that dark puckering soul of it, looks very capable of being applied to the use I have for it. I pull the cheeks apart and stare into it. You'd think I'd never seen one before . . . Toots giggles at me. . . .

The damned thing moves. It's alive, it wiggles and appears to breathe. Assholes, I should imagine, might make a very interesting study. You might not discover the secret of the universe in one, but it would be a fuck of a lot more interesting than the study of your own navel.

Toots doesn't need instruction in any of the minor perversions, in so far as I've been able to learn. Certainly, since I've screwed her in the ass before this, she knows what to expect from me and how to prepare for it . . . . She turns onto her belly and offers the thing to me . . . . it's there before my eyes, spread out like a feast. I climb on and give John Thursday the scent. He's in like a shot and Toots begins to moan again.

I really screw Hell out of Toots this time. And she's happy enough about it with the exception that I don't have enough hands to please her. She wants her trap played with, she wants her bubs pinched, she wants to be felt up and down, from head to foot and all at once. In the end she makes up for my lack by playing with herself. My God, what a capacity for enjoyment that cunt has! Orally she's applying herself to marvelling at her bitchiness, which she seems to appreciate as much as I do, and chewing on a corner of a pillow. . . .

When I have her well browned on that side and turn her over to go after her cob, Toots sets up a howl. She wants to be fucked, she insists, but she wants my cock in her rectum, too. Since I'm not one of Alexandra's demons I don't quite see just how that's to be managed . . . but Toots finds a way. On my bureau there's a brush with a round, smooth and quite stubby handle. She wants that.

I finally hand her the brush . . . I've found there are two ways of getting a good screw . . . one is to pull the strong arm act and the other is to let the bitches follow whatever screwy notion comes into their heads . . . . . so I give it to her. She lies on her side, lifts her leg to get things into the shape she wants them and, zingo! Right up to the damned bristles!

I get my dong into her fig as soon as I can . . . I'm afraid she'll come without me, she's showing such dexterity with that brush handle. And that's how I screw her . . . fucking little Jesus out of her cunt while she wallops Hell out of her ass with the brush.

She's so hot, thermally as well as sexually, that I could operate the entire Metro system three hours on the energy she's burning up. Her skin becomes slippery and, because she's naturally a lively bitch to begin with, we're soon lying together in a pose that must look like a nest of double-jointed eels. But I still have my dong under her legs, shoving away at that itch, until we both come.

"That was wonderful . . ." she begins, and that's as far as she gets. She hasn't taken the brush handle out of her rectum yet . . . she's still twisting it a little, moving it back and forth. I leap across her and shove it back in, all the way, and start giving her the rest of the fucking that John T. isn't up to.

What a Hell of a racket a cunt can make! If she keeps up

like this she'll have everyone within four blocks coming on the run to watch the fun. I throw a pillow over head and go on ramming her with the brush. She can't stand it, of course, and I'm killing her, etc., etc., I must admit that she's consistent too. All the time that I'm giving her the brush she keeps up the same line . . . . but her tone changes and gives her away. She's having a splendid time imagining she's being foully mistreated and she's perfectly within her rights . . . I am mistreating her, and in a foul manner in the bargain. But it's a mistreatment that ends when she comes once more, and I know that she's really enjoying the party.

I sit on her back and look up her ass when I've finished. She's limp, exhausted and those two big, fat cheeks are simply too much of a temptation. I turn the brush bristle side down and smack her with it. She gasps, but doesn't quite howl . . . . and then says "OH," and sighs.

"Do it again," she whispers.

I begin to spank her quite hard, and at first she whispers "Do it again . . . again . . ." each time that the brush lands. She begins to whimper . . . . it hurts but she still likes it . . . Her ass turns pink, a mass of tiny dots that remind me of printing mats. Finally she no longer whispers. . . . . she simply sighs. . . . .

When I toss the brush away and put my hand on her ass the skin is fiery hot. Tomorrow she'll have bruises. I leave the bedroom to get a bottle of wine and when I come back she's still lying exactly as she was when I left her. We each have two glasses of wine in silence, and just as silently, she dresses. When she's ready to go, as she stands with one hand on the knob, she turns to me and kisses me passionately.

"Thank you," she says, "Thank you, thank you!"

Good-bye to Toots.

Ernest has arranged everything. He has been worrying for a couple of weeks now about his crazy inventor. Not the inventor himself so much as his women . . . . his wife and daughter. Since he has found that the old boy doesn't give two hoots who fucks either of them, or why, Ernest has been unhappy. There's something wrong he maintains, they must have a dose or something like that. Or perhaps the old duck has detectives stationed around, all ready, when he gives the signal to them to go ahead, to pop out of somewhere with flash-cameras and get the needed evidence for a divorce. When I point out to him that the man would hardly be in need of a divorce from his daughter, Ernest is merely more than ever convinced that there is something screwy going on. He wants to lay both of the cunts, but be damned if he's going to play old Snitzgrass's game. There's even something wrong with the name, Ernest says. Did I ever hear of anyone named Snitzgrass? It's obviously a fake . . . there's something strange about it all . .

But, as I said, Ernest arranges everything. He'd like me to go to see just how the land is laid out. Maybe we can take turns in taking Fitzberg or Whistfast out for a walk to look at Orion or something, and the other one can screw whichever one of the cunts seems to need it the most. So he wangles an invitation for both of us to go to dinner.

I'm supposed to be going with the idea of getting material for an article on "Whence Is Science Leading Us?" Ernest has as much faith in the power of the press as a Parisian madam.

Mutzborg, as the name proves to be, is a hopping little cricket of a man with a fluffy red beard, trimmed short, which he uses as a combination pen-wiper, napkin, monocle-polisher, and general catch-all. Since Ernest and I are there on an ostensibly serious errand, we are made acquainted with his inventions first and his brace of cunts afterward. He has them all strewn about in his cellar, one

124 ·

hundred percent of them either in disrepair through having their parts purloined for something later or not yet completed. The majority of them run to improved potato-peelers or devices to combine half a dozen handy tools in one. The only thing of any possible practical use is an improved feather-weight cement, and that crumbles to dust at the slightest touch. All in all, it's as messy a collection of junk as I've seen in a long time and wholly uninspiring. Mutzborg himself is slightly more interesting, and as he talks I really regret that I'm not going to write an article on what he says . . . he's so damned earnest about it all.

His wife and daughter are much better. The girl is seventeen or eighteen, I should say . . . her mother is somewhere between thirty-five and forty. Ernest tells me that it's Mutzborg's wife who has the money. Why a cunt as handsome as she is with cash in the bank, should have picked this bearded flea is one of those things which is quite beyond me . . . Possibly it's because he wears his horns so casually. . . .

Everything is very proper and polite during dinner, nothing indiscreet. Shit, from what Ernest told me, I thought that they all sat around playing with each other between courses. Instead it's talk about the future foreign situation, the climate of southern Italy and the wonders of America.

After dinner the fun begins. Mutzborg confesses shyly that he's been holding out on us . . . there's one little invention of his which he hasn't yet made us acquainted with. He brings in a bottle and holds it up to the light for our inspection. It's filled with an inky black liquid that I at first suppose is ink or a liquid explosive. In my second guess I'm not far off the track. . . . It's a drink which he's invented, distilled from a combination of wormwood, grains, certain field plants and God knows what else. Afterward I'm positive that those little green Spanish flies were included in the recipe.

He passes the stuff around in tiny liqueur glasses which hold about as much as a thimble might. It has the raw woody taste of American bootleg gin plus a few indefinite but unpalatable flavors of its own. But the potency is something I've never experienced before . . . Mutzborg, who tells us that he's never dared drink more than one sip of it before, is persuaded to join in the second round he offers us, and he immediately begins to sing. The conversation loosens up, and Mutzborg's wife begins to show signs of becoming quite lively.

After the third one, Ernest is the one who is singing, and the daughter is making eyes in my direction. Mutzborg goes out of the room to get some soda water, for the drink is pretty cloying after the first sip, and he's away long enough for another glass to be emptied all around.

My hands and feet begin to buzz. It's more than just a tingle. . . . I can feel the nerves stretch when I move my fingers and toes, and they vibrate like tight piano wires, all on different notes. The colors of the room become excessively bright. I'm surprised to find that I'm not paralyzed. My skin has become excessively sensitive.

Everyone's enthusiastic about this invention, including Mutzborg. In an hour or a little longer we've finished the bottle. Mutzborg's daughter is being very clever, she thinks, about showing her thighs to me without anyone else's knowing it. Ernest is sitting on the couch beside Mutzborg's wife; he has one hand behind her and is feeling her ass. Mutzborg wanders in and out along the borders of the conversation, hopping around to get cigarettes or this or that, and pretty soon he has hopped himself dizzy. Muttering something about free love, he slumps in his chair and passes out.

His wife says something about showing Ernest the garden by moonlight. They make a marvellously dignified exit . . . the strange thing about this liquid drop-hammer of Mutzborg's is that it doesn't seem to interfere with the powers of locomotion. Ernest rather spoils the effect by giving the woman a pinch on the ass and making her squeal just as they are going through the doorway. . . .

Rational conversation had been abandoned long ago, so Mutzborg's daughter and I sit and shout nonsense at each other for another five minutes or so. I had begun to get an erection as soon as Ernest and the woman were gone, and by the end of those five minutes it's the finest example I've ever had to offer. It's not wasted on that cunt, either . . . . she has her eyes open, she knows what's there. . . . She moves around on her chair like someone with a bug under her ass, showing me everything right up to her white, silk pants. Mutzborg snores on.

Five minutes, and then . . . shall we. . . . . ? Like that . . . . shall we. . . ? She turns off all but one dim light in the room while I sit there with my dong jumping in my pants, then we move to the couch. The bitch, you'd think she'd at least have the decency to suggest a bedroom . . . even her mother goes off to the garden . . . . but she has to do it right there, with her old man asleep in the chair . . .

It's nice to get one of these young bitches again. She's not so young that she's underdone, but she hasn't reached the ripeness of most of the cunt I've been using lately. Her legs have a firm feeling against mine . . . her belly is flat but not her teats . . . . and she's willing . . . but not too willing. She's a nice girl.

We have a short argument over almost everything that I want to do. I want to undress her, but it's something that has to be done piecemeal. But the longer it takes, the bigger John Thursday appears to get, so I don't mind. I'm not going any place. . . .

Her shoes come off . . . then I have to lift her skirt and give her a good feeling up before I can go any further. Her stockings . . . . I have her skirt up to her middle and I'm pulling off her pants when good old Ernest comes back with mother. . . . . .

"I beg pardon." The woman takes Ernest's arm and wants him to exit with her, but he stands and stares at the girl and me. No use pulling down the girl's dress now. She blushes and looks at the wall. It must have been damp in the garden.

The woman begs our parden again but she stops tugging at Ernest's arm. Apparently her theories haven't extended to the precept that people should fuck openly, like dogs, and it's evidently a new experience for her to see her daughter being undressed for love. She's uncertain, but she's drunk or doped, whichever Mutzborg's concoction has done to us—and she comes in with Ernest.

The girl's terribly embarrassed, but she's thinking, too, I still have one hand between her thighs, and the same display of principle that keeps her from pulling her skirt down and covering herself keeps me from taking my hand away. I notice that two buttons of Ernest's fly are open. . . . .

There's some talk of being perfectly natural. This from Mutzborg's two cunts . . . Ernest and I haven't any thoughts on the subject . . . and while this is going on Ernest drops into the chair that the girl had and pulls the woman onto his lap. Ernest I know, is ready to see the whole show, and from the looks of things, the girl's mother is too. Ernest slips his hand under her dress and after a long look at Mutzborg begins to play with her. The girl blushes some more. . . . .

It requires about ten minutes for me to screw up my courage to the sticking point and for Ernest to get his cunt's dress up so that she's showing her bare ass to the world. Then to Hell with it. I wouldn't give a damn if the whole Chamber of Deputies wanted to look on. The girl appears to feel much the same way . . . the liquor is still working.

The woman has taken Ernest's dick out and she's playing with it, but most of her attention is turned to what's going on where we are. She watches quite calmly while I finish stripping her daughter, but when I undress too she becomes anxious about something, it appears.

"Oh, my God!" she exclaims, wringing her hands. "Oh my God!" She falls suddenly through Ernest's knees, and before he can catch her she's on her ass on the floor, her dress up and her fig spread out in my direction as though she were taking my picture with it. Ernest can't lift her and she's too much preoccupied with what's happening to her daughter to give him the attention he thinks he deserves. Finally, since he can't do anything else, he takes her dress over her head. She doesn't mind that . . . doesn't even seem to notice what he's doing. And there she sits on her big ass, wearing only stockings and shoes as casually as though she were fully dressed.

The girl tries to hide her little fig from me at first. Her hand covers it and she keeps her thighs together. But after I've felt her up a bit, after she's had the feel of Johnny's whiskers rubbed up against her belly, she comes out of her shell. It's all right if I feel of her cunt, it's all right if I tickle her rectum . . . anything's all right now.

The girl is a wonderful screw. . . . . She has life in her body and experience, too, but there's none of the desperation that I've found in Tania. She loves to be laid, that's evident, but she's not looney about it.

She makes a tight fit for Jean Jeudi . . . . getting him in is more than just throwing his head in her general direction. But when he's well up there, with his nose into the center of the itch that's making her ass wiggle, everything's perfect. She's still blushing, and each time she looks over towards her mother she lets go with one of those long Ooh's of embarrassment, but, if anything, it simply helps to make her a better lay.

When we've been fucking for perhaps five minutes, the girl's mother experiences a yen to see things at close range. The fact that Ernest is sporting a good sized dong is not enough to keep her where she is, either. . . . . She starts to get to her feet, but that is too much effort. She toddles over on her hands and knees, then lays her head on the edge of the couch and peers over like a big collie bitch. In the spirit of the moment, I turn the girl on her side, with her ass toward her mother's face, so that everything may be observed.

I've been fucking the girl in that position for less than a minute when I feel something besides a cunt around my cock. It's the mother feeling around and playing with me, and when Ernest sees what's going on he begins to assert himself at last. What the fuck is wrong with his prick, he wants to know? He starts up and throws his clothes angrily on the floor. Next he's dragging the bitch off and across the room by one foot. Right in front of Mutzborg, almost on his feet, he jumps on her and wags his dick in her face. He's howling like an Indian, yelling that he's going to make her suck it until she has some respect for it, and she's trying to quiet him, telling him that he'll wake her husband. But Ernest is sore by now . . . he doesn't give a shit or even half a shit, he says, if this little hoptoad does wake up . . . in fact, he hopes that he will. . . .

The girl wants to see what's going on, of course. She's so shocked at the sight of Ernest squatting over her mother, sticking that imperial dong of his at her mouth, that she forgets to fuck. But when Ernest has his reward, when the bitch finally gives in and takes it the way he wants her to . . . . when she goes after it as hard as she can and is definitely and beyond any argument sucking him off, the girl is even better than she was before. She doesn't take her eyes from Ernest and her mother . . . not one second. But she takes me for a swell ride.

Zingo! My cock has exploded up in the headwaters someplace. I feel as though my stomach had fallen through my ass and my guts were draining away inside that grasping little fig. The girl wraps me up in her arms . . . she squeals that she's coming, that her belly is ignited, that her bonne-bouche is turning inside out . . . Mutzborg has developed one worthwhile invention, it would appear.

Ernest, in the meantime, has at length succeeded in interesting his cunt in his dong. He no longer has to sit on her bubs to keep his dick in her mouth . . . she wouldn't let it go now under any circumstances. He's lying on his back both hands under his head as a pillow, and she's bending over him, giving her oral all. . . .

Has she ever done that, I ask the girl as we watch this. Oh, no, of course . . . . never that. She's lying, the bitch . . . she's a cocksucker if I ever met one. Besides, she answered too quickly . . . . I slide up on the couch so that I can use forcible persuasion if necessary, but when she sees what's coming she drops off the couch and onto her knees in front of me. Then . . . . right in.

Mama takes a look over at this new development. My prick hasn't had time to become erect yet, and the girl has the whole thing in her mouth. The mother's eyes widen and she is evidently about to say something, but just then Ernest comes. He holds her head down, and there's nothing for her to do but swallow it . . . . the two bitches, both of them on their knees, each with a cock in her mouth, eye each other wordlessly. What in hell they're thinking about I can't for the life of me imagine. . . .

Ernest suggests a trade. Not, he says tactfully, that he doesn't like what he has, but he's in favor of variety. I'm as willing to try mamma as he is to take a shot at the daughter, and the cunts themselves can't object, so it's arranged. The only disadvantage of the trade is that Ernest gets the couch along with the girl. . . .

It's my suggestion that the Mother and I ought to try one of the bedrooms, but she won't hear of it. She wants to stay and watch her little girl get hers, that's plain to see . . . besides, I think she likes the idea of all this screwing going on directly under her husband's untidy whiskers. When I cross the room to get her she puts her arms around my knees and begins kissing my balls . . . then she puts her lips over John Thursday's neck and begins sucking him, apparently to show her daughter how it ought to be done. He isn't soft any longer when I finally take it from her and turn her over and put him in her rectum. . . . .

The girl is still holding Ernest's prick in her mouth and

she almost bites it off when she sees what I am intending to do to mother. It's quite possible she's heard of that way of doing it. But her mother has . . . she knows all about it, and she's had enough of her husband's elixir to eat to display her knowledge. She holds her ass up in such a way that I can get at it easily, and then she cuddles her head in her arms like a kitten about to go to sleep.

Once John T. has begun to nuzzle under her tail she lifts her head . . . there's not a chance of them going to sleep when they've got a cock up their asses. She bends her head down and looks along her belly, under her swinging teats to see what's taking place back there. I set my dong in easily, she evidently doesn't get screwed this way as a regular thing. Her asshole is as tight as her daughter's cunt, but like it, it spreads after you've fucked it for awhile.

It makes her wiggle, that prick in her rectum, and when I really fuck her it makes her chatter like a lemur. She gets excited and hops like a rabbit whose legs are tied. Her arms wave and suddenly one of them strikes her husband's shanks quite hard. He wakes up and stares stupidly down at us . . . the woman claps her hands to her mouth in dismay. Then he spots his daughter and Ernest. The girl is still on her knees and she hasn't even taken Ernest's dong from between her teeth. . . .

I don't know what we're all waiting for . . . no one moves for several seconds. Then Mutzborg yawns, closes his eyes and begins to snore again.

"Did he see us?" That's what the girl and her mother both want to know and they both ask the question at the same time. My own opinion is that he saw us but he won't be able to remember it. Ernest claims that he is so far gone that he doesn't even recognize what he sees. The cunts are comforted. . . . Ernest puts his dong into her mouth and she recommences sucking . . . mine urges me on to go on with what I was doing.

She comes just before I do, and for the last few seconds it's a fight to keep my cock in her . . . she wants to get it out

of her rectum as quickly as possible once that vast surge of
sensation has washed away. But I keep it in . . . I lock her
hands behind her back and let her howl as loud as she cares
to. By the time I've come too she's quiet again.

Ernest is sore. He and the girl were so busy watching
me that they forgot themselves, and she's sucked him off,
leaving his cock limp and apparently out for the rest of the
night. . . . . .

I'm not in any condition myself to do anymore for several hours although both of the cunts would like the party
to go on for at least another round. Besides, Ernest and I
have suddenly developed ambulatory difficulties and find
ourselves bumping into the furniture and each other with
monotonous and bruising regularity. We make our excuses,
dress and take our leave.

For once, there's not a taxi to be seen. Clinging desperately to each other in the midst of a world that is both fear-
ful and seasick, we walk to Ernest's place. In the morning
we both have the worst hangovers of our lives.

Anna wants a party. She makes the proposition to me
quite frankly as we are sitting in a café one afternoon. She
would like to arrange to have a few very dear friends fuck
her by wholesale some evening soon. . . . . very soon. From
now on it's to be take what you want and to Hell with being
something you don't want to be. This is not Anna as I knew
her a few months ago, but Anna has changed a great deal in
a short time. One thing, she makes a perfect type for the
sort of thing she proposes . . . . she looks and acts like a
lady, she's neat as a pin, dresses well and has some money.
In other words, she enjoys all the expensive necessities for
conducting herself like a ten-franc whore.

I ask her who she'd like. . . . Ernest, Sid, Arthur . . . .
would they do? Yes, she thinks, that would be just about
right . . . . not too many, but enough to make an interesting

time. And will everybody be drunk and make things very gay.

I don't have the slightest trouble in arranging things. No one even objects to being touched for money to buy liquor. That bitch, to make a proposition like that! Well, I'll see that she gets what she's asking for . . . . I keep away from women for four days before the date, swallowing raw eggs and oysters by the dozen. . . . .

I'm with Anna during the whole latter part of the afternoon on the day of her party She acts nervous . . . . she never did anything quite so baldly before. As a sedative I suggest that perhaps we should go up to my place and try a quick one before the main event, but the bitch won't give in. Not a smell, she says, until it's time . . . . it would be like playing with your toys before Christmas. . . .

I take her to dinner, and afterward we spend a long time butting the liquor, so when we get back to my place Sid and Arthur are already there. Ernest arrives one drink late, but that's all right . . . he's more than made up for it at the bar he's been in. . . .

You can't just jump into these things . . . Drinking slowly, talking a lot to make the thing seem somewhat less raw than it is, we use up three hours before the party takes on form. Everyone by that time is thoroughly stinking, at the stage where one more drink goes a very long way. Arthur is showing us for the fourth time, the trick of taking off your coat without removing your vest. Anna circulates from hand to hand, never staying in one place for very long. She sits on your lap, gives you time to get an erection started, and when she feels it getting stiff she goes off somewhere else . . . . all, of course, in the guise of simple good fellowship. . . . .

Then she's gone for a few minutes. Everybody looks at me . . . when the Hell are we going to fuck her, they all want to know? Isn't it up to her to break the ice? If she doesn't say anything about it when she comes back, Sid declares he's going to grab her and rape her. Shit, an evening like this is as bad as one with Miss Cavendish. . . . .

In the midst of this Anna returns. One look at her and there's no need for further speculation. She's wearing pants and shoes . . . . nothing else. Those magnificent bubs of hers are bare except for a long string of black beads that hang down between them, hugging the skin and bouncing slightly when she walks.

"Here it is," Anna says.

Ernest whoops and makes a grab for her . . . misses and falls off his chair. It's Arthur who gets her. She falls into his lap and lets him play with her while an argument develops as to who's going to screw her first. I claim the right of host; Sid, for lack of any better claim, proposes that he needs a fuck more than the rest of us. . . .

It's not for nothing that I learned to play crooked cards . . . I get a deck and we cut for Anna. My king gets her . . . Arthur had a jack, Sid a six and Ernest a three. As a consolation prize Ernest demands the right of taking off her pants, either that, he says, or she'll have to put them on again before he screws her.

The four of us carry her into the bedroom and Ernest pulls off her shoes and her pants . . . While he's at it he manages to get his finger into her fig, trying to bribe her into letting him on first, but Anna sticks to the bargain.

There's a great deal of free advice floating about while I'm undressing. Anna's the only one who doesn't seem to have an opinion about how she should be handled. She lies on the bed and watches us taking off our clothes . . . for some reason she looks scared.

I haven't the sort of a hard on that I ought to have, but Anna is the girl to fix that. As soon as I'm on the bed she has my dick in both hands, giving it a treatment that begins to work immediately.

When I do start to fuck her I'm not on her very long. It's fast and it's hot but it simply doesn't last. I'm so keyed up,

I've stuffed myself so full of seafood and dairy produce that I come almost before I start to fuck her . . . Perhaps it's true that dishonest gains are soon squandered. . . . Oh, it's nice enough while it lasts and I can see that Anna can feel John T. all right, but it's gone before I have a chance to appreciate it.

As soon as I'm off, Arthur hops on. He looks like a rabbit fucking her. I even have the impression that his ears are laid back. To Hell with the rest of her, just give me her cunt, seems to be Arthur's idea. He doesn't even bother to look at those wonderful teats. In goes his cock, and Arthur almost follows it. Well, Anna wants evidently to be made to feel like a whore, and if anything can do it it ought to be having someone screw her the way Arthur's handling it. She could have a bag over her head . . . . shit, she could be sewed in canvas with just one small hole at her cunt, and Arthur would be just as happy.

Anna looks around with an eye that has already begun to look glassy. She waves her legs and hugs Arthur against herself, fucking just as hard as she can. Sid and Ernest are both standing with their dongs sticking out like iron pipes . . . my cock hasn't completely collapsed yet . . . Such a lovely, lovely party, Anna lisps drunkenly. . . . .

How one small cunt . . . or even a big one . . . can stink up a room with the smell of itself is really remarkable. Jesus, if anybody were to call on me now they wouldn't have to come into the bedroom to know there was a bitch in the neighborhood . . . the wonder is that it doesn't attract people in from the hallway. And the bed . . . it's a good thing that tomorrow is the day I'm supposed to get clean linen. . .

Anna still hasn't come, although Arthur is pounding his prick into her as though he were committing murder with it. He smacks her ass to make her fuck faster, orders her to turn this way and that way, do that or the other, as though he had laid out good, cold cash for her. She thinks that's just dandy, the bitch. She's willing . . . she'd try to walk on the ceiling if she were told to now. . . .

Ernest steps closer to her and as soon as his dong is within reach she has her hands on it. Sid goes around the bed and lets her take his from the other side . . . she squeezes them both purple, she's so hot that she's liable to tear them off and stuff them into her ears if she's not watched. . . .

Arthur ends up with a kick that almost drives the footboard from the bed, and he really does his best for Anna in those final seconds. He's filled her with jism but he hasn't made her come. Sid is sore when he wipes his cock off on her belly . . . who the hell, he wants to know, wants to screw in a puddle of that stuff? He makes Arthur mop it up with a handkerchief before he gets on for his ride.

Sid has hardly put his prick into Anna's fig when she comes. She "ohs" and "ahs" a few times and for several minutes afterwards she's too groggy to do anything but lie still and let Sid go on by himself. If he minds having her act half dead he doesn't let it interfere with his fucking . . . . he screws her until he's pushed her almost off the bed, then rolls over and screws her back over on the other side. About halfway through the performance Anna seems to remember what's happening to her . . . she wakes up and begins to show a little life again. Pretty soon she's as good as ever, or perhaps better, and while Sid is finishing up it looks for a couple of minutes as though she were going to come again. Sid grunts and puffs and slaps her belly and pulls her teats, but he can't get her the second time. Trying to work her up, he gets himself too enthusiastic and at last he has to give up and let fly.

Anna presents as messy a looking figlet as I've ever seen, when Ernest spreads her legs. Jism and her own juice are oozing out of it . . . her legs are messed up . . . all in all, I don't blame Ernest for raising a howl. But he pushes her knees wider and gets between them anyway. Anna is still a little timid with Ernest . . . she hasn't forgotten the last party she attended with him. As though to make up for it she acts especially nice to him. She takes his dick in both hands and puts it in. . . . Ernest doesn't have to do a thing. She'd even do all the fucking if he wanted her to.

Ernest must have been following my regime of the past few days . . . at any rate, he doesn't last much longer than I did. But now that Sid has taken her over the first hurdle, Anna may be coming easier . . . she comes with Ernest, just as he gives her the first squirt of his own, and they're both satisfied.

You'd think that after a session like that Anna would be through, if not for the evening at least long enough to get her breath. But not Anna. Her cunt is still twitching from the last screwing it's taken but she's just as interested in our cocks as ever. She crawls onto me when I sit on the bed and begins licking my dong and my balls.

"Why don't we make the bitch suck us all off?" Sid suggests. Anna's willing, and as though to prove it she puts mine in her mouth. It's sticky because both the jism and her juice are drying on it but after she's sucked it for a moment it's as clean as a new penny whistle.

There's some argument. Ernest thinks we ought to let her clean our cocks off until she's had them all in her mouth. What Anna thinks of any of this isn't of the slightest importance, and apparently she's quite willing to let her fate be decided for her, because while this is going on she continues to suck my dong without once even bothering to look up.

Finally it's fixed up . . . Anna is to get a taste of all of us before we go any further . . . a breathing spell for us and it's decided that the ceremony will be held in the other room because the liquor is still there. We haul Anna off the bed and back to the other room in the same way that we brought her in, but ass-upward, with her legs and arms spread-eagled. The black beads drag along the floor. Ernest stuffs her pants in her mouth, and lets her carry them in her teeth. Her shoes are left behind with the rest of our clothes. . . .

With someone she didn't know very well, with people she never intended to see again in her life, I could understand Anna letting herself go completely. But with people that she sees every day, that she meets on the street and at parties . . . . to me it looks as though being a bitch with friends was worse than being one with complete strangers. Shit, that way she's not degraded just the one time that she shows herself to be a filthy cunt . . . it happens every time they speak to her and use her name. What's in a name? Hell, there's everything in a name . . . Anna won't mean "hey, you," after this . . . it will be a one-word summary of all the slobbering bitchiness she displays. . .

We all have another drink . . . Anna throws hers down as quickly as she can, and goes on her knees at once for the prick that's nearest . . . which happens to be Arthur's. She has all the encouragement in the world, both from Arthur and the rest of us. Does it stink of her cunt? Anna doesn't mind that. She doesn't mind anything . . . not the choice of names that are used to address her nor the fact that Arthur is demanding she call him "sir" when she speaks to him. Then she goes from one to the other of us giving us all the same treatment.

She stays on her knees in front of Sid for a long time . . . She remembers that he wanted to be sucked off. But while she's giving it to him I discover that her cunt is leaking and she's losing a puddle of jism and juice on my rug. Sid knows what to do about that he says . . . He makes her salaam in front of him and lick it up . . . then he makes her put her fingers into her fig and chew the juice off them afterward. That, however, isn't as practical as it is interesting, so he finally chases her into the can to wash herself.

When she comes back through the door on the way in, Ernest, who is sitting on the couch, grabs her. He's going to fuck her in the ass, he tells her, and he begins trying to do it. Sid sets up a howl . . . he's going to have his prick sucked.

Anna settles what has begun to look like a serious difference. All that has to be done, she says, is for Sid to come over to the couch and they can both be satisfied. In fact, she adds, it might be interesting if everybody came over. . .

She doesn't have trouble getting customers . . . not when it's free. Sid lies on the couch on his back and she spreads herself out on her belly over him with her ass close enough to the edge of the thing so anyone can stand behind her and fuck her from the back. She lets Sid put his cock in her mouth at once . . . . then Arthur and Ernest and I all take a short turn at screwing her ass.

Sid has decided that this arrangement is all right . . . . Anna is a very fine cocksucker when she has a prick rammed into her ass. And, conversely, she makes a better fuck when she has a prick in her mouth. It works both ways; it's simply a matter of which end you prefer, I guess.

Arthur decides when he's taking his second try at Anna, that it would be a fuck of a lot of fun to piss up her ass. Ernest tries to argue him out of it . . . he'll have to lick it up like Anna, he warns him . . . Arthur turns to me. . .

"Fuck the rug," I tell him. "Go on and piss up her ass . . . . I want to see it."

"Sure, go on," Sid encourages him. "Shit, maybe we'll make her lick it up . . . . "

So Arthur lets go. For the first time Anna registers something that looks like a protest . . . but she can't do a thing about it. Sid holds her down and keeps his cock in her mouth, Ernest and I hold her legs to keep her from kicking and Arthur fills her. He keeps his cock in her afterward, and not a drop comes out . . . her ass, he informs us, is doing the quaintest things he ever felt . . . .

Anna is making choking, gurgling noises in her throat . . . Sid appears to be trying to feel out her ass from the top down. Ernest has been interested by Arthur's description

. . . . . he wants to try that business himself. I remember that I haven't been able to get rid of that bidet yet, so I dash in to get it but when I get back I find that the change has been made . . . they held her rectum with their thumbs and Ernest's dong is acting as stopper.

Anna raised Hell when Arthur pissed in her . . . she raises twice as much when Ernest does it. Sid inquires gently if I intend to take a shot at it too . . . . it's beginning to come up around his prick, he says . . . Ernest says that he's been cheated . . . Anna's ass feels no different from any other ass he's ever had his prick in. If this were a whorehouse, he swears, he'd ask for his money back.

But Anna with an ass full of piss is something of a problem. Sid, after he's come and seen to it that Anna swallowed what he had to give her, offers the best solution. The neck of a bottle is very gently shoved into her rectum for about an inch and then we leave her to her own devices. Balancing her buttocks carefully, she walks to the bath. . . .

In three minutes she's back again . . . telling us we've played a dirty trick on her but fresh as ever . . . and willing as ever . . . as soon as she's had another glass of rum. In her absence Sid has helped me load the bidet . . . Anna doesn't find that out until she's put Sid's prick into her mouth again. She gives herself completely away . . . she knows the taste of piss, she says. Sid who probably knows the story already, drags out of her the evening details with Ernest and Arthur and me . . . and how she enjoys those juicy details.

There hasn't been a window or a door open for hours . . . the air is heavy and hot and filled with cigarette smoke. For me, things begin to lose their sharpness, and time begins to lurch heavily. A drink clears things up for a while, but that's only a temporary measure . . . it requires a great and frequent dosage to keep things straight. I watch Anna suck both Arthur and Ernest off lying on the couch as before and working on them both together.

After what seems like an age she has them both on the point of coming. Sid is sitting on the couch playing with her trap, and she's almost ready to come herself. Then, masturbating both of them, she pushes and shoves until she has both cocks into her stretched mouth at the same time. Bang! they both let go, almost together, and Anna goes on playing with them to give them encouragement while she swallows the double dose of jism. . . .

Sid wants her to suck his prick so he can screw her in the ass . . . but he won't put his dong into her mouth, he says, until she's washed it out. The only way to wash it out, it develops, is with piss that Sid himself will provide. . . . he drags out the bidet and gives it to Anna to hold under her chin . . . then he brings his dick to within a few inches of her mouth and lets fly. Anna takes it without batting an eye, in the face, over her chin and straight in the mouth . . . . after which Sid tosses her on the couch and polishes her off as he said he would.

It's time I had another shot at her, myself. I let her work my dong up while Sid is finishing off on her, and when he's through with her I have only to take his place and screw her cunt from the back. I give her a fine fucking . . . she comes twice before I take John Thursday out. . . . .

In the meantime Ernest has had an idea. While I am screwing Anna from the rear he lies on his belly with his ass under her face. It takes Arthur's aid and some pretty violent persuasion to convince her, but Anna is finally brought to see reason. . . . She licks the cheeks, kisses them . . . at last she put her arms around Ernest's thighs and puts her mouth on his rectum. Soon she's kissing and licking it . . . she sucks it and runs her tongue into it when she's coming. . . . The pace increases . . . we're averaging one drink to each shot at Anna . . She's getting two lays for each drink. She's so groggy that she can't stand alone, but we keep on. Every bar is down . . . she'll do anything now, she sucks our asses, one after another, gratefully licks Arthur's toes when he sets her on her can for asking him to play tete-beche . . . There are usually two of us on her at once. She can't have anything to complain of after this party.

Finally we've exhausted ourselves. Anna has a hard time finding a dong in shape to screw her, and she goes doggedly from one to the other of us, sucking a succession of wet, soft pricks until she finds a brief spark of life in one . . . then, when she's found one, she flings herself down, apparently in a half coma, until the life has been fucked out of it again. She's been battered about until she's silly . . . I'm positive that she doesn't know any longer who fucks her. Her beads are broken and are underfoot. Arthur stuffs a handful of them into her cunt and fucks her . . . She loves that . . she thinks it's a tickling stripper and she's worried when he takes his prick out of her with nothing on it.

The liquor is exhausted now . . . the inexorable indication is that the party is over. But Anna wants one more lay. She tries all of us, but Sid's the only one who has any dong at all, and he can't get it up. Anna begs . . . she tries everything.

"I don't care how you do it . . . beat me if you want to . . ." Somehow she gets to the bedroom and back again. She pushes a belt into Sid's hands and throws herself across his lap, offering him her fat ass and the white backs of her thighs. Sid begins to strap her, and the welts rise criss-cross over her skin . . . Anna doesn't move, doesn't kick, doesn't seem to feel the belt. Suddenly Sid throws the belt down and leaps on her. . .

Anna is too far gone to dress herself. With every one helping we manage to get her clothes on after a fashion. There's a small safety pin left over when we're finished. . . . . Ernest insists that we have to be certain to give back all her accessories, and he uses it to pin her dress up in back, leaving her ass bare. We've forgotten her pants. I give them to her to clutch in her hand, along with her purse.

The three . . . Sid, Arthur and Ernest . . . manage to get her downstairs and on the street. From the window I watch a taxi driver help them into his car. They have the address of the old fart who keeps her, and they're dumping her off on his porch, they say. It will be a wonderful surprise for him. . . . .

Going from one bottle to the other, I manage to squeeze out one more drink. I stare into the glass . . . the light coming from it swells out and illumines the whole room. I toss it down and when that tiny glint of amber light is gone, darkness drops over me to blanket everything. . . .

VOLUME II

"Balls," said the Queen, "If I had them I'd be King!"
—Canterbury.

BOOK 1

A Black Mass and
a Midget

For anyone in Alexandra's condition I know of just one prescription . . . . a liberal dosage of two great specifics, liquor and a lay. Her experience at Charenton's mass has left her trembling and incoherent, but she's able to find the brandy she keeps in the car. We drive away as fast as we can. I don't know the roads and Alexandra is too hysterical to be much help, but from this place where she has brought me they all lead to Paris.

Charenton . . . there's a man! At least his entertainments aren't boring, which is more than you can say for his more respectable brethren. And since he apparently doesn't go to extremes, since there's no slicing up of babies and no cannibalism, his evil seems innocent enough. A bit more spectacular than the usual brand of evangelism, undoubtedly, but not very much more dangerous. I respect his vitality, and to Hell with the ends toward which it's applied . . . too many of the people I know are more than half dead, both ways from the neck.

Alexandra's opinions on the subject remain her own. After tipping the brandy bottle a few times she becomes quiet. She snuggles across the seat against me, still naked, and offers me the brandy. I take just one drink. I don't need brandy half as much as I need to screw somebody . . . the dong I had back at Charenton's begins to come back after we've driven a few kilometers. In a closed car with the windows up, you really begin to get an idea of the potency of that stuff women are continually brewing between their legs. . . .

Alexandra can't relax . . . won't, probably, until something's been done for the itch she's worked up. The brandy has settled her but a very little bit, and she feels like something which might explode in your hands. She claws my clothes open and grabs my cock . . . not to play with but to hold, as though to be sure that it was still there and that it stayed where it was.

I suggest several times that it might be a good idea for Alexandra to put on at least some of her clothes . . . I don't care much to drive through Paris with a naked cunt in the car. But when I bring the car up to the curb in front of her place she's as naked as when we started back. Even then she won't put on anything. Holding her clothes in a bundle she gets out of the car and marches around in front of it before I find the light switch. Then we stand for all of five minutes while she looks for her keys.

I've never seen Alexandra do anything like this. She's been a bitch since I've known her, but she's always been one of those discreet cunts . . . . the kind that get up on their horse if you try feeling them up anywhere but in their bedroom. But I'm not tremendously surprised. I don't try to figure them out anymore . . . . . I just fuck them. It's a great saving of effort. You can screw a cunt in twenty minutes, but if you consider your time as worth anything you can't afford to answer all the questions that come up in those twenty minutes.

Alexandra takes me directly to her bedroom, going up the stairs ahead of me with her ass wagging in my face, grinding away like some wonderful machine. Christ, they have no respect for you, these cunts . . . . . they'll wag their tails under your very nose without the slightest concern for what it does to you. Alexandra's thighs are slopped up with cunt-juice halfway to her knees . . . I'm tempted to set my teeth into that fat ass she shows and see what happens when I bite out a steak for tomorrow's lunch. . . .

In the bedroom she's as tense as before. She tries to lie down and wait for me to do the honors, but she's too nervous. She sits with one elbow propping her up and fiddles with her bush while I'm undressing. And she's still taking pulls from the bottle although she stopped trembling long ago.

Since Alexandra began playing with it in the car I've had a dong as big as my wrist, and my balls feel as though somebody had tied them into knots. It's such a wonderful erection I have that, after I've gotten my clothes off, I stand in front of the mirror and admire myself for a couple of minutes. A man ought to have a photograph taken of himself when he's in shape like that, just to keep around and look at when he goes in to ask the boss for a raise in salary. Then too, it would be nice to have around and show your grandchildren.

Alexandra admires it with me, but she has her own notions of what to do with it. She grabs for it first thing, and before I'm on the bed she's trying to fit it into her mouth. That cunt . . . after all the trouble I had getting her to suck it at first . . . She fits her head into my lap and begins making love to John Thursday. She moans . . . she could suck my prick all night, she tells me . . . but I have a reason for believing it won't be that long . . . I pull the pillow under my shoulders and take the pins out of her hair.

Did I notice the woman who formed the altar at the mass Alexandra asks . . . and I wonder how you can believe women to be anything but a race of idiots when even a supposedly intelligent one can frame a question that way. But I tell her that I believe I have some recollection of such a person being there. . . .

"She's married, has a child . . . and nothing of what goes on reaches her husband's ears. Charenton even goes openly to her house . . . the husband believes him to be his wife's confessor, and is happy to have them shut themselves off for hours at a time. . . . ."

She bows her head again and licks my belly while she rubs John Thursday's red head over her chin. Her tongue is like a very small snake scurrying down my belly to hide in my mop. . . . Somehow I can't help wishing that I had been around on one of the nights when Alexandra was taking a more active part in Canon Charenton's Hallowe'ening . . . she's such a cool, dignified piece of cunt when you see her out of bed.

At times there's something about Alexandra's features that remind me of the Egyptians. It must be the way she holds her lips, pouting them, when she's close to my prick. Or perhaps it's the angle from which I see her when she's put her face against my belly, because I don't think of it unless she happens to be washing John Thursday's whiskers. But Alexandra should have a band of gold about her head, a viper to play with, and a peacock feather to tickle her cock. . . . . .

She lets my dong lay on her hand while she touches the head of it with her lips . . . . she doesn't hurry, there's plenty of time for everything. Alexandra's nothing like some of these young cunts that hop all over you like a flea. She's mature, she's a big woman, and there's too much meat on her bones for her to go bouncing about like a rubber ball. You get a sense of satisfaction with Alexandra and it's only when you've been screwing someone like that that you can really see how little you get out of those fucks that come off like an explosion. Fireworks may be pretty, but to keep your ass warm in the winter there's nothing like a slow burning coal fire. . . .

When she puts John T. into her mouth again I know at once that he's going to be soft when he comes out. I push Alexandra's hair over her ears so that I can watch her face . . . then I lock my ankles around her waist. It's not until then that Alexandra realizes that Johnny means business, and she doesn't care at all for having my dong go down before she had a feel of it under her ass . . . . she tries to get away, and I have to hold her head and push it down until we come to an understanding about this matter. John Thursday finally settles it himself . . . . with his nose shoved almost into her throat he suddenly comes. Once that begins to happen, Alexandra gives up the battle and makes the most of the bargain. I feel that pints of jism are being sucked out of my cock, and Alexandra acts very much as though she were trying to suck my balls inside out. Her mouth gurgles like a straw at the bottom of the glass . . . she's not content to swallow my jism . . . she wants to swallow my prick and me after it. . . . .

152 ·

She's hotter than ever when she's exhausted me. She hops off the bed and has another spot of brandy, gets back on and tickles her fig by holding it against my bush. At last she throws herself back on the pillows, and laying her bonne-bouche within a couple of inches of my nose, she spreads her legs and starts playing with herself. She obviously expects something of me . . . After spending several minutes in showing me how that part of her anatomy works, Alexandra sighs wistfully. There are times she tells me, when she does wish that the children weren't off in the country. . . . If her Peter were here now he'd know what to do, he'd make her happy . . . or even Tania . . . Soft little Tania with her wicked mouth and quick tongue . . . Yes, sometimes, although she knows she did right to send them out of Paris, she wishes they were back again.

Which makes it unanimous as far as the family are concerned. Tania and Peter, I know, would do almost anything to be back in Paris, even without the privilege of going to bed with their mother. It all seems pretty silly anyway . . . I've never noticed that solitary confinement had any particularly moral effect on kids . . .

Alexandra's hinted invitation is overlooked, and finally the cunt comes out and asks me directly . . . will I suck her cunt? The answer is that I won't. I haven't any idea of when Canon Charenton was fiddling around Alexandra's abricot-fendu with his pontifical prick, and I'll be damned if I'm going to be argued into Peter's habits. To make her happy I do lick her thighs . . . they taste of her cunt, and since a large part of Alexandra's happiness is in anticipation anyway, she's almost contented with that. She keeps one finger in her con, almost splits herself trying to spread her legs a bit further, and goes on diddling her tail while I lick all around it.

But that can't go on forever . . . Alexandra gets too hot to keep at it for more than a few minutes. She wants to be screwed, and a finger in her fig is a poor substitute for what ought to be in there. She tickles John Thursday's beard, makes him promises, bribes him with kisses . . . and shortly she's teased him into lifting his head again. And doesn't she get excited when she sees him coming to attention again! She flounders around the bed until it begins to look as though half a dozen boy scouts had been camping out under the covers for the past week . . . she climbs over me and under me, through my arms and between my legs, leaving streaks of juice and the stink of her trap everyplace. Finally I grab her as she is going by, throw her on her ass and jump on. . . . .

She isn't contented to spread her thighs and wait for my dong . . . she hooks her fingers into her split fig and pulls the lips so far apart that for a moment it looks as though the slit might spread right on up her belly. Then she throws herself downward and tries to snag my cock by herself. She couldn't miss . . . not with her cunt spread the way she has it. My dick slides into her bush, between those juicy, stretched lips, and right on in until it feels as though it must be swimming in oil. Alexandra puts both arms and legs around me, and her con snaps back to hug Johnny. . . . . . .

So far as I know, Alexandra wasn't screwed at Charenton's party. Certainly she doesn't act as though she had been . . . . from the way she takes the fucking I hand out you would say she'd been alone for weeks. There's the possibility, of course, that her goblins haven't been screwing her so well as she would like to have me believe . . . . the spirit may not be sufficient to the needs of the flesh. . . . She wiggles like a hula girl with chiggers in her skirt . . . grabs her teats and sticks them in my face, begging me to suck them. . . . She's panting like an overheated steam engine, and I expect the safety valve to go off at any second. I grab her ass, give it a pinch and spread the cheeks . . . she almost throws both of us off the bed when I begin tickling the fuzz around her rectum.

My God, the amount of hair that cunt carries around her tail is astonishing! Before you can find her rectum you have to go through that forest with a lantern . . . If she ever got crab lice she'd be host to them for the rest of her life . . . you have to take a machete and tear a path through her hair when you go exploring back there, blaze a trail on the way so you can find the route out again . . . I manage to get to her rectum finally, and I poke around until I am sure of the place to wiggle my fingers into. . . . Alexandra squeals as though I were scalping her, but I have three fingers up her ass anyway. . . . . From the way it feels back there, I could put three more in without anything very awful happening. . . .

Suddenly my cock is pouring jism into her womb. . . . . . Alexandra takes the hot shock of it in her stride, squeezes her legs tighter around me . . . and she's coming too. . . . We lie wrapped into each other and I wring my fingers up her rectum each time that I feel her wriggle . . . She's never going to stop coming . . . . and neither am I. . . . . .

One screwing isn't enough for Alexandra tonight. She rests long enough for me to have a bit more of her brandy . . . . then she's back again catting for another lay. She lies up against me and rubs her mop over my legs, diddles her fig against my bush, covering me and the whole room with that hot, sweet stink which pours out of her. She's so juicy that when she rubs her brush on my belly it feels as though she were daubing at me with a brush full of paint . . . then, as they dry, each single hair curls stiffly, much as though they had been starched. . . .

She demands to know, Alexandra does, if she's not a better lay than Tania . . . That little play-with-herself, Alexandra calls her. Why would a man like me want to screw Tania as much as I did? For boys, yes, she could understand how a young boy like Peter would like to fuck Tania . . . and she wouldn't really mind so much if Tania would let herself be fucked by youngsters of her own age. But all this filthiness with grown men . . . it's not good for the men and it's certainly not good for Tania. Whatever will the girl do when she grows up? What will she find to satisfy her then? But to get back to her original question . . . isn't she better, a grown woman with everything possible to satisfy a man's passion, than that little flat-chested cricket, that little puppy cunt, that. . . . . .

How in Hell can a man answer a thing like that? Tania is in a class by herself . . . you can't judge her by ordinary standards because there's nothing like her anywhere. I answer by asking Alexandra why she is attracted to the girl. . . Ah, but that's different! It's the incestuous motif which has Alexandra where the hair is short. If Tania were someone else's daughter she wouldn't have a thing to do with her . . . not a thing. Ah yes, she could parade herself before Alexandra all day and all night too, and nothing whatsoever would happen. Nothing. Which, of course, is a lot of shit. It undoubtedly helps a lot to have a relationship with a cunt like Tania salted by the fact that you're related, but daughter or not, Tania would be able to climb into Alexandra's bed anytime she chose.

Alexandra goes on to review some of the high points in her misadventuring with the girl . . . Tania it seems has dragged from her mother all the juicy details of the playing around that's been done with the men Tania knows. . . . and she's traded back a few of her own experiences. What I find most interesting, however, is the news that Canon Charenton has been putting pressure on Alexandra to turn her daughter over to him and the devil. She's been putting him off on one excuse and another. . . Now, of course, that's all over . . . . but if I hadn't been with her tonight, Alexandra says with a shudder . . . ah, that would have been the end itself . . . yes, that must surely have been the end. . . .

She's worked herself up by this time to the point where she simply has to be screwed again, and she hasn't been forgetting to do a bit for me too. . . My dong is hard and she's holding it between her thighs, rubbing her split peach against it. Without either of us doing very much about the matter, my dong is worked up into the open trap. . . . I'd be quite contented to lie there and lazily fuck away at Alexandra, but that's not at all in her line, and certainly not what she wants right now. She becomes enthusiastic . . . . at last she climbs on top of me and shows me how she thinks it ought to be done.

I can think of any number of things which are not so pleasant as that . . . lying comfortably on your back while a hot and hefty bitch works over you. I don't have to do a fucking thing . . . . Alexandra knows all the tricks herself, so it's not at all like trying it with some young, ignorant cunt who has to be shown how the machinery works. And she gives me a swell ride, really letting herself go, and evidently saying to Hell with her dignity. A woman really fucking you in that set-up has less dignity, I suppose, than in any other position you can arrange . . . . shit, they can even be dignified about sucking your prick, but in all the bounce and flailing of an upside-down screw . . . . not a chance.

I've never yet had a woman fuck in that position without wanting to see what things looked like. If you stay on top you can screw them week in and out without having them get curious, but once you let a woman get into the saddle she begins to look around for a mirror. Alexandra's no exception . . . after she's been screwing for awhile she hops off and grabs a hand glass. Then she's on again, the first peep she takes at what's happening down there almost finishes her. It shouldn't look like THAT she exclaims, but after she's watched for a few minutes she likes it better. She has, she decides, a very handsome cunt, and one that shows up very well in action. . . . .

She wants to watch what happens when we come, Alexandra says . . . but when it does happen she's so glassy-eyed that I don't believe she has any notion of what she sees. . . . .

For a few minutes after that she's quiet. She lies next to me on the bed, her legs as far apart as she can get them so that her fig will cool off a little, and wants to tell me about Charenton. It gives her a tickle to talk about it, obviously, even though she wants me to believe that she's horrified by all that now. . . . Charenton's laid all the cunt in his flock, of course. . . . he'd be an absolute dope if he didn't . . . and if anyone in his congregation has missed screwing someone else in it that's pure accident. Ah, and that horrid image! She'll never forget. She was frightened that first night, and she screamed when they carried her to it. . . It was a device which I probably missed . . . . consecrated wine is contained in a vessel within it, and may be released through the huge member . . . later in her first mass she became quite tipsy on consecrated wine.

I'm interested in knowing what she intends to do now . . . is she going back to the Catholic Church? No, she doesn't believe she can . . . it's as though whatever drew her to mysticism in the first place had been all used up. She doesn't know what she will do herself . . . . but do I think it would be a good plan to have Tania entered in a convent?

The thought of Tania in a convent is simply too absurd. She'd corrupt the Mother Superior herself, that baggage . . . in two weeks the heads would have a class of cunt suckers on their hands and there wouldn't be a candle in the joint that didn't smell funny when it was lighted . . . Alexandra sighs and agrees with me . . . but what she will do, she doesn't know . . . . she should have sucked their father's cock those times, she says.

She wants to be fucked again, finally, and to get my prick up to where it ought to be she lets me put it into her mouth again. It takes her a long time to pull John Thursday out of his trance, but she's determined, and after she's done everything almost but swallow him alive he begins to stretch again. Then, when I have something to give her a respectable fuck with, Alexandra gets an idea which isn't the best of all possible ideas. I try to warn her, but before I can stop it, she has rubbed a few drops of brandy into her fig . . . . to see if it won't make things different.

She becomes absolutely crazy as soon as that stuff touches her. She drops my cock from her mouth, jumps completely over me, and begins to hop around the room, howling. She has both hands pressed over her bush . . . she fans herself with a handkerchief, showers herself with powder, and even, for some unexplained reason, climbs up on a chair and jumps off. . . If it were Tania or even Anna, it wouldn't be so funny . . . but Alexandra's such a husky, placid-looking cunt that it's hilarious.

At last she jumps back onto the bed . . . . if I put my prick into her, it may stop burning she thinks . . . I ram my dong in and she howls louder than ever . . . . all that she wants now is to get away from me as quickly as possible. I simply set my cock in deeper and hang on . . . I fuck her until I'm dizzy, and the louder she squeals the better I like it. . . .

Coming into a bitch who's making such a Hell of a rumpus as Alexandra is might be even more fun if it wasn't like trying to ride a bicycle on a catboat in a squall. When I've finished pouring jism into her, Alexandra's still trying to kick her way through the bedsprings, but I still have my dick up her tail. Suddenly, without giving her any hint as to what I'm about to do, I begin to piss into her.

Alexandra's raving as soon as she knows what's happening . . . I'm scalding her, her womb's bursting, it's deranging her internal anatomy . . . . but she loves it, that bitch, and suddenly she stops squealing and flings both of her arms around me, begging me to do it some more. She's going to come . . . . she wants me to make it squirt hard. . . Inside her belly I can hear something gurgling. . . .

They're crazy, these bitches . . . . every fucking one of them. . . No matter what you do to them, it's fine, it's marvellous. . . Do you want them to bring you their sister, or their daughter or their grandmother? Wonderful! Do you want to beat the ass off them? Ah, they'll rush right out and buy a whip! They're grateful for everything, and anything you do to them is fun. There's no other explanation . . . . all cunts are queer in the head. . . . . . .

Ernest is in bed with a bottle, and about his head he has a garland of withered rose leaves. He puts down his Flato and he calls for the dancing girls as I enter the bedroom, but no one appears.

"Hmmm . . . . no dancing girls," Ernest says. "I must be getting over it." And he takes a swig from the bottle.

He doesn't remember exactly how long he's been drunk, Ernest tells me, but he'll know as soon as he goes back to work. They're very good at keeping track of those things at the office. He does remember, however, why he's drunk . . . . a neat triumph for Ernest. He got drunk out of sympathy for a friend, and then the friend made up with his wife and left him to carry on alone.

"He took me home to dinner," Ernest tells me, "and guess what we walked in on? That cunt of his was there being laid, and not only that, but right on the table that we were supposed to eat dinner on! Did you ever hear of anything like that? Right on the very table with her ass bare and this guy whamming it into her. . . ." Thinking about the guy whamming it into her agitates Ernest so that he has to have another drink. This time he remembers to offer me one, and he also offers to braid me a wreath if I'd like it.

"Let us dispute," says Ernest. "You will contend, if you please, that marriage is a noble and holy institution, while I will hold the opposite view." He props himself up on one elbow and drags the sheets around him like a toga, but before the argument can begin Ernest has forgotten what it was to be about. "What do you think about a cunt like that?" he demands. "Wouldn't you think she'd have the decency to do it so that her husband could at least bring someone home without being embarrassed? But no . . . . there she was, wiggling and squealing like a pig on butchering day and this cocky frog ramming his dong right up to her ears. And me, Alf, just like always, I walked into the room first. So what was there to do? How did I know that it wasn't the regular thing: that maybe we weren't supposed to line up behind this guy, and get a turn, too? How about that,

Alf? All I could do was wait to see what happened; if her husband took off his pants, too, then everything was right and maybe later we'd have dinner, after we laid her. Listen! Did you ever have a bozo showing off a new radio, or a car maybe, and right in the middle it wouldn't work? What does he say? He always says, 'that's funny, it never did that before.' And that's what this guy kept saying only he said 'she' all the while that we were drinking our dinner of rye whiskey. . . . ."

Ernest is at last obliged to pause for breath; then he begins aria da capo, and tells it all over again.

"Then when we got drunk, we found some cunt, and everything was all fixed up for us to lay her . . . only then what do you suppose happened, Alf? This guy decided that he can give his wife a Hell of a lot better screw than this frog who was fucking her, and he tells me he is going home to show her. And he doesn't even invite me to go along! Jesus, wouldn't you think, after he'd invited me to dinner and all, he'd at least do that much? But he just swallowed a couple of those peptonic pills they sell you at bars and goes off by himself. . . . That just goes to show you how a cunt can ruin a fine man. . . ."

Somewhere on his way Ernest has picked up a batch of fancy photographs. They're on his bureau, and while I'm listening to his story for the third time I start to look them over. They're really high-class stuff, with cunts that look like cunt instead of a bunch of aunties trying to be cute . . . . and right in the first half dozen . . . . there's Anna. I let out a howl, and Ernest has to see what I've found . . . he didn't even know he had the things.

Well, it's a small world, Ernest says, looking them over and finding a couple more of Anna . . . that must be why he bought them, because she was in the lot. And Anna's another bitch on horseback, he tells me. Do I think that Anna's going to do me or anyone else of us any good? Anna's not going to do anyone any good, least of all Anna.

When I leave I have the pictures of Anna in my pocket

and a large part of Ernest's quart of rye in my stomach. Ernest has taken another pint from his bureau and he's still talking, calling for his dancing girls again. I walk down to the office, and, since there's never anything for me to do there, write a couple of letters in order to make it look as though I were working for a half hour or so. Then I sail out again to see what I can find.

Just as I'm going out to the street I bump into Arthur. He's been looking for me, he says, and he's so excited that he can hardly talk. Before he can tell me what it's all about he has to have a drink, and he can't even wait to cross the street to a place where I have credit . . . . we go into the bar next to the office, where my credit has been exhausted for almost a month.

It develops that our little friend Charlotte has been to call on Arthur. He wasn't at home, but she left a note . . . . an invitation for both of us to drop in and see her. Arthur is shitting his pants over it, and he insists on reading the note aloud so that I'll be certain not to miss the good parts.

"Imagine that little cunt coming up to my joint," he stutters. "Jesus, I can't imagine what they thought when the bell rang and she was standing there at the door. . . . They'll think I'm nuts at my place. Look, read this part again . . . what does that mean if it isn't an invitation to come around there and throw a fuck her way? Jesus, didn't I tell you that she was a bitch? Didn't I?" He gulps down his pernod and calls for another. "Look, Alf, how's your nerve today? Do you have your nerve? My God, I haven't got the guts to go there and face her alone . . . . but if you were there it would be all right. . ." He looks anxiously at me to see how I'm taking all this. "Listen, Alf, I'll tell you what . . . . you can try her first. We'll both go up there and you can screw her and then I'll hop on . . . Christ, I didn't have to let you know anything about this, you know . . . . I could have just gone up there and laid her myself. But that's not my way, Alf . . . . Only, did you ever hear of such a thing in your life? Who the fuck ever heard of a midget who was a bitch? Hell, I never ever thought about the sex life of a midget before. . . ."

I'm not at all sure that Arthur isn't talking through his hat. He's reading a lot more out of that note than was written into it, and the only thing that is definitely suggested is a drink. But I have faith in Arthur's hunches, if not his reasoning, and the midget business is so crazy that it's appealing. In short, we make the call. . . . .

Charlotte looks like a doll when she lets us in . . . but they don't include all of what she has on a doll. If she's surprised to see both of us she doesn't show it . . . . She's so glad that we've come, she says . . . she didn't know what to do with herself today. Then, just as we've settled ourselves into a couple of chairs, in comes a man-sized police dog who shows every intention of eating both Arthur and myself.

If we weren't in such immediate danger of being devoured it would be funny to see the girl wrestling with that brute. She grabs him by the collar, and without half trying he lifts her off her feet and swings her around. But Charlotte bats him on the nose, tells him that his manners are deplorable, and he quiets down almost immediately. If he even so much as barked at her he'd knock her down, but he puts his tail between his legs and slinks out.

Charlotte says that she wants to shut him up, so she runs out after him, wiggling her tiny ass as efficiently as any full-sized woman. Arthur whispers to me . . . there's no question about why she keeps an animal like that, is there? If she kept a toy bull or one of those nasty hairless Mexican things it would be just for a pet . . . but, Jesus, did I see the dong that son-of-a-bitch had?

After the second drink there's no question about it. . . . . Charlotte's catting to be fucked. There's not a hell of a lot of difference between the way she acts and the way any other cunt would do it, either. Everything Arthur and I say is very amusing, and sometimes it's amusing when we don't intend it to be.

That little cunt! She's fascinating, sitting up in a chair that's a mile too big for her, crossing her tiny legs and drawing her skirt up to give us a peep at what's under there. . . . . But how the fuck to get a midget into bed with you is something I've never had to worry about before, and I don't know what to do next. I look at Arthur; Arthur grins back at me. We go on drinking Charlotte's very good scotch . . . . she's taking shots down with water, and it shouldn't take many of them to do something to her. . . .

The liquor hits her very suddenly . . . one minute she's all right . . . the next she's completely up to the ears in it. I don't realize what's happened until I've gotten up to pour her another. . . I'm leaning over the chair with my back to Arthur, and before I know what's going on she has reached for my dong and grabbed the front of my pants. It's an amazing feeling . . . . those baby fingers tickling around your fly . . . I simply stand there and let her fiddle with the thing. She pats it and strokes it the way some women handle a piece of fur, holding her glass in the other hand and smiling as though we had a secret. But we haven't any secret for very long . . . . Arthur gets a squint at what's going on, and he lets out a howl.

"Hey, what about me?" he wants to know . . . . . and nobody thinks he's asking for another shot.

That little cunt doesn't even stop playing with me. She has such small hands that she can put them into my fly without so much as opening a button, and she shows how it's done while she turns her doll's smile on Arthur. . . .

"You didn't come over to me," she says.

It looks as though Arthur had forgotten all about our agreement. He's off the couch and sitting on the other arm of Charlotte's chair in as fast a move as I've ever seen him make.

"Don't pay any attention to that guy," he tells her. "Here feel this . . . Isn't that a beauty?" He takes the glass from her and places her hand over his fly. "You don't want to fool around with anything he's got. . . Anyway you never

164 ·

can tell anything about a guy like that. . . . Where's he been in the past week? Do you know? Does anybody know? Hell, probably even he doesn't know. . . . Here . . . just squeeze it, like, and see how big it's getting."

Charlotte giggles and gives us both a squeeze. He's being silly, she says . . . they're both too big. . . Can't we see that she's just a very little girl with very small ambitions? And Arthur immediately wants to see her ambitions. It's the first time he's heard it called by that name, he says. Arthur must be drunk . . . . he thinks he's funny.

But Charlotte won't show us her ambition . . . she'll show us all around it though, so that we can get some idea of the size. . . . . She pulls her dress up and shows us her dainty thighs . . . . Arthur says that's not enough, and he and I have found one point to agree on. So Charlotte holds her legs together and shows us what she's like all the way up to her pants. And those pants are something to remember once you've seen them . . . they must be made of fairy wings . . . they look lighter than the sheerest silk stockings . . . I'm afraid to touch them . . . they'd fall to pieces under my hands. But her thighs look more substantial . . . I have to get a feel of them, and she doesn't seem to mind. . . .

Charlotte stops diddling our pricks and places her two forefingers on her thighs, up in her crotch. Do we see? That's how wide she is there. How could she have anything big enough for what we have in mind? And as for the other way . . . . it runs from here . . . oh, someplace down underneath. She holds up one hand, measuring with her thumb and finger . . . . no bigger than that. . .

"Listen . . . how about letting us have a feel of it?" Arthur says, "There's something I have to find out about that thing. . . Here . . . you can feel my cock some more . . . I feel you and you feel me, see?" He's talking to Charlotte as though she were a child and couldn't understand things very well. "Maybe it is too small, like you say, but there's something else I have to find out about it. . ."

She won't let him put his hands under her pants. . . . .
He bites his fingernails, and he'd start runs, she says. So
she'll just have to take her pants off, and she hopes we won't
mind. . . We wouldn't care to look the other way, would we?
No? Well. . . She pushes her little high-heeled pumps into
the chair cushion and lifts her ass. . . . I hold her dress up
and keep her belly bare while she squirms out of the
things. . . .

Arthur and I look at each other . . . she does have hair.
She sports a swell little bush down there . . . I grab for it,
and Arthur's too late. . . . Charlotte settles back and plays
with his dong while I find out what that fuzzy mop is hiding. . . .

It's a perfect little cunt . . . and not so fucking little
either. It's a hell of a way from being full-size, but it's nothing that makes you think of kiddie-kars, either. It's really
smaller than Tania's, I suppose, and it's softer, but the hair
around it is denser and longer . . . It's a woman's cunt,
all right, pint-sized . . . I run a finger into the split and
squeeze it into the lips . . . and when I glance up at Charlotte to see how she's taking this, the little cunt winks at
me. . . . .

Do I think she's nice? Someday I'll find some cunt who
doesn't ask me that question while I'm feeling her up, and
the chances are ten to one that when that happens I'll find
out that she's swallowed her false teeth and choked to
death. . . . It's like asking if you think breathing is nice . . . a
cunt's a cunt and they're all nice. . . But Charlotte is really
an exceptional bitch. . . I don't mind telling her what a
swell piece of machinery I think it is. You have to admire it,
just as you'd admire a very tiny, but perfect, watch. . . .

Arthur is going nuts waiting to get his paws on Charlotte's bonne-bouche. She's opened his fly now, and she has
his dick out in her hands, but he's not half so much interested in that as he is in what is going on down below. I'm
patting Charlotte's behind. . . It's as soft as a goosefeather

166 ·

pillow. . . I hope she doesn't bruise easily, because I can't keep from pinching it.

Arthur's amazed when he takes over. The first thing that comes to his mind is to ask if she has any pictures of it. . . . . She could make a fortune, he advises her, just by selling pictures of it, maybe with a measuring rule in the picture to show how big it is in millimeters. . . In the meantime, Charlotte's opening my fly and taking John Thursday out for the afternoon air. She sighs . . . . she thinks he's wonderful . . . . Charlotte may be a squirt but she has a full grown itch under her tail.

Arthur wants to take Charlotte over to the couch and undress her. . . .

"It'll be all right," he assures her. "Hell, that's a pretty big cunt . . . . I'll bet I've fucked smaller ones lots of times. Look, I don't have such a big prick anyway . . . in fact, when you really get down to measurements, it isn't big at all; it just looks that way at first. Ask Alf, he'll tell you."

All this time he's trying to rub up with something that looks like a piece of red fire hose. . . But it all sounds perfectly logical to little Charlotte. She looks us both over; she isn't even able to get her fingers all the way around my dong, but she nods her head. . . Well, perhaps. . . And Arthur says that if we can't fuck we can lie around and play with each other. . . . .

Charlotte lies at full length across the couch. She's so tiny that her feet don't come to the edge of it after we've taken her shoes off . . . . Arthur can hide her shoe completely simply by closing his fist over it. Jesus, the sex that's wrapped up in that small package! She has enough for any normal cunt, and it all has to be packed in, crammed into that hot, tiny body. . . . You can feel it oozing out when you touch her. . . . .

Most of the midgets I've seen were like Shetland ponies . . round and fat and pretty shapeless. But just as you'll see, now and then, one of those animals that look just as clean and well-proportioned as a horse, with a head that fits the rest of them, this cunt is a real woman in miniature. She has the shape . . . . and a swell one, too . . . and she even uses her body the same way as a woman of twice her size. Before we've gone very far I'm beginning to feel too big and too clumsy.

She has wonderful teats. . . They're so small that when you put your hand over one of them it's hidden, but for her size they're regular showpieces. There's not a chance in the world of taking a fuck between them . . . Arthur's cock looks like a baseball bat when he tries it later. . . . But it's an entirely new sensation to suck some bitch's bubs by putting the whole works in your mouth. . . . .

Arthur's found something to bitch about. . . He wishes he had his Kodak with him. He doesn't want to take dirty pictures, he tells Charlotte . . . all he wants is just one picture of her on the couch next to him, so you can see the cock he's got and what she's got to take it with. Charlotte is peeved by that. . . . What kind of a girl does he think she is, anyway? But that doesn't keep her from grabbing his dick as soon as he has his clothes off . . . Arthur and I lay side by side and Charlotte sits up between us, playing with us both. . . .

It's easy to get a finger into that split under her ass. Charlotte is as juicy as anyone else, and it's no trouble at all when you do it right. . . . And she likes to play that finger game. . . . . She lies back and spreads her legs and tells us to go right ahead.

Arthur sits sniffing his finger. . . He starts to say some-thing a couple of times, breaks off and looks first at Char-lotte's fig and then at me. What he's thinking about is obvious, but Arthur's being fastidious. . . . Finally he has jacked up his nerves . . . he bends over and takes a good sniff of Charlotte. She closes her legs around his neck and rubs her figlet in his face. Arthur looks up at me and says that I can go fuck myself if I don't like it. . . He runs his tongue into her conillon and begins to suck it . . . . I lie beside Charlotte and play with her bubs. . . .

She's a doll that I could play with all day. But Jean Jeudi can't appreciate things in abstract . . . there's just one idea in that hairless dome of his, and you can't get it out. Johnny wants to fuck and it's useless to argue. But I have to wait until Arthur takes his nose from under Charlotte's ass . . . she still has her legs clenched around his neck, and they're both having a swell time. It tastes sweet as a Texas banana melon, Arthur says . . . that's something he's picked up from Ernest, but after a few months here all Americans begin to talk that way. There's not one in Paris who doesn't pretend to know the United States as completely as his own face. . . .

Charlotte wants to know if we thought anything like this would happen when we came here. I give Arthur the sign to keep his trap closed, but he goes on like a dope and tells her . . . we had it all figured out that I was going to fuck her first. That makes two strikes on Arthur; she's sore at both of us, but mostly at Arthur. She makes him stop sucking her cuntlet, but it's all right for me to go on playing with her. . . It takes another shot to put her back in a good humor.

Arthur goes on prying . . . you can't blame him for wanting to know things, but he hasn't a hell of a lot of tact. Charlotte finally asks him to get them all off his chest . . . she'll tell him what he wants to know, and from then on he can either stop treating her like a freak or get the hell out. I agree with her about six hundred and seventy-five percent. I'd have thrown both of us out long ago. . . .

Arthur's first question is about cunt, of course. He wants to know if all the small people . . . a term which he thinks is very delicate . . . have cunts like Charlotte. It seems that they haven't. Some of them have cunts as big as your hat and some of them have little slits without a bit of hair on them. The men are the same way, Charlotte says, and the big problem is to find a good fit. . . . .

Then Arthur wants to know if Charlotte has ever been screwed by a full sized man before. She won't answer that one, and I can tell by the look in Arthur's eye that he's going to ask about the police dog next. . . Sure enough before I can stop him he's popped it out. I grab Charlotte before she can get sore and tell Arthur to go chase himself into the other room and ask the dog. . . . . Shit, he'd be asking her if she ever sucked off the rubber man next. . . . . .

Something of what he's doing seems to squeeze into Arthur's noggin. He takes a shot glass and moseys out of the room and it isn't until he's telling Sid about it a couple of days later that I learn that he's just gone off to take a look at the bathroom to see if the crapper is half size too. . . . . . .

Charlotte seems to like the way my dong smells . . . . she lies with her face in my mop and keeps sniffing at it while she tickles my balls. Finally she puts her tongue out and takes a taste of the end . . . . . she opens her mouth as wide as she can to let me try to put it in . . . we're just able to make it . . . . she's more of a cocksucker than a grown cunt could be . . . . no grown cunt would ever find a prick that much too big for her to handle. Charlotte can't be very delicate about sucking your cock, not when it's almost choking her.

When she gets under me and spreads her legs to be screwed I simply can't do it at first. I just lie and look at her until she begins to wave her legs and whimper for it. Then I'm between them, and she has one tiny thigh on each side of me while John T. goes nuzzling against her cuntlet. It's like trying to screw a child . . . . . shit, it's worse than trying to fuck a child because Charlotte has a real itch for it, and if it won't work she's going to be nuts. . . . .

I'm afraid that I'll pop her wide open like a ripe peach . . . but my dong goes in without a squeak from Charlotte. I try to look at it . . . . it's bulging like a squeezed balloon when it's fitted into her . . . . it must be bulging inside her too.

She bites my nipples and tells me to fuck her . . . she's

so hot now that she would tell me that even if I had a cock twice as big as this one. . . . .

Once she's opened up there's nothing to it. She may never be the same again; her cuntlet may never be quite so pretty and perfect as it was before we started, but that does not matter so much as having it work . . . a pretty little figlet is not much better to boast about if you can't fuck with it . . . . I give it to her up to the ears, and she begins to ask for more whoopee. You'd think she'd be scared, a tiny cunt like that . . . but not a bit of it. She's all bitch, what there is of her, and if she's afraid of anything it's the possibility that she won't get all the screwing she wants.

Where in hell she's putting my cock once it's in her figlet, I don't know. If it isn't coming up her gullet now, it never will . . . . so I grab her by that fat bunch of ass, turn her on her side, and give it to her the same as I would anybody else. There isn't room for so much as a hair to get into her . . . I've got her cunt stretched so far that you couldn't lay a pin between the edge of it and the edge of her rectum. And who the Hell is going around laying pins there anyway? I've got her . . . . I've got her good, and she's taking a fucking that whoever made her never intended her to have. . . . Suddenly she begins to squeak . . . she kicks my sides with her feet . . . . She's coming, and she shows me that she can fuck, too. . . .

Charlotte is one of those cunts who seem to be able to go on coming, once they've begun it, for just as long as you'll screw them. The couch is having the stuffing kicked out of it . . . . for a little girl Charlotte can raise an uncommon amount of hell. She raises her little voice along with her baby ass and lets go with both of them as hard as she can. It's a good thing the concierge is deaf . . . . he'd be in here looking for a murder if he heard this bitch howl. She grabs her teats and seems to simply lay them in my hands to be squeezed . . . . the dog begins to bark and raise the roof from wherever she has him tied up . . . Charlotte has juice in her thighs and juice on her ass and even on her belly . . . . I must have opened up a new spring in her cunt. . . . .

John Thursday hiccoughs a couple of times. He's not used to such cramped quarters, and he doesn't seem able to make up his mind. But then he lets go . . . . and I'm fucking Chrlotte so hard that she doesn't even squeak any more. She opens her mouth, but no sounds come out. I'm made aware that I've got a load of alcohol in my system . . . the furniture swings around the room in a slow gavotte.

Arthur comes back balancing his dong in front of him like a pole. I'm sitting in the center of the couch, trying to keep it quiet so it won't teeter so much, and Charlotte is lying on her back, playing with her bush. As soon as she sees that erect cock, Charlotte jumps off the couch and runs to Arthur. Fickle little cunt! Both arms go as far around his ass as she can get them and she hugs herself up to his crotch. She's just tall enough so that when she stands flat-footed and looks down, the end of his cock touches her lips. . . . She kisses Arthur's belly and the bush that grows halfway up it, and then she stands there and opens her mouth. She simply stands there and lets him put it in.

Arthur must have been playing with himself while he was out. Either that or he's losing his control, because Charlotte hasn't been sucking his prick for more than a minute before he spills. One instant Charlotte is gnawing away at him as hard as she can, and they're both happy; in another they're ecstatic, and Charlotte is trying to swallow a pint of jism in one gulp. I get the impression of watching a moving picture that's been speeded up several times. . . .

Charlotte comes dashing back to me. . . . Would I like to have my prick sucked, she wants to know . . . . and before I can answer she's climbed over me and has it in her mouth. She'd like to have me suck her figlet too . . . she throws her ass almost in my face, and I lie staring up between her legs. But I never was attracted to a cunt with jism in it . . . I bite her thighs instead, and she's almost as happy. She slobbers and coos over my prick until it's too big to be cooed over. . . .

One of my balls is all that one of her tiny hands can hold. She likes to squeeze them for some reason . . . . perhaps she thinks that she'll get more jism out of them that way. So with one hand she squeezes my balls and with the other she tries to choke John T. into being nice to her. In the meantime I'm playing with her ass. She has a little rectum that's not half as big as a dime, and I find out that she likes to have it tickled. Arthur is interested in it . . . he looks it over and thinks that it would be nice to give Charlotte a cock in there, but there's not a chance. . . .

Those baby fingers are driving me nuts. . . And that tight, doll's mouth . . . Jean Jeudi wants to show his stuff again, and I don't keep him waiting. It's the damnedest feeling, letting your jism come into that cunt's little lips and watching her swallow it. . . . .

I've just finished with her, and Arthur is giving her a feeling up, when there's suddenly the most startling racket I've ever heard. Then that damn police dog comes scrambling in from the other room, trailing a leash and acting as though he intended to finish up a job he should have done earlier. He's as big as a house, and he makes straight for the couch. Arthur and I both tumble off in opposite directions, but it's not us he's after. He lands squarely on Charlotte and pins her down.

Arthur grabs the first thing that's handy . . . the bottle of Scotch . . . but the dog isn't eating Charlotte after all . . . . he's only raping her. She can't do a thing . . . he knows how to handle her, and he's really being as gentle as he can under the circumstances. And Charlotte's not being afraid of him . . . she's only dreadfully embarrassed.

"Go on and drag him off," I suggest to Arthur. "He won't hurt you much."

Arthur politely asks me to go to hell . . . he's not going near that son-of-a-bitch. And in the meantime, the dog has managed to get the end of a very red and juicy looking dong between Charlotte's legs.

"It looks like he's going to go in," Arthur says. "Hey, Alf, do you suppose we ought to ask him to have a drink with us after it's all over? I'll bet that bastard has some experiences that would be worth hearing."

"Please . . . . go . . . . away. . . ." Charlotte gasps. "Jacques, oh, Jacques, don't do that! Go away, you wicked, wicked dog."

"Are you going to sit there and let that animal take the meat away from you?" I ask Arthur. "Aren't you going to do anything?"

"I'm going to sit here and take this thing in," Arthur tells me. "Did you ever see anything like this before? Well . . . . in a whorehouse show, maybe. But you never saw a dog actually rape anybody. . . By Jesus, if you think I'm going to get that horse mad at me, you're crazy . . . . he's bigger than me."

Charlotte keeps asking us, whenever she has a breath to spare, to get the hell out. The dog has a good grip on her now, his cock's in, and he's fucking her a mile a minute. . . At last she can't do anything but spread her legs for him and let him have it. . . . .

"Look dope," I tell Arthur after we have watched for a few minutes, "that thing is going to be through in a couple of minutes, then what's going to happen? I'm telling you he has a mean look in his eye. . . . After he's through fucking her he's going to be hungry as hell. I don't give a fuck in hell what you do, but I'm getting away from him, beginning as of two minutes ago."

I sneak over to the couch to get my clothes. Arthur thinks it over for a few seconds and then he dresses too. We manage to grab off another shot of the scotch, and we try to say good-bye to Charlotte. . . But she doesn't hear us . . . she has her arms around that pooch of hers and she's loving him back. I think women are such charming people when you get to know them. . . . .

Arthur and I don't have much to say about our visit when we get on the street. We walk about half a block and then Arthur grabs my arm.

"My God, Alf, look at the size of that bitch, will you? How'd you like to try laying her? Boy, you'd get lost under that ass . . . that's the kind I want in my old age, to keep me warm nights. . . ."

She looks like a big cunt. But when I close one eye and look at her again I see that she's just about five foot three . . .

Anna is depressed. The old geezer who keeps her is getting to be a pain in the ass, she tells me, and she doesn't know exactly what to do about it. He gives her plenty of dough, and all that, but he's still a pain in the ass. We're out having lunch and she reads me the record.

First of all he wants to meet her girl friends. He thinks he's a very gay old buck, and first thing, as soon as Anna's introduced him to some cunt she knows, he puts on the stuff and wants to get the girl in bed. Which would be all right, I suppose, except for the fact that they all want to get some of his cash, of course, and that makes him sore. He thinks that Anna tips them off and that he's being played for a sucker . . . he gets peeved when he finds that he's not getting any free cunt. . . .

Then there are a couple of other little matters. . . . He expects a new and better Arabian Nights for his money. Anna has to tell him stories about her sex life, and she's going nuts trying to think up new adventures. The other night, for instance, when the boys dumped her out at his place. . . He was absolutely delighted about that. . . Anna says he almost hopped out of his nightie as soon as he saw her, because there wasn't much question about what had been happening to her. So he fucked her, of course . . . it must make him feel that it's really that last one he gives her that finishes her off . . . and not only then, but afterward, he had to know all about what went on. . . . He kept her awake for hours trying to find out just how this was done and that was done, and Anna was so full of liquor and so much fucked out that all she wanted was to go to sleep. And when she simply couldn't stay awake any longer he was sore. . . . . if she could stay awake while all those things happened, why couldn't she stay awake long enough to have some fun with him?

Then when he has some business acquaintance in, Anna's supposed to put on another act. He likes to show her off, to let people see what a swell cunt he's got, and that's all right, but Anna's supposed to show everybody that she's got a continental case of itchy tail . . . . and all for him. So she has to slink around and show her shape and act like a bitch in the spring, rubbing up against him, and letting him feel her ass and maybe giving him a feel around his balls now and then. Then, when this has gone on for awhile, she calls him from another room and he excuses himself and struts out to play with her for a half an hour . . . . sometimes he even manages to get it up and screw her, but usually all he accomplishes is to take half her clothes off and rumple her up. Then . . . back they trot, together, and maybe he's even buttoning his pants when they go into the room, and Anna looks . . . and is supposed to act . . . as though she's just been through the washing machine. . . .

Now he has another marvellous plan. He'd like Anna to bring some big-cocked young bozo in and take it from him, let him give her the whole works, complete, while her daddy dumplings hides in a closet and peeks out at them. Anna refuses absolutely. What he'd actually do, Anna says, is hide in the closet and play with himself until he'd seen it all and then hop out playing the outraged lover. Because he'd be in his own house, Anna says, he'd probably have enough courage to slap the other fellow in the face, and he might even take a shot at him . . . even if he hit him, a French court would back him up on the defense of honor gag. It sounds fantastic, but Anna says that I wouldn't think so if I knew this bastard.

While we're having our coffee I flash the pictures that Ernest bought someplace. Anna almost pisses her pants when she sees them . . . she might have known those friends of hers would do something like that. They wanted to take them just for fun . . . . . well, just for fun she'll cut their balls off if she meets them again. There are people who should never see those, she says . . . . but by now every half-wit in Paris is diddling himself silly over them . . . . . Anna sees the whole city passing them from hand to hand and pointing her out on the street. However, this ought to make her meal ticket happy for awhile . . . . this is just the sort of thing he likes. . . .

Raoul runs into us just as we're about to leave. Since he has something to say to me, we stay for a liqueur. Raoul is a bit shy about getting it off his chest while Anna's there, so she takes a skip to the can to give us a chance to talk. . . . . .

Raoul's sister-in-law is back in Paris now, and he's fixed things up to pay for those Spanish lessons I gave him. Raoul gave her a line about me, fixed it all, and she was quite reasonable about it. I don't know what he could have told her, but whatever it was must have been pretty good . . . she doesn't know me from Adam, but on Raoul's recommendation she's willing to pass out a free fuck. Raoul hopes that someday he may be able to go to America and sell vacuum cleaners. . . . .

It wouldn't be so good for me to go to her house, Raoul says. Too risky, and besides, she might not want me to know where she lives. That suits me . . . I'd just as soon she didn't know where I live either . . . at least not until I get a look at her and find out what she's like. So we arrange a meeting place . . . corner rue Cuvier and the quai St. Bernard, eight o'clock tomorrow night.

"But if there's some old bag waiting there," I tell Raoul "I'm just going to turn around and leave her there. We're not agreeing that I have to fuck her, now. . . . What we're agreeing is that she has to fuck me if I like her. . . ."

"She's not a bag . . . she's nice, Alf. Wait until you see her . . . She'll be a nice fuck, you see if she isn't. . . . My brother, he still thinks she's a nice cunt, and he's married to her. . ."

"Does she know my name? Maybe she thinks I'm rich or something . . . what the fuck did you tell her that she's so ready to hand herself over to me?"

"Ah, I told her, Alf . . . I fixed it up all nice. She does not think you're rich or anything. . . . I just told her your first name. But she thinks you're wonderful. . . . I told her lots of good shit about you. Just fuck her good, that's all she wants from you. Anyway, maybe I have a little something on her, see Alf? Maybe there's something she wouldn't want my brother to know about. . . . It's a little thing about the groceryman, perhaps . . . maybe he brings some of the groceries without ever putting them on the bill. . . .".

"I don't care about what she does with the grocer . . . what's she going to do with me? I don't want to get into any mess. . ."

"She won't get you into any mess, Alf. She's a nice girl. I ought to know. She goes to church. . . ."

"Is she a cocksucker?"

"Sure, she's a cocksucker. She's a nice girl I'm telling you. She goes to church."

Anna comes back and Raoul runs along, for Anna and I are going visiting. . . .

Anna's two girl friends are not at home when we arrive at their place, but they have hung a note on the door asking us to walk in . . . . for they'll be right back. So, while we're waiting we sit down and Anna wants to see the pictures again. Oh, it's really awful, she says, to think of those being scattered all over Paris . . . . and the lord only knows where else. She sits shaking her head and licking her chops over them until I can't stand it any longer. . . . . all she's doing is working up an itch under her ass, and I know of a fuck of a lot better ways of doing that than looking at dirty pictures of yourself. . . .

Anna keeps telling me that we shouldn't do it . . . but she doesn't do anything to stop us, and pretty soon we're on the couch playing with each other. I have her pants down and her ass bare; she has my dong out and is combing my brush . . . and in walk the two cunts. Young cunts, too . . . they might be around twenty.

Everything's very chummy right from the start. With an introduction like that it couldn't be anything else. Anna manages to get John T. put away after some fumbling, but nothing can be done about her pants. At last she stands up, hoists her skirt to full mast, and pulls them up to her ass again. I'm introduced to the cunts who turn out to be Americans . . . one named Jean and the other with a regular Lesbian tag. . . Billie.

Jean is a little blonde cunt who must buy all her clothes a size too small . . . she just manages to fit all of her shape into them. Billie has the shape too, but with her it's a tai-lored suit and a necktie. Later Anna tells me that Billie has some money and Jean hasn't, so Billie takes care of the bills and Jean spreads her legs at the right times.

Jean is just as hot as she looks. Since everyone else is standing, I have to stand too, hard or not, and Jean stares at my fly as though she expected a jack-in-the-box to come popping out of it. She'd like to know, she says, if that thing she thought she saw is real or if she is imagining things. Anna tells her that it's very real, and asks if she would like to see it again. Jean says she thinks she'll wait awhile. . . She smiles and winks at me. . . .

I don't know why we came here in the first place . . . Anna told me that I was going to meet two of her friends, but it looks as though we came to play with each other. Billie shows off a couple of books she illustrated . . . for some reason it appears that Lesbians can draw better pictures of people fucking than anyone else can draw. We go on from there. Anna takes a look at one illustration . . . . anyone who ever sucked a prick would know that the artist never did, she says. Billie demands a demonstration, but Anna isn't bothered by that . . . she drags out her postcards and shows Billie how it looks. That cunt . . . . and she was pretending to be worried about them being made public!

We've fiddled away the better part of an hour before Jean has the nerve to say what's on her mind. Billie has been doing everything but undress her right there, and every time that Billie passes her and gives her a feel on the ass Jean turns and makes eyes in my direction. . . Why don't we all, Jean says, change into something more comfortable, or is everybody going to beat around the bush all afternoon?

"Every time she sees a man she wants to undress," Billie says. "I can't do a thing with her. . . ."

"She's jealous," Jean explains. "She thinks I ought to undress for her, but not for anybody else. . . . But I like to take my clothes off, Billie . . . I want to take them off right now. . ."

She looks over in my direction. My dong is up like a dirigible, and I've given up trying to shove it down my pant leg. I don't know what I'm supposed to do . . . I've never run into a set-up like this. With any one of them I'd know how to act, but the three of them are simply too much for me. And Jean isn't the only one who's catting for a fuck . . . Anna wants it, and Billie has something on her mind, though Jesus can guess what it is. . . .

Billie takes things out of my hands, and neatly, too. That cunt . . . she couldn't bear to have her Jean looking at a pair of pants. . . She suddenly grabs Jean around that tough looking little middle and tosses her onto the couch like an Apache.

"Fight, you fucking little bitch," she howls when Jean

begins to kick and keep her away. "So you want him to see you. . . Well, I'm going to undress you so he can. . . ."

Myself, I wouldn't want to get within three feet of those wicked looking heels of Jean's . . . she acts as though she'd like to kick Billie's head off. But Billie isn't afraid of her . . . . maybe they play this way a lot of times . . . . shit, you can't tell anything about people like this. Anyway, it makes a nice show . . . Jean pulls her skirt up to her pants so she can kick better, and she has thighs which are just as juicy as the rest of her. But Billie gets between Jean's legs, and Jean hasn't a chance from then on. Billie smacks Jean's thighs and that part of her ass that's bare, and while Jean's trying to wiggle away she jumps on top of her and goes to work.

It really is exciting to watch those cunts wrestling, and I'm not at all surprised when Anna comes bouncing over to sit on my lap. She had juice between her legs when I was playing with her before, but there is twice as much there now . . . . I find it on her thighs almost to her knees, and she smells the way your bed smells when you've had cunt in it for three nights running . . . . She grabs my dick and begins to play with it, and I don't have to take her pants down again . . . she takes them down herself . .

Jean is putting up a nice battle. She knows she can't keep Billie from undressing her now, so she's putting everything she's got into stripping Billie too. In a couple of minutes they've both lost their skirts, and they're squirming around with their asses bare before they've lost anything from the top. Even if Billie is a Lesbian, she's got a swell shape, and just knowing that she's not interested in me can't keep me from getting hot about her when I get a view of her cunt thrown at me. That bushy pink place was meant for a prick to go into . . . even if Anna weren't pestering him John T. knows it, and he'd be up and about. . . .

Billie finally gets all of Jean's clothes off . . . and she has damn few of her own on now. She yells over for Anna and me to get a good look at her bitch. Would we like to hear her squeal? She pinches her bubs. Or maybe we'd like a better look at her bonne-bouche . . . so she pulls Jean's bottom around and tickles her crotch. She must want us to count the hairs . . . . she begins playing with Jean's fig and runs her finger up in it . . . Jean is becoming very quiet. . . .

Anna has her dress up to her belly and she's opening it at the top to take those marvellous teats of hers out. Billie lies across Jean and looks over at Anna's cunt while she plays with Jean's. Jean has her hand between Billie's thighs, but I can't see just what she's doing. Anna wants me to play with her teats . . . she leans over and shakes them at me.

"Did that cunt ever go to bed with you?" I whisper to Anna. "She's looking at you as though she'd like to gobble you up. . ."

Apparently that's none of my business. . . . Anna shakes her finger at me and won't answer. Then she spreads her legs farther so that Billie can see her fig better . . . Jean and Billie have stopped fighting, and now they lie and quietly pick the clothes from each other until they're both as bare as plucked chickens except for one little spot . . . . Anna rolls down her stockings. Then she decides that it's time for her to get out of her dress. I'm not one to be out of step with the rest of the world, so I undress too. And while I'm doing that they stop, those three bitches, and do nothing but watch me . . . Jean squeaks and bounces on the couch . . . she wants some of that . . . some of THAT! She tells the world.

Billie tells her that perhaps she'll get some if she's a good girl. . . Shit, I'd rather give her some if she's a bad girl. . . Anna has slid down between my knees and is playing with my dong, rubbing her head against it while she looks over at the two cunts on the couch. Jean suddenly grabs Billie by the ass and hugs her; they're kissing each other like high school lovers, and if you just looked at one pair of hips you'd swear that the girl was fucking. They lie there rubbing their bellies and teats and cunts together, and it's enough to make you tear your hair, seeing them go through all the motions and not getting anyplace.

"Show them what you do to me," Jean says. Jesus Christ you'd think they'd at least have some reticence about what they do to each other . . . but not those bitches! Jean spreads her legs and lies on her back; Billie isn't much more self-conscious about her part . . . she slips her hand down to Jean's belly and lets us in on the big secret.

Billie has a swell time playing hide and seek in Jean's bush. Most of the blonde cunts I've run into didn't have much hair around their figs or anyplace else, but Jean has all you could ask for, unless you were looking for something to stuff a mattress with. Billie wipes her face into it, bites Jean's belly, and finally she kisses her squarely in the middle of her split. Then Anna and I might just as well not be there at all . . . Billie begins to suck Jean's fig, and she doesn't pay any attention to anything else. . . You'd think that she'd be a little less brash with strangers about . . . but then, one look at a cunt in a suit like that and with that mannish walk and you'd know that she likes to sniff under a cunt's skirt . . . she has it well advertised already. . . . .

Anna begins to play around my prick with her bubs. She keeps one eye on the couch, but she's not neglecting Jean Jeudi, either. She puts him up in that harbor between her teats and tries to rock him to sleep. Anna has teats that make better fucking than a lot of cunts that I've tried, and Johnny's happy about the whole thing . . . especially since Anna bends over every couple of seconds and kisses his red, alcoholic nose. . . . .

Jean gets tired of having Billie lick her fig . . . . after all, she probably gets that every night of her life, or all but a handful of nights every month, and I suppose you can get tired of that just as you can get tired of anything else. Jean wants to know why she can't be screwed now . . . she thinks it's time that everybody changed over.

Billie agrees with her. It certainly is time to change

over, she says . . . and she hops up and sets her ass over Jean's face before Jean can guess what's going on.

"I know you, you bitch," Billie says, rubbing her con over Jean's nose. "You want him to think that you're a NICE girl! You wouldn't be nasty and suck a cunt, would you? Why you dirty juice licker . . . what happened when my sister visited us? Yes, and on the very first night. And what did you let Annette teach you? Didn't I find you with your head under Bebe's skirt? Didn't you let Meg play with you? For that matter, who of my friends haven't you sucked? Damned few . . . I'd say. Oh, you bitch, you, don't try that game! Every time you go from here to the corner you come back either with your pants full of jism or your nose smelling of cunt. . ."

Anna goes on shaking her teats against my cock, but suddenly she has her mouth open and she's letting me put it in. I'm in such a hurry to get there that I almost put it all down her throat. . . . All I can see of Jean is her ass and her waving legs, but from the sounds that are coming out from beneath Billie's ass I can guess all that I can't actually see. Billie holds her legs close to Jean's head, like a jockey . . . . she's leaning forward and she's bouncing up and down . . . . all she needs now are spurs and a small quirt. . . .

Anna jumps up . . . and just in time, for inside of another minute I would have come. She goes to the couch and I follow her. Jean has her eyes closed, and she's sucking Billie's cunt as though it were a peach . . . . she's feeling Billie up while she sucks her, and whatever else, she doesn't look as though she didn't like do that stuff.

Anna has a crazy idea. . . She wants Billie to suck my prick. I'd never have suggested such a thing myself, but Anna has an argument . . . . she's perfectly normal herself, but she's sucked cunts and she's not backward about admitting it. From what she said it sounds as though Anna might have had something to do with Billie's bonne-bouche at some time or another . . . and if Anna can suck a cunt, there's no reason why Billie shouldn't be able to suck a prick.

For a Lesbian, Billie's a remarkably reasonable person. Most of those bitches would go through the ceiling if you made them a suggestion like that . . . . but Billie listens very carefully and seems to consider it for a long time. At last she throws her leg over Jean . . . she dismounts, that's all I can think of . . . . and takes a good long look at my dong.

"You know . . . I think I will do that," she says. "If it's all right with you, Alf, of course. . ."

If it's all right with me! Christ, I'm fairly reasonable myself . . . I can't remember ever having refused an offer to have my cock sucked. I park my ass on the couch and wait to see what happens.

Billie doesn't want any coaching from the gallery. She understands this thoroughly, in theory, she says, and she won't need a bit of help . . . . She kneels in front of me and crawls between my thighs, and after she's looked at my prick for a second she looks up at me. She has that lovesick, moon-gazing look down perfectly . . . if I wasn't pretty certain of what she is I'd swear she was nuts about my cock and the thought of getting a suck of it. . . Then she begins to play with it . . . not because Johnny needs any playing with, but because it's part of her theory, I suppose. Then . . . in he goes.

That cunt can be damn convincing . . . she begins to coo and slobber over it as though there wasn't anything in the world she liked better. She puts her arms around me and hugs me, she rubs her teats against my knees, she plays with my balls . . . and when she isn't actually sucking my cock she's either kissing my balls or she's shampooing my belly.

By her own standards Billie is being a particularly filthy cunt. You see them hanging around the bars sometimes, these bitches, eyeing all the cunt that comes along, and

buying drinks for those they're trying to proposition . . . .
and I always wonder what would happen to them if they got
a good fuck. But you can't get near them. Some of them are
swell looking bitches, too, but they'd no more think of letting a man get under their skirts than you'd think of asking
the bozo next to you on the Metro to take down his pants so
you could jerk him off . . . I know . . . I've tried to pick up
some of them. . . .

Even Billie, if her theory is any good, must know what's
going to happen if she goes on sucking my prick that way.
Jean and Anna are almost pissing their pants, waiting for
me to come. . . . I don't want to disappoint anybody . . . I
hold it back until my balls are turning handsprings: I want
to give it to her all at once, if I can. . . .

Billie knew what she was talking about when she said
she wouldn't need any help. I'm ready to grab the bitch's
head and hold her if she gets smart when she finds her
mouth full of jism, but I'm wasting my time. You'd think
that she loved the stuff. She takes one look at Jean when it
starts to come, and when she finds her cunt watching her,
she swallows it. Jean grabs Anna around her teats, and it
looks as though something interesting was about to begin
there . . . . but she remembers herself before Billie catches
her at it. . . As soon as I've stopped coming, Billie grabs
Jean . . . but not to suck her fig, as I thought she was going
to do. She puts her arms around Jean and kisses her on the
mouth. They hug each other and lie running their tongues
into each other's mouths . . . Jean whispers to Billie again
that she's a dirty, perverted cock sucker.

Anna breaks into the party with the way of someone
who feels that they're being left out of things. Her cunt
itches, she says, and what would somebody like to do about
that? Billie puts her arms around Anna and begins feeling
her up . . . . pretty soon they're playing with each other's
tails, and it's no surprise when Billie puts her head between
Anna's thighs and starts licking that juicy trap.

Jean is behind Billie, tickling her crotch and pushing a

finger up her cunt . . . Christ, with all that display of ass, I can't simply sit there and watch them fiddling around with each other. I hop in too and grab Jean. . . John T. isn't up to form, but that bitch knows what to do about it, she has the stuff to fix him . . . she spreads her legs so that I can play with her fig, and she begins massaging my dong.

She's a hot young parcel, that Jean. A few minutes with her and I have a dong that would be in danger of being shot and stuffed if it happened to be seen in the wrong place. She's so hot that she's panting like a dog . . . she'll split herself if she tries to spread her legs any farther . . . and her conillon has been opened up so much by what Billie was doing to it that my fingers seem to fall in as soon as I touch it. . . It's a nice fat cunt. . . If there's one thing I don't like it's one of those bony bitches with just a bunch of hair and a hole that looks as though it might have been poked into them with a stick.

Billie doesn't mind what I do to her Jean. Probably she wouldn't anyway, but she's so much wrapped up in Anna— literally—that she hasn't time for anything else. Anna's watching us, but Billie never notices when I climb onto Jean.

Jean doesn't fuck at first. She has her knees up, making it easy for me to get into her, but that's about as far as her cooperation goes. She's being screwed rather than screwing . . . and she's being screwed damn well. My dong is all the way in with every jump . . . . I have the edges of her cunt tucked in and the cracks plugged up with hair. I fuck her until her tongue is hanging out . . . and when she's almost coming she starts fucking too; then it's like screwing the Furies.

Watching me ride that ferocious little cunt like that seems to put an extra measure of pepper up Anna's ass. She pulls her cunt open as far as she can, until the damn thing actually yawns, and Billie seems to have most of her face inside it. Then she comes: when that happens she can't stand having Billie trying to climb in . . . . she pushes Billie away, but lets her come back again to lick up the juice that's pouring down her thighs.

When Billie comes out from all that and sees what game Jean and I are playing she lets go with some invective that's too neat to be as masculine as Billie wants to be. Only a female could scatter the language about so recklessly and still have it seem to mean something. She's not angry, exactly . . . but from what I've seen it looks as though this brace of cunts have their best fun when they're either spitting in each other's faces or kicking each other around. Jean doesn't pay much attention . . . she fucks harder than ever. Then she throws one leg up almost to my shoulder, shoves her ass out so that Anna and Billie can see just exactly what this game looks like at close range . . . and we both come . .

She wants my address! That's the first thing that Jean says after she's come, and she sounds as though she means it. Shit, I'm not going to refuse my address to a cunt like Jean . . . and from Billie there's not so much as a dirty look. It's Anna who acts jealous, if anybody does . . . she asks Billie if she's not afraid of losing her little cunt. Not Billie. . . .

"She has to be screwed," Billie tells Anna, playing with Jean's hair and pushing it out of her eyes. "I don't mind when she goes out and gets laid . . . . it's these bitchy Lesbians she takes up with that I can't stand. But you know what you'll have to do, Jean, if I say it's all right. . . ."

Jean knows . . . and right then and there she shows us what it is. She shoves her hair back over her ears so that it won't get in the way and then she bends over and kisses Billie's cunt. . . . . She's still breathless from the screwing I gave her, but she sucks Billie's cunt until Billie comes. . . . .

Last night, eight o'clock on the nose, I keep my appointment at the entrance of the Jardin des Plantes. Fifteen minutes . . . . half an hour. . . . Nine o'clock and that bitch hasn't shown up yet. Jesus, people who break dates ought to be jailed. It's like taking money from you . . . it's worse than taking money. They waste your life . . . . an hour here, fifteen minutes there . . . it must add up to years after a while. So another hour has been stolen from me, and where am I going to get another one to take its place? My great Jesus, I'm not going to live forever, I don't have so many hours left that I can go tossing them away like that. But women never think of things like that. I don't think that women ever think about coming to the end of their life someday. Certainly they don't in the same way that men do. You can depend on it . . . . if a man's unpunctual he's usually worthless, shiftless and at least eighteen assorted kinds of a prick besides. But even a smart woman, or what men call a smart woman, will keep you cooling your heels without any compunction. . . .

At nine o'clock I give that corner the shake. I've got better things to do than hold down the sidewalk all night. A hell of a fine job of fixing it up Raoul did. . . . One thing, though . . . in Paris you never miss the boat. If one cunt doesn't show up another will . . . . in every café shit-house there is a fine list of addresses on the walls, and they're not all phoney, the way they are in America. (What kind of a cunt would you find at one of those addresses? I'll have to try it sometime. . . .) There's cunt all over the place . . . . you can pay for it or you can have it for nothing, depending on how badly you need it, and while your belly may be empty just as often here as in America, your bed doesn't have to be. . . .

So even if Raoul's sister-in-law hasn't shown up I'm not worried about finding a fuck. About an hour later, when I've had a few drinks, I pick one up. She's not a whore, really, she's simply hungry. She's not a beauty but she's not bad; she's young and she looks as though she used soap once in a while. So I give her a feed and then we go home and I try to ram it back out of her again . . . . but I'm still sore about that other cunt. . . .

Then this morning Raoul comes prancing in, bright as a daisy. He's going to be funny, the son-of-a-bitch . . . . and how did it go last night, he wants to know. . . .

"Oh boy! Oh! Alf?" he says, wagging his finger at me. "How did you like her? Was she a baggage like you thought? See . . . . . when I fix it up . . . . maybe you'll believe me next time. . ." He runs around the room and finds a cigarette. "She likes you, Alf . . . . I saw her today, first thing, and she's nuts about you . . . . . only she thinks you're a little bit crazy. One thing is bad, though . . . . very bad. All those bruises on her behind, Alf . . . . how is she going to explain those to my brother? Ah, but she likes that too . . . . at the time. She's headstrong, Alf, and she forgets about tomorrow . . . . you shouldn't spank her so hard next time . . . And for Christ's sake take her to a better hotel . . . . she has friends at that place. . . ."

"Stop being cute, damn it. Listen, Raoul, you can tell that cunt . . . Oh, tell her any fucking thing you want to! She kept me waiting there an hour. . . ."

"An hour? No, not an hour, Alf. . . . Eight o'clock, that was the time we said. . . ."

Raoul goes on talking until it begins to come to me that he really thinks I was out with his sister-in-law last night. Shit, he even has all the details about it. . . Finally I put him straight and I have a hell of a time making him see that I'm not kidding. . . . He even climbs onto the bed and sniffs the sheets when I tell him I was home with another cunt last night. He's wild when he's convinced.

"But she got laid, Alf . . . honest she got laid good! You ought to see her this morning! I thought you were just shitting me, Alf. . . She isn't smart enough to try to shit me. . . Do you know what's happened, Alf? . . . She's been screwed . . . she's been cheated!"

He wants to know who I'd told about that date. I hadn't told anybody. Then what corner was I standing on? Yes, that's where she was . . . etc., etc., for ten minutes. Raoul doesn't see anything funny in it, and it's too early in the day for me to laugh.

"Well, what about that fuck I was supposed to get?" I ask Raoul. "How about tonight? Can she make it?"

Raoul gets sore. To hell with the fuck I was supposed to get he says . . . what about the one she got? How is he going to explain that to her? Do I think he's going up and say, hey, that was the wrong one, and ask her to do it over? When she didn't even get paid?

"What kind of a son-of-a-bitch could have done a thing like that, Alf? It must have been one of your friends . . . nobody else would do a thing like that. What a prick he must be, eh, Alf? Taking advantage of an innocent girl like that . . . and not even paying her . . . not even paying her, Alf? And in a cheap, lousy hotel where she could get lice or things! My own sister-in-law!"

He won't stick around any longer . . . he's got to rush right back and try to straighten things out. Do I have a picture of myself he can show her? No? Well, maybe he can call me up later in the day and I'll meet them some place so that he can show her she was fucked by the wrong guy. . . . Raoul says that maybe if she sees me she'll like me and want to give me a screw anyway, but he can't say that he's very hopeful. There's always bad luck like this in his family, Raoul says. . . He has a cousin who went with a girl . . . nice girl. But the girl got a job and pretty soon her boss was after her. . . Well, Raoul's cousin found out that she had to be nice to her boss, and he didn't like it. Up he goes to tell the old fart off. And then what do I suppose happened? I can't guess, but I imagine it was something catastrophic. . . . The old man thought he was there looking for a job, Raoul tells me, and he hired him on the spot. So now they both have to kiss his ass, and Raoul's cousin has to answer the phone and say the boss is in conference when he knows fucking well he's back there with his girl friend on the couch, screwing the pants off her. . . . Nothing but bad luck in their family Raoul tells me.

I've just closed the door after Raoul when Alexandra comes dashing up the stairs. Have I got Tania here, she wants to know. Well, if I haven't got here here, where have I got her? Tania, it seems, got tired of playing with her puppy and disappeared yesterday. She ought to be somewhere in Paris by now, and Alexandra has simply come to the most likely place to look for her.

What about Peter, I ask Alexandra when she's calmer, is he gone too? No, Peter is still out in the country, waiting to see if Tania comes back . . . . he doesn't know anymore about where she's gone than anyone else does. But have I had any notes from her? Do I have any idea of where she might have gone?

What Alexandra seems to want is for me to organize a searching party, rouse the country through the columns of the paper, and send boy scouts out. I've never seen her go so completely up in the air, and it's useless to try to talk to her until she's got some sense. I tell her that I'll do what I can, and Alexandra goes hopping off somewhere else. She's completely off her nut today, but she needn't be. If I know Tania, she's taking very good care of herself. . . . . .

BOOK 11

France
in My Pants

So it's true. Tania is bald as an eagle, bald as an egg. All that's left to show that she used to have a sprouting young rosebush down there between her legs is a soft bristling when she's rubbed the wrong way. And it's not only her cuntlet that's been shaved . . . she's shaved her ass too, or had it shaved . . . . not that there such a hell of a lot there to begin with. . . . .

"Peter did it," she tells me, "and Snuggles helped. Isn't it funny?"

She spreads her legs farther apart, slips down and pulls her dress up higher so that I can see it as well as feel it. It's as smooth as her face . . . smoother, because on her face there's still a light down which you can see if you get the light just right.

"I looked so strange when it was being done," Tania giggles. "Like a horse foaming at the mouth. Peter said he wished I could make juice that way."

I can see what it must have been like. . . Snuggles holding the bowl of warm water, using the lathering brush, Peter holding his sister's ass cheeks apart while he ran the razor down the crack. . . . Yes, that must have been a swell party.

Tania can't sit still on my lap. She wiggles her ass from one side to the other, squeezes my hand between her thighs. She's got that itch in her tail again. . . . taking her muff away from her hasn't done much to cool her pants. We could play a game, she says archly, to see if Jean Jeudi still recognizes her bonne-bouche. . . .

He'll recognize her. . . . That thing is the face of Medusa where he's concerned . . . . one look and he turns to stone, even without the snaky whiskers. I've got a rock in my pants already . . . . but Tania knows how to soften it up . . . . she turns it to lava in that furnace of hers, and pours it out.

Tania's wet between the legs. She doesn't have any hair to mop it up with now, all that juice, she says . . . perhaps she'll have to ask to borrow mine . . . . and into my pants she goes, grabbing a handful. The bitch, she doesn't even ask for things any more, she takes what she can, and what she can't get for herself, she demands.

Johnny, she thinks, would look very queer without his beaver. She opens my fly, pulls him out, and gives him the eye. . . . Yes, he's got to have his whiskers to keep his dignity, she says. She tickles him under the chin. . . . If he didn't have that fancy overcoat, Tania thinks, he'd probably hide his head for shame and never get big . . . . . he'd lose his spirit. Peter, she goes on to let me know, wouldn't let Snuggles and her shave him. . . .

Tania has my cock in a death grip . . . . she'll never let it go now until the life has been choked out of it. But she's like a kid with a new toy about her cuntlet . . . . she has to use one hand to investigate it even while she's playing with me. She likes it so much, she tells me, that she can't keep from playing with herself all the time. But Billie, she says, tells her that a little bare figlet like that isn't the playing kind. It's not the fucking kind, either . . . . it's the kind you eat. . . . . .

She likes Billie, oh yes, she thinks that Billie's great. Billie's almost like a man sometimes, when she gets rough in that playful way she has. Billie tells you to do something, and if you don't jump Billie makes you do it. Billie is very strong, especially in the legs . . . . once she gets her thighs around you there's no escaping . . . and she has lots of nice whiskers to rub in your face. Oh, Billie sees to it that you keep in line when you play tickle tail with her!

Of course she likes Jean too, but in really a different way. With Jean you know all the time that it's just playing, whereas with Billie . . . that's all Billie wants, and she's dead serious about it. But then, Jean has such a soft, teasing way of boring her tongue into you. . . . She really thinks, Tania says, that every girl should live with a Lesbian for a while, even if she intends to marry and settle down and be a very nice girl afterward. Ernest was right . . . the Lesbians will yet inherit the earth.

Tania crouches with her hands covering her figlet, watching me undress. Do I want her to suck my prick, she asks? I don't answer. Oh, then I must want to put my prick in . . . . here! And she throws her legs open, both arms over her head. I'm on her before she can get her legs together again, my dong in one hand and my pants still held in the other. . . . .

John Thursday has a little trouble. When Tania had hair all he had to do was find the place where there wasn't any and run in . . . . now there isn't any place, and he's lost. I pull her legs farther apart and take a look to refresh my geography. Jesus, no wonder Nature put hair on cunts . . . one look at a thing like that would scare the piss out of you if you hadn't been in them before, if you didn't know that it was perfectly safe, no more dangerous than crossing a busy street. It takes a brave man to trust his cock to a thing that looks like that. The damned thing looks ravenous . . . . snap-snap . . . . and you're gobbled up.

Another thing . . . . when there isn't a bush to keep it in the shade, fucking looks positively deadly. My dong hasn't a chance in the world of going into that tiny hole without splitting the works wide open . . . a five year old child could see that . . . . but neither Tania nor I is five years old, we're willing to give it a try . . . . I give Tania a pinch on the ass and shove John T's nose against her tail when she jumps. He gets his head in and the rest of him crawls in like a snail going into its shell. I don't suppose that he really knows where he's going, but he seems to be in a hell of a hurry to get there. . . . .

Fucking Tania now is almost like fucking a grammar school girl, except that a grammar school girl wouldn't look quite so naked. My belly rubs her, and there isn't anything to rub but her bare skin. Between her legs there's nothing but slipperiness and a smell and a heat like a blast furnace. She's more naked than a plucked chicken, because a chicken would at least have pimples. But she's taking my dong the way she always has . . . . like a grown woman, only more so, right up to the end.

Try to sound bottom on a bitch who really has a yen for fucking! There isn't any bottom, you could pay out prick to them like cable, and they'd always have room to tuck in an extra inch or so . . . . . telescopic dicks, pricks that expanded and pricks that blew up like balloons . . . . she just smiles sweetly at you and looks as though she were disappointed but too polite to mention it. . . . .

She puts her legs around me, gets a solid hold . . . and zingo—she's slapped herself against me as smoothly as wallpaper. My cock is in her as deep as my arm, and it finally does succeed in squeezing a squeal out of her. Then she starts to wiggle, pulls my head down, and shoves her tongue into my mouth.

I know that it's only imagination, but that doesn't make it seem any less real when I taste cunt on her tongue. As long as it's only cunt I don't mind, so I let her go on running her tongue against the roof of my mouth while I screw her. It's a sweet, fruity flavor, not at all the fishy thing it smells like . . . someday it will be found that this juice which women are so free with contains all the vitamins necessary to prevent falling hair . . . if only because some excuse will have to be found to salve the conscience of the Americans who indulge.

I can't fuck Tania with my prick alone . . . that bareness is too astonishing, I have to feel it, play with it, get my fingers into it. I put both arms around her, under her ass and between her thighs, playing with that spread open figlet while I ram my dong up it. I tickle her asshole, poke, squeeze, pinch . . . . finally without taking my cock out, I have my fingers in her conillon too. Tania thinks that's grand . . . not a peep, not a word . . . . she wiggles all over the couch; she's like a live basket of snakes. . . . We roll over and over, and she never once lets those warm, bare legs loosen. I've got my cock in her, and she's taking no chances of having it taken away from there. We're the great gymnastic success.

Tania doesn't want me to forget those growing bubs she sports . . . . she hasn't had them for very long, and she's proud as a pigeon about them. I've got to play with them; I must bite them, give the nipples a chew now and then or she'd feel that I didn't appreciate her. That's the one thing that Tania will sometimes stop fucking for . . . . to have those teats of hers played with. Not for long, of course . . . ten minutes and she's had all she wants. She'll be back again to get your prick in her tail and take you for a ride. I suspect that she still believes that they'll only get big if they're played with, and I'm almost certain that she uses some kind of a supposed developer on them. . . Hell, I was older than she is when I tried that stuff on my prick . . . . I thought at first that it worked, too, but later I decided that it was simply the massage . . . jerking off, to be frank . . . that accompanied the treatment. . . .

When Tania stretches her arms above her head and arches her back her teats almost disappear. She wants me to take my dick out of her . . . but only for a minute . . . while she does it.

"Look at me . . . I'm just like I was when I was a little girl. Aren't you sorry that you didn't know me when I was a little girl? I'd have let you fuck me just the same . . . yes I would! I was a pretty little girl, with long curls . . . and I used to look every day to see if I had any hair down there . . . . and now I have it I've shaved it off, isn't that silly?" She rolls over and looks down her shoulder at her ass. "But I didn't have such a big rear when I was little. It didn't have any dimples on it. . . "

We examine the dimples on her ass . . . but I'm more interested in that dimple between the cheeks. I kneel behind Tania and she spreads her legs when she feels my dick back there. . . . .

"Put it in! Put your cock in my funny bare hole and

screw me. . ." She hides her head in her arms, and her voice is muffled; "It's all bare and tiny . . . you can pretend that I'm still a little girl when you fuck me. . ."

Tania can play her games with herself. . . But I don't have to pretend . . . she isn't much more than a little girl, any angle you look from, and from the rear, with only the pink split of her bonne-bouche showing, she's younger than ever. It seems disgraceful to fuck anything as young as that, but with her asshole winking up at him, Jean Jeudi is unmanageable.

From the way it stretches her rectum you'd think that Tania would be satisfied just to have Johnny's head in there . . . . but she wants it all, the whole works, and she wants it bad. . . All the way in, she keeps howling . . . . so in it goes, I'm not one to be stingy with what I've got. Then she wants me to play with her cuntlet . . . and if I won't, she'll play with it herself. She's going to give me lessons sometime, Tania says, on how to play with a cunt.

"I know all about playing with cunts," she tells me. "Big ones, little ones, hairy ones, fat ones . . . . if you ever find any that you don't know how to handle, you bring them to me . . I'll show you."

Then . . . no more talk, she's howling with a prickful of jism in her rectum, and she's coming. She hops like a cricket, with me after her with each jump, still screwing her . . . I'm determined not to take my cock out of her ass, but she finally falls off the couch and gets away. . . .

"If you did that to Snuggles she'd be so frightened that she'd hide from you as long as her folks kept her in Paris," Tania says. "You must promise not to fuck her that way if I get her for you."

I still have a hard on, and Tania plays with my dong to try to keep it that way. She lies on her back and diddles me, and I can see the jism and juice squeezing out of her bald figlet. Clam broth. . . . .

Tania wants to know all about Snuggles' mother and me. I have fucked her, haven't I? No answer to that. Well, do I fuck her the way I have just fucked Tania? Does she suck me off? Have we played tete-beche? Does she have as nice a shape as Tania's mother? But I'm not talking. . . Tania can make enough of a mess without any information. Very well, she says . . . . but I needn't think that it's a secret. Snuggles is keeping her eyes open; she'll know things soon enough.

"Does she know that you've been fucking around with her father?" I ask.

Tania's astonished to find that I know about that. How did I find out? Through Ann? Tania grabs my dong as though she might tear it off . . .

"Did he tell his wife about it?" she demands. "Does she know what we did?"

I'm not talking about that, either, and Tania is annoyed. How is she to know how to act if she doesn't know these things?

"He gave me a check, just as though I were a whore," Tania says. "But I didn't cash it yet because I didn't want to buy anything."

Then she wants me to have the check. She'll pass it right over, so that I can buy something I want. If she's to be paid off like one of those girls from the hotels she might as well act like them and hand her money over to some man, she sighs. And wouldn't I have a time trying to explain that to Sam . . . . my signature on that check! I suppose that what I ought to do is try to get it away from her and give it back to Sam . . . but the money doesn't mean anything to him, and he has eased his conscience a little, so to hell with it. I tell Tania to shove it up her ass and paste it there, the first money she ever earned. She will, she says, if I'll wrap it around my cock and do the shoving.

Still I want to know if Snuggles understands about Tania and her father. Tania takes a long time in getting to the point, which is that she hasn't said anything about it yet. She's saving it, she smiles, saving it to find out just how Snuggles feels about her father. If he wants to screw Tania, he must have a certain feeling abut Snuggles too, don't I think so? Who knows . . . perhaps they're pining away for each other. . . .

That bitch! I can see that she's already engineering another mix-up there. I feel sorry for the Backers . . . if this filthy cuntlet gets on their tail there's no telling what may happen. They'll take more than Backer's art collection back to America with them. . .

Tania's tickling her tail with my dong. She'd have it in herself in a minute, but I pull her to the edge of the couch. She lies there on the edge, with her ass balanced and her thin legs out straight and apart. Her feet are on the floor and her fig as wide as a barn door. She doesn't move . . . she stays that way and lets me put my prick in and screw her. . . . . .

"Snuggles is going to be jealous when I tell her," she says . . . .

"Why in Jesus' name do you have to tell her?"

Tania doesn't say . . . . perhaps she doesn't know the answer herself. She wiggles closer to the edge of the couch in order to get my cock all the way in, and she plays with her teats, shaking them under my nose. . . . . .

"I'm going to see later . . . I think I'll take her to my room and make her lick me. Yes, that's what I'll do. . . . . I'll make her suck my con, and I'll rub all that jism in her face and on her nose, and I won't tell her what it is until later, after she's sucked me. Then I'll tell her that you were screwing me and that she's been eating your jism. Oh, big Jean Jeudi . . . get in, get far in . . . and make lots of jism in me, because I'm going to make a pretty little girl eat it all up later. . . ."

At Backer's hotel . . . . the bell-boy doing his best with his kitchen English!

"We not 'ave the *Humanity*, sir. We have the *Intransigeant* and *Paris-Soir*."

"No," says Backer, "I want the *Humanity*, it has a good name. Humanity, it means, doesn't it?"

"Yes, sir."

"I like its name; I want that paper. Order it for me tomorrow."

Off goes the boy, hugging his tip, and in a minute the porter is saluting us. The porter is very dignified, very certain that he can handle the situation.

"Excuse me, sir. The boy tells me that you want the *Humanité*. You will not like that paper, sir. Will I order the *Matin?*"

"No, I want the *Humanité*. I like the name. The French are admirable people, a great revolutionary people. . . . I came here because I admire their free spirit. I want to get your paper about humanity."

The porter looks cautiously, heavily, about. It's impossible to tell what he imagines Backer to be, but I know he doesn't approve of me or Carl.

"Je vous demande pardon, monsieur, but it is not about humanity . . . . it is about politique. It is for working people."

"Well, I work, you work . . . get it. Get it in the morning."

"Monsieur!" the porter cries desperately, "you don't understand! It is the journal of the reds!"

This could go on for hours, but Carl catches sight of Severin, the bozo we are here to meet. He represents, so Carl has told me, various large and unnamed interests. Through Carl he's been trying to jockey some scheme with Backer, and Carl is beside himself. All his life Carl has been waiting to be in on one of these deals, the scandalous money-making schemes of which you hear whispers and speculation in the Bourse cafés.

Severin is really the man that Carl would like to be. Handmade shoes, a beautiful dental plate, a pocket full of Corona-Coronas and a gold lighter to touch them off with, the ruddy complexion of a man who eats and drinks well and reestablishes the balance with months spent bob-sleighing at St. Moritz. He and Sam spent twenty minutes in feeling each other out, sizing each other up . . . . they're like two people tactfully trying to decide if they should spend a weekend someplace or simply run to a hotel for a quick fuck. . . . . .

Perhaps they're showing off a bit for Carl. At any rate, he's left completely in the cold while they're establishing a common plane to work on. Severin, since he heard the last part of Backer's little joke with the porter, begins to talk about recent riots. They called out the Republican Guard and two Negro regiments, he tells Backer.

"The old Roman way . . . . suppress the Romans with provincials, the barbarians with Romans. Oh, the French are wise in their way as the British in their particular brand of politics. Usually an attempted coup d'état is sufficient to rout the questions in the French mind. Lagny and Stavisky almost brought the state down . . . . the coup of the sixth of February was nicely managed to make people forget about both. But now . . . . the people are beginning to feel that Stavisky wasn't the only speculator in France, merely the most exhibitionistic. And the French, like all Latins, are mad gamblers . . . . . one-tenth lottery tickets when they're poor, Bayonne bonds when they're rich."

Backer and Severin agree on the venality of the French press soon after that beginning, and Severin's plan begins to shape.

"The point is," says Severin, "everyone nowadays wants to get something for nothing . . . . that's why there'll never be communism anyhow. But the French are the only peo-ple who study how to lose money on the Stock Exchange. Every newspaper here runs its financial page, and there are dozens and dozens of little daily and weekly sheets giving Bourse tips and notations. But take the English . . . they're mad about horse-racing. . . ."

"Even the workshops have their weekly sweepstakes,"

Carl interrupts eagerly. It's pitiful to see him trying to edge his way into this thing, and I don't see why he doesn't either leave or shut up.

"You see chalked up in a few places," Severin continues, " 'Shining Light to win the 2:30,' but what do you have for information sheets? The tipsters' envelopes, very dear, and a couple of bi-weekly or weekly sheets. In France the local financial news comes out every day."

"You do the Teutonic countries an injustice," Backer puts in. "You forget that they can't read or write . . . if they could, they'd undoubtedly read the newspapers. I tell you they're smart. When you hear a bus conductor figuring out how he'll win fifty pounds through five races with an initial outlay of a tenner, you realize that was the race of Newton. I hold that the people are the unexplored mines of intelligence of the country."

"I don't think so. If they were smart you couldn't get money out of them, and we wouldn't be sitting here. If they weren't dumbbells could any business man make a living? But as I was saying, the French Bourse gamblers will read any tip, good or bad, and any sheet, no matter how suspect and despite any rumors concerning it, because of a third fact . . . . the incredible venality of the parliamentarians and the judiciary . . . . they always assume that these little sheets can get information from high sources through sheer blackmail. And even if they are pool papers, the little speculator thinks he might as well be in the pool. He reasons that the minister giving information may or may not be telling the truth . . . in either case the rumor will lead to a change in the market, and he may as well get in at the beginning and out again before the ripple dies out . . . . the same with a ramp. It may be a canard, they think, but someone owns it and someone will pluck it . . . I'm smart enough to get some too. It's a republican sentiment, you see. . ."

Carl nods wisely. You'd think that he was an old market

juggler . . . if you mentioned American Can to him he'd look around for the girl from the States . . . .

"The fourth point of my plan," goes on Severin, "is based on the fact that the French press hates to pay for cables. They'll print bad news, a week old . . . . they'll crib, steal, invent, anything to get out of paying cable service."

"And Havas?" Sam asks.

"I'd pay Havas part of the boodle, that goes without saying. The point is I'd have New York backing from Wall Street pool workers."

"Well, you'd need just one paper. You could buy some cheesy, bankrupt sheet, spread the rumor through the red light and Bourse cafes that the backer was Wall Street, and make a rip-roaring success overnight. You've only to start the fashion . . . the other papers will pick up your information and advertise it for you."

"No. To sell the shares en masse we've got to have all the financial papers behind us. This thing has to be good, good enough to catch all the suckers, to draw all the good coins out of the famous country wool stockings, out of old maids' cotton bosoms, out of funds held in trust by family lawyers. I don't want only the smart alecs who take a flyer, the beachcombers who wait for a turn in the tide, the wise guy who cut a loss and cut a profit . . . . I want investment money. . . ."

In other words Severin's idea is to pose as a private cable service while buying the cable service from one of the companies. Another of his ideas is that his gang will call themselves a Committee of Economic Survey or some shit like that, pack the advisory board with big names.

Carl is frowning at his cigar to keep from grinning. His face lights up at the mere thought of money, and this thing has him almost hysterical. Perhaps he expects Backer to rush immediately to the bank while Severin goes off to rent the offices, because he's disappointed when the conference breaks up with nothing definite having been done.

Sam and Severin are to meet again, Severin shares a taxi

with us as far as the Capucines. We drop Carl off a few blocks farther on. Then Sam and I are on our way to Alexandra's. . . . . . . Snuggles is supposed to be there and it makes a good opportunity for Sam to meet Alexandra. He's still worried about Tania.

"Do you think that there's any chance that she might have become frightened and said something to her mother?" he asks again. "I don't want to walk into any trouble, you know. You've known her mother a long time, haven't you? Is she all right?"

I spend the rest of the ride in reassuring him, but he's nervous when we stop at Alexandra's. If there's any trouble, he says, he's going to leave everything to me. . . . . . .

Snuggles isn't there, and neither is Tania. They've already gone back to Backer's hotel, and they're probably out for the evening by now. Alexandra asks us to come in. . . . .

Sam beams at first sight of Alexandra. He hadn't expected her to be such a good-looking cunt. He pouts up and begins to show off his feathers like a pigeon, and his efforts aren't exactly wasted. Alexandra warms up to him right away.

"Say, she's wonderful," Sam exclaims as soon as we're alone. "You never told me she was like this. She likes me, don't you think? And she knows what it is about her that I like . . . watch how she shows it off! Tell me, what kind of a woman is she really? Is there a chance of going to bed with her?"

It's no use for me to stay around in an atmosphere like that, but I want to be sure of how things stand before I leave Backer alone with her. After a lot of jockeying around I manage to get a few minutes alone with Alexandra. We stand in the hallway and she lets me feel her up . . . . even lets me take John Thursday out and rub his nose between her legs. But she doesn't want me to put my cock all the way into her cunt.

"I wouldn't want you to take it out again for a long time," she says, pushing me away and putting my prick farther down on her thighs, where the juice is wetting her. "And I can't be rude to my other company . . . . we'd better go back now."

"He wouldn't mind if you were rude to him for a while if you were rude to me too, later," I tell her. "He wants to screw you."

Oh what have I been up to now? Yes, what have I been telling the charming Mr. Backer about her? Does he know that I lived with her? And do I perhaps think now that I'm free to bring my friends and offer her to them . . . . as though she were my wife, perhaps? So I have to explain that Backer knows nothing at all about her except that she is Tania's mother, and that all he knows about her is what he can see . . . . which is plenty to make a man want to fuck her.

Alexandra stands there and we play with each other while she thinks this over. . . Does Mr. Backer have a wife as well as his pretty daughter? Oh yes, she's heard the girl mention her mother. Then, is his wife pretty, are men attracted to her? And lastly . . . how well do I know his wife?

I answer all but the last question . . . Alexandra pretends not to notice the omission . . . She's very . . . . filled with yearnings, she tells me. Yes, she'd like a fucking tonight, and if I had come alone we should have had a wonderful evening. But since I have my friend with me it will have to be abandoned, for she does certainly not intend that the two of us should screw her. And something else she will tell me . . . if my friend had come alone . . . perhaps she would have allowed him to stay. Either one of us, do I see? Yes, that's how badly she wants to go to bed with a man, to get a cock into her con. . . . But not two . . . no, never. . . . Since her experience with Canon Charenton she has seen that one must be discreet. . . . .

Back I go to talk to Sam. It's all right, I tell him. I've been sounding her out, and I think she'll let him fuck her. . . She likes him, I tell him, and I make up a lot of

pretty things that she didn't say. So now it's up to him . . . .
all he has to do is remember that she really wants him to
screw her and not be afraid to go after it. As for myself, I
have a date, and I will leave now. I don't tell him that my
date is with his wife. . . . .

Ann thinks that my apartment is very quaint and very
cozy. Everything about it is so private, she says . . . she
doesn't know about the parades that troop in and out of
here at the most inappropriate times. Such a place would
be just the thing for a woman who wished to conduct an
affair, wouldn't it? And are there many such in the neighborhood? Of course she was merely wondering. . . . .

Ann wants to know Paris better, and she has a list of
questions as long as your arm. Where is this? Where does
one find that? Which is the best neighborhood for thus and
so? And for this first half hour that she's in my place she sits
and scribbles into a notebook all the answers. She still has a
lot of Paris to see before she goes home, she exclaims, and
she wants to know the city from all angles. Now, where
does one buy those awful postcards?

I tell her where she can buy dirty pictures. . . . Although how she's been here as long as she has and not met
the hawkers I don't know. Then she wants to know if they
are actually as bad as they're supposed to be . . . . or are
they just . . . risqué? She's never seen any, of course. . .
Well, would she like to see some. Oh, I have some? Now,
that's embarrassing . . . . but she supposes that it's part of
life. Yes, she ought to see them; one's education should be
well rounded. . . . . .

I show her the ones of Anna, give her the whole handful
of them and let her go through them. She blushes as soon
as she glances at the first one. Oh . . . they are rather
strong, aren't they? She looks at them all very quickly and

then looks at them all again, very slowly. . . . She becomes warm, glances at the fireplace, and loosens her sweater. She drinks many glasses of wine. . .

Getting her out of her clothes after that isn't very hard at all. A few feels and she's ready for anything . . . . or so she thinks. Once I've got my hand under her skirt it's clear sailing. She spreads her thighs when I feel them up and lets me take off her pants without as much as a raised eyebrow. And she's really gotten into the spirit of those pictures, the bitch . . . . she's so juicy between the legs that her pants are soaked, and that big cunt of hers is like a firebox.

Perhaps I would have preferred her to wear a girdle, she asks? She thought of it when she was dressing, but it seems so perverted to wear such an article of clothing only because it was sexually exciting. . . . Still, if I would like her to, she'll always wear one of them after this, even with sport clothes. . . .

I'm satisfied with her the way she is . . . . that big ass of hers is enough to give my cock a stiff neck, with or without the girdle. Leaving her stockings and shoes on make it seem bigger than ever. . .

Ann rolls back and forth on the couch while I feel her up. Oh, what would Sam think, what would he do, if he saw her now! She sticks her fist into my pants and grabs my dick. What would Sam think! This is really shameful of her . . . coming here to be fucked by me, leaving poor Sam to himself. She ought to be at home screwing her husband rather than here giving it to me. . . . . I don't disillusion her . . . but by my reasoning Sam and Alexandra ought to be very good friends by now.

Ann pulls my pants down and plays with my bush. Oh, that hair! She runs her fingers through it and tickles my balls. When has she ever seen so much hair, she exclaims! And do I know what it makes her want to do? It makes her want to lay her head down by it . . . . yes, put her very cheek upon it. . . But after telling me that, she gets coy. I finally have to grab her and hold her head down. . . . . .

It bristles, she complains . . . but it's a nice bristling, she adds soon enough. Would her hair bristle my cheeks, she wonders . . . She's sure that it's very soft . . . . I'm fairly certain that the pictures of Anna playing tete-beche with her boyfriends have stuck in Ann's mind, but she's afraid to say so or even to think of sucking my prick. I put my arms around that huge behind of hers and put my head against her thighs. She wiggles . . . she's so hot that she can't talk straight . . . . but still she's afraid to put that thing into her mouth. . . .

Hell, I could make her take it, I suppose. . . . Almost any cunt, if she's hot enough, will open her mouth when she feels the end of a cock shoved against her lips . . . . but I want her to take it herself . . . or think that she's taking it herself. I begin to lick her belly and thighs . . . . she spreads her legs and kisses my belly shyly. I'm moving my hips as though I were slowly fucking . . . and Ann is doing the same thing.

These cunts! How they love to get something for nothing! Ann would like nothing better right now than to have me stick my tongue into that axe-split and try to lick it dry, but she doesn't want to get any more familiar with my prick than she already is. . . . But I can be as stubborn as she is. . . . I lick around the edges of her cunt, bite her thighs, tickle her mop with my nose. When I come very close to her fig she whispers excitedly . . . there . . . . kiss it there . . . . why don't I put my tongue out now. . . Oh, we must look just like those awful people in the pictures, mustn't we? Yes, we're doing almost what they were doing. . . . .

Finally I let her get a taste of what she wants to feel. I kiss her squarely on the cunt, slide my tongue over the lips and in . . . . her thighs swing wide, like a double gate that will never close again, and she gasps when I suck the juicy, hot fruit. . . . Oh, what a feeling! I mustn't stop again! My tongue can go in deeper . . . I can suck harder . . . . she'll spread her legs further . . . . She's trying to wring John Thursday's neck,' but she still isn't sucking him. . . . .

She can't believe that I've stopped again. How . . . oh, how could I stop when it makes her feel so good? Here . . . . she'll lie another way to make it easier for me. . . And this is how she'll play with my prick while I do it . . . . Isn't that all right? Why don't I begin again? Oh, why don't I put my mouth on her cunt and suck it some more!

She pulls her head away when I rub my dong on her mouth. The second time she lets me do it . . . then she kisses it. What is it that I want her to do, she whispers? As though she didn't know, as though she hadn't the least notion of what it was that I expect! Do I want her to kiss my balls as well as my belly? Is that it? She'll do that if I want her to. And so on.

You can stand just so much of that shit. Imagine a woman with a daughter as big as Snuggles, a cunt who's been married as long as Ann has, pretending that she doesn't know that you want your cock sucked! I decide to give her one more chance . . . . . then, if she doesn't open her mouth when she opens that cunt of hers, I'm going to put my foot in one or the other and my prick in what's left. I begin to lick her fig, and I roll on top of her, jabbing my dong in her face. Suddenly I feel her tongue on it . . . she opens her mouth and takes Johnny's head in. . . . Then she has both of her arms around my waist and she's sucking as hard as she can . . . I'll give her all she can handle. . . . .

Ann isn't as well equipped to take a cock in that end as she is to take it in the other . . . . she chokes, but she hangs on to it grimly. Her cunt is open so wide that whatever is inside ought to be falling out, but nothing happens . . . she must be well stitched together in there. She may not have a cast iron belly like Tania or Anna, but she's solidly anchored. That's another way in which the American amateurs have it all over Parisian professional whores . . . . you can turn them upside down without worrying about having their wombs drop out on the floor. . . . .

Ann wants me to tickle her rectum while I suck her fig. She hasn't noticed, apparently, that I already have two fingers shoved up her ass . . . I stick another one in and she's happy. I act as though I were trying to eat her cunt, she giggles. . . . She doesn't know that it's because I'm afraid that that big mouth will eat me. . . . . .

I could have come almost as soon as Ann took John T. into her mouth . . . . I've been keeping it back because I want her to be all ready to come when she finds her mouth full of jism. I wait until I'm sure that she's on the very edge, until she's trying to smother me with her thighs and drown me with her juice . . . . She's got an ant up her ass and a fire in her belly, and if Sam himself were to walk in now she wouldn't be able to stop. Then, when she's like that, I let John Thursday have his way about things.

Everything stops for the briefest moment. Ann looks panicky . . . . she can't believe that she's really sucked me off, and it's a terrific shock to her. Still the jism keeps coming into her mouth, and she doesn't know what to do about it. I yell at her to swallow it . . . . threaten to stop sucking her cunt if she doesn't. I run my tongue along the inside of those bushy tips, and Ann suddenly makes up her mind. Down goes the full dose, all at once, and she's still sucking my prick. I put my mouth on her bonne-bouche again, and she's coming too . . . . she's losing juice by the quart. . . . .

As soon as she can talk Ann says that she isn't going to come to my apartment again. No, this time she has gone too far . . . . much too far. Do I realize that she has a husband who believes in her, a little girl who simply adores her? She has to think of them. Oh, a wife and mother can't act like this! The time for such adventures is past . . . a woman of her age, and in her circumstances, is mad to embark upon such seas, etc. etc. . . .

She wants to leave at once, but I won't allow it. I persuade her to stay for another glass of wine, then a second. She picks up the pictures again. The ones of Anna sucking various pricks and having her cunt licked seem to attract her more than before. Such depravity as there is in France . . . . it must be something in the atmosphere. Certainly she has never done anything such as that which we have done tonight . . . do I understand?

I understand perfectly I assure her . . . . and now if she will come into the bedroom . . . or does she prefer the couch? She thinks the couch is very nice, but she really shouldn't. . . . . Poor Sam. . . . Poor Sam . . . . it isn't right for her to deceive him so . . . . . . and she rolls onto her back and spreads her legs. . . . . . .

Carl thinks that I ought to do something to influence Backer in this Severin deal. There's money in it, he assures me, money for everyone who's connected with it, and he and I could each pick up a nice bit of change just by kissing a few asses. Carl has kissed asses for so long now that he doesn't really know that he does it . . . . . . he thinks he's a magician pulling rabbits from a hat. Carl has a hard time making a living the easy way. . . . . . .

He's a royalist, is Carl, and he believes in patronage. How the hell else, he wants to know, is someone like him going to make a living? That's a hangover from the year he spent at the Beaux-Arts. They kicked him out, but they forgot to let the hot air out . . . . they turned him loose talking cinquecento, Renaissance, Great Pandora and Little Pandora, the Genius of France . . . . . all of which comes straight from the crummy crowd hanging around the Deux-Maggots, where they read *Action Française*, the deadest sheet on earth. . . . .

Anyway Carl thinks that I have the advantage of influence——or at least proximity, to Sam. . . . . . .

"What the fuck do you talk about all the time when you're running around to these joints?" he demands. "Don't you have any ideas at all? Why this is your golden opportunity . . . . there are a thousand . . . a million ways to make money. Do you mean that you never talk about money? Why Jesus, you could even make a nice piece of graft of those dumps you take him around to . . . he wouldn't mind if he was overcharged a little . . . hell, he wouldn't even notice it. . . ."

We are interrupted by Raoul, who says that he has been looking for me for days, and who has a funny story to tell us. It happened to a friend of his, he is careful to explain . . . . a friend whose name he will not mention since he would not know it anyway. . . . But Raoul looks so relieved when he has finished the story that I'm sure the friend is himself. . . . .

"She was just a little girl . . . . you know, a very little girl, and my friend had a very good time in teaching her all the things that a little girl of that age certainly should not know. Then she goes away . . . perhaps my friend pays her something to go to the movies . . . . . and it is all over. It's to be forgotten, or perhaps just to be remembered sometimes when he doesn't have a woman and has to play with himself. . . But in three weeks the girl is back. My friend has to do something . . . well, what is wrong? Why, she is pregnant . . . she is going to give him a baby unless something is done. Pregnant? Impossible! Oh, horrible. And my friend is very disturbed. . . Finally he thinks to ask . . . how does she know she is pregnant? Has she been to a doctor . . . has she been talking to her mother about it? No . . . . no . . . but she is bleeding. Bleeding? Where? Ah, well, where do women bleed? He puts her on the bed and pulls up her dress . . . it is only a monthly that the little girl is having. So my friend gives her a towel to tie around herself and gives her some money to go to the movies again. No more little girls for him! What the fuck do you think of that?

Since neither Carl nor I finds it so funny as Raoul believes it to be, he turns the subject to his sister-in-law. She is out of Paris, now, he says . . . . too bad, but she will be back again, I'll get my chance to take her to bed. In the meantime, he would like to meet some nice Spanish girl, someone he could practice the language on. But one who wouldn't want money, he is quick to add. Do I know any nice Spanish girl who doesn't have the clap or bad tempered brothers? One who earns her own living would be nice, and a whore would be especially nice, he says . . . I tell him that I don't know any Spanish girls any more, but that Ernest might have one or two that he doesn't want any longer . . . I'll find out. Raoul is very grateful . . . he buys Carl and me a drink and gives us cigarettes. Any girl will do, he insists any one will do at all, just so long as she doesn't have a disease and has most of her front teeth. . . . . . .

Later on, when I've given Carl the shake and Raoul has gone off to the funeral of one of his many relatives, I meet Sam. He's feeling very gay, he's full of talk about Alexandra.

What a woman! Oh, what a woman, the mother of the little girl! Do I know, he stayed at her house all night, didn't get home until nine in the morning! Of course he had to tell Ann something . . . . so he told her that he was out with me. If she asks me anything about it I can tell her some story of getting into a card game. . . .

I can't tell him that it was a mistake to tell Ann that, any more than she can tell him that she knows he's shitting her. And besides, he's so excited about Alexandra that he probably wouldn't hear anything I said.

"She knows how to fuck!" he tells me. "Lord, does she know about fucking! Alf, you hadn't been gone a half hour before we were at it! Honestly! Hell, you know how those things happen . . . . one minute you're talking and having a drink, next minute you're putting your hand under her dress. . . ."

We stop while Sam wakes up a bum who's asleep in a doorway and gives him five francs. He waves away a woman who comes up whining, head wrapped in a shawl, skinny hand extended.

"'We'd better go upstairs,' she said," Sam goes on, "so up we went to her bedroom . . . just like that! Isn't that a hell of a thing, though . . . . going there to see what she's like because of that business with her daughter and ending

up in bed with her? First the daughter, then the mother
. . . oh Lord! And let me tell you something . . . you remember what I told you about the girl? That she sucked my
prick? Well, so did her mother . . . what do you think of
that? Yes sir, the first time she ever saw me, and I didn't
have the slightest trouble in getting her to do it! By God,
Alf, I don't know whether I want to go back to the States or
not . . . when there's cunt like that in Paris. The only thing
is, now I don't know about the daughter . . . I'm not so sure
that I want Snuggles running around with her. . . ."

Sam worries about this for a few minutes, but he comes
back to Alexandra and what a wonderful cunt she is. She
read him poetry he says, in between times, and he wants
me to guess how many times he screwed her.

"Four!" he says triumphantly. "Oh, maybe that doesn't
seem to mean much to you now, but wait . . . . wait until you're my age and you'll see. Especially if you're married, if it's the same woman every night. You don't fuck a
woman four times a night when you've been married fifteen, twenty years. . . Russian love poems . . . and Chinese, too . . . . did you know that she speaks Chinese?
Well, she does . . . at least, she said it was Chinese. . . .
Why the Hell didn't I come to Paris when I was twenty?
What was wrong with me then? But maybe it's just as well
that I didn't . . . . I wouldn't have appreciated it . . . just as
you don't appreciate it yet. How old are you, about forty?
Listen, take my advice, go back to America and make a
million dollars, then come to Paris and live for the rest of
your life. . . But don't get married . . . don't get married,
whatever you do, because you can always find plenty of nice
cunts like this Alexandra to read you poetry and suck you
off if you have a million dollars. . . ."

The advice is good, but Sam doesn't think to tell me
how to make the million. He has bigger things on his mind.

"I'll never forget what she looked like when she got her
clothes off, and was lying there on the bed showing her
cunt and waiting for me to do something about it. She

wasn't backward about asking for it, either . . . only she was saying it in Russian. What a hell of a language to talk about fucking in! I'd rather hear her speak French . . . at least I can get the sense of what things are about. But when she looked at my cock, spread her legs, and looked at me through her knees, she could have used any language and it would have sounded the same. . . ."

"Suppose," Sam says later when we're in a bar, "that I might have expected her to be like that. After all if the girl is so easy, the mother must have hot pants too . . . . it's in the blood. But listen, Alf, I'm going to be seeing a lot of Alexandra from now on . . . so any time that I call you up and say something about a card game, you'll know that I'm going to be out all night and want you to cover me up with Ann. Just tell her anything if she asks you about it . . . she won't be interested enough to ask for details."

"Look, Sam, I'm not so sure about this. . . ."

"Oh, nonsense. It's all right, I tell you. All you have to do is remember that you and I go out and play poker some-times. By God, Alf, I came to Paris to have some fun . . . . you're not going to let me down, are you?"

"No, I don't want to let you down, Sam, but still I don't think. . . . ."

"Well, hell, if that's the way you feel, all right . . . I suppose I can get Carl to do it;. . . ."

"No wait a minute, Sam, don't get me wrong . . . . . . I didn't say that I wouldn't do it . . . I was just. . . ."

"Then let's have another of these and forget about it. Hey, Alf, listen to my accent, see if I say this right . . . Garçon! La même chose! How was that? Better?"

Sam is doing all right . . . he's learned to ring with his spoon . . . to call an order across the terrace so he can be heard without seeming to call hogs . . . even his accent is right, at least for ordering drinks. Now he wants to know all the forms of the verb foutre. . . . .

Ann has rented a few rooms in my neighborhood, and she gets me out of bed one morning to come and see them. I don't know why the concierge can't be trained not to let anyone in before noon, but the most astonishing assortment of people are allowed to walk up the three flights to my place at any time of the day or night. Anyway, I'm allowed to stop a few minutes for breakfast, for which I am thankful.

Ann has found herself a regular little nest, a real hideaway, tucked up under the eaves of a rickety old joint a few blocks from my place. And it's very cheap, very very cheap, she tells me again and again while she shows me around, explains how things work. They told her that Verlaine lived here once, she says, that it was here he wrote some of his finest sonnets. Do I believe that? I tell her that I suppose he did . . . . after all, the poor son of a bitch had to live someplace, and only a broke poet or a million-dollar American ass could afford the atmosphere of a hole like this.

She decided to rent it, Ann confides, the morning after she came back from my place. Where do I suppose Sam was while she was there being fucked? Where? Shit, I don't tell her . . . well, she doesn't know either, but she knows that he wasn't playing cards with me . . . not when I was screwing her all evening.

"Yes, that's what he told me . . . that you and he were out playing cards! And he simply reeked of some other woman! Well, I'll show him! Two can play that sort of a game . . . so I'm going to have this place to come to and do exactly as I choose. . . ."

She shows me how she's fixing it up . . . nothing fancy, because she won't keep it very long, but very bohemian. She wants some dirty pictures to hang on the walls . . . do I know anyone who does that sort of thing well? She wants watercolors, she thinks, perhaps an engraving or two in the seventeenth-century style. And she's going to have albums of those photographs which one can buy . . . . in short, a whole cozy part of her life will be tucked away here. . . . . .

Who's going to come here, I want to know. . . Well . . . friends . . . or perhaps no one. It's just to have a place, do I see? She might use it only to put Sam out . . . let him find out that she has it, and then try to find out what goes on here. She'll teach him to bring her such stories about card games!

Something else comes up . . . . do I know where Sam might have been that night? I? Of course not! Perhaps he really was playing cards with someone, perhaps it was only an accident that he said he'd been with me instead of somebody else. Ann merely sniffs at that. He was with a woman, she insists . . . it's not hard for another woman to tell. . . . .

I'm all for putting the place to use right then and there, but Ann avoids it. It's all right if I feel her up a little bit, if I raise her skirt and slap my hand on her bush while we're talking, but that's as far as she'll let things go. No, she tells me, it's no use to take that thing out of my pants because she isn't going to do anything about it . . . she won't even touch it . . . . well . . . she'll feel it just a bit, but nothing else. She won't take off her pants and she won't let me take mine off, so there's no use hanging around there after we've seen the place. Besides, I have things to do, so I put her into a taxi and send her back to her husband for lunch. . . .

There's nothing doing at the office, so I spend some time composing letters to the editor, which I will post on my way out with company stamps. I suppose that some of them are printed occasionally . . . I never think to look. . . .

At two I meet Ernest and Arthur at a place where, if you don't like the food and aren't drinking, you can go upstairs and lay the proprietor's wife . . . hence, a most respectable place, because none of the whores will go there . . . it's unfair to their trade, they complain . . . certainly they don't try to sell you something to eat when you take them to a hotel. But it's a quiet place to sit when you don't want to be disturbed . . . . without any whores there aren't any journalists either.

Ernest wants to know what about all the rumors he's

heard about me. Is it true that I'm taking some American around, showing him all the whorehouses so that he can go back to America and open a big chain? Is it true that some nutty art collector has lost his daughter and we're going through the sewers of Paris looking for her? Is it true that I'm working with some bunch of American financiers to start a new paper which I will edit? Well, what the fuck is true?

"You shouldn't disappear that way, Alf," he says. "I've tried to find you a couple of times . . . we've been taking Anna out and fucking her, but you never were around."

Perhaps it's just as well that I wasn't around . . . Arthur has been playing with that Kodak he bought, and he has a mess of some of the rattiest pictures I've ever seen . . . . Anna and Ernest, Sid and himself with their pants down and their pricks up . . I'm not so sure that I'd care for that kind of advertising even if it is strictly private

"I only show them when I'm trying to make some virgin," Arthur explains fondly as he puts the pictures away. "You see, the way these pictures came out, it looks as though I had a prick twice as big as anybody else. . . ."

I remember that Raoul wanted to meet a Spanish cunt, and I ask Ernest about it. Hell yes, Ernest knows plenty of Spanish cunts; what kind does Raoul want?

"Listen," he says, "I've got one that's a real Spanish Fly . . . . . . one bit of her and your cock stays stiff for a week. What does he have to trade?"

"Aw, now look, Ernest, he don't want any trades . . . . all he wants is to meet some nice cunt . . . he'll do the rest."

"No trade? Oh, hell then . . . I couldn't help him out. No, Alf, any time. I hand over a cunt I have to get something back. Doesn't he have a jackknife?"

"He has a sister-in-law."

"I don't know, Alf. Sisters-in-law are mighty undependable . . . . you have to know your people pretty well. Besides, you know these Spanish cunts yourself. Didn't I get a knife just because you threw one over too fast? You can't give these spics the go-bye, just pass them around the way you can an American girl or a Russian. They don't have the temperament, you're taking a chance with them."

"Well, Jesus, Jesus, Ernest, look at some of the things I've done for you. . . . Didn't I fix it up for you with Tania? Yes, and her brother too . . . . and how about Anna? My God, isn't it time that you did something for me? It isn't as though I were asking you for some cunt that you really wanted or liked. . . ."

"Hold on now, Alf . . . where did you get the idea that I didn't want this cunt? She's a fine cunt and she has an ass on her that broad. Why Christ, if I hand her over to this frog friend of yours, he'll never appreciate what he's getting. Shit, she'll lick his boots for him if he wants her to . . . . any old boot will do . . . she'll take it home and lick it there. . . ."

"Just so she fucks, that's all he wants. He isn't looking for anything fancy, Ernest. . . All he wants is somebody to go to bed with him and talk Spanish in her sleep."

Ernest finally says that he'll see what can be done about it. And when the Hell, he wants to know, is he going to meet my rich American friends? If he had any rich American friends he'd have introduced me long ago. . . Well, that's something I'll have to see about: maybe Sam and I will run into him in a café.

"Listen, to Hell with the husband. I want to meet the wife. You tell her that you have a friend who wants to show her Paris; the real Paris, the Paris of Villon, of Manet, of Guy de Maupassant. . . Tell her I'll show her the Regecem where Napoleon played chess . . . and Alexhine too, the champion . . . does she like chess? Does she like to eat? I'll take her to dinner . . . she pays. . . . Oh, we'll have a fine time together! Tell her I'll take her to a place in the Place de l'Odeon called the 'Sucking Pig,' only in French, then to coffee on the boulevards . . . perhaps the boul' Mich' where she can see the students. . . Listen, Alf, you must be busy taking the husband around. . . . . I'll show her a good time:

'here you can get a lovely soft Chambertin; there they make an entrecôte Bercy . . . oo, la, la!' Why not? Does she like books? I'll take her to the stalls . . . there's a motherly old soul in a black apron . . . and a shawl . . . who left off drinking a bowl of bread soup to sell me Brantome's 'Gay Ladies' at thirty francs, the crook! My first day in Paris, too . . . I want to get even with that old witch . . . I'll take her to the Capucins and she can look at the Baron de Rothschild . . . or maybe she knows the Baron. Does she like art? Look, you tell her that I have a lovely engraving in my hotel. . . . 'The Last Roll-Call of the Girondins in the Conciergerie' it's called . . . Does she like politics? We'll sit somewhere in the rue du 4 Septembre with *La Verité* under our arms and talk about Trotsky . . . . look, I can say all the right things about politics. . . 'I believe that perpetual revolution is the only cure for thermidorian degeneration' . . . . 'Without a Robespierre we will have no ninth thermidor' . . . Does she like to listen to stuff like that? When am I going to meet here?"

"What about blackmail?" Arthur wants to know. "Maybe if Ernest took her around he could find out something that she doesn't want her husband to know."

Arthur would probably try to blackmail his grandmother for going to bed with his grandfather . . . Ernest tells him that he should not talk that way . . . . someone is liable to think he's serious and turn him over to the police!

"Just fix it so that I can meet that rich cunt," Ernest says, "I'll show her how to have fun again . . . I'll make her young. . ."

Jean has been to my place and, finding me gone, left a note saying that she may be found in the bar around the corner. I go there and discover her at a table with a dark, tired-looking Lesbian who has been buying her Amer-Picons.

"They always hang around me," Jean says while we're walking back to my place. "Even if the place is full of women, you'll find all the Lesbians at my table. It's as though I wore a little ticket . . . . do you suppose they have some way of sniffing out each other's girl friends?"

No need to ask why Jean has come to see me . . . she runs up the stairs ahead of me, wiggling her cute ass at me, hurrying a bit faster when I reach up to pinch it. She's looking for a lay, and those Amer-Picons have made her anxious to get it as soon as possible. While I'm finding the right key for the door she's tickling my crotch . . . She intended to come and see me before this, she says, but Billie has kept her very busy . . . . and she's had to be nice to Billie recently because of certain complications. . . . . .

Is one of her complications named Tania, I ask? Ah. . . . . Tania, that very young, very bad, little bitch? Jean kisses me, running her tongue, which is sticky with the first glass of wine, over my lips and into my mouth. Yes, Tania has been complicating things . . . . she and that other, that very, very young girl. They're both so young . . . . and so pretty: but so bad and so complicating. . . . .

Jean is wearing a sweater which is so tight that her nipples show . . . and her skirt is so close around her hips that in front there is a bulge where her bush must be. . . Feeling her up with those clothes on is to feel her up with nothing on at all. You can really get acquainted with a cunt in an outfit like that . . . . put your hand on her belly and you feel her navel; let it drop a little and you find a slit under your fingers. . . . She sits on my lap, and I've played with everything without even reaching under her skirt. . . . .

Jean tries to explain things to me. With Billie, she says, girls like Tania and the other one, Snuggles, are a vice. Like a man, Billie likes to get a very young girl and play with her, tell her pretty lies, and seduce her; make a bad girl of her. It's a game, just like the one men play, getting them early, innocent and teaching them all manner of vice. . . . But in

Tania, Billie has found competition . . . that too-wise bitch is as imaginative, if not so clever, as herself, and she is corrupting the younger girl at an amazing rate. So Billie and Tania, competitors of a sort, play with Snuggles as girls play with a doll. They teach her all manner of dirty things because she is innocent . . . . but when they lie together, Tania and Billie, they are wise and experienced; they play like grown cats play, not like kittens, warily, and sometimes showing their claws. . . . .

Which is not exactly the same story which Tania told me, but which helps to round off the picture of what is going on among that gang of cunt suckers. Jean plays in their games too, but she is still more of an observer than anything else . . . . because she's Billie's mistress. The etiquette of vice is very complicated. . . .

Jean has grown tired of being felt up. She pulls up her skirt and wraps one naked leg around me, feeling in my pants for something to tickle herself with. When she gets my dong out she sticks it against her bush and, with both arms around my neck, sits and rocks back and forth while she faces me, sitting on my lap. She has a tiny pair of pants on, but my prick slides up under them and rubs back and forth against that hairy mouth . . . . up and down, without ever going into it. . . .

She wants her teats played with. What good has it been for her to work on them all these years, plan for their future, give them the best of care, if I'm not going to play with them? So off comes the pullover sweater, under which there is nothing at all but Jean. . . That's how we're sitting when Tania comes to the door. . . . . .

Jean knows it's Tania as soon as I do . . . she always knocks in the same way. But we haven't time even to pretend that we're not there, because Tania tries the door and finds it open. In she walks, and Jean and I are still there with our tails touching and our mouths open.

Well, well . . . . Tania waltzes around the room. . . .

Romance, romance! She didn't know that she'd find anyone here, least of all, Jean . . . She would have waited to be let in if she'd known I was entertaining.

Jean slides off my lap and pulls her skirt down. She's peeved because she feels that Tania will go back to Billie with a story, and she didn't want Billie to know that she was here today . . . . I ought to use the snap lock on my door, she says. . . It wouldn't do any good . . . . if Tania wanted to get in she could go out the hall window and over the roofs to my bathroom.

Tania hopped off my lap . . . not bashful, surely? Not embarrassed? They do know each other, after all . . . . the time for being embarrassed has gone past . . . Jean blushes as Tania becomes explicit . . . .

"But Jean, you have sucked my con . . . I've sucked yours. . . Why should we be embarrassed before each other? I've seen you do such worse things than this! Oh, you should have seen her with Snuggles one night. . . ." (This to me.) "She became so excited that we couldn't make her stop sucking! And poor Snuggles . . . . she'd come, it was real torture to her to have Jean's tongue still pushing into her abricot, still licking all the wet, pink places. . ."

"We finally had to pull her off by strength," Tania says, "and let her take turns sucking the rest of us while we tickled her until she came. . . Oh, it would have taken more than an opened door to stop her then!" She sits on the arm of my chair, reaches for my cock and pets it. "And it would take more than an opened door to stop her if I had been doing what you were doing just now. . . ."

Jean doesn't like the familiar way in which Tania takes over John T. She pushes her aside and sits on me again, puts my hand under her skirt. If Tania is going to carry tales to Billie, she says, she may as well have a good story. She pulls her skirt up and shows her thighs . . . she wants me to feel of them, and she says that she wants Tania to watch it. . . . .

"See, I asked him to feel me up . . . . you can tell Billie

that, if you want to . . . you can tell her that I did it all myself, that I came here and asked him to screw me . . . . and a lot of good it will do you!"

I try to pacify them . . . I don't want a pair of squabbling cunts on my hands. Now if everyone will just calm down and have a drink all this can be smoothed over. . . .

Jean says that it doesn't need any smoothing over . . . it's all very simple . . . Tania wants me to fuck her and she wants me to fuck her. The choice is up to me. . . . .

Tania isn't disturbed. She's so accustomed to those fierce, Dostoevskian scenes at home that she probably considers this a mere slight difference of opinion. While Jean is still talking, Tania bends forward and kisses one of her lovely, bare bubs. . . If only she had teats like that, she sighs. . . . . . She knows how to put Jean in a good humor . . . within five minutes they're both on my lap feeling each other's bubs while I feel them both up. . . . .

I'm not going to complain. If they can settle their differences I'd just as soon lay both of them. With two strange cunts it wouldn't be easy to do that unless we all happened to be drunk, but these bitches know each other and they know me, and they're making each other hot with all the feeling up and playing that's going on.

Tania wants to gamble. A flip of a coin to settle matters, she suggests . . . the winner to be licked by the loser and fucked. Jean is cautious . . . she suspects a trick, and I don't blame her. But it's the only way to settle something like that without hard feelings.

Considered coldly, that's a hell of a thing to do . . . to suck another woman's cunt merely because a coin came down one way instead of another. It's a bitch's gamble, and I feel relieved when Tania calls the spin wrong . . . even though I know that Jean's bread and butter comes directly through her ability to suck a cunt well. Somehow Jean doesn't seem to be the right girl to lose that gamble.

Jean's out of her clothes quickly enough . . . . and Tania too, for that matter. They stand in the middle of the room and undress. Then, hand in hand, they tip-toe over to the couch. Hand in hand! That's what gets me. . . You'd think they were two girls on their way to school . . . . they ought to have bonnets on their heads and baskets under their arms.

They make a swell show, those two. Jean has the shape; Tania looks like a miniature beside her. Two pink asses receeding across the room, two little bushes showing where there's something else which can't quite be seen . . . it's a beautiful sight, especially when you know that both of those bitches belong to you, more or less, and I hope that I never forget what they looked like.

Jean lies on the couch. Tania sits near her knees, squeezing her legs. They both look over at me as though I were supposed to drop a handkerchief, give the signal for the entertainment to begin. I sit there with a bottle of wine at my elbow, my feet propped on a stool, and my dong hanging out of my pants. I feel like Claudius. . . . .

Tania dips her fingers into her glass and sprinkles a few drops of wine over Jean's belly, over her thighs, and into her rosebush. The wine isn't sweet enough to her taste, she explains prettily . . . then she bends over and picks up the drops with her tongue.

Jean is hot already, but in half a dozen minutes she's burning up. She's used to this stuff, it's the way she gets her pants warmed every night, and she likes it. And Tania is no amateur . . . . she lies and presses her little mop—that mop which is already growing back—against Jean's knee while she sucks her nipples and tickles her sides. Her fingers run up and down Jean's thighs . . . . then she has one fist shoved between Jean's legs and is massaging her fig. . . She tickles Jean's bonne-bouche until her legs are spread, and the ends of her fingers become juicy.

John Thursday is standing out of my fly like a lopsided pole. He's bloated with importance, apoplectic with frustration. I take off my clothes to give him more air, to let the breeze run through his whiskers and cool him off a bit.

Jean has been lying on her back while Tania played with her. But Tania is kissing her thighs now, and Jean sits up to see it better. Tania teases . . . . she puts her mouth almost on Jean's juicy abricot-fendu, but never quite touches it. Jean becomes impatient . . . suddenly she grabs Tania's head and shoves it between her thighs. . . . . .

"Suck it, you little fiend!"

She's made no mistake. Tania is a fiend. Tania's arms go around her ass and her tongue disappears in Jean's traplet. With your eyes closed it would sound as though some-one were sucking an orange, someone who hadn't had an orange for a long time. She sucks, she licks, she bites . . . and everything she does makes both of them hotter. I'm afraid that Jean will come before I have a chance at her. . . . Hell, at this rate they'll both come in a few minutes. . . . .

But Tania knows when to stop. She hops up and shakes her hair out of her eyes, leaving Jean gasping and moving her legs back and forth. She bounces over to me and kicks my feet from the stool so she can kneel on it. The juice is really dripping onto her chin. . . Then she's kissing my prick, licking my balls . . . . she slips off the stool and licks my toes . . . she grabs my cock and puts it in her mouth, sticking her cunt-stinking fingers under my nose.

"Fuck her! Fuck her!" she howls . . . and before I know what's happening she's jumped up and licked across my mouth, leaving the smell and taste of Jean's cunt on my lips. . . "Fuck her before she has to play with herself!"

Jean's legs are wide open when I jump on her . . . and so is her cunt. Johnny rams his head into her without even looking, and he doesn't stop until he's all the way in. She has her knees up and her ass turned almost to the ceiling . . . when she fucks she wiggles all over; there isn't a part of her that is still. . . . . I'm not sorry now that Tania came bursting in on us . . . . not when she's gotten Jean into such a state as this. . . .

Tania's delighted. Her eyes are big and shining, and she has parked her ass in the warm spot I left on the chair; she's diddling herself while she sits and watches us screw. If only her friend Snuggles could be here to see this, she exclaims! How much that little innocent one would like it! Poor Snuggles . . . she has yet to know another cock besides Peter's . . . . She's never seen a grown man screwing a girl. . . .

Tania has been carrying tales again . . . Jean wants to know if the things Tania has told her are true. Do I fuck Tania's mother, as she says?

"Certainly he fucks my mother," Tania says indignantly. "And Snuggles' mother, too! Yes he does! Snuggles won't believe me, but she'll find out. . . ."

And her brother, that effeminate . . . is it true that when the mother takes a man to bed she takes the boy in with them and makes him suck her lover's prick? Oh, what a world! What a wicked family! Then I've had the boy suck my prick, the enormous prick which is in her now. . . What a revelation!

"I'll show you what Peter sometimes does," Tania says . . . . and she's out of her chair, and on the couch with us. "And I do it sometimes when he's fucking my mother. . . ."

She's upon us, between us, under us . . . she crawls about and wiggles through my arms like an eel. . . There's no holding her still, no pushing her aside. She licks Jean's teats, she licks my ass and bites Jean's . . . . finally, as we lay on our sides, she's behind Jean with her arms around her waist.

Jean's thighs are kept apart, because I won't stop screwing her for long enough to throw Tania on her ass. She buzzes around us like a gadfly, but I'm too hot to swat her. Tania licks between Jean's thighs . . . she licks my thighs and balls. There's nothing she won't do, the filthy bitch . . . She kisses Jean's rectum . . . . I can hear her lips smacking and I can hear her sigh. Her nose is in my crotch, my dong rubs it . . . she's begging us to be still for just a moment . . . . one small moment.

230   ·

"Let her do it," Jean pleads. "Do what she asks . . . I want to know what she'll do. . . ."

The couch stops bouncing. I have my dick half out of Jean's cunt, and Tania is kissing it. Her lips flatten on it, and she begins sucking it . . . . then her mouth slides down and clutches Jean's fig too. . . . She's sucking both of us at once, and even though I begin to screw Jean again she won't stop. At last I can scarcely tell which lips I'm fucking and which are sucking my cock . . . . when I take my prick out and then shove it back into Jean's crotch it's as often in Tania's mouth as in Jean's cunt.

Jean moans that she's coming . . . . I fuck her until my belly aches . . . . and John T. goes off. Tania's sucking him like a pig, and I take my cock out of Jean long enough to give her a mouthful to smack her lips over. . . . Then, back in Jean's cunt. It's all the same to Johnny now . . . he's too drunk to know where he is. I give him back to Tania . . . then to Jean again. . . Finally I let Tania suck the last jism out. . . . .

Things are already so badly fucked up that they couldn't be worse. But I have to make my contribution to the general disorder. . . . . Ann wants pictures for her little nookery, so I advise Billie to call her. It doesn't matter to Billie that this is the mother of a girl she's been playing with . . . she has her pictures to sell and a customer is a customer. Next time I see Ann she's somewhat shocked.

"That artist you sent to see me . . . . she's a Lesbian! And such a shocking Lesbian! We had lunch . . . . you should have heard the remarks she made about women who passed by! Really, I hardly felt safe!"

This from a woman who is buying pornographic art to hang on her walls. . . . Ann is still a tourist and will remain one, no matter what happens to her in Paris. To hear her talk you'd think that cunt-sucking among women was something which sprouted only on this side of the ocean. . . But at any rate she's bought some pictures and commissioned more; she likes them and she's getting her money's worth, which is something that can't be said about all of Sam's art-buying ventures.

In the meantime, Billie and I have talked about things other than art. She came to my place to talk about Jean. What she had to know, she said, was just how I felt about Jean. . . . Did I have any noble ideas, perhaps about re-forming her and leading her to a better way of life? Had I been thinking of taking her for a mistress? Man to man, now. . . . .

Relief, when she learned that my intentions towards Jean are not at all honorable . . . . she doesn't mind if I lay the girl, she explained, just so long as I don't try to take her away from her. In fact, she likes to have Jean come here because she knows where she is and that she probably won't catch anything. And it makes Jean contented to be fucked, too. There, she says, is the reason why she herself continues to make pictures, even though she's long ago re-alized that she's just a capable craftsman and no world beater . . . . even for a Lesbian there's not the satisfaction in having her cunt sucked . . . . not the satisfaction that a normal woman gets out of a good lay. So, she's always dissat-isfied, she has to do something, and she makes herself al-most an artist.

Billie and I become very good friends when she's con-vinced that I have no designs on Jean other than casual designs. As a man, she asks, what do I think of her? Her as a woman, she means. . . Does it give me hot pants to look at her? Do I think that she ought to be a good lay, or would I think so if her hair wasn't cut that way and if I didn't know she was a Lesbian? Since I know that she's not anything but what she is, and since I know that she doesn't give a damn about attracting men, I can tell her the truth. . . . .

The truth is that Billie happens to be a very luscious looking package, no matter how it's wrapped, and I tell her so. For perhaps half an hour we sit by my window and talk about Billie as though she were someone else who wasn't there just then.

Then Billie looks at her watch . . . . she has an appointment soon . . . but before she goes, would I like to fuck her? I can't believe that I'm hearing straight. . . . Yes, that's what she said . . . . would I like to try screwing her; shall she take her clothes off for a few minutes before she goes?

She explains . . . she likes me, and she's grateful, for the way I'm handling Jean. What do women give men when they're grateful? So if I like her, if I really think that she's a nice cunt and would be nice to fuck, she'll let me. If I don't want to . . . if I think that her being a Lesbian would interfere (although, she points out, it didn't keep me from wanting her to suck me off the first time I met her) . . . . that's understandable, and no hard feelings either way.

I couldn't say no to a proposition like that, even if I hadn't been thinking already what a nice fuck she'd be if she only weren't queer. A cunt's a cunt, and it's what's between a woman's legs that matters to John Thursday, not what's in her head.

"I like to be screwed once in a while," Billie confesses, "I get a feeling that I'm cheating my destiny if I don't. Don't think I'm like those women who can't stand to have a man touch them . . . I could marry a man and be a pretty good wife if I had to. But I wouldn't have much fun."

We undress in the bedroom, and because Billie is so dark and so odd I pull my Chinese hanging from the wall for her to lie upon. She likes that . . . it's an erotic touch that she hadn't expected. And it's perfect for her.

Billie has an appealing awkwardness about her . . . when she is taking her clothes off she tries to be feminine and seductive, and it's like watching a very innocent girl who's trying to be sophisticated. She steps so cautiously out of her dress as it lies around her ankles . . . she's so excruciatingly delicate about letting down her pants and giving me a peep at that black-fringed bonne-bouche . . . . that

I feel like some cradle snatcher who's bribed a ten-year-old with Woolworth jewelry. Then before she's taken off her shoes and stockings, she comes across the room to me and lays everything she's got into my hands. She presses her belly against me; she stands on the tips of her toes and rubs her pussy on my fly. She's come to be felt of, and the invitation isn't rejected. . . She laughs embarressedly when I pick her up and carry her to the bed.

Hell, I'm embarrassed too . . . I drop her on the spread, on her ass and she rolls over with her legs apart to show her split fig. Do I want a bite, she asks? Then, when I lunge at her . . . no, she was joking; that's a girl's business.

My dong isn't up as high as it might be, and we lie there diddling each other until it's hard enough. There's a Hell of a lot that Billie doesn't know about playing with a prick, but Johnny only needs encouragement, not persuasion. . . . .

"Is Jean very nice to screw?" Billie asks me while we're still fiddling with each other's tails. "Does she do that as well as most girls?"

Then she wants to know other things. . . Does Jean suck me off by herself or do I have to make her? Does she ask me to suck her cunt? Do we play tete-beche? Does she ever talk about Billie? Does she ever speak of other women she's been to bed with? Lastly . . . . do I think she's happy with Billie?

I give all the right answers, and Billie's happy. Jean, she tells me, is the nicest cunt she's ever lived with. For one thing she isn't messy. Ah, if I haven't been married or lived with a woman for a long time, I don't know what that means. Hairpins in bed, piss and paper in an unflushed toilet, Kotex pads left in clothes closets . . . . these are the things that most women bring you. But Jean is as clean as a cat; if you didn't sleep with her, you could live with her for years and never know when her flag was out, and whenever it's time to make love she has her little box as fresh as a flower.

Billie could talk about Jean all afternoon, and to hell

234 ·

with fucking, but I have a bug up my ass. Finally I get her back to where we started and let her feel what Jean Jeudi is like when he rubs his head between her thighs. She spreads them and I climb on . . . . is she ready? Does she want to be fucked now? Yes, yes, I can put it in, but not too quickly . . . she's not used to it, I must remember.

I've never laid a cunt who was so damn uninterested in what was happening. She's bored, that's it . . . and after I've been in her for a couple of minutes she doesn't care about it one way or the other. And the next thing I know she's opened her purse, taken out her lipstick and a pencil, and is sketching on the wall by her head! Drawing pictures while I'm fucking her! A hell of an insult, and she's completely unconscious of it. . . . . she lies across the bed, humming a little to herself, and you'd never think that I was ramming my cock into her. . . . .

In addition to which, the picture she's making is upside down and if anybody wanted to look at it they'd either have to lie as she is or stand on their head. . . . .

"Are you through already?" she asks . . . because I've stopped screwing her.

Then she yawns in my face, the bitch! Oh you lousy upside-cunt. I'll see to it that you wake up . . . I've got something to make you open your eyes! You won't ask if I'm through again . . . . you'll know when I'm through, and you'll be damned glad when it's over.

I pull my cock out of her fig, fling her lipstick across the room, and throw her belly-side down under me. She's amazed at the strong-arm tactics, but she looks a little pleased, too . . . . until she sees what I'm trying to do. Then she raises hell. . . . .

No! She's very emphatic about it . . . she won't be screwed in the ass! It's . . . . it's a perversion, and besides, it would hurt! If I want to do that I can do it to Jean . . . if Jean likes it. But not to her! And she tries to hop off the bed.

If Billie were like any other cunt I probably couldn't handle her. But she fights like a man, without biting or pinching or scratching, and she doesn't try to kick you in the balls. It's a matter of weight and strength, and as long as I'm behind her I have an advantage, and when I manage to get my dong where I want it, struggling merely helps me . . . every time she wiggles, John Thursday looks into her rectum.

Billie threatens me . . . if I don't stop, she'll see to it that Jean never lays me again. She'll tell everybody that I have the clap. She'll scream and bring the concierge up. . . Well, if she tells people I have the clap I'll spread the rumor that I got it from her. If she rouses the concierge I'll tell him that she's a whore who tried to cheat me . . . he's a sympathetic fellow; he'll probably help me hold her (the old bastard would throw me out on my-ear, that's what he'd really do).

There's no squirming out of this for you, Billie. . . Now, you cunt sniffer, why don't you draw some more pictures? Yes, I know that you're not used to this. I can feel how tight your rectum is where my cock shoves into it. . . But it will be big enough: it will be bigger when I've finished, when you've felt all of my prick in there, and when I've oiled up your machinery with jism. . .

Billie bites the bed with anger. I'm a bastard, she says, a son of a bitch, uncle to a family of idiot shit-eaters. . . . I look at dirty pictures and play with myself, I sleep with old Kotex pads under my pillow . . . . she has a colorful imagination, and it's a pleasure to have her come to life. A cock in the ass works wonders sometimes; it's a great stimulant.

Before I've finished I've screwed bloody Jesus out of her. She isn't demanding that I stop now . . . . she's begging. But I keep at it. She becomes limp and lies moaning . . . . it's a trick, and when it doesn't work she pounds the bed with her fists.

"No more," she pleads, "No more! Alf, listen . . . I'll get you girls . . . oh, such girls! I know lots and lots of nice cunts who are looking for a man, Alf; I can get them for you. . . . I'll give you their addresses now . . . I'll call them up for you. . . Take your cock out of my ass now, Alf. . . . "

And more of the same. Probably she does know some nice cunts . . . . . these Lesbians pick up everything nice in sight. But she could promise me a weekend with a barnfull of virgins and I wouldn't stop. I screw harder and begin to play with her fig. I'd give my left ball to make this bitch come right now, but there doesn't seem to be a chance. . . . .

Suddenly I seem to have lost both of my balls . . . they've turned inside out and shot out my dick, into Billie's rectum. I shove my fingers into her cunt and diddle her until she howls, but she won't come, the bitch. I've filled her ass with jism, and feeling as I do I'd like to piss up her ass too . . . but I can't bear to take a chance with that lovely old hanging. . . . . .

Billie snaps back into good humor almost immediately. Well . . . I certainly take what I go after. She'll know better next time; she won't come here again without police protection. Or, at the very least, she won't offer to let me screw her; not without thinking twice about it. The whole thing becomes a joke to her . . . she doesn't know if she should tell Jean or not. But did I have a good time? And am I satisfied now? Good! Then, could she please lie down on the bed to rest a minute and to finish her upside-down sketch?

Sam has made some sort of a deal with Severin. I don't know the details exactly, but Carl sees all of us making money by fistfuls.

"I don't know what's wrong with me, Alf," he moans over a glass of Perrier water, which seems to be his expression of repentance for an evil life, "It must be my time of life . . . . but Hell, I don't feel any different than I ever did; I really gave that girl a hell of a screwing, too. . . . ."

Why to Jesus Alexandra had to break that date Sam can't understand. If she hadn't done that, everything would have been all right . . . he'd have had a good time with her and no headache afterward. But now, now he's really in the gravy.

"Ann would forgive me if I ran around with the mother," he tells me. "She's broad-minded enough to understand things like that happen; that a man needs a little diversion once in a while. But how in hell could I tell her that it was a kid . . . just a little girl hardly older than my own daughter? And the worst part of it is that I want to fuck her again! Right now, while I'm sitting here talking to you, I can see her as she stood after she'd let me take off her clothes . . . she didn't know whether to cover herself so that I couldn't see her, or cover her eyes so she couldn't see me." Tania must have given him a wonderful line of bullshit—or else she just kept still and let him make up the beautiful background, because Sam is full of astonishing ideas. "She was so innocent about everything . . . . she trusted me completely, you could see that. And yet she was so full of life, so eager to do anything to please me . . . she's just a babe in the woods. . . ."

As things are now, anything I could say would just make Sam mad. Either he'd think that I was slandering a sweet innocent child or he'd feel that I'd let him make a fool of himself. My best bet is to keep still and hope that when London Bridge comes down I'm off to one side with the newsreel cameramen. I let Sam talk . . . I've listened to a lot duller stories for the sake of a few drinks. . . . . .

"I don't suppose she's a virgin," he says thoughtfully. "She didn't act quite like one. . . I suppose some boy has taken her on a picnic or something like that. But it's really wrong to take a girl like that, with all her illusions, and do to her what I did. But I couldn't stop, once it was started! I had to screw her, and because she was young and innocent and little I acted worse with her than I did with her mother . . . I made her do everything that her mother did. . . . God! Mother and daughter I've screwed them both . . . . and I can't forget either of them. What a situation! Alf, you know Alexandra; what would she do if she found out? Do you think she'd go to Ann? Would it be very bad?

Christ, Almighty. I'd tell her myself, right now, if I thought it would do any good. . . . . ."

That's what Sam has been doing with his time. As for Ann, she has another story and a hell of a story too. For some reason she wants me to believe that she has really jumped off the high board . . . perhaps she thinks that I'll tell Sam and make him jealous . . . . . she won't forget that card game he didn't go to. . . . . .

There are two vague males . . . . so vague that Ann can't even keep their names straight. And these two bozos, with Ann, are alleged to have promoted some very high jinx at her little hideaway a couple of nights ago. According to Ann's story, she took them up there intending to let them fuck her, one at a time, and then got scared. Then, when they found out that she didn't intend to take down her pants after all they got sore, tied her to the bed, and gave her the works. . . . . .

If she'd picked better names! If these birds had been called Sid and Ernest, for instance, I might have believed her. But these guys are a couple of tough frogs . . . . perhaps Apaches . . . . and the whole, glittering picture is obviously a piece of cerebral adventuring.

"The way I was treated!" Ann exclaims, managing a shudder. "The filth I was obliged to endure! It's impossible to speak of it. . . . . I shan't even remember it! Tied to a bed! Helpless, and at the mercy of men without mercy! What would Sam say if he suspected!"

Ann, unless she is careful, is liable to talk herself into something. In America, when a woman begins daydreaming like that, she goes to a psychoanalyst and has her mind felt up. In Paris she's more likely to end up in a hotel bedroom with two thugs and a pimp with a movie camera. . . . . . .

BOOK III

Cherchez
le Toit

Sam has plenty to say about the French these days. It's a fake, says Sam, all this you hear about the indolent good living of the French. The indolence he is willing to concede . . . as to the good living, he wants to make speeches about it.

"An hour and a half for lunch," he snorts to me . . . "I used to think that it must be a wonderfully carefree people who lived that way . . . until I found out how they spent that hour and a half. Backbiting, penny-pinching . . . do you really want to know why they take an hour and a half for lunch? Because they figure that they're safe in a café, that they won't be tempted to spend any more money than they've allowed themselves. If they stayed in the office maybe somebody would come in and sell them a new ribbon for a typewriter. That's the whole idea . . . they shudder at the thought of doing business because it costs something to do business. Here, look, I'll show you something. . . " He finds a scrap of paper in his pocket and throws it on the table. "There's a receipt I got this morning from a supposedly reputable business house. Do you see what it is . . . . the back of an envelope. That's French business for you."

And so it goes. Sam can find a thousand reasons for disliking the French, but the real trouble is that Sam has had his life somewhat upset since he's been in Paris. I don't pay much attention to all this as long as he doesn't threaten to go home to America. Let him say anything he pleases . . . just so long as his wife and his daughter are here to fuck and he's around to buy me a drink he can talk his head off for all I care.

Not that I don't like Sam . . . . considering all the years I spent back in New York kissing the asses of men like him, we get along beautifully. He tells me all about his adventures with Alexandra and Tania; I tell him nothing about my adventures with Snuggles and Ann. It works perfectly that way.

Something new is happening to Ann . . . or so Billie tells me. Ann is still avoiding me, so I have to take Billie's word for it. But I've no reason to believe that Billie might be shitting me. . . . .

Billie's story is that Ann is trying to make her . . . and Billie should know, I suppose. She stops in one afternoon just after she's been to see Ann with another delivery of those fancy watercolors that Ann's collecting and gives me the lowdown, the real dope. Billie's amused, but I think that she's interested too. After all, Ann is a fine-looking woman, and while Billie usually goes for the sweet young things like Jean and Snuggles I can imagine that she likes a change now and then

According to Billie, Ann tried to flatter her pants off for a change, told her how lonely it was in Paris without any women friends, and practically asks Billie to teach her what *The Well of Loneliness* was all about. Billie thought it was just curiosity at first, but by now she's decided that Ann really wants to go to bed with her. She wants to know what I think about it . . . . not that it will make much difference in the end.

Well, why not? Ann probably figures that she's gone overboard so completely in Paris that it simply wouldn't make sense to neglect an opportunity to find out the answers to all the questions she's been asking herself. Paris, for Ann, is something that never happened before and probably won't happen again once she's on a boat for New York. If she wants to know what it's like to sleep with a woman it's now or never.

Billie nods, pleased because those are the things she wants to hear. What's Ann like in bed, she wants to know. Is she a hot fuck? Is she as good as Jean, for instance? She wants me to tell her all about Ann, the way a man would want to be told. And what about the guy who foots the bills . . . what about her husband? She throws one leg over the arm of the chair, not giving a fuck that I can see everything she owns, and throws questions at me.

"For the love of Jesus, will you put your leg down?" I finally have to interrupt. "I haven't had a lay in almost a week."

Billie looks pained. She's full of sympathy. Why don't I call Jean? Or do I want her to ask Jean to come around when she goes home? That bitch! If she isn't careful she won't get home . . . I'm in a mood to lock up her clothes and keep her here a week, Lesbian or no Lesbian.

"What are you going to do about Ann?" I ask, when I've answered more questions than she can remember.

"I haven't decided . . . . I'll think about it. I'm wondering about Snuggles."

Then she's made up her mind to leave, and she's gone before I can work myself up to raping her. . . . . . .

Ernest calls me. What have I been doing, he wants to know, about fixing things for that date at Ann's? I have to tell him that I haven't been doing anything . . . I haven't seen her long enough to talk to. Well, then, by all the fucking names of a name, he'll take care of it himself . . . where can he find her? I tell him a couple of places where he might run into her and he hangs up.

He sounds as surprised as I am when he calls me back a couple of hours later. He's found her, they're in some joint on the rue St. Jacques, and he wants me to come right down.

"What do I want to do that for? Look, Ernest, you just fix things up. . . . I have to go out and eat pretty soon. . . ."

That won't do at all, it seems. He has to go home and get the camera, and he can't take her with him and he can't leave her alone. He's afraid she'll sober up too much if there isn't someone with her.

"Did she say it was all right about the party?" I ask him.

"Well, no, she didn't exactly say that, Alf, but it's going to be all right. Once we get her at her place we can fix that. What's the matter . . . . don't you want to fuck her?"

"Yeah . . . yeah . . . I want to fuck her all right, Ernest, but I'm not so sure about taking any pictures. It's likely to spoil everything if you show up with a taxi full of lights and wires and things."

"It won't spoil anything . . . she'll think it's swell when we get her in the right mood. Wasn't it her idea to begin with?"

In the end, of course, I go out to meet them. If I didn't Ernest would be sore. And there might be something to it after all . . . . free drinks, anyway.

It's growing dark as I walk along and the whores are creeping out for the night's trade. Who in Hell picks up a whore at this time of day, I wonder? Tourists, probably . . . . . . anyone else would know that if you picked one up now you'd have to feed her. One falls in step beside me and gives me her little sales talk. . . . .

"It's so nice, Monsieur . . . and costs so very little . . . . wouldn't you like to know how they do it in Havana? Yes, I was in Havana, Monsieur . . . this is not my regular line . . . not at all! But the times being what they are. . . . Perhaps you will buy me a small Pernod. . . . ."

I give her the shake and walk for a couple of blocks behind a blonde cunt. Picture under her arm . . . must be an art student, but she walks like a chorus girl. After the first fifty feet I have a hard on just from watching that ass sway back and forth, and I whistle a couple of times to see if she'll turn around. She won't.

How many times, I wonder, have I done this . . . gone chasing through the streets after a cunt like a dog sniffing after a bitch . . . . with not a chance in a million that she'll give me a tumble. That ass moves like a pendulum, ticking my life to pieces. Here I am chasing a cunt that I'm not going to get . . . . a million other bozos must be doing the same thing at this minute . . . while that pendulum goes on swinging. I'm glad that I have someplace to go. If I didn't I'd turn around and find that whore again . . . she wasn't so bad.

The girl turns into a shop and I still haven't seen her face . . . but I still have that erection she gave me. It's like finding money on the street, getting that hard on and carrying it off with me. The difference is that nobody's lost anything. I make a note that if I ever run into that cunt again I'll have to go up and thank her, have to try to explain how wonderful it is that you can get something for nothing and nobody's out anything. But I won't see her again. . . . I never see them again, all these beautiful cunts who lead me down the avenues.

I nurse that erection along until I'm with Ernest and Ann. I follow one cunt after another, dreaming about them. Shit, I must be cunt struck . . . here I am talking to myself again . . . something I haven't done since I first came here, when I used to get so fucking hungry just for something to eat that I was a little delirious most of the time . . . A fuck . . . hell. When I saw a big, juicy ass I wanted to eat the damned thing. But I learned one thing . . . . you can be starving to death and old Johnny down there can't keep his mind off cunt. He still comes up strong when your knees are so wobbly that you can't walk straight. It may be different when you get really bad and your belly starts to bloat. I never found out about that . . . I panhandled instead.

Ernest hadn't told Ann that he called me. As soon as he sets eyes on me he sets up a shout. Well, well, well . . . . . imagine finding me there! He claps me on the back and shakes my hand . . . . they were just about to start talking about me, he says. As for Ann, she's confused and embarrassed, but she has to make the best of things.

Christ, what a lot of shit there is to getting a woman to bed with you! Some women. It would be so much simpler if you could just thump Ann on the ass and say "Let's go to your house and fuck." . . . . . Ann maybe you could, if she were drunk enough. Instead, we have to finagle and fuck around. Ernest decides that it's his birthday.

"Everybody have a drink on me!" he says, "My birthday. . . ."

. . . . Since there are only the three of us the celebration won't cost him much. Ann is as surprised as I am to hear about his birthday. Ernest insists that it's his birthday, but he forgets how old he is.

"I'd have a party," he says mournfully, "but my place is so small. . ."

"Oh yes, mine too, mine too," I tell Ann.

"Well. . . ." Ann says doubtfully.

"Fine!" Ernest roars. "Just the place to have a little birthday party! Now you two just stay here . . . I have a little errand to do. But I'll be back . . . I'll be back!" Aside, as he's leaving, he says to me: "For God's sake, keep her drinking. . . ."

"Sure . . . . keep her drinking! How the fuck am I going to do that if she decides that she doesn't want to drink?"

"Stand her on her head and pour it in her asshole . . . that's what I've been doing. Just don't let her sober up before I get back."

"What a fuck of a nuisance this is! Why don't we go out and pick up some whore? There are lots of nice girls on the street tonight."

"Now, Alf, don't start that. . . . Do you know where Sid is?"

"No, I don't know where Sid is, and I don't give much of a damn. Do you realize that this used to be my cunt before you and Sid came sticking your fingers in the pie? Where's that suit she was going to buy me? Is she going to buy it tonight? No, you're going to gyp her on some camera deal you rigged up! By Christ, Ernest, there's a limit to friendship! You and Sid are going to fuck up everything before you're through."

"Sh, she'll hear you. . . . Listen Alf, I never pulled

anything on you in my life . . . . if I make anything on the camera I'll see that you're taken care of. Of course if you don't want to screw her you don't have to come along. . . ."

"What do you mean, if I don't want to screw her? Who has a better right to screw her? Who got her started?"

I'd like to remember what I said to Ann in the next half hour. I poured. . . . I overflowed. I pissed conversation like a weak bladder. I talked about every fucking thing . . . . that came into my head, and every time I caught the garçon by the coattail that was a period. She forgot that she was sore at me, and she sat there with her teats hanging over the table and her mouth open a little while she tried to guess what it was all about. She even let me feel her up a little under the table while I sang her a song in Russian. But she wouldn't feel me back, the bitch . . . still too much of a lady. Anyway, she didn't stop drinking.

She begins to get restless, though. There aren't enough people in that joint to suit that tourist mind of hers. Couldn't we go somewhere else for awhile and leave a note for Ernest? I think that's a splendid idea, so we settle up and leave a message with the waiter and go down the street.

Ann is getting gay. Two drinks in the new place and she's had enough of that. We write another note and try another. By this time I'm beginning to feel those drinks a little myself. Another note. Ann doesn't like one place because it's full of sailors. The next one has too many whores. Then she counts six cats in one place, and she can't stand cats. Christ, I've given up trying to let Ernest know where we might be. . . . I just leave a note each time to tell him we've been there and gone.

"Is it really Ernest's birthday?" Ann asks me every few minutes.

Shit, I don't know if it's his birthday . . . . it might be. For that matter I don't suppose that Ernest knows when it is. I'm wondering if I ought to come right out and ask her for some money . . . this drinking is beginning to get expensive. And every time I want to leave a note at the bar I have an argument with the patron who can't understand why we don't want to stay in such a nice place as this to meet our friends.

"If it's Ernest's birthday," Ann decides, "I'll have to get him something. . . . ."

Out of that place we go and into the nearest men's shop. Ernest's birthday! Shit! Why couldn't he have made it my birthday, I'd like to know? My heart sinks when she begins to buy things. She simply walks around the store and jabs her fingers at things, and the clerk puts them in a pile on the counter.

Shirts, neckties, socks . . . . my God, it's criminal! And here I am with a suit that's getting shaggy at the cuffs and a hat that looks as though I polished my shoes with it. . . . . Underdrawers . . . what size? Well, what size do I take? That son of a bitch with his birthday! Shoes! We have to go to another store for those, and to make it more insulting I have to carry the packages. We have another drink, which I pay for, and buy the shoes. Well, that bitch, if she wants to spend dough, I'll help her . . . but Ernest's going to answer to me for this night!

"Why don't you buy him a suit?" I ask her, "And maybe a coat and hat?"

A suit? But how can she get his measurements to a tailor? And it always takes three or four weeks for Sam's suits to be made. Finally I argue her into buying a ready-made one . . . if it doesn't fit he can bring it back. I'm so fucking mad now that I don't care what she does. I even let them use me as a clothes dummy while she picks out what she wants. But I've decided that I won't carry those damned packages another stop. I plunk them down in front of the spider who runs this joint and tell him that he can send everything. Of course it's going to cost a little something to send them tonight, he tells me. . . . .

At the next bar we turn into I steer Ann far to the back, in a corner, and face her toward the wall so that she won't see anything she doesn't like . . . . I want to rest my ass for a while. But we haven't been there ten minutes before Ernest comes in . . . with Sid.

"We got your notes," Ernest yells, and he waves them. A light bulb drops from somewhere on him and the report almost precipitates a panic at the bar. He's carrying a suitcase and all his pockets are bulging. Sid has a tripod and a half dozen reflectors and some stands for lights. He's like a man who has been split open and is trying to keep his guts under his coat . . . miles of coiled black tubing keeps popping out of him. Light cord, when you take a second look.

"You dope," I say to him as soon as I get him out of Ann's range, "do you want to scare her away altogether? Why the fuck didn't you leave it in a taxi?"

"Nuts . . . she doesn't know what it is. I'll tell her its machinery to make root beer . . ." He turns to Ann and tells her: "It's to make homemade root beer. . . ."

Ernest wants to go for a drive after a couple more drinks, so we get into a fiacre and cross to the right bank by way of the Ile de la Cité. But I make damned certain that I get a place next to Ann. She's all right now . . . she's warmed up, and in the dark of the musty smelling cab she's quite friendly. We go as far as the Place de la Bastille, and when we get to Ann's place, where the horse immediately takes a piss, we've finished one of the bottles which Sid has brought. Passing Notre Dame on our way over, I had my hand under Ann's skirt and she was feeling of my fly . . . . . coming back she had my dong out as we passed the morgue at Place Masas, I had her pants half off, and what she was doing with her other hand I couldn't say.

All the junk which Ann bought arrives just as we do. As soon as we're in her place she hands everything over to Ernest. He's in a fog, he doesn't know what it's all about.

"It's for your birthday, you dope!" I yell at him. "For your God-damned fucking birthday!"

He can't look me in the eye, but Sid takes everything in his stride. Sid slaps Ann across the ass and tells her it's his birthday too.

"How about a present for me too?" he keeps asking her. "I don't want much. . . . Just a few minutes of your time. . . ."

He gets her off in a corner and starts playing with her. Ernest looks at them and then at me. He shakes his head.

"I can't understand this . . . . . I just can't understand it," he says. He shakes a box that's among all the crumpled wrapping paper and another necktie falls out. He puts it absently in his pocket. "You know me, Alf."

Just then Ann lets out a screech. Sid has her on the floor and he's sitting on her. Her dress is over her head and he's pulling her pants off her ass. When he gets a nice juicy place bare he smacks her a couple of times.

"She won't take her dress off," he explains. "I think she just likes to have her ass warmed."

"Thought we were coming up here to have a drink or two," Ann wails. "If I'd have known you intended to try this. . . . ."

Ernest begins to stumble over his wires and lights. He sticks the camera up on the tripod and takes a squint through it.

"Wrestle with her some more, Sid," he says, "We want her to look real mussed up, like, for the first ones."

Ann gets really sore at that. We're not going to take any pictures of her, she insists. But Ernest goes on setting the lights around and trying them and Sid musses her up some more.

"Hey, Ernest . . . . you want her cunt showing? You want her legs open: what do you want?"

"Just show me plenty of belly . . . . . yeah, one of her bubs, too . . . . just let her brassiere hang down. Maybe you ought to get in this too, Alf. . . ."

"Fuck that! You're not going to get my picture committing rape! Do you know what that picture's going to look like?"

It's going to have plenty of juice no matter what else it has. Ann's half naked, while Sid still has his hat on and is

252 ·

chewing what's left of his cigar, and they both look just about as stewed as they are. Ernest finally presses the button and gets some kind of a picture. Sid lets Ann go then, but she still lies on the floor wringing her hands and kicking her feet.

"To think of such a thing happening to me!" She howls. "Oh, if Sam ever found out! Oh my God, if Sam ever found out!"

"Let her enjoy herself as long as she doesn't make too much noise," Ernest says while he's opening another bottle. "She'll come around."

Ann takes a drink when it's passed to her and sits up with her back against the wall. She wants to try to reason with us. A woman in her position really can't afford to have such a picture of herself taken . . . . can't we see that? Ernest swears that they're only for her own collection . . . . she said she wanted to buy a camera and take some. . . So here is the camera and here we all are. . . . .

"Here's another drink for you," he says. He sits down beside her and begins to feel her up. I felt like sitting down myself, so I take the other side of her. One more drink and she lets us put her dress up to her belly. Ernest and I take turns feeling her bonne-bouche while we try to get her to play with our cocks.

"All right," she says suddenly, "you may take your damned pictures. . . . ."

She puts her empty glass between her legs and runs one hand into my fly and the other into Ernest's. Out comes Johnny and out comes Ernest's dick. I have a sweet dong on, and it's getting bigger by the minute. Ernest's isn't exactly a peanut, either. Sid chooses that moment to press the camera button. I'm too drunk by now to think much about whether or not I want my physog recorded for the ages.

"Undress me," Ann says, and then the bitch throws herself across our knees.

From then on it seems that every time I turn around

that fucking camera is clicking in my face. It has an attachment, which Ernest tries to explain to me, and which I'm too drunk to understand, that delays the action so that the guy who presses the button can get into the picture before it goes off. After the first few times it doesn't bother us much.

As soon as we have Ann's clothes off she's after our dicks. The bitch can't even wait for us to undress. While she's still squirming around on her belly, and while Ernest is taking off her stockings, she pulls my fly wide open and shoves her face in it. She curls her tongue around my balls and licks them, jerking me off while she's doing it, and in about ten seconds she's grabbed John Thursday in her mouth and is washing his face.

"Feel my ass!" she yells at Ernest, "Feel me up good!"

She spreads herself and shows us everything she has between those big thighs. Ernest tickles her fig and pokes his fingers into it, and back into her mouth goes Johnny. She rubs her teats on my legs and tries to crawl into my pants head first. Then she hops up and shakes her ass in front of our faces like a hula dancer.

"Come back here, you bitch!" I yell at her. But it doesn't do any good. When I make a grab for her she runs to the couch. She bounces on it and turns her belly to the ceiling, lies there with her legs wide open and shows us her con. She wants to be fucked, she wants to feel a prick under her ass, and she's not at all bashful about telling about it. She pulls her fig wide open and rubs her fingers into the split. She ought to have a rain gutter to take care of that cunt when it starts to leak. . . . . she has a river of juices coming out of her forest, feeding the flowers, that grow around her ass. . . . .

Sid has been taking off his clothes, and he's on the couch at the same time that Ernest gets there.

"Don't you fuck her, Ernest," Sid argues. "Don't you try to fuck her with your pants on . . . you'll get them so soaked with that stuff that you'll have to bury them . . . Let me screw her while you get ready."

Ann doesn't care a fuck of a lot who screws her . . . . she has her legs open like a trap, waiting to hook the first cock that comes close enough. Sid hops on her and the trap springs. She gets her legs and both arms around him, and her ass comes up into position. Sid has a dong on that looks like something you ought to go after with a horse and a lariat, but that's just the kind that Ann is looking for. She gives her rear a wiggle or two and gobbles it into her belly. Ernest runs over to the camera and starts snapping away while Sid rides her. . . . .

"My God!" Ann squeaks after a minute, "I'm going to come! Somebody give me a prick to suck while I come. . . . ."

I'm not crazy enough to give my cock to a bitch who's as wild as Ann is . . . Jean Jeudi has to last me for the rest of my life, and I'm not taking any chances of losing half of him. She acts nuts enough to eat him. She makes a grab for me, and I won't let her put my dong into her mouth, so she yells to Ernest. He's there in nothing flat, stuffing it down her throat while she coos and gurgles over it. As soon as she has it Ernest begins to look desperate, as though he'd made a mistake, but he goes on jabbing it into her mouth.

"For Christ sake," he pants at Sid, "make the bitch come, will you!"

He grabs her teats and squeezes them until the nipples turn almost purple. Sid is sticking his fingers up Ann's ass, and every time he wiggles them she howls and tries to swallow Ernest's bush. Then, bang . . . . bang . . . . bang. One after the other, Sid, Ann and Ernest.

Ann keeps her legs around Sid until she can't squeeze another drop out of him. Then she's ready to let Ernest go too, but he goes on frigging away at her mouth.

"What the hell are you trying to do?" Sid asks, watching him, "Piss?"

"Sure," Ernest says . . . and Ann jumps up quicker than you'd think a woman of her size could move.

It's time for everybody to have another drink, and Ernest fools around with the camera. Ann is beginning to get ideas about the pictures she'd like to have. First of all she wants pictures of her sucking each one of us off.

That's easy enough . . . we put her on a table and take turns. I'm first, and I stand at one end of the table with my dong up while Ann, on her belly, sticks it in her mouth and puts her arms around my ass. As soon as her lips close on my prick I'm ready to forget about the pictures and simply work on her.

"Look," I say to Ernest, "why don't we forget the art and just screw her? Just let me take her off into the bedroom for half an hour, then maybe we'll take some pictures. . . ."

But that wouldn't do, it seems. Even Ann is against that idea. She wants the pictures and she wants a lot of them, and it's Sid's turn now. For once he doesn't have a hard on, but Ann fixes that. She hangs over him and kisses his nuts. Then she licks his belly and his thighs and his bush. By the time Ernest has the camera ready Sid is ready too. Ann pulls the skin back from his prick and cleans around the head of it with the tip of her tongue. In it goes. . . . . .

Ann's really hot again when it's Ernest's turn . . . you can see that in the way she grabs for his cock. And she has another idea for a picture . . . . she wants to lie on her back and let Ernest hang his balls into her mouth. Ernest looks doubtful . . . I don't blame him after the ferocious way she was sucking him off a few minutes ago . . . . but he lets her have her way. His balls are too big for her to take both of them at once, anyway . . . . and if she bites one off he still has a spare. Ann lets her head hang over the edge of the table and Ernest drops one of his nuts into her open lips as neatly as though it was a cherry . . . . she's using both hands to jerk him off . . . she has her legs apart and her ass is wiggling.

It suddenly comes to me that this catting bitch is Ann. Not Tania or her mother and not one of Arthur's or Carl's cunts, but Ann Backer, out to see Paris. My Christ, the adaptability of a cunt is a wonderful thing . . . . when I first knew her Ann would have jumped into the Seine before she'd have done anything like this. It just goes to show what a fine thing travel is. . . . .

Ann has another idea . . . she's thought of a way to suck two pricks at once, she says. Ernest and I will have to lie on the couch. . . . .

I've never heard of such a thing before . . . . but, strangely enough, it works. Ernest and I lie with our heads at either end of the couch and our asses together, my legs over his. Ann licks my dong and then she licks his . . . she gives him a suck and then puts mine in her mouth. Finally she puts her fingers around them and squeezes them together. . . . .

It isn't easy, getting both of those cocks in at once, but Ann is determined. She twists her head from one side to the other keeping her mouth as wide as she can. It's the bitchiest thing I've ever seen, the way she struggles to get both of those big dicks in together. . . . .

She manages it somehow . . . . and I'm ready to come long before she starts to suck them. I sit up and look at her better, and so does Ernest. Sid is so pop-eyed that he's pushing all the wrong buttons on the camera . . . he's taking pictures all over the place. Ann is slobbering all over us, wiggling her behind and trying to rub her bubs against our balls.

"For God's sake," I yell at her, "if you stop before I come I'll strangle you with the damned thing."

She starts playing with both of us, bouncing her head around so that it feels as though our pricks were in a tight cunt. Sid can't stand any more . . . he leaves the camera and rushes over with his dong up. He gets behind Ann and rams his cock against her rectum. Ann jumps as though she'd had a hot poker stuck into her ass, but she sucks us twice as hard when she catches on to what's happening.

Sid goes on poking at her, and in a few minutes, he's got the end of his dong in her rectum. He starts to fuck her, pushing the rest of it in, and Ann hops around so much that it's all we can do to keep her on the couch. She can hardly catch a breath of air, because each time that she tries to lift her head Ernest rams it down again. And those two pricks haven't grown any smaller, either. Sid yells at her to smile at the camera because it's to go off. . . . .

"Smile, you whore," he yells, "or I'll shove this cock into your mouth, too. . . . ."

The camera isn't the only thing that's ready to go off . . . . . . I can feel Ernest's cock jump against mine, and in the next minute Ann's mouth feels very sticky. The jism is running out and over her chin and over everything else . . . . she can't stop it.

"My ass!" she manages to sputter, ". . . . my God, it's on fire!"

Sid is fucking himself cockeyed, shooting that jism up her rectum, but she hasn't come yet. She's trying to swallow Ernest's jism and she's damned near swallowing my cock along with it . . . It's halfway down her throat when I come, and that first taste must go directly into her bowels with no stops on the way. Sid's given up trying to fuck her into coming . . . he takes a deep breath and starts to piss inside her. He's determined to either make her come or kill her, and he comes close to doing both together. . . . . .

For half a minute Ann is completely nuts. Neither Ernest nor I can get our cocks away from her, and she seems to be trying to suck our balls out through them. She doesn't quite get our balls but she gets everything else. She's choking herself on the jism she's sucking out, but that's too unimportant to bother her. Her ass is full of piss and her mouth is full of cock . . . . she's daffy as a loon, and completely happy.

When she's through sucking us I can't move, and neither can Ernest. I'm so glad to have my prick back in one piece that I simply lie there and sigh while Ann, who seems to be still coming, licks the juice from my cock and my balls and hair. She's got plenty of cleaning up to do . . . . there's jism from my navel to my knees, and Ernest is in the same condition. But she licks it all up, and then she's got to make a run for the bathroom to get rid of the little present Sid gave her.

You'd think after that she'd be ready to sit down and take it easy for awhile . . . . but not Ann. She takes time out to pour another drink into herself and then she's ready to take some more pictures. Doesn't anyone want to fuck her now, she asks brightly.

"How about sucking our asses?" I suggest.

Oh no! That is the one thing of which there will be no pictures, Ann says. So of course that becomes the one thing we're determined to get pictures of. Sid and Ernest grab her. . . . . I turn my ass toward her and they rub her nose in it. She fights like hell, but she's as drunk as we're fucked out. I feel her nose rub my rectum, and then I hear a smack as Sid slaps her ass with his bare hand.

"Kiss it, you bitch." he says, "or you'll have a blistered ass to show your husband tomorrow. . . . ."

Ann finally kisses it. She pushes her lips up against it, and her tongue shoots out. She's still objecting, but an occasional bat on the behind keeps her in line. At last she begins to suck . . . . she puts her arms around my waist and starts to pull Jean Jeudi's neck.

Five minutes ago I was sure that I would never get another dong on, but when I feel her tongue slipping up my rectum and hear her sucking in that sloppy way she has, up comes Johnny again. It's such a marvelous restorative that Sid and Ernest want to try it too, so she has to give them both an extra long ass-sucking while they try to ease themselves into condition again. Ernest wants to try pouring a bottle of wine into his rectum and letting Ann suck it out again, but Sid argues him out of it . . . . Ann is so stinking drunk now that she'll pass out on us if we give her much more. But she insists that she isn't drunk . . . . she takes two more drinks one after the other to prove it. She wants me to fuck her, and I'm ready, so after she's licked my ass some more I jump on her and throw my cock in. Jesus, that's a deep, hot hole she's got! The hair around it must be to pull yourself out with in case you fall in. . . . But John T. loves it . . . . he comes almost as soon as he's in. I go on screwing her and come again before she does.

Ernest wants to fuck her when I'm through. But Ann still wants to prove that she isn't soused, so she tips the bottle up and takes an enormous drink before she spreads her legs for him. I go into the bathroom, and when I come out again Sid is riding her and Ann has passed out cold.

Ernest sits in a corner among his new suit and his new shirts and things and swears at Ann when Sid is finished with her.

"Look at all these fucking things the rich bitch bought me," he says. He snaps his fingers. "Just like that . . . And here I am fucking around trying to get her to buy a camera so I'll have a little extra next week. . . . That cunt. God damn the rich cunt!"

"It's a fucking shame," Sid sympathizes. "A dirty bitch like that!"

Ernest swears some more but gets up to take some pictures of Ann while Sid and I pull her around to the positions he wants. She's like a log . . . .

"Look," Sid says after a few shots have been taken, "I'm too old for all this exercise. . . . Why don't we go out and get a couple of bozos to help us? Shit, if we let a few guys come in and screw her you could get some fine pictures. We'll surprise her . . . a damned rich cunt!"

"Aw Sid, that wouldn't be nice. . . ."

"What the fuck do you mean, wouldn't be nice? Is it nice to let people take pictures of you sucking assholes? What makes you think she's nice? She's just rich. . . . . Hey, how about it? We could even charge a little something, just to keep the bums out. . . ."

There's an argument about how much we ought to charge, but it sounds like such a good idea that we put our clothes on and go out to see if we can find any takers. I'm for the idea because it seems like such a good joke on Ann . . . that's how stinking drunk I am.

"We won't have to tell them that she's passed out or that we want to take pictures," Sid plots as we're falling down the steps. "We'll just tell them that we have this rich cunt who wants to be screwed. By Jesus, she's going to be surprised when she takes a look at those pictures!"

Snuggles comes to see me . . . . Snuggles of the raspberry nipples and the progressively hot underpants. It's in the afternoon. . . . I've just taken a bath so she finds me in nothing but a bathrobe . . . . which seems to be just right for her purpose. She's come looking for a lay . . . . and to tell me an amazing story.

Sam has laid her. She still acts dazed about it, which I suppose is how she ought to act, considering that he's been just her father for a good many years. It must be pretty much of a shock, one way or another, to have your father suddenly pull out his dong one day, wave it in your face, and lay you.

Of course that isn't just how it was done. Sam being what he is, it couldn't have been done that way. But the result is the same. . . . . . .

Tania is at the bottom of this, as usual. She's probably been working on poor Sam for weeks, putting the idea into his head, pounding it in with every hump of her hot, bitch's ass. And of course she's been putting the idea up to Snuggles almost from the very minute they knew each other. So one afternoon the pot boiled over.

I thought, when I heard someone at the door, that it might be Ann. . . . Ernest was going to take the pictures of her today. And I thought I was ready for anything. But I wasn't ready for the greeting Snuggles offered. . . . . . ."

"Daddy fucked me yesterday. . . . . . ."

That doesn't sound so good out in the hall where everyone might hear, so I get her inside and lock the door just in case someone should come. Then she sits down and tells me the whole story. . . . .

That bitch, she doesn't forget a single, inflammatory detail. She can't simply tell me that he screwed her and when and where . . . . no, she has to almost show me how it was done. Another trick of Tania's.

As I said, it was in the afternoon. Snuggles came back to the hotel and found her father there alone . . . . although she's pretty certain that Tania had just been there because she smelled Tania's perfume when her father kissed her. That's quite possible, especially if Tania knew that Snuggles was coming back soon. . . . I can see how she's teased poor Sam until he was almost nuts and then left him with his cock up and his guard down. Anyway, Sam followed Snuggles into her bedroom and like a dope . . . or a bitch . . . . she began to change her clothes in front of him. In two minutes he was feeling her up and in three he had her on the bed. In five they were fucking and by the time fifteen minutes had passed Sam had something to feel lousy about.

"Well what the Jesus did you let him do it for?" I yell when Snuggles gets that far. "You didn't have to, did you? He wouldn't rape his own daughter!"

"I imagine that I wanted him to," Snuggles said, giving me that wise, kid look of hers.

She wanted him to! Yes, damn it, I suppose she did. And she can't see why I'm so upset about it, either. What the fuck does a kid like that know about economics. Does she know that if things get much messier her family is going to go shooting back to America, where they should have stayed in the first place, and leave me with nothing to show for their visit but a sore dick and a thirst for better liquor than I can afford? Like so much shit she does. . . . So she goes on telling me how much she wanted him to and what she felt like while he was feeling her up and how big his prick was. . . . All that stuff, until I simply can't stand it any longer. I go out to the kitchen to find something to settle my nerves, and I make the trip both ways with a bump on the front of my bathrobe that looks as though I had elephantiasis of the balls.

"What are you going to do about it now?" I ask her when I'm settled with a glass and have given Snuggles a much smaller glass.

"Fuck him again, I suppose," she says, "And then again . . . if he wants to."

If he wants to. How to Jesus can a man help himself? All I have to do is look at her . . . . she sits crossing and uncrossing her legs, showing the new pants she's wearing . . . . and I have a dong on . . . . . and I'm not her father, by Christ!

"I thought you'd be glad to hear about it," Snuggles adds in a minute. "Tania said that you liked girls who were real dirty bitches."

I simply put my head in my hands. There isn't any answer any more. This whole affair has gotten out of my hands and is moving too fast for me. Then, while I'm sitting there, Snuggles comes over and sits herself down on the floor between my knees. She sticks her chin on my thigh like a dog and looks up at me. Her fingers are sticky when they go under my robe to touch my leg . . . . she's spilled wine on them. . . .

"You know why I came to see you, don't you," she whispers. "Of course I could go home and see if Daddy's there . . . "

She keeps feeling up my leg, running those nails that she's learning to keep pointed now up my thigh. Jesus, and to look at her! Butter pigtails and inkstains on her fingers instead of nail polish. But that bitchy little red mouth is going to begin to give her away soon . . . . that cock sucker's mouth, that cunt licker's mouth. . . . It's beginning to get that look that you learn to watch for. . . . I don't know what it is, but it's beginning to show. . . . .

Snuggles rubs her teats on my knees. . . . Teats? Her chest, I should say, but there's a softness there, you can tell that there's something started, and she pulls my bathrobe apart, a little at a time, looking at my legs while she uncovers them. John T. is holding up the tent, waiting for the big show. She slides her hands under the robe and tickles his whiskers. . . . . .

I almost drop my glass when she pulls the bathrobe completely open . . . . . she's so suddenly vicious about it. I set it down and she sits on her heels looking at my cock with her eyes looking a little bit daffy. She puts one hand around it and squeezes until the end is red and bulging.

"For God's sake, don't sit there looking at it," I tell her, "put it in your mouth if you want to suck it . . . "

"You can't make me. . . ."

It's not hard to make her. All I have to do is put my hand on her head and push it down . . . she does the rest. In goes Jean Jeudi, and she leans up against me while she unfastens the front of her dress. Then she has those teatless teats of hers rubbing against my balls, and she's giving a remarkable imitation of her mother.

"Are you going to fuck me?" She rubs my prick across her mouth and on her nose and looks up at me innocently. "Shall I take my clothes off now . . . or do you want to?"

I stand up, but I don't know what I want to do. She's on her knees with my cock in her mouth again, and there doesn't seem to be much reason for not letting her keep it there, letting her suck me off then kicking her to hell out. But I don't . . . I pick her up and chase her into the bedroom. . . . . . .

She lies crosswise on the bed and looks at me. Her dress is up to her hips and she's managed to keep her bubs uncovered too. One shoe hangs to the floor and then the other as she pushes them off with her toes. I leave my bathrobe somewhere on the floor and jump on the bed with her.

How these little cunts love their underdone bodies! Shit, even if it wasn't so damned exciting to look at them, it would make you hot just to see how much they think of themselves . . . I get Snuggles out of her dress and yank her pants down . . . . She turns to see if I'm getting a good view of her ass. . . . .

"Fuck me with my stockings on!" She says, "Fuck me with my stockings on!"

So she's learned that. From Tania, most likely. The little whore. . . . . I'll fuck her with her stockings on! Perhaps she'd like me to go out and buy a top hat and fuck her with that on. . . . She grabs my cock and throws her legs open. That little red fig stares me in the face like a danger signal. It's bare as an apple, and much the same color. Christ, but it's a juicy apple. . . . .

"Lick my prick," I tell her. "Hey, did you do that to your old man?"

No, she tells me, they just fucked. He put his cock in her cunt and fucked her, and that's all there was to it. But perhaps next time. . . . .

I grab her by the waist and yank her belly against my chest, rubbing my dick all over her face. I may be a baby fucker, but who the Hell cares . . . . Snuggles is a damned fuckable baby . . . I lick her hips and bite her thighs. She squeals like a young pig, and wiggles like one, too, but she likes it . . . . as, come to think of it, why in hell shouldn't she? How many girls of her age, after all, have a chance to get their conillons sucked? Plenty, I know, but not such a fucking lot of them at that. . . . .

She really throws that fig of hers at me when she understands what I'm after. Her thighs go around my head and she smacks me in the face with it. It's something like being slapped in the mouth with a warm, wet dishcloth . . . but no dishcloth ever had fuzz growing on it, and no dishcloth ever had a smell like that juicy peach. I dig my tongue into it . . . . and lick up a mouthful of juice . . . . and poke my dong into her mouth at the same time. She loves the tete-beche game . . . she twists around me like an eel, tying knots into herself and into me. My cock is twice as big as anything she ought to be familiar with yet, but she's having a fine time with it. She slobbers over it like a vet, making everything nice and juicy. These young bitches always surprise me that way. When you get a woman with a good bush and a heavy pair of bubs . . . one of those heavy mares with an axe mark under their tails . . . you expect them to be wet between the legs. But girls like Tania and Snuggles . . . . it's astonishing, the amount of that stuff that they produce from their wee splits. . . .

Snuggles has a nice little belly. It isn't broad and soft like her mother's . . . . you wouldn't mistake it for any feather pillow . . . . but the skin is smooth, and it's hot as your cock, and it moves continually when she breathes. You know you've got something alive on your hands. And it makes her squirm when it's licked. . . . .

I slip my tongue into her figlet and suck it for awhile. Snuggles is holding my dick in both hands, keeping Johnny's head in her mouth but jerking him off more than she sucks him. She tickles his nose with her tongue and tells me that he's too juicy. She always thought, she tells me, that if she didn't have to suck Tania's and Billie's and Jean's cunts but sucked cocks instead she wouldn't have to get her face all wet . . . . but a prick is almost as bad. . . . .

Between the cheeks of her ass Snuggles is almost naked. Her rectum is pink and tight, and for some reason it's a hell of a temptation. I run a finger over it and poke at it. Snuggles wiggles a little more, but she doesn't seem to mind. Finally I push my finger into it, just to see what she'll do. . . . . . and the little cunt, she begins to hop back and forth against it, trying to fuck herself on it.

Suddenly I stop sucking her cunt and begin sucking her rectum instead. Don't ask me why . . . . it's just because it's there and it looks as though it ought to be sucked . . . I lick it a few times, kiss it . . . . and shove my tongue up it. Snuggls almost tears my cock off, she sucks it so hard then.

She doesn't have to tell me that she's going to come . . . . I know she is . . . . and I am too. I climb over her so that I can hold her better, so that she can't suddenly change her mind and leave me with a pot of jism to spill over the sheets, and put everything but my balls into her mouth. I manage to get one finger into her conillon and my tongue too . . . . and we both come.

"Swallow that, you crazy cunt!" I yell at her as John T. lets go. "Swallow it, or by Christ I'll make you wash it down with a mouthful of piss!"

"I'm . . . . . . trying . . . . to . . . " is all she can say. She's got such a dose that it's practically coming out of her ears, but she's doing the best she can with it.

The room settles back on its ass again after a long time. I've been sailing around like a bird, and I come down with a jolt. Snuggles is still sucking my prick, still swallowing the jism. And some son of a bitch is trying to break down the door. I shake Snuggles off . . . she's like a leech on that cock . . . . and listen. It sounds like Sid, but it might be anybody. It might even be Carl, which would be a fine mess.

I've read about these things, but by Jesus this is the first time I ever really was in a situation where I had to hide somebody. We've been making so much noise that whoever is out there must know I'm in. And I'd like to see who it is, just in case. . . . .

She's under the bed like a flash, taking her clothes with her. And I can't get her out again. I even grab her leg and try to pull her out, but she's like a snail in a shell. Why the fuck didn't she wait until I had got her into a closet? Well, there's nothing to be done now . . . . that door will be off its hinges if I don't answer it. . . .

It's Sam. For the first time in his life he comes to my place, and it has to be when I'm fucking his daughter! He gives me a funny look and walks straight in.

"Are you getting deaf?" he asks me. "What was the row about, anyway?"

"Exercise," I tell him, Hell, I must look as though I'd been exercising. I pound my chest and take a deep breath. Then I suddenly remember that I haven't anything on and that my dick must still be wet. I tell him I'll get him a drink, and I go out to the kitchen where I can wrap a towel around my ass.

When I come back from the kitchen Sam isn't in the living room. He's in the bedroom, sitting on the bed. I almost shit my pants.

"Hey, Sam, come on out here and sit down. . . ."

No, no . . . . he couldn't think of interrupting my exercises. Best thing in the world . . . . . keep in trim. He wants me to come in and do my exercises while he has a drink. It's no good to tell him that I'm all through . . . . . he's positive that he interrupted me, and besides. . . .

"Come to talk to you," he says, "Rather you were doing something while I tell you about it."

So I have to go into the bedroom. I haven't the faintest fucking notion of how people exercise. I swing my arms a few times and try a few squats.

"You've got this bed mussed up plenty," Sam notices. He seems to be wondering about something.

"Yeah. . . .sure. . . ." I try hopping over the foot of the bed to show him how I get the bed mussed, and I land on my puss. Suddenly I realize that if I don't keep exercising Sam is likely to hear Snuggles under the bed. Christ, I can't keep up this bending and stretching and floor thumping forever.

"Sam," I beg, "let's go into the other room. I've done all the exercises now."

It's a struggle but I get him out of there. I can't close the bedroom door because there isn't any. There used to be one, but that was before I ever moved in.

What Sam has to tell me is the same thing that Snuggles has already told me. But it takes him the better part of an hour to get his little confession off his mind. And all that time I'm waiting for Snuggles to make a noise . . . maybe a fart or something. I'm farting myself. In the first ten minutes I'm a nervous wreck.

The worst part of it is that I have to be patient and sympathetic with Sam, when what I'd really like to do is toss him out on his ass. And I have to give him advice. . . . . I haven't figured out yet why a man who can make money in the best American tradition . . . . rags to riches . . . . . could be coming to a half-assed newspaperman for advice on anything, but Sam seems to have the notion that I know all there is to be known about this sort of thing.

"Should I put her in school and just drop her out of my life?" He asks me, "Or should I ask Ann for a divorce? First that other little girl . . . Tania . . . and now my own daughter! Alf, when I get back home I'm going to have my head examined."

I have to cheer him up. I have to give him some wine and assure him that it will all be all right, that everything will clear itself up in the end. And I'm a Hell of a long way from believing that it will all be all right in the end. From where I'm standing this looks like one of the fuckingest stews that anybody ever got themselves into . . . . . and that includes me. . . . .

Sam talks his head off, and when the hour is up he hasn't gotten anywhere. The only thing that's been accomplished is that I've argued him out of confessing everything to Ann. Finally he looks at his watch . . . . he has an appointment and I don't try to keep him. I get him out as fast as I can, promising that I will talk to him some more about this matter . . .

When I'm sure that he's gone down the stairs and won't come popping back in I go into the bedroom and look under the bed. Snuggles is lying on her back playing with herself, having a fine time. I drag her out, and she climbs into bed, wiggling her ass at me.

"Why the Christ didn't you leave things alone?" I yell at her. "Hell, you could have fucked anybody but your father. . . ."

"I'm a bitch," she says. "I thought he'd have a big cock. He did have a big cock. I'm going to try to get him to fuck me again. . . . . ."

"You little bitch of misery, I hope he gets wise to himself and smacks your ass off! What do you suppose your mother married him for? So you could fuck him? Like hell! So she could screw him! It's her business to screw him, not yours! She can give him all he needs. . . . ."

"Well, she's busy fucking you or somebody all the time. And why shouldn't I let my father fuck me? He's nice. . . . . I've known him all my life! How long have I known you? Why you're almost a stranger. . . ."

Stranger or not, she pounces on my dong and starts jerking me off. She kneels across my legs as I sit on the bed and rubs the raspberry nipples of her bubs on my cock and my balls. Johnny begins to come to attention, and she slides farther over, rubbing him with her belly. And there's her little soft ass just waiting for me. . . . .

She doesn't know what's happening until about the third time my hand comes down on her bare behind. Then she starts kicking and squalling as though she were being murdered. I spank her ass and her round thighs so hard that my hand aches. . . .

"You're not going to fuck your father again! Promise!"

Like hell she'll promise. She's an obstinate cunt, and the more I paddle her ass, the more obstinate she becomes.

"I will fuck him! I will I will I will I will I will I will!"

I spank her some more. And much good it does. Her ass turns pink, but she just sings louder without changing her tune much.

"I will fuck him! And . . . and I'll suck him off too! I don't care how much you spank me, I will! I'll fuck him right in front of my mother if I want to! Spank me harder . . . . see if I care! Spank me as hard as you want to . . . . I'll do it even if you do make me promise not to!"

Spank me harder! The bitch! I give up. I should have learned by now that you can spank a cunt into fucking you or sucking you off but once they've had a piece of ass you can't spank them out of wanting it. I stop mauling her and Snuggles crawls over me on the bed. . . . . .

"Now fuck me!" she sobs. "You've made my ass hot . . . . fuck me!"

I'll make her ass a hell of a lot hotter than it is . . . . I turn her onto her belly and get behind her. I squeeze John Thursday's head into her fig and fuck the rest of him in after it. She's small, even though she just sucked me off, and it's a tight fit, but there's plenty of juice and he goes in all right. I fuck her until I've got her squirming, until she's groaning for the next shove up in her womb. Then I pop Johnny out.

She doesn't have a chance now . . . . I put one arm tightly around her middle and grab my cock with the other hand. Zingo . . . . up against her rectum. She hops like a sparrow when she feels the head of my dong going up her ass, but she can't stop it. Christ, I don't see why she doesn't split . . . to hear her carrying on you'd think it already had.

She won't fuck her father, she wails . . . . she won't do anything I don't want her to . . . . if I'll only take my prick out of her rectum. She'll be a good girl, she howls. She'll promise anything. . . . .

I'm past caring whether or not she lets Sam screw her. She can shit in his soup for all of me. What I want is to keep my cock in her behind and get some more of it in there. I want to fuck the piss out of her, but all I'm succeeding in doing is fucking a river of juice out of her fig. . . . .

"Play with my cunt if you're going to do that!" she gasps. "I can't stand that feeling inside me. . . . . "

I tell her to play with her own cunt . . . . and she does, the dirty little bitch! She opens it up with one hand and uses the fingers of the other to poke herself with. Finally I stick a couple of fingers in too. Then I'm filling her ass with jism and she's coming, raising the roof. . . . .

Ann is up in the air and Sam has the shakes. I can't say that I really blame either of them very much. Of course

Ann helped to bring on the things that are bothering her, but poor Sam. . . . . . .

Ernest delivered the pictures to Ann. Wonderful pictures, when I consider how drunk we were at the time. But Ann simply couldn't appreciate them. Especially, she was horrified by all the pictures of herself with a half a dozen bozos she'd never seen in her life. First she accused Ernest of faking them, but he knocked that idea out of her head immediately. When she finally caught on that she'd actually been laid by those boys, that there were half a dozen strange men running around Paris with as intimate a knowledge of her anatomy as is possible, she raised a marvelous rumpus. So Ernest says . . . . I haven't talked to her myself, and perhaps it's just as well I haven't. He was afraid, at least so he tells me, to let her know that we'd charged them a little something for the privilege. . . . . .

Anyway, she bought that camera from him . . . . and if I know Ernest she probably bought the negatives as well. Also if I know Ernest, she probably didn't get the negatives until a few thousand prints had been made from them. Ernest says she turned green when she saw the first one . . . . a nice juicy one of her with one cock in her mouth, another in her cunt, and three guys lined up waiting in the background. And she didn't appreciate at all the trouble it was to get her to suck those dicks without completely waking her up. . . . .

As for Sam's little trouble . . . that's Snuggles, naturally. A couple of days ago he was taking a little afternoon snooze and woke up to find her sucking him off. He's been more or less drunk ever since. Every time he begins to sober up he decides that he's going to make a clean breast of it to Ann and then I have to get him started again. It's beginning to bother his nerves . . . and mine too. This can't go on forever . . . he's either got to stay stinking for the rest of his life or figure a better out than he's found so far. He keeps telling me about it. . . .

"I half woke up, Alf," he'll say . . . and here we have a

drink, . . . "and I felt her working on my cock. Christ almighty, I thought I was dreaming . . . . I thought it was Ann . . . I don't know what I thought. But I didn't move. I let her go on . . . . I closed my eyes for a few minutes more and let her suck it. . . . She was pulling the skin back . . . you know how a woman does, I don't have to tell you that . . . . and she was rubbing my balls in her hands. . . . My own daughter, God damn it! That sweet little girl! By Jesus, I know who's at the bottom of this . . . . it's that Tania bitch! She put her up to it, one way or another! Oh, God damn that Tania! I wish I'd never fucked her! Why didn't you tell me not to let Snuggles go out with that dirty little pervert? Why didn't I have enough sense to see, when Tania began to act the way she did, that I had to get Snuggles away from her?"

We think this over, Sam and I, for a few minutes. Since there doesn't seem to be any satisfactory answer to most of the questions that come up we pile up another pair of saucers and I wait for Sam to go on. Hell, I could tell him the whole story backward by now, but it does him good to talk, I suppose.

"I let her suck it," he repeats. "I let her go on until I was almost ready to come, waking up little by little. Then, gradually, I began to realize that it was Snuggles who was doing that. . . . God, what a moment! I hope to Christ that you never have to live through a moment like that, Alf!"

I hope so, too. In fact, I'll take damned good care to see that it doesn't happen that I do.

"Then, when I did realize what was going on, I. . . . . . I don't know what got into me. I must have been crazy for a few minutes. I looked at her . . . and she winked at me, just like that damned Tania cocksucker . . . and I grabbed her head and sat up. She was on her knees beside the couch, and I kept her there . . . I began to call her filthy names. . . " At this point Sam usually becomes pretty vague about the details but it all comes to one thing: the girl sucked him off, finished it the way a sucking ought to be finished . . . . "and then I saw that she was swallowing . . . . she'd almost sucked my nuts dry. . . ." But here's something that bothers him almost as much as what he himself did to her. . . . "How did she ever learn to do such a thing? From Tania, of course . . . . but who could the man be? Or men! How many men do you suppose . . . . oh it's awful to have to ask yourself such questions about your own daughter! What man could be low enough to do a thing like that to a girl as young as she is? Except me . . . . her father. . . ."

Sometimes when he says that Sam gives me a very peculiar look, which I wish he would get over. I don't know whether he's really suspicious of me or not. There's a question on his mind, but he can't quite make up his mind to ask it.

"I tried to learn that when she was doing it . . . . when I was calling her those names . . . . and . . . all that. I kept asking her who she's sucked off before, how many men . . . . but she wouldn't answer. . . . ."

I breathe easier here, but I still don't feel very damned comfortable. If they get in bed again Snuggles is likely to spill the soup . . . . . and something tells me that there's a Hell of a good chance that they will get in bed. Once something like this is started it doesn't simply die overnight.

"Of course I could take a strap to her and beat it out of her," Sam says. "That's what my father would have done to me if I. . . . . I mean . . . . you know what I mean. But I can't bear to even think about asking her. I'm almost afraid to go back to the hotel at all. . . "

All I can do is hope that whatever happens happens damned quick and gets itself over with. I can't stand having my nerve up like this and I can't stay drunk much longer; I can't eat a thing when I'm drunk this way, even though I manage to get a little soup down when I go to the office and do my act which is called working, and I'm slowly starving to death.

Billie calls, bringing Jean as a sort of present to me, or perhaps I'm the present for Jean . . . . I haven't got that quite straight yet. Billie may be trying to soothe Jean for what happened with Ann.

It's in the evening, and I've just gotten up after being in bed for two days. I wasn't sick . . . . I was sleeping. I simply couldn't take it any longer, so I managed to give Sam the shake at last. I ditched him in a whorehouse . . . he's in safe hands, it's a high class dump . . . . and I hope to Jesus he stays there for a few days. They'll take good care of him in that place, they're nice girls and I know them all. . . .

As I was saying, Billie arrives with Jean, and I've seldom been as glad to see anyone in my life as I am to see that Lesbian bitch and her cunt. It's not only that I feel that I need a good fuck to get some of this bad blood out of my system . . . . I want to see somebody who isn't too mixed up with the things that have been happening these past few days. Then I find out that Ann and Billie have been playing tag with each other. Oh well . . . . I'm still glad to see them.

It's been a long time since any cunt has made a meal for me. I think that the little Chink was the last one. But when they find that I've just gotten up and was going out to feed myself Billie and Jean get busy and get something started. That means that somebody has to go to buy things, and going to buy things means that Jean goes. Billie sits down and tells me about her affair with Ann.

Billie isn't very explicit about the juicy details . . . the main point is that Ann found out what she wanted to know about women like Billie. Billie went to see her with some more sketches, they went out somewhere in the evening, and Ann screwed up her nerve to ask Billie to stay all night. They hopped into bed and there the fun started. Now Ann knows all. Don't I think that's interesting?

I certainly do think it's interesting. I'd also like to know if that's all there's going to be to it . . . . . or does Billie plan to carry on a love affair with Ann? On that point Billie isn't positive. It appears to be one of those things which is simply left up in the air when somebody goes home in the morning. But she's amused because Jean has acted a little jealous ever since.

Jean comes back and the two cunts put together a meal for us all. Luckily I've got a table and some dishes . . . one place I lived in had a couple of planks that you were supposed to put across chairs. A table is a nice thing to have because you can always feel somebody up under it. Jean and I play with each other all through the meal. Billie knows what's going on, but she doesn't mind. Pretty soon she gets interested, though, and begins to play with Jean too. There we sit, me with my cock in Jean's hand, Jean with her skirt up to her ass, and God only knows what Billie's doing . . . but we all go on talking about how hard it is to get good bologna or some fucking thing like that. It's idiotic.

Jean breaks down first. She doesn't want a second cup of coffee, she says. She's got hot pants, and she wants to take her clothes off. She gives my dong an extra hard squeeze and gets up from the table, giving her ass a shake to straighten her skirt. She goes to the couch and lies down, giving us plenty of bare thigh to look at while we decide what to do about her.

"You brought me here so that he could screw me," she says to Billie at last. "Why don't you go away so he can do it?"

Billie doesn't think that she ought to be chased out. After all, she says, she's watched me lay Jean before.

"You always want to watch me get fucked," Jean complains. "I believe you like to believe I'm a pig."

Billie says that she is a pig . . . . a particularly dirty kind of a pig. And all this is being said in the most pleasant way imaginable. It's a sort of nice and soothing thing to listen to. . . . .

"You're a promiscuous cocksucker," Billie tells Jean.

"So are you," Jean fires back. "Don't forget, I watched you suck Alf off. . . . ."

"Not a promiscuous cocksucker, Jean . . . . I've never yet come home with jism on my brassiere where it dribbled off my chin."

"No, I notice . . . . you swallow it, don't you?"

This sort of thing goes on for some time. It could go on all night, and I'd just sit there and listen. It's so peaceful, sitting there with a dong on and listening to those two beautiful cunts saying sweet, nasty things to each other. . . . .

"Tell us about the boy who rubbed shit in your face," Billie suggests gently. She sits next to Jean and starts feeling her up, pulling up her dress to give a pinch on that sweet ass we've both been squeezing.

"I'm not going to talk to you," Jean says . . . and she's blushing, too. Shit, maybe somebody did do that to her.

Billie gives Jean a good feeling up before she begins to undress her. She knows just how to make Jean hot too, and pretty soon Jean is reaching under Billie's skirt, feeling for that hairy fig she's always eating and never finishing. Billie pulls Jean's pants off and holds her skirt up.

"I'm going to show Alf your cunt, Jean," she says, "because I don't think he wants it at all. What will you do if he doesn't want to fuck you?"

"I don't want you to show it to him," Jean says. "If I want him to see it I'll show it to him myself! Why don't you show him yours, you bitch?"

"He's seen it," Billie assures her, "And he's fucked it, too. . . ."

She pulls Jean's skirt up to her belly and turns the works towards me. Jean kicks, and the red light flashes on and off. Billie tickles her in the crotch. Jean grabs Billie's skirt and pulls it half off, baring her ass. Christ if my dong got much harder than it is now I could break rocks with it. . . . .

"What are you trying to do?" Billie demands. "You want him to see that thing you suck every night, is that it? Then I'll show it to him . . . but you'll have to show what you use it for, you little pervert! You dirty little cunt sucker!"

"I'm more of a woman than you are," Jean yells at her. By this time she's gotten Billie's skirt so tangled up that Billie simply kicks her way out of it. Both of them are bare-assed, they wrestle across the couch. Billie is trying to push Jean onto the floor, and Jean is trying to get the rest of Billie's clothes off. It occurs to me that if they play like this every night it must be hell on their clothes. . . . . .

"You're a dirty ass-licking whore!" Billie insists. "Would you call a man a man . . . . a real man . . . . if you learned that he was a cocksucker? Then why do you think you're a real woman? Bitch lover! Teat chaser!"

Suddenly in the midst of all this they quiet down; it's exactly as though someone had pressed a button. They seem to melt into each other's arms, and they begin to pet and kiss each other. Jean is rubbing Billie's cunt and Billie is opening Jean's blouse. When she has Jean's teats out Billie kisses them and sucks the nipples.

"I'll suck you off now if you're ready," Jean whispers.

"No . . . I'll suck you off," Billie says.

"No, I'm the woman," Jean says, "You're my husband. . . . . I have to suck you off."

They take the rest of their clothes off and then Jean slips off the couch and between Billie's legs. Billie lies back and raises her ass so that Jean can get at her con, and Jean starts to kiss her. Jean begins at Billie's toes and works up to her bubs, then licks her way back down to Billie's fig again.

Jean may be, as she says, all woman, but she likes Billie as much as she could like anyone. Christ, she almost eats her up. She bites Billie's belly, licks her teats and kisses her thighs . . . . soon she's rubbing her nose into Billie's split fig, holding the thing open with her fingers so that she can get her nose further into it. Then she shoves her tongue into it and really goes up in it.

"Oh, it's nice and juicy tonight!" she says as soon as she's gotten a taste of it. "And you have that Orange Blossom perfume in your hair, haven't you. . . ."

"You gave yourself away that time," Billie says, pressing

her knees together to hold Jean better. "That's Ruth's perfume! I thought you'd been sucking her! Admit it now, you lying little fucker . . . . you let her put you on her knees, didn't you?"

"Just . . . . just a little . . . . . ," Jean has to confess.

"Just a little! I'll have to put a leash on you, like the bitch you are, if I don't want you running around with your tongue out! You just wait . . . next time Ruth comes to see us I'm going to make you suck her off right in front of whoever's there . . . . . and I don't care who it is! Put your tongue in now! Lick it! Now, that's enough . . . . you're going to suck my ass now. . . ."

Jean doesn't even argue about that. Billie turns over and sticks her rear out for Jean to kiss , and Jean simply lays her hands on Billie's ass and goes after it. She licks every part of Billie's ass, the backs of her legs . . . . even her heels this time. Then she puts her lips over Billie's rectum.

I'd come in my drawers if I didn't get into this soon. Jean Jeudi is on the warpath. He's bristling his feathers, and he acts as though he might crow at any minute. I might be patient, but he can't be; he isn't as smart as I am.

Neither of these cunts know I'm after them until I'm on top of them. Then Billie turns around, and probably because she saw me first, I hop on her. I jump onto the couch and wave my prick under her nose.

Billie doesn't want to have anything to do with my dick, but I wrap myself around her like a monkey on a pole and rub it in her face. That doesn't make her like it any more, but I'm not worried about whether she likes it or not. I stick the end against her red mouth and wet her lips with it. Jean looks up at us from somewhere under Billie's ass . . . she's still sucking like a good girl. . . . . .

It takes some persuasion and a hell of a lot more actual force before I get what I want. But Billie isn't a bad sort at heart . . . . she thinks of herself as being almost a man, so she can sympathize with the way I feel. . . . Finally she lets me put it into her mouth and she starts to suck it. But while

I'm trying to decide whether I'll let Johnny blow his head off that way or not, Jean hops onto the couch too. She wants to be screwed, she says, and it's a shame to waste that cock on Billie when Billie doesn't really appreciate it.

"You like my little whore, don't you?" Billie asks me. "Just wait until I get her broken in right, though . . . I'll make a real bitch of her yet. . . ."

I don't know what she means by that . . . . Jean is a bitch if I've ever seen one . . . not the nasty kind; the fucking kind. Whatever Billie does to her, she couldn't be much of an improvement over what she is right now . . . . I start screwing her and she wiggles back at me, reaching up to give Billie a pinch on the teats. . . . .

Billie wants to have her cunt sucked, so we roll over, on our sides, and she wiggles her ass down between our faces. Jean pokes her face between Billie's thighs and I lean my head over Billie's hip so that I can watch her.

Jean likes being watched, and she does a really nice job on Billie. She licks her bush and then digs her tongue into Billie's wet split, and the wetter Billie's cunt gets the better she fucks me. She gets her nose soaked, she gets cunt juice over her chin . . . . and she makes a noise which occasionally sounds vaguely like a toilet plunger. . . . She makes it seem so nice that I begin to feel like trying some of that myself. I bite Billie's ass and stick my finger up under her tail to tickle the place that Jean is sucking.

Billie seems to guess what's on my mind . . . she turns over and gives her ass to Jean, throwing that soaked mop and that open, dripping con right in my face. She doesn't try to push it onto my mouth . . . she just waits to see what I'll do. Hell, this isn't any time to be formal . . . . Jean and I look at each other between Billie's thighs. I've got my tail into her to what I should say was about three feet, but which probably isn't more than two and a half, and we're both so completely hot that we're off our trolleys.

Jean sticks her tongue out and takes a very deliberate lick at Billie's ass. Then she takes another one. Then, next thing I know, she's reached across and stuck her tongue into my mouth. That lousy, dirty cunt! I'm so sore that I can't think of anything to do but to lick Billie's cunt and spit the juice at her . . . but I only think about it.

Billie's cunt has a wonderful smell. I put my nose into her mop and just lie there sniffing it for a couple of minutes. If Orange Blossom, as Jean says, then I like Orange Blossom . . . . but to me it just smells like a nice clean con . . . I kiss it finally, and then lick it. Jean's tongue and mine meet between Billie's thighs. I start to suck, and so does Jean. Billie goes wild. . . . .

Suddenly Billie's come. She's come and she's pouring juice. There's too much for me to handle by myself, so each time that I get a mouthful of it I move back, Billie shoves her ass towards Jean, and Jean gobbles some of it up.

Jean must be screwed silly. She begins to laugh, and for a minute I think that she's going to become hysterical. I give her a slap on the ass and she doesn't laugh quite so hard.

"Don't worry officer," she giggles, "I'll come quietly."

She does, too. I don't know when she begins to come or when she stops, but somewhere in between I come. My cock simply pours into her, and I stick my face back against Billie's cunt and suck at it while I fill Jean's womb. That Lesbian and her girl friend have given me the most satisfactory fuck I've had in weeks. . . . .

End of the ride. End of a long, long ride. Finish, all over, all done. Now I'm beginning to wonder where I got on this merry-go-round, and why this is the particular place where I get off. Well, one place is as good as another, I suppose. The trick is not to get so dizzy while you're going round that you can't walk straight when you get off. This way to the Ferris wheel, and the roller coaster. They take you nowhere in an even more breathtaking manner.

Today I went down to the paper and got that little slip that I've always been looking for and never expected to see. Two weeks pay too, which went to pay up the little bills I've run up here and there in the two years I've been on the paper. That makes me even.

The amusing part of it is that I was fired for a story I didn't write. So they tell me, anyway. Somehow there was a news story written and it said something about somebody who is a friend of somebody upstairs. I never saw the piece, but the point is that I was supposed to have done it. It was assigned to me on one of those days when I was helping Sam get drunk, and since there's no record of me being off . . . . things on this fucking sheet being as screwed up as they are . . . . I'm the bozo who's credited with it. No use kicking, of course . . . . I'd just get some other poor bastard fired, some guy with a wife and eight kids. It's always the guys with a wife and eight kids who are doing somebody else's work . . . . they're always so scared of losing their own jobs that they can't bear to see anyone else get in bad. So I'm even all around. I've been drawing my checks for a long time without doing anything, now I get sacked for the same reason. It's uncanny.

Well, I have my walking papers, so I sit down to clean out my desk. Can't clean out my desk . . . . there's nothing in it; I never put anything there. All I really want to do is goose the snotty looking blonde who comes through the news room every now and then with her tail feathers in the air, but she's not around.

On the street I begin to feel wonderfully exhilarated. Even though I never spent much more than an hour a day at that office I feel marvelously free of the place. I mooch along the streets wondering where I'll go first . . . like a kid who's playing hookey. It's a fine day: I feel great. . . .

Suddenly I remember that I'm going to be broke when I pay my rent. Just for the hell of it I decide to go and see Sam. Sam ought to be good for some kind of a shakedown. There are a thousand things I can do for Sam. Shit, if I have to I can bounce Carl out of this phoney art racket of his, but I don't think I'll have to do anything like that.

I walk to Sam's hotel, trying to figure out something to sell him. Or, maybe, I think, I ought to just tell him I've lost my job because I got drunk with him . . . . . he'd have to support me then. Anyway, I'm not worried.

I ring the bell at his place a couple of times, but nothing happens. I'm just turning away when the door pops open and there's Sam, wearing a union suit. He seems to be pretty drunk. . . . .

"Come in . . . . come in . . . ." he shouts at me. "Do you have any friends with you? Bring them in if you have!"

He closes the door after me and picks up a bottle from a table, motioning me toward the bedroom with it.

"She's in there," he says to me, "Go in and fuck her. . . ."

I don't know what he's talking about until I get into the bedroom. . . . Tania comes into my mind. But it's not Tania. Ann is lying on the bed, stark naked.

"Go ahead . . . . fuck her," Sam urges me. "Have a drink first."

"Hey, now look, Sam . . . . "

"Don't tell me she's not worth fucking," he says, "I know better. I have proof!" He grabs a pile of papers from a drawer and shoves them under my nose. They're not papers . . . . they're the pictures we took of Ann that night. He pushes them into my hands and goes to the bed. I look toward the door to be certain I can get there in a hurry if I want to . . . . but it doesn't look as though Sam was going to wave a pistol or anything like that. He pulls Ann off the bed and gives her a shove in my direction.

"Suck him off now, you whore!" he yells at her. "I've seen all the pictures . . . now let me see you do it!"

Ann's pretty drunk too. She wobbles toward me and goes down to her knees in front of me. I try to break away from her, but she's got my legs in her arms. She kisses the front of my pants and puts her fingers into my fly.

It's so crazy and frightening that I seem to have become

petrified. I don't know if they've gone nuts or I have. I watch Ann take my dong out and lick it. . . . Then she puts it into her mouth. . . . .

"Snuggles!" Sam roars.

Snuggles comes hopping in from another room. She's naked too, but she doesn't look scared. That's a good sign . . . if Sam had gone nuts she'd be pissing in her pants.

"Come on over to the bed," Sam says. "You, too, Alf. Come on, fuck them both . . . you've done it before. I'll fuck them both too . . . . I've done it before. . . ."

"Listen, Sam," I say, "what the Jesus is this? . . . What's going on!"

"Why this is Paris, my boy!" he shouts. "Paris, where everything happens, where you learn things you never knew about yourself! And your family!" He pulls Snuggles to him and she grabs his cock. He sets her on his knee and plays with her figlet while he's yelling at me. . . . . "I want to meet these friends of yours . . . . this Ernest fellow, and Sid. And that fairy brother of Tania's, too . . . . I think I'd enjoy watching a fairy fuck my wife! Maybe I'll let him suck me off afterward, if he does a good job of it! Bring them all around . . . . all but that bastard Carl. I just want to meet the people who've been fucking my family for me!"

He pushes Snuggles on her ass and yells for Ann to come over and suck his prick for awhile. Then he decides that he wants them both to do it, taking turns.

"We're going to have a big party tonight, Alf," he says. "Lesbians and everything . . . . somebody named Billie took my wife to bed with her! AND my daughter . . . . mustn't forget Snuggles! Champagne and cunt for everybody! I'm going to have Tania here . . . . . and Alexandra! I'm going to out-Paris Paris. . . ."

"Sam, I think you're making a mistake. . . ."

"Not any more, Alf! Here, why don't you fuck somebody, why don't you screw one of these bitches for me? I'm killing myself trying to handle both of them . . . . if they wouldn't suck each other off I'd be dead already!"

284 ·

"Sam, look, if you act crazy like this you're going to make a lot of trouble for yourself. . . . You've got a business to take care of. . . ."

"Business? What business? I don't have . . . oh, you mean that thing with Severin? Well, fuck Severin! And that piss ant Carl, too. That bastard Carl always did get on my nerves. . . . No, that's gone overboard. . . ."

"But Sam, what to Jesus are you going to do?"

"Do? I'm going to have some fun. I'm going to find out just what these two bitches of mine are. . . . . I'll drag out every fucking bit of slime in them! I hear that you fellows made a little profit on this whore wife of mine the other night. . . . . maybe I'll try that myself! No . . . I can think up something better than that. . . . And when I've found out everything there is to know about them, do you know what I'm going to do? I'm going to beat the ass off both of them and take them back to America! They wanted Paris. . . . I'll give them the Paris they can stand!"

I'm standing there with my cock hanging out not knowing what I'm supposed to do or say. I've never run into anything like this . . . . I didn't even know that things like this happened. I still have a feeling that all isn't right in Sam's upper story. He wants to know if I'd like to to see Ann and Snuggles play tete-beche.

"Sam. . . . I haven't got the time right now. I just came around to tell you I'm off the paper. . . ."

"Got kicked out of your job, did you? Well, it's about time that they caught onto you. How much do you want to borrow?"

"I don't want to borrow anything, Sam. I want you to give me some money."

"Now you're talking, by Jesus! Come right out and ask for it! How much do you want? Say it in American money. . . ."

He's waving a check book already. I take a chance and name twice the amount I really need for what I'm going to do. Then I translate it into francs for him. I grab at that check like a drowning man grabbing for a nice big life-boat. . . . . .

"If you want some more money tomorrow come around. . . Oh, that's right . . . . you'll be around tonight to help me screw these cunts, won't you?"

I run for the door before he can change his mind. And on the street I run for the taxi to take me to the bank. I am running away, and I am not going to stop running. I am not going to stop running until I have bought a ticket to America on Sam's money and am on the boat. And when I get to America I am going to run some more. I am running away, and I am not going to stop running until I have put a lot of ocean between me and Sam Backer, Ann, Snuggles, Tania, Alexandra and the rest of these crazy bitches who have slowly been driving me nuts for the last year or so. I am going to America and I am going to buy or make or have made a good mechanical cunt, a fucking machine, which runs by electricity and which can be pulled out of the wall socket when the fuses begin to blow and the trouble starts.

EPILOGUE

The following is an affidavit filed by Milton Luboviski at the United States Embassy in Paris on March 10, 1983 affirming the circumstances under which he commissioned Henry Miller to write *Opus Pistorum*:

In the summer of 1940, I was a partner in the Larry Edmunds Bookshop at 1603 North Chuenga Boulevard in Hollywood, California. In September of that year, Henry Miller arrived at the bookshop on a Sunday afternoon when the shop was closed. He knocked on the door, introduced himself and I admitted him to the shop. That began a friendship which lasted some thirty-five years or so. At that time, Henry had little or no money and knew very few people in California. I befriended him, helping him with money from time to time, introducing him to people and, at one point, finding him a place to live.

On September 1, 1941 Larry Edmunds died and I became sole owner of the bookshop. In those days the shop was not doing well and I supplemented our income by selling various items of pornography whenever it was possible to obtain them. My customers were mainly studio producers, writers and directors such as Joseph Mankiewicz, Julian Johnson, Daniele Amfitheatrof, Billy Wilder, Frederick Hollander, Henry Blanke, and others.

Henry, being in need of money, offered to write material for me that I would be able to sell. I offered to pay him one dollar per page in return for all rights to the material he would write for me. Shortly thereafter he began to bring in several pages at a time and I paid him in cash at the agreed rate. Within a few months the pages had accumulated into a complete book which he entitled *Opus Pistorum*.

When he gave me the last pages, around the middle of 1942, I recall his saying "Here is the end of the book. I hope you make a few months' rent from it."

I retyped the entire manuscript, making four carbon copies. I then had all five copies bound by a book binder and, thereafter, sold copies to Julian Johnson, Daniele Amfitheatrof and Frederick Hollander. A few years later, I gave a copy to my friend, Robert Light, and kept the original for myself.